NEVER GOING HOME

NEVER GOING HOME

a tale of extraordinary people in today's formidable times

My Best Regards
Jy Lewis
nghjerrylewis@gmail.com

Jerry Lewis

Copyright © 2017 by Jerry Lewis
All rights reserved.

ISBN: 1537443682
ISBN 13: 9781537443683
Library of Congress Control Number: 2016914743
CreateSpace Independent Publishing Platform
North Charleston, South Carolina

Dedication

*To my friends Lori Kay and Elizabeth Anne and my
loving daughters, Adriin and Casey Lee.*

*There is a demand in these days for men who
can make wrong appear right.*

—*Terence, Roman philosopher, speaking about the Roman senate*

*"The more and more varied the experiences,
the wiser one becomes... sometimes."*

-- Jerry Lewis

Foreword 1

The story Jerry Lewis tells reinforces my own disgust. Sadly, like everyone else, I am too busy with the everyday demands of family and self to engage in a plan of action to challenge the fallaciousness identified in *Never Going Home*.

I too rationalize that someone else will eradicate these damaging wrongs we the people regrettably tolerate. Even more disturbing are the many Americans who have no idea what unscrupulous politicians are doing behind their backs to this great country of ours.

Most amazing is Jerry's weaving of many need-to-know subjects into an exciting, action-packed story with an interesting cast of intellectual characters. Paramount to me was his narration of diet and disease prevention. I never knew healthy eating and avoiding disease could be made so easy.

I cannot go away without mentioning Ruby Ridge. Her characterization is of the perfect man's woman. All eyes are always on Ruby. Her constant need to entertain supports her admitted exhibitionist behavior.

In conclusion, I thought I was on my way to recovery. Jerry, you just reignited my anger with the "State of the Union" of this country I love! Every American citizen should read *Never Going Home*.

—Benjamin Bernstein

Foreword 2

Jerry walked up to me on the beach, introduced himself, and asked if I read. I hesitated. He quickly said he was looking for a stranger to read his manuscript and give an evaluation that he intended to include in the book.

He reached into his backpack and pulled out a piece of printed-paper. "Take a minute and read the introduction."

He said nothing as I read. The moment I lifted my eyes from the paper, he asked, "Will you?"

I said, "Yes!" He then pulled from his backpack a freshly printed manuscript.

I was on vacation and had intended to spend most of my days bathing in the sun. I agreed to finish it over the next three days. "How long do you think it will take for you to write a short review?" he asked.

"Not long," I replied. "That is kind of what I do. I write property description listings for realtors."

Wow, I really enjoyed reading *Never Going Home*. I do admit falling in love with Lenny. He was the kind of man a woman adores: intellectual and a perfect gentleman. He was gracious and loyal because he knew what being alone and having a hard life were really like. Lenny and Mary's first encounter did challenge my sexual morality.

Every page I turned produced excitement or useful knowledge. I am a strong proponent of *Never Going Home*.

—Robin Jones

Foreword 3

Jerry and I were in Vietnam at the same time. We have spent many a day discussing our Vietnam experiences. We both have 100 percent service-connected disabilities related to the war. The topic that will not go away is the incompetency of the VA, which we have been discussing for several decades. Every so often it becomes a heated topic with the public. Congress gets involved and promises change. The news media then loses interest, the public is diverted to some other problem, and Congress does nothing…and the same problems live to hurt veterans another day.

Jerry and I have seen more than our share of combat. We never run out of war stories; a few are included in *Never Going Home*. Between the two of us, we could have filled the book with combat stories. However, we agree that only a small constituency likes to read war stories. Jerry wanted to try to make a difference by informing others about the effect institutions, corporations, and government corruption have on our lives.

The number-one wrong we believe should be memorialized is the condemnation Vietnam veterans faced when they returned home. I congratulate Jerry for the way he presented their struggle in *Never Going Home*.

—William "Bee" Holden

Contents

Foreword 1 ·ix
Foreword 2 ·xi
Foreword 3 · xiii
Introduction · xxv

Paradise · 1
   The Youthful Invasion of Paradise · 1
   Times Square Survey · 3
   Survey Results · 3
   The Veteran, Betty, and Lenny · 4
   Betty's Husband Died On Iwo Jima · 7
   Enter Gloria, Ruby, Harold, and Jojo · 8
   Gloria's Financial Problems and Late Husband · · · · · · · · · · · · · 11
   The Veteran's Guilt · 12
   Betty's Career and the Origin of Her Ill Health · · · · · · · · · · · · · · 13
   Americans Are Hoodwinked and Robbed · · · · · · · · · · · · · · · · · 14
   Murphy's Law and the Peter Principle · 15
   Why Simplify the Big Bang? · 16
   Being Alone · 17
   My Commonality with the Veteran · 18
   Betty's Problem · 19
   Betty's Diet-and-Exercise Routine · 19
   Shake Contents · 20

Lenny's Friendship with the Veteran	20
Faulty Surgery	21
Conditioning People to Believe in Hoaxes	24
Doctors Know to Treat Only the Symptoms	26
The Veteran Speaks Out	27
Doctors Are 008 Agents	28
An Obese Nurse Lectures Lenny at Starbucks	28
Plans to Take the Veteran to the Regional VA Hospital, and Ruby Returns	33
The Veteran Tells His Story	34
The Veteran, Imprisoned for Something He Did Not Do?	37
The VA Hospital	39
The Veteran Is Dead	41
Ambushed	41
Devastated	42
Can Lenny Make It to the Hospital Before He Bleeds Out?	43
Return to the Emergency Room	44
Detective Ray Investigates the Attempted Robbery	46
Enter Will Johnson and Selma, Alabama, 1965	46
Ruby Saves the Day	49
How Does Lenny Carry On?	51
The Next Morning	53
Commemorating the Veteran	54
Lenny's Assailant Is Arrested	56
Police Officers Are the Lawyers' and Judges' K9s	56
Checking Out of the Hospital	59
Enter Will, Betty, Gloria, and Ruby	59
Ruby Tells Her Story to Lenny	61
Ruby Plots a Murder	63
Ruby, the Streetwalker	65
Ruby's Break-Dancing Performance at the University	66
Teaching Dance in Fort Myers	66
Ruby Goes to Vegas	67

Ruby's First Love, James Rogers · 68
Will Is Home, and Lenny Is Never Going Home · · · · · · · · · · · · · · · 70
Betty Returns from the Hospital's Mortuary · · · · · · · · · · · · · · · · · 71
Will Johnson Suggests a Slogan for the Family · · · · · · · · · · · · · · · · 71
Will Accepts the Position in Cape Coral · 73
Stopping at a Truck Stop for Food, Fuel, and Ruby's Show · · · · · · · 73
My Ruby Daydream · 74
The Theory of Ignorance · 75
Breezy Meets Jojo · 77
Gloria Goes to the Bank to Stop Her Foreclosure · · · · · · · · · · · · · 78
Gloria Reunites with Her First Love, Bob Richburg · · · · · · · · · · · · 78
Betty Selects a Scattering Urn for Lewis's Ashes · · · · · · · · · · · · · · · 80
Betty Reveals Ruby's Interest in Lenny · 81
Will Is the Man at Starbucks · 82
Ruby and Will Become Best Friends · 84
Ruby Purchases a Honda Odyssey and Sells Will Her Honda Fit · · · · 86
Identifying Lenny's Assailant · 88
Raining Rockets · 89
Enter Adolf, the German Industrialist · 91
Ruby Asks Lenny Out · 93
Ruby's Sexual Dysfunction Is Exposed · 94
A Nice, Clean-Eating Restaurant · 95
Ruby and Lenny Discuss Why They Don't Have Partners · · · · · · · · 96
The Gut Microbiome · 99
The Chemicals in Our Meats · 100
Ruby Explains Her Relationship with Adolf · · · · · · · · · · · · · · · · 101
A Possible Cure for Ruby's Sexual Dysfunction · · · · · · · · · · · · · · · 102
Watching the Sunset · 104
Rehabbing Ruby's Sexual Dysfunction · 105
The Therapy Is On · 109
Ruby's Sexual-Dysfunction Therapy Continues at the
Adult Toy Store · 110
Physical-Dysfunction Therapy at the Pink Shell · · · · · · · · · · · · · · 116

Gloria's First Date with Bob · 117
Will Meets Bailey at Work · 119
Betty Introduces Will to Healthy Foods at Whole Foods · · · · · · · · 120
Betty and Will Bond Over a Bottle of Champagne · · · · · · · · · · · · 123
The Health Manifesto · 126
Back to the Story · 132
Betty Takes Charge of Sunday Brunch · 133
Bailey and Bob Meet Betty's Family · 136
Betty Welcomes New Family Members · 138
The Perils of Conventional Health Care · 141
The VA Delivers the Veteran's Ashes · 143
Betty's Eulogy · 145
Ruby's Influence on Lenny · 146
Betty Informs Ruby of Harold and Her Plans · · · · · · · · · · · · · · · · 147
Betty Wants a Driver's License · 148
Dining with Detective Ray and His Wife · 149
Betty Explains to Lenny Why Ruby Chose Him · · · · · · · · · · · · · · 155
Ruby Takes Betty Driving, and Lenny Vacates His Apartment · · · · 156
Establishing a Lifelong Habit of Exercising · · · · · · · · · · · · · · · · · · · 157
An Unfortunate Gym Experience · 160
Everybody Knows How to Exercise · 161
Ruby's Dance Career, and Channel Six News · · · · · · · · · · · · · · · · 162
Lenny Leaves His Apartment and Moves into Betty's House · · · · · 165
Lenny's Lyrical · 166
What Is Going on with Betty, Ruby, Gloria, Bob,
Harold, and Lenny? · 167
Betty Updates Bob on the Community-Bank Charter · · · · · · · · · · 170
Bob Is Enlightened About Betty and Harold's Finances · · · · · · · · 172
Bob and Lenny Talk Personal Matters · 173
Betty Meets Bailey and Joni · 174
The Family Dinner · 176
Welcome Home from Vietnam (1969) · 177
In Search of a Home · 179

Vietnam Veterans Have Their Reasons for Disliking Authority · · · · 180
Caught by a Cop Being a Vietnam Veteran (1969) · · · · · · · · · · · · 181
Goons from the United States Treasury Department (1969) · · · · · 182
Living in a Box for Thirty Days (1969) · 184
Who Dies and for What? · 185
Betty Secures Her Driver's License, and the Family Comes
Together (Presently) · 186
The Rise of Civilization and the Agricultural and
Industrial Revolutions · 188
Ruby Teaches the Family Members to Dance · · · · · · · · · · · · · · · 191
Released from Wrongful Incarceration (1969) · · · · · · · · · · · · · · 192
The First Category of Sociopaths · 192
The Second Category of Sociopaths · 193
The Third Category of Sociopaths · 193
Lenny Meets Eric, a Naïve and Gullible Government
Loyalist (1969) · 194
The Evil the CIA Does · 197
Finding Callie, a Vietnam Veteran, at a Truck Stop (1969) · · · · · · 198
Callie's Vietnam Tour · 199
Callie Educates Lenny on the Slander of Vietnam Veterans (1969) · · 200
Callie's Truck-Stop Story (1969) · 201
Saigon Tea and an American Atrocity · 203
The Veterans' Dilemma · 203
Callie and Lenny Connect (1969) · 204
Betty Goes Car Shopping (presently) · 206
Betty and Bailey Drive the New Escalade to Bowditch Park · · · · · 207
Bailey's Fascination with Water · 208
The Origin of Mismatched Diseases · 211
Betty and Bailey Discover a Tortoise Family · · · · · · · · · · · · · · · · 212
Betty Confesses to Bailey, Not Marrying Harold Was a Mistake · · 213
Betty's Advice On Willy Johnson · 213
Betty and Bailey Shop at Neiman Marcus · · · · · · · · · · · · · · · · · · 214
The Burning Car · 216

The EMT Crew Insists that Betty Go to the Hospital · · · · · · · · · 217
Betty, Bailey, and Señor Gonzales, Hold a Press Conference · · · · · 220
Betty Returns Home After the Rescue and News Interview · · · · · · 222
Harold's Residence's Furnishings · 224
At the Truck Stop with Callie (1969) · 225
Cal Introduces Lenny to the Gym (1969) · · · · · · · · · · · · · · · · · 233
The Remodeling Is Complete, and Betty and the Family
Return Home (Presently) · 236
Betty and Harold Reinvest Their Money · · · · · · · · · · · · · · · · · · 237
Betty, Ruby, and Lenny, Leave Downtown Fort Myers
and Go Home · 238
Inspecting Harold's Addition · 239
Betty Gives Bailey a Blue Topaz Necklace · · · · · · · · · · · · · · · · · 241
Harold's Supercondo and the State of the Family · · · · · · · · · · · · 241
The Family's Intelligence · 242
Ruby Sizes Lenny Up · 243
Ruby and Lenny Go to the Beach at Sunset · · · · · · · · · · · · · · · · 245
Ruby and Lenny Are Privileged · 247
The CT Scan of Lenny's Heart · 248
It Is Time for the Beach · 250
Shopping for a Swimsuit for Ruby · 251
Ruby's Unofficial Swimsuit Fashion Show · · · · · · · · · · · · · · · · · 253
What Lenny Knows About Ruby · 254
Return to the Pink Shell's Honeymoon Suite · · · · · · · · · · · · · · · 255
The Cause of Ruby's Sexual Behavior · 255
The Superaphrodisiac Combination at the Pink Shell · · · · · · · · · 256
Ruby's Sexual-Dysfunction Therapy · 257
The Morning After · 259
Checking Out of the Hotel and the Photo Shoot · · · · · · · · · · · · 260
Revisiting the Manatees · 261
Ruby's Shrimp-Boat Photo Shoot · 263
Where's Lenny Now? · 266
The Dolphin Hunt · 267

Ruby and Lenny Talk at Starbucks · 269
Ruby's Confession and Apology· 271
Beginning a Life with Callie at the Truck Stop (1969) · · · · · · · · · · 272
Cal and Lenny Go Shopping, and Lenny Dreams of Bagging
Dead Soldiers (1969) · 276
The Government's Thirty-Year Denial of the Existence
of PTSD (1969) · 279
Lenny Goes to Jail (1966) · 281
Lenny Escapes from Jail (1966) · 282
Peach Tree Street (1966) · 284
Thank Goodness for Jane (1966)· 285
Basketball at the Park and Lori (1966) · 287
Jane Takes a Mother's Interest In Lenny (1966) · · · · · · · · · · · · · · 289
Shopping for Tires and Groceries with Jane (1966) · · · · · · · · · · · 291
Lenny Talks to the Atlanta Army Recruiter (1966) · · · · · · · · · · · 293
Second Day at the Park (1966)· 294
Cal Is Upset About Lori's Part in the Story (1969) · · · · · · · · · · · · 296
Back to Lori at the Park's Pond (1966)· 300
Knowing Lori (1966) · 301
The Psychology of Deprivation (1966)· 304
Sex-Education Talk On the Walk to Lori's House (1966)· · · · · · · 305
The Unexpected Return of Lori's Mother (1966) · · · · · · · · · · · · · 307
The Sex Discussion with Lori's Mother (1966) · · · · · · · · · · · · · · 309
Mother-Daughter Threesome (1966) · 312
White Slavery? (1966) · 315
The Final Deal (1966) · 321
Defending Lori's Honor (1966) · 322
A Recapitulation of What Went On with Lori, Ms. Gibson,
and Lenny (1966)· 325
The Arrangement Sidebar · 330
Leaving Cal at the Arizona Truck Stop (1970) · · · · · · · · · · · · · · · 331
The Return to Atlanta (1970)· 334
Lenny Has a Daughter and Lori Overdosed (1970) · · · · · · · · · · · 335

Lenny Decides to Stay with Mary Gibson in Atlanta (1970) · · · · · 336
Hormone Supplementation for Mary Gibson· · · · · · · · · · · · · · · · · 337
Mary Discusses Her Prior Relationships and Suggests that
Lenny Attend a University (1970) · 337
Mary, Annie, and Lenny, Pledge to Make a Life Together (1970)· · 338
Bringing a Family Together (1970)· 340
Lenny Could Not Help Being Pissed Off (1970) · · · · · · · · · · · · · · 345
Accomplishments (1975) · 346
Mary and Annie Approve of Lenny's Next Goal (1978) · · · · · · · · · 347
Lenny Receives Two Lifetime Awards (1983) · · · · · · · · · · · · · · · · 347
Slick-Talking Government Pundits Trick the Public· · · · · · · · · · · 348
Mary and Annie Agree that Lenny Should Stay Home and
Continue to School Annie · 349
Mary is Hesitant to Approve Lenny's Thesis on Sexual
Dysfunction (1989) · 349
Christianity, Hypocrisy, and Persecution · · · · · · · · · · · · · · · · · · · 350
The Final Plan (1990) · 351
The Drive Back to Atlanta and Memories (1990)· · · · · · · · · · · · · 351
Mary Cruises Through Menopause with
Hormone Supplementation · 352
Spending the Summer in Florida (1990) · · · · · · · · · · · · · · · · · · · 353
Purchasing a Motor Home for the Florida Trip (1990)· · · · · · · · · 354
What Does "Normal" Mean? (1990) · 356
The Cottage on the Beach (1990) · 359
Annie Leaves for Korea · 360
Departing Fort Myers Beach (1991)· 361
In Retrospect (1991)· 362
Setting Up Camp in Key West (1991) · 363
Catching Spiny Lobsters in Key West (1991) · · · · · · · · · · · · · · · · 364
Lightning Strikes (1991)· 366
The Final Arrangements (1992) · 369
Preparing to Break the News to Annie (1992) · · · · · · · · · · · · · · · 370
The Day After Mary's Death (1992) · 371

Informing Annie of the Death of Her Mother (1992) · · · · · · · · · · 376
Facing the Inescapable (1992) · 378
The Final Chapter in Atlanta (1992) · · · · · · · · · · · · · · · · · · · 379
Fort Myers Beach (1992 to Present) · 382
The Latest Family News · 383
The Windy Beach Store's Fashion Show, the Shrimp-Boat
Shoot, and Walmart· 385
Ode to Harold · 386
Ruby Returns Her Phone Calls · 387
Family Gathering· 389
The Bank Charter's Details and Bob and Gloria's
Marriage Announcement· 391
Betty and Lenny Discuss Adolf and Harold· · · · · · · · · · · · · · · 392
Le Moiré Café · 393
Lenny's Final Recipe for Good Health · · · · · · · · · · · · · · · · · · · 397
The Drive to the VA Regional Hospital · · · · · · · · · · · · · · · · · · 401
Reflections of Lenny's Life · 402
The VA Regional Hospital with Harold · · · · · · · · · · · · · · · · · · 403
Ruby Confesses Her Disgust · 405
Waiting-Room Scuttlebutt· 406
Harold's Debut · 406
Every Family Member Becomes a Millionaire · · · · · · · · · · · · · 408
Harold Enjoys Country Cooking at Betsy's · · · · · · · · · · · · · · · 409
Harold and Betty Take Vows · 412
Harold's First Day · 414
The Citadel Bank Building · 416
Tragedy Strikes · 418
Memorial Hospital· 418
The Show Must Continue · 422
Cracking the Safe and Ruby's Confession · · · · · · · · · · · · · · · · 423

About the Author· 427

Introduction

Never Going Home is a tale of passionate love, intrigue, despair, and tragedy. The characters in *Never Going Home* are alone and have been alone for most of their lives. They find their way to one another and create a family. Betty, an eighty-five-year-old retired librarian, is the head of the family. Lenny and Lewis remove the debilitating pill therapy prescribed to her by her doctor and design a successful rejuvenating diet-and-exercise program for Betty. Within a year, Betty stops using a wheelchair and starts walking. With her new lease on life, she directs the family forward.

Everyone knows what goes on with lovers behind closed doors today. For that reason, I do not apologize for the beautiful twenty-first-century acts of love portrayed by Lenny, Mary Gibson, and her daughter, Lori. Lenny, a Vietnam veteran who first studied psychotherapy to understand his PTSD, has flashbacks of his combat experiences. Ruby, hearing of Lenny's thesis in psychotherapy, surmises Lenny could be the key to curing her very private dysfunction. Ruby worked as a showgirl in Las Vegas for five years after obtaining a master's degree in dance from USC. She was voted "the best of Vegas" for five years running. She returned home wealthy.

Lenny, a lifetime critic of the practice of treating only a person's symptoms and not his or her disease, exposes the many hoaxes in conventional health care. He creates a common-sense program that allows people to understand healthy eating and the prevention of diseases even if they have never studied the topics.

Years earlier, Callie, a woman at a truck stop in Arizona, rescued him from the United States Treasury Department goons who robbed and incarcerated him soon after he arrived home from Vietnam. Lenny reminds the reader of the deplorable treatment Vietnam veterans received from the public, law enforcement, and the government when returning home from Vietnam.

Betty's son, Lewis, know to all as "the Veteran," dies from a botched surgery at the VA hospital. Betty's lifetime Michigan-based lawyer-boyfriend, Harold, files a lawsuit against the Veterans Administration for twenty-five million dollars.

The family accepts a new family member, Willy Johnson, a sociologist who works at the VA. Willy asks that he be called "Will." He contends that "Willy" sounds too ethnic. Will suggests that the family adopt the motto of Alexandre Dumas's three musketeers, "all for one, and one for all."

Will introduces Bailey to the family. Bailey has a master's degree in finance and works in administration for the VA. Bailey lost her husband in Afghanistan and has a three-year-old child named Joni. Her late husband impregnated her on a thirty-day leave and died in combat, never knowing that she was pregnant.

Betty's husband died in combat in World War II on the island of Iwo Jima, in the South Pacific. Her husband impregnated her on leave and never knew that she was pregnant. Bailey and Betty become inseparable.

Gloria, Ruby's mother and Betty's best friend, lives next door. She rents her apartment to Will and Bailey. Gloria, an administrative assistant with a master's degree in business administration, meets Bob Richburg, the president of a local bank. They eventually wed.

Betty reveals the enormous wealth that she and Harold accumulated by investing in the Military-Industrial Complex off a tip from an aircraft-manufacturing lobbyist whom Harold defended in court prior to the Vietnam War. They made millions as crony capitalists. They later felt guilty and reinvested their money in ways that they could live with. Betty admits that they disingenuously kept the money.

There seems to be no challenge that the family can't overcome. Author Jerry Lewis exposes through his 'can-do' characters a wide variety of issues facing Americans today: war, religious intolerance, racial issues, corporate and government corruption and deception, culture evolution, mismatch diseases, and diet and exercise.

Paradise

It was a typical Florida day in mid-February, seventy-two degrees and sunny, with a slightly cool wind blowing in from the ocean.

My name is Lenny. I lived on a small island off the coast of Southwest Florida. I found the fresh and toxic-free air that blew in from the Gulf of Mexico to be psychologically and physically medicinal.

The scientist Rachel Carson states in her theory of environmental pollution: "For the first time in the history of the world, every human being is subjected to contact with dangerous chemicals, from the moment of conception until death."

This transgression against humanity disturbs me. For more than two decades, this community had been my refuge. Not much went on there. It was mostly a retirement community, with a population that became three times larger during the winter, when the snowbirds arrived, and it became a sanctuary for those from the Midwest. The most popular saying was "another day in paradise."

The ocean is the primal source for all living things on earth. The drive to return to the beach is innately ingrained in our species.

Once upon a time, we left the ocean and crawled up onto the beach and into the forest, where we learned to become land creatures.

Charles Darwin's theory of evolution basically states that all present-day species evolved from simpler forms of life through a process of natural selection.

THE YOUTHFUL INVASION OF PARADISE

March was spring break. I had witnessed spring break for over twenty years. Things had changed on that little island. The sheriff's department plundered the kids with fines to the point that most never returned.

Fining kids for public displays of intoxication was the best source of revenue for the sheriff. The sheriff would sometimes set up a sidewalk sobriety check. The kids doing nothing would be stopped and given the balance test—they would stand on one foot and touch their noses with one finger while looking up.

If they failed, they were fined a few hundred dollars for public intoxication. I understood why more and more kids went to Mexico. The college kids very seldom caused any trouble. It was the local high school kids who caused the majority of the problems.

A competition had developed between the high school kids and the college kids over the last decade. Recently the high school girls had been winning over the college girls in the bikini contests around the island.

The college girls were overweight and, in some cases, obese. The high school girls wore less, were firmer, and had less body fat. The large amounts of steroids and growth hormones given to livestock had hastened their growth. The result was physical and sexual maturity at a much younger age than in the past and a greater biological drive to reproduce.

The competition among the sexes caused verbal arguments that often turned into physical fights. The newest group to "act out" in public were lesbian, gay, bisexual, transgender, gay, and queer (LGBTGQ) people. They were out of the closet, and they had their verbal and physical fights in public too.

Youthful hormones are raging at that point in kids' lives, and their reproductive hormones dictate their needs. Such disputes are natural at that age. The reactions of authority figures, though, were unnatural.

I had just completed a touch football game on the beach with some of my younger friends. I asked three of the younger males if they would assist me with a survey in Times Square. When I explained the survey to them, they eagerly volunteered to help.

Times Square was designed with a walk encircling the merchants. Some people casually strolled round and round the square for varied personal reasons, like to exercise, to have conversations, or to take in the sights.

TIMES SQUARE SURVEY

Our objective was to survey ten women in four different age groups. A young man of twenty-three years whom we called Mr. Rip was going to stroll the square in his bathing attire.

Mr. Rip had the typical Hollywood look; he had long blond hair, he was tall, and he had a perfectly tanned, sculpted physique.

My role was to decide which unescorted women would be observed and then questioned. They would be identified by the colors of their bathing suits and blouses.

The second young man would sit with me and record the reactions of these women when Rip passed them.

The third young man would approach the same women and tell them that we were doing a survey on the average age of the people in Times Square.

I felt that we must lie in order to extract true answers.

The real purpose was to record the women's sexual attraction to Mr. Rip when he walked past them and to categorize the women by age.

The results of our survey are displayed below.

SURVEY RESULTS

Anecdotal Results Based on Four Age Groups

(1) Women between the ages of 15 and 25 out of 10 women)
   a. Looked 9
   b. Looked more than once 7
   c. Turned and looked or stared 4
(2) Women between the ages of 26 and 36 out of 10 women
   a. Looked 7
   b. Looked more than once 5
   c. Turned and looked or stared 3
(3) Women between the ages of 37 and 47 out of 10 women
   a. Looked 3

      b. Looked more than once.. 2
      c. Turned and looked or stared 1
 (4) Women between the ages of 48 and 58 out of 10 women
      a. Looked 1
      b. Looked more than once.. 0
      c. Turned and looked or stared 0

This survey might give you some idea of the effect that age has on women's sexual drives. It could possibly raise some questions about the change of life that women go through known as menopause. It raises more questions and proposes no solutions.

Don't think I'm picking on women! I did a similar survey on men's andropause. Basically, the findings were much the same or worse. Furthermore, it suggested that menopause and andropause, the changes of life in both sexes, could be major causes of middle-aged divorce.

That topic was one of the many health-related topics that I explored over the last twenty-five years that no one really cared to read about.

The story that follows is a story that I have wanted to tell for a long time.

■ ■ ■

THE VETERAN, BETTY, AND LENNY

It was a perfect day to ride my Honda scooter. My best ideas always came while I was riding out of contact with the perils of society. Cruising the highway with a therapeutic, gentle salty Florida wind in my face could expedite my recovery from a substandard day.

When you're living in paradise, the comfort level is very high. The subtle high caused me to pass my destination. I made a U-turn and pulled into Starbucks to satisfy my desire for a cup of hot coffee. I had some thinking to do.

On my mind was Lewis, an old Vietnam veteran who had called me earlier. He had been an army airborne ranger and had seen a lot of combat during the Vietnam War. The Veteran, my very first Florida friend, had been a very dear friend for many years.

The Veteran's mother's health had been deteriorating for years, and he was her only family member, so he'd taken on the responsibility of caring for her. The decision to not dump her into an assisted-living facility said much about the man's character.

Her need for twenty-four-seven care put limitations on his lifestyle. The Veteran could leave her side only for a couple of hours at a time. An airborne ranger never leaves behind a soldier in distress. This code of behavior was ingrained in him. In civilian life, the same man refused to leave distressed loved ones behind. In this case, that loved one was his mom. It was a code that transcends generations.

In battle you must rely on the soldiers around you, and they must rely on you. Watching one another's backs creates a bond like no other experience creates. Every combat soldier, regardless of his age or the war he served in, is your brother. Trust is a common denominator among combat soldiers. This type of bond is rare among the civilian population.

The Veteran's mom's name was Betty, which was a popular name during the 1930s and the 1940s. Some days I would sit with Betty to give the Veteran time off to handle personal business or just to run free for the day. Betty's health was steadily improving.

Later I will discuss the reason for Betty's premature health problems and the adjustments that the Veteran and I made to her routine that enabled her to feel vibrant again.

Betty was in her mideighties. Her mind became strong and clear after the Veteran and I slowly took her off the five medications she'd been taking. The medication served only the financial interests of her physician.

Betty cooperated fully after the Veteran presented her with a copy of *Fortune* magazine's interview with Henry Gadsden, who served as the CEO of Merck from 1965 to 1975. Merck was the largest pharmaceutical corporation in the world at that time.

Gadsden said that it had long been his dream to make drugs for healthy people so that he could sell drugs to everyone. Three decades later, his dream had come true.

Doctors started prescribing drugs based on corporation-sponsored public-awareness campaigns that created illnesses by suggestion.

Betty took a strong interest in our discussions of the impact that the environment has on health. She realized that it might be too late to correct her arthritis but that it could be possible to arrest and minimize the pain.

She worked diligently on her own to restore her physical fitness. Betty's effort to reclaim her health greatly pleased the Veteran. She hated her wheelchair and refused to sit in it.

She declared that it was worthless because of her inability to roll herself. She complained that the arthritis in her shoulder caused her so much pain that she was unable to push the wheels. The Veteran and I agreed that Betty would walk when she was willing to. For months she closely followed the strength-training and nutritional-diet plans that the Veteran and I had devised for her. She began to mention her shoulder pain less and less.

The Veteran and I formulated a strategy that would give her the best chance of reaching her goal. After beginning the program, Betty increased her weight from 95 pounds to 110 pounds, mostly by gaining weight in her legs and shoulders.

She bragged often about how strong she had become but didn't mention anything about walking. We knew that when we were not present, she exercised her legs and practiced walking. How else could her legs have doubled in size?

Betty had been without her son for decades. The Veteran had returned home when she'd lost her mobility. Our analysis was that Betty feared that the Veteran would leave her if she walked. Whether or not his decision was the right one, the Veteran had decided that he wouldn't leave her side ever again.

The Veteran secured a self-powered wheelchair on a trial basis. Betty would have nothing to do with the electric wheelchair. She preferred to sit and read in the dilapidated ancient rocker that her late husband had bought her.

Betty ardently proclaimed that the rocker fit her like an old shoe and was a precious honeymoon present from her late husband. It was obvious that her sentimental attachment to the old chair was greater than the physical comfort that it provided.

The Veteran and I never challenged her feelings for the chair. We confidentially referred to the chair as "Betty's shrine."

BETTY'S HUSBAND DIED ON IWO JIMA

Betty's husband was a marine during World War II. He was killed in February 1945 while fighting the Japanese in the battle of Iwo Jima in the South Pacific. He was responsible for flushing the Japanese out of the caves they were holed up in. He carried a flamethrower and tanks containing highly volatile liquids strapped to his back.

When he pulled the trigger, liquids under pressure were expelled from the tank and ignited. Very few Japanese soldiers surrendered; most chose to burn.

While her husband was performing his duty, a Japanese sniper shot his tank with a projectile with a pyrotechnic charge known as a "tracer round." The tank exploded, incinerating him and three other marines who were close to him. His sergeant explained what had happened in his letter to Betty, and she shared the contents of the letter with me.

After viewing the letter, I handed it back to Betty, and she placed it on her heart and sat motionlessly for a minute or two. This letter was sacred to Betty.

William Tecumseh Sherman, a Civil War general, said, "War is cruelty, and you cannot refine it."

The battle of Iwo Jima was the only battle won by the United States, whereas, the United States suffered more casualties than the Japanese. Betty's husband, Bill, had a thirty-day leave before he shipped out. During that time, the Veteran was conceived.

Betty told me that they were newlyweds, and she said with tears in her eyes that he'd died not knowing that she was pregnant. She hung her head to hide her expression and told me that when his body arrived home, it was sealed with a warning that she should not look at it under any circumstances. The rumor was that that meant that the fiery explosion had disintegrated his body. She cried out in emotional pain nearly seventy years after his death, and I quickly surrounded her with my arms in an effort to console her. Betty had become like family to me. She quickly gathered her composure and spoke. Betty said that she could never remarry and that the very thought of her son being raised by another man repulsed her.

I asked Betty if she had friends who visited her on occasion. She hesitated, and when I saw the puzzling look forming on her incredible, beautifully aged face, I quickly said that what I meant was that I would enjoy meeting them.

"That was a white lie," I quietly said. And I wondered whether I'd turned into an investigative reporter.

I mean the kind of reporter who asks any question, no matter how hurtful it is, to get a story. A reporter who believes that the story is more important than the pain caused by the insensitive questions that he asks the victim. Now the trend is to report certain sentences out of context in order to spin the story and to make it sound worse than it was, which creates higher network ratings and thus, greater profits.

ENTER GLORIA, RUBY, HAROLD, AND JOJO

Betty answered my question about her friends with a displeased facial expression; she said they were all dead except for Gloria, the crazy woman who lived next door.

"Gloria's daughter's name is Ruby. I liked her," Betty said. "She's a wild thing! She's very smart." Betty told me that she was the smartest kid in her senior class in high school and that she earned a full academic scholarship to a prestigious university for dance.

"When Ruby was in high school, her friends were street people with no directions or goals. Most of their parents were ignorant and lived on welfare. Ruby never sought employment. Betty was told that Ruby hung out on the streets, hustling tourists for money.

"Gloria admitted that she'd been too busy with her own troubles to spend time with her. She justified not being there for Ruby by saying that she was an adult and that it was time for her to grow up and become responsible.

"When Ruby was young she would come over to escape her stepfather, who she claimed was sexually molesting her. I should have called the authorities, but I didn't know if Ruby, a teenager with a bad reputation, was making the story up," Betty said. "The rumor was that Ruby was a streetwalker, you know; she wasn't a full-time prostitute, but every now and then, when she needed money, she'd walk the streets.

"Her mother had gotten drunk and had a one-night stand with a man she'd picked up in a bar. She didn't remember his name or see him ever again," Betty said. "Ruby informed me that she had no idea who her father was."

Betty continued. "Ruby took off with some guy and has never been seen or heard from since. She left her dog behind, and it shows up here when Gloria is too broke to feed the dog or just forgets to. Ruby found the dog half starved, brought it home, and nursed it back to life.

"That indicated that Ruby was a caring individual. After Ruby left, I paid to have one of those dog doors installed. I keep a bowl of dog food in the kitchen. The dog's name is Jojo. When she gets hungry, she comes here to eat and then leaves. Ruby's disappearance is just one more thing that's driving Gloria crazy," Betty said.

"After all of those years working in the library, you never had a man friend?" I asked.

Betty blushed, looked straight up at the ceiling lamp, and said, "Sort of. His name was Harold, and he was fifteen years younger than I was."

"Do you still speak with him?" I asked.

"He still writes to me. He lives in one of those old historic homes. In his letters he tells me that he lives there because his parents lived there. In his last letter he said that he still has a car and a valid driver's license. He came to visit me the first year I was in Florida. I had just bought this house with my retirement money, and my focus was on the house. I guess he felt ignored.

"Harold left with an obvious look of rejection on his face. A couple of years later, I sent him a birthday card and apologized. I admit that was damn rude of me, especially after he drove so far to visit me."

"You knew when his birthday was?" I asked.

"For years we exchanged birthday and Christmas presents," Betty said. "He was good to Lewis. Took him to movies and to school when I was busy with work.

"I kept the relationship platonic. I never allowed Harold to sleep over. I know he wanted more intimacy, but it wasn't in me. I can say now that I regret my actions. That was then, and this is now. Things have changed—especially with my health."

Betty took a deep breath and continued. "Three years after he'd left Florida, I received a letter from him. I was surprised! I thought he'd moved on with his life. Now he writes me a letter once a year, asking if he can come see me again. I write him back but don't invite him down. He tells me what's going on in his life, and I tell him what's going on in my life.

"Our conversations are never personal. We talk a lot about the weather and the books we're reading. Harold loves to read," Betty said.

"Why not invite him down?" I asked. Betty went silent. I repeated my question.

Betty took a deep breath and said, "He doesn't know I can't walk!"

I could tell that Betty was tiring of the conversation, so I decided to move on to another subject and to come back to this part of Betty's life another day.

I did notice a glimmer in Betty's eyes when she said Harold's name. I wondered whether the Veteran's living with her had anything to do with her not inviting Harold down again.

I remembered her telling me that she would not ever think about marrying or having another man raise her son. I also remembered that I hadn't recorded Betty's husband's name.

"Betty, what was your husband's name?"

Betty was quick to reply. "William, but everyone called him Bill." I waited for a moment…. She said nothing more, so I left it there.

GLORIA'S FINANCIAL PROBLEMS AND LATE HUSBAND

I asked what Ruby's mother was like.

"Gloria married when Ruby was young. Her husband was a compulsive gambler. He refinanced the house to keep his legs from being broken by the loan shark's thugs. One night he was driving drunk, and he crashed his car and was DOA at the hospital. That was not long after her older brother had died and left her one hundred thousand dollars to pay off her mortgage." Betty shook her head and said, "Instead of paying off her mortgage, she spent her inheritance. She bought an expensive car—a Mercedes—jewelry, fancy clothes, and new designer furniture for the house with the money. That's pretty dumb, huh?"

I couldn't help but nod my head. Betty continued. "Gloria is in an irritating 'panic mode' that affects everyone she comes into contact with. She has no idea how to handle her situation.

"Gloria has only her unemployment to live on, and that won't even cover her basic living expenses. She has tremendous skills, but her age is certainly an obstacle that prevents her from securing a gainful job.

"If Ruby turned tricks, and I have my doubts that she did, it would have been to help her mom to pay the mortgage. Ruby was Gloria's cash cow, and when she left, the money went with her.

"Gloria admitted that she'd accepted money from Ruby but never asked how she'd earned it. That doesn't necessarily mean that Ruby was hooking, though.

"Gloria's house is in foreclosure as we speak. When the foreclosure notice came, her behavior became intolerable. I could no longer endure her whining and complaining.

"She would not listen to reason. I tried to console her and to offer her advice or maybe a solution. Her personal misery dominated the conversation. You know, it's not like I can jump up and leave when I've had enough.

"I told Gloria not to come back after her last visit, although we've been friends for many years. I know I'll miss her."

I wanted to laugh out loud when Betty commented about jumping up and leaving. However, I could only snicker to myself.

I knew at that moment that I wanted to meet this Gloria. I was sure her story would be full of interesting drama. Living with a compulsive gambler must have been difficult; gamblers are high when they're winning and low when they're losing. I saw Gloria's life as an emotional yo-yo. I wanted to record a slice of it. Furthermore, I wanted to hear more about Ruby.

I thought I saw Betty's knee jerk. Interesting.

THE VETERAN'S GUILT

I always looked forward to being with Betty one on one. I surmised that Betty could tell me more detailed versions of the trials and tribulations that had shaped the Veteran's life. Betty's story would definitely allow me to gain insight into his upbringing.

I've always relied on facts, but I know that emotion is the engine that drives every story.

Between Betty and the Veteran, I always had plenty to record. Betty was formally educated at a Michigan university. She was a surviving spouse and used the GI Bill to obtain a degree in library science.

Betty was a librarian in a small Michigan town for thirty years before she retired and moved to Florida. The Veteran told me that she had been in Florida for five years before he'd found out where she was.

"I guess it was my fault—I was young and caught up in a fast-moving life," the Veteran said.

I tried to comfort him. "I've been there too. That's a requirement for being young, right?"

The Veteran nodded.

BETTY'S CAREER AND THE ORIGIN OF HER ILL HEALTH

Betty was an overachiever, as were many others of her generation. Her job required a forty-hour work schedule. She took it upon herself to be at work seven days a week, from opening to closing.

In those days people didn't spend their evenings watching television. They read and socialized more with their families and friends. Some contend that those interactions create stronger and more confident individuals.

She once told me that she worked seventy hours a week or more if the staff members had meetings. The library had a small café that had a reputation around town for being one of the least expensive places to grab a quick meal. Another known draw was the fact that the café's proceeds were donated to the children's library.

This commitment to children made the library well known in that area of the state. Some parents would drive one hundred miles so that their children could spend the day in this library.

Betty's son, Lewis (the Veteran), grew up in the children's library. The children's library opened up to the outside, where there was a playground. The playground had been planned out very well. Betty had been its chief designer. The kids loved it.

The presence of an adult in the playground made it possible for parents to allow their kids to play while they explored the library. The library had an infant nursery staffed with volunteers, most of whom were older, well-qualified women whose children were on their own.

Children's meals were free at the café. The library and the café were the town's pride and joy. Betty had built both, and then she maintained them for thirty years. Betty had definitely left her mark on the sleepy little rural town. The children's library now bears a plaque commemorating its founder, Betty Anderson.

She showed me pictures of the retirement party that the town threw for her. For three months before the party, a registration book was displayed in the library for people to sign that were planning to attend Betty's retirement ceremony. In that length of time, fifteen thousand people wrote messages to Betty to show their appreciation for her service to the community at large.

The party was held in the high school's football stadium, which was able to accommodate the thousands that attended. There were concessions, music, fireworks, and, of course, plenty of entertainment for children.

Lewis joined the army when he was eighteen and did not return home until Betty retired in Florida and became physically impaired.

Betty had been the head librarian for twenty-eighty years. She'd been at the library for only two years before she'd assumed that position. "It was all about being in the right place at the right time," Betty said. I did not buy that. She earned her position, and the beneficiary of her work was the city. She had started as an assistant librarian and had worked closely with the head librarian.

The head librarian had become mentally incapable of doing his job during Betty's second year on the job. Betty did his job for most of that year. When he finally resigned, his job was given to Betty. His diabetes had advanced to the point that he was unable to fulfill his responsibilities.

Betty was promoted to librarian by the library board. They had been well aware that she had been running the show for the last year. The head librarian was given the benefit of eating for free at the library café.

Betty was always present at the library except during the few hours she slept every night. She ate at the café for thirty years. The café served precooked and processed food and an abundance of pastries.

Thirty years of this toxic diet caused Betty to have nutritional deficiencies, diabetes, and arthritis. What happened to Betty has happened to millions of other Americans who eat toxic processed foods and too much sugar.

AMERICANS ARE HOODWINKED AND ROBBED

There is no way that the average person can understand or keep up with the industrial developments in food technology. Some of the best scientists work in the food-processing industry. Their jobs are to formulate chemicals that make cheap, bad-tasting food taste great.

A category of chemicals, known as glutamates, was developed during World War II by Japanese scientists to enhance the taste of the Japanese soldiers' field rations. When the Japanese soldiers were captured, the United States soldiers set aside their rations and consumed the better-tasting Japanese rations.

American scientists discovered that monosodium glutamate, a taste enhancer, had been added to the Japanese rations. This might be the time for me to offer some words of wisdom about health. The Veteran and I have spent many hours discussing this topic. It's a pleasure for me to have a friend who shares my passions.

The average American would rather watch television than take a few minutes a day to educate him or herself on matters of health. So sit tight for a moment, and listen. You might find the facts that the Veteran and I studied interesting, and you might not have noticed or thought about them before.

The average American spends his or her day working long hours. During the evenings, he or she worries about money or relaxes by watching mindless programs on television. Then it's time for bed, and the vicious cycle starts all over again. Most people don't have time to notice what is going on in the environment and how it is affecting their lives and health.

In America you are on your own when it comes to health. I refer to health in America as the "Wild West." If you pack up your wagon and go out West, you are on your own. You must protect yourself from indigenous people, bandits, and the many other dangers of the frontier.

Today, you must protect yourself from the health-care industry's pills, the food processors' toxic additives, the chemical corporations' environmental poisons, the sheriffs, the IRS, the lawyers, and the government.

They all are competing for your hard-earned money and taking it any way they legally can—and sometimes, if you are poor and defenseless, they take it illegally too.

MURPHY'S LAW AND THE PETER PRINCIPLE

The Veteran developed his great storytelling skills from his many exploits. He quotes Murphy's Law often.

The law states that anything that can possibly go wrong will go wrong. He was the first person to show me the law's mathematical formula, which is 1+1×2, where × stands for "hardly ever equals."

Another law he speaks of is the Peter Principle. This is when employees within an organization advance to their highest level of competence and then are promoted to and remain at levels at which they are incompetent.

According to the Veteran, this can also apply to one's status in his private life. The Veteran realizes that these thoughts are not really laws, but they add entertainment value to conversations.

WHY SIMPLIFY THE BIG BANG?

The Veteran was impressed when I explained my version of the big bang theory. I told him I had memorized a condensed interpretation of it so that I could explain it to the not so intellectually endowed, who often demand simple explanations for some of science's most complex phenomena. I received a nod of agreement and a chuckle from the Veteran.

I was examining inexpensive watches in a discount department store when a lady in her late fifties approached me. She asked me how I'd gotten in such good shape at my age. I responded by saying that fitness is not the result of one or a couple of things. It entails multiple things that one must understand and coordinate. She gave me a disappointed look when I told her my answer. I said nothing more and waited for her next question.

"My husband is younger than you, and he has a huge stomach. He tells me that because of his age, nothing can be done about it. I don't believe him. Lately I've been noticing that other men his age and older do not have grotesque stomachs," she said.

I felt that I shouldn't say anything more. She then lashed out at me. "People like you don't want to help others!" I quickly turned and left the department store. When I was sure I'd escaped the impossible situation, I ran over her statement in my mind.

How typical that mind-set is among the illiterate masses. Shallow thinking demands simple explanations for complex problems. The lady had been expecting me to tell her everything that she needed to know in a couple of simple sentences.

When the forefathers were creating the United States, they agreed that it should be a republic. That meant the people of an area would elect a person to represent them in a larger body made up of elected representatives from all of the areas. It was generally understood that each area would elect the smartest and wisest people to represent it.

Today too many individuals think that they are smart and insist that they are right. I must remind the reader that ignorance means not knowing what you don't know! I have also devised a condensed and simple version of the big bang theory for your shallow friends.

The universe began when a single point of infinitely dense and infinitely hot matter exploded spontaneously. The debris caused by this explosion began to fly away from the explosion point and is still flying and will keep on flying indefinitely. All of the galaxies, stars, and planets were formed from this debris.

BEING ALONE

Betty and the Veteran had both been on their own for their entire lives. Their exemplary lives made me believe that one can have a good and productive life without friends and family. What am I questioning? Is it possible to maintain acceptable social behavior without the constant social stimulation that a loving relationship provides? I believe it is.

To focus on my writing, I must be selfish with my time. When another indelibly shares my space, I am accused of ignoring him or her. Not having family and being alone for extended periods of time make it easy for me to view my solo existence as normal.

My rationale for this idea can be described by a cliché: What you never had, you never miss. When I asked the Veteran for his opinion on this perplexing personal matter, he said, "Do what makes you happy."

I thought, "I guess this is one I have to go alone on."

I never told him that I had been alone from the beginning and that I would most likely be alone in the end.

It's all I know.

MY COMMONALITY WITH THE VETERAN

I once complained to the Veteran that my ability to write transcended my ability to speak. His response was that I needed to practice verbalizing my thoughts in order to become an eloquent speaker.

Most of the conversations the Veteran and I enjoyed were over a cell phone. I truly took pleasure in our discussions and always looked forward to his calls. The Veteran's experiences were esoteric and diverse and often similar to mine.

The Veteran had worked many different jobs, owned several dissimilar businesses, twice become a millionaire and twice become broke, and bought and lived in five dwellings, three of which he had personally remodeled, in five different cities.

After three tours in Vietnam he worked his way through a prestigious university and had educated himself in many different disciplines. He was well traveled and well read, and he could converse at any social level. He had an extraordinary ability to empathize with almost everybody, whether they were young or old or rich or poor.

Sometimes when he told his story, I would think he was telling my story. When I mentioned the similarities, he said, "You know what? It's the same with me when you're telling me a story about an event in your life."

The Veteran was initially attracted to me because of his interest in my knowledge on the prevention and causes of mismatched diseases, diseases caused by our environment. He was on to them when we met. We each had something that the other one wanted: more knowledge!

He was mesmerized by my years of research on these vital subjects and referred to my knowledge as "life-or-death information." He spoke of me as though I had a wealth of information.

I have to admit that his acknowledgement of my learning felt good. We often discussed disease prevention and the reasons why there was little interest in preventing disease.

We both agreed that the main reason is that there is no money in preventions and cures. Once a person is cured of a disease, the cash flow stops. The money is in the indefinite treatment of chronic maladies and in the drugs used to treat them. The Veteran had a unique way with words. I once heard him say that the average American man knows more about his automobile than his own body. You would think that a person would realize that an automobile could be replaced if abused but that he would receive only one body and that it would have to last for his whole lifetime.

He was chock-full of information that he accumulated during hands-on life experiences. I never once heard him tell the same story twice. His "fly by the seat of his pants" life came to an abrupt halt when his mom became chronically ill.

BETTY'S PROBLEM

The Veteran blamed himself for not being there sooner to take care of her. He said to me that years of ill health had caused her to give up the fight for life and that by the time he'd gone to see her, her diabetes and arthritis had taken a toll on her. However, her mind had still been sharp.

I was certain that Betty was a victim of conventional health care and that drug therapy was the culprit of her ill health.

He was quick to agree. We did learn that after she started her new eating regimen, she had no need for insulin injections. That inspired the Veteran. Her pancreas was capable of producing an adequate amount of insulin but only if she restricted her intake of carbohydrates to no more than fifty grams over a twenty-four-hour period.

We speculated that with the right diet, in due time, her pancreas would recover and begin producing a normal amount of insulin.

Betty's diet-and-exercise regimen was based on common sense. Told to rely on others for information about health for her entire life, she became conditioned to not listen to her body and to not think for herself on health.

BETTY'S DIET-AND-EXERCISE ROUTINE

The following was Betty's diet-and-exercise routine:

1. Get 15 minutes of direct sunlight 3 times per week.
2. Take a 1 mL injection of B12 and folic acid containing 500 mcg/mL hydroxocobalamin acetate and 15 mg/mL folic acid weekly.

3. Take a 10 IU injection containing 5 mg of cypionate testosterone weekly.
4. Take a 10 IU subcutaneous injection containing 1 mg of IGF-1 every day.
Note that no supplemental estrogen or progesterone is needed.
5. Drink 2 ½ cups of grass-fed and finished organic bone marrow broth each day.
6. 6. Take a Mercola women's formula whole-food vitamin each day.
7. Take a 50 mg pregnenolone capsule each day.
8. Drink as much Fiji brand water or organic tea as desired.

SHAKE CONTENTS

1. Drink 2 cups of grass-fed raw organic milk per day.
2. Take 1 ¼ ounces of wild Alaskan salmon oil per day.
3. Take 15 grams of blue-green algae twice per day.
4. Take 2 ½ grams of astaxanthin powder twice per day.
5. Take 10 grams of organic whey protein powder twice per day.
6. Eat ¼ ounce of pulverized raw almonds twice per day.
7. Eat ¼ ounce of pulverized raw walnuts twice per day.
8. Add Fiji water as needed.
9. Add a serving of organic fruit for flavor.

Note that only Himalayan salt is allowed.

Complete daily in-chair exercises for the upper and lower body. These will be changed weekly, and no resistance exercises are required.

LENNY'S FRIENDSHIP WITH THE VETERAN

I owe the Veteran for repairing my worst character flaw. After twenty years, I learned patience from him, which has been instrumental in helping me finally become a good friend to myself in spite of the horrid mistakes of my past.

The Veteran and I were in Vietnam at the same time, although we didn't meet each other until I received his number from a mutual friend and gave him a call. Our friendship has developed over the last twenty years.

Not long after we met, he said that I was a good listener. I took his comment as a compliment. I look at listening as an art, and I practice it. I write stories, and it's necessary for a writer to be a good listener. The better I listen, the more precise I am when I record the necessary details of a story.

Every individual has a story, but very few have amazing stories that take others to places they have never been to and will never go to. It is a rare incident when an individual meets another individual who has had an esoteric life similar to his or her own.

The Veteran's life experiences ran parallel to mine. In my sixty-seven years of being on this earth, I had never imagined meeting a person who could understand me as well as the Veteran could. That is why our friendship is like no other friendship.

His mother's misfortune unfortunately caused him to willingly incarcerate himself, which left him with nothing but time to tell his stories. So he told them to me, and I visualized and recorded them.

FAULTY SURGERY

Several months earlier, the Veteran had had serious complications from a botched surgery performed by the VA. Why was I not surprised?

He'd had a congenital inguinal hernia from birth. Years of picking his mother up and carrying her from place to place had finally caused his weak abdominal area to give way, which had allowed the contents of the area to protrude through his skin.

During the simple operation to net the protruding abdominal contents, he mysteriously got an infection. It appears that the infection had become a mystery to the attending physicians.

Over time the chronic infection wore down his immune system. In the last few months, he struggled with pain and related illnesses every moment of the day. The Veteran requested that I drive him to the main VA hospital in Tampa, which was 150 miles from where he resided.

At first I assumed that his request was not out of the ordinary. We had ridden to the VA together on many other occasions. We always tried to schedule appointments on the same day in order to split the costs of traveling.

When it was not possible to schedule our appointments on the same day, the one without an appointment would go along for the ride. The VA pays for travel, giving veterans a certain amount of money per mile. Riding together cut the cost in half and gave us a little extra money—enough to pay for a good meal.

We always tried to eat at a different restaurant. We made a game out of hunting for unprocessed foods along our way. When real foods were not available at one exit, we would drive to the next exit.

I'd had a sense that something was very wrong when he called. There was a long pause after my hello. I could hear him breathing heavily. I know the sound of someone gasping for air. After a long pause, the Veteran said in a stressed voice that he did not trust himself to drive.

He asked me if I would drive him and offered to pay me. I immediately said I would, and without hesitation, I let him know that I was offended by his offering me money. I knew, though, that his offer to pay me had been a courtesy.

Something was terribly different with this situation. The Veteran had called me a thousand or more times before, and none of those calls had been as alarming as this call. I could tell he did not want to discuss the matter at that time. I said good-bye and hung up.

The trip conflicted with a VA appointment of my own. I couldn't have cared less. I intuitively realized the seriousness of his situation. Besides, how could a 100 percent service-connected disabled Vietnam veteran have refused care to another 100 percent service-connected disabled Vietnam veteran?

Combat veterans share thoughts unimaginable to the average American—never-ending horrid thoughts of death and war. I am privileged to have a friend of his distinction. My long-awaited VA appointment would have to be rescheduled. To me, seeing a shrink was far less important than the obvious emergency at hand.

I knew that for the last few months, the Veteran's health had been in a steady decline. I regretted my hesitance to say something about the VA's negligent postoperative care. My failure to verbalize my discontent to the Veteran really bothered me. The fact that the Veteran had never asked for my opinion was my excuse at the time.

The simple operation had definitely moved him closer to his expiration date, and we both knew it. I wondered how this could have been happening. To tell this story, I need to share additional information and be expeditious.

My last appointment had been with my primary physician for a blood test. He hadn't thought it was necessary, because I hadn't had any pending symptoms to complain about. My thoughts are always on prevention. I insisted, and he reluctantly ordered the test. I informed him that I would pick up a copy of the test results in the records department.

He resented the fact that I had no interest in his interpretation of the test results, and I resented his ignorance of the topic of prevention. I did not need to make an appointment to discuss the results. I read blood test as well as anyone.

I had been teaching the Veteran to read blood reports, and I am proud to announce that he was getting good at it. I had become increasingly dubious of the medical practices at the VA. The fact that the Veteran's simple operation had morphed into a life-and-death situation didn't do much to help matters.

A physician is trained to look for disease. He does that by ordering a cascade of tests. Many of these tests are completely irrelevant, although they do increase his income. If you take these tests and no disease is present, you will be most likely told you are well.

By studying on my own for years, I learned to look for indications of a disease or a malady in order to prevent its manifestation. The word on the block is prevention! You know what I mean when I say that an ounce of prevention is worth a pound of cure.

I never understand why a person would totally rely on a stranger (a doctor) for advice on the most important thing he has: his life! Furthermore, a doctor's financial interests are best served when you are sick or prescribed toxic drugs that mask your symptoms and require a follow-up appointment, more times than not, that serves only the doctor's financial interest.

Everyone in our society is conditioned to do as doctors say and to never question their diagnoses.

CONDITIONING PEOPLE TO BELIEVE IN HOAXES

The Veteran and I reviewed Ivan Pavlov's study. Pavlov demonstrated the classical conditioning process of responding automatically without hesitation or thought in his theory of conditioned reflexes.

In his experiment, Pavlov rang a bell and then fed a dog. He repeated this procedure over and over. Before long he could ring the bell, and the dog would start salivating.

People get sick and are told to see a doctor over and over again for years. Before long their reflexes are to see a doctor without investigating on their own why they are feeling a little different. This human-conditioning process is similar to Pavlov's dog-conditioning process.

The Veteran admitted that he had become conditioned. He went to the doctor for his hernia, and without thought, he did exactly as he'd been told. Thinking that the surgery would be a simple in-and-out procedure, the Veteran gave little thought to the possibility of any complications. He regretted not saying anything about the dirt he noticed under the operating physician's nails.

I didn't see any reason for concern either. However, if the Veteran had told me about the dirt he'd noticed under his operating physician's nails, I would have convinced him to complain about it. We were both blindsided by the unexpected complications.

The Veteran did question me about why I'd never mentioned my years of studying conventional health care on my own. "I knew you were well studied, but I had no idea of the extent of your study," he said. My response to him was that I had learned from experience that what I said made no difference to people—they would listen only to their doctors. I recognized their conditioning; they believed that their doctors knew best.

After losing too many debates to people who thought they knew everything but actually knew nothing, I learned to give advice only when asked. Every person, regardless of his or her level of education, insists that he or she knows everything about health, disease prevention, exercise, and diet. The only explanation I can come up with is that the human species' health knowledge is inborn stupidity.

The only authorities who pretend to know more about exercise and diet than they do are their doctors, even though doctors' medical school curricula are virtually devoid of training in these areas.

My conclusion is that you are living in a society in which the majority's misinformation is right regardless of whether it is wrong. My advice is to do your own investigation before you act on hearsay or any authority's advice, especially when it comes to your personal health.

Suppose that you do know more than most, and suppose that you know more than the average doctor about the cause or the prevention of a disease. The only thing you will accomplish if you speak out is ensuring that you will be considered a fool in your circle of peers.

The Veteran seemed to be satisfied with my answer and never brought the subject up again. People don't think. Instead, they believe and do what they are told. Some contend that state supported education is synonymous with indoctrination.

I have to admit that I stole that statement from a different conversation with the Veteran. He also said that changing the mind-set of the average adult is more difficult than cooking a twenty-pound ham without a meat thermometer. Now I can't help but laugh when I see a ham.

I regretted not flaunting my knowledge to the Veteran. He would have considered my knowledge. "Damn," I thought. I was a day late and a dollar short! Timing is everything! The Veteran and I had so much information to exchange and so little time.

When my daughter was twenty-three years old, she had a glucose reading of ninety-two. Her doctor said that score was good and that she had no problems with sugar metabolism. When she told me that, I said, "Hold on—you are prediabetic! Simply put, a number over eighty-nine could mean that you're on your way to becoming diabetic. It's time for some lifestyle changes, exercise, and different food choices."

She ignored my information and said, "Dad, you are not a medical doctor."

DOCTORS KNOW TO TREAT ONLY THE SYMPTOMS

Doctors receive money and expensive vacations from pharmaceutical corporations when they overprescribe drugs. For most, this practice is a little hard to believe. But it's true—big pharma spends more money on advertising their drugs than on researching their drugs.

Furthermore, some say that doctors are guilty only of being ignorant (that is, not knowing what they don't know.) The only people who are more ignorant of prevention than doctors are patients. Unless a pill is developed for prevention, there will be no significant progress in eradicating diseases. The doctors can take that to the bank!

The causes of diseases are rarely discussed in medical schools. Doctors definitely practice what they were taught; they treat the symptoms of diseases with drugs in order to mask the conditions.

I can't imagine some young student who's grateful that she's been accepted into a medical school ever insisting that her professor direct her to the science that supports what he is saying. This conventional practice of treating the symptoms, not the causes, ensures that doctors will be paid for their services almost indefinitely. This fact is so transparent. Why can only a few see it?

Even presidents have been duped by the drug-therapy cartel. I noticed that in his State of the Union address, a recent president mentioned that doctors were curing more and more people with new drugs and technologies. Someone needs to educate the president. Drugs can't cure. They only mask the symptoms

THE VETERAN SPEAKS OUT

The Veteran jokingly said, "Once they tore me open, they were addicted to cutting on me." I couldn't help myself—I laughed out loud! He said he'd lost count of the entries into his abdominal cavity and that every time they operated on him, they would go back in to repair what they had done before.

He experienced continuous painful contractions and believed that they were caused by the battery-powered infection pump that had been implanted in the side of his abdomen. Later his doctors agreed the pump was responsible for the infection that was filling his side bag too often and removed it. Oops—they'd made a serious medical error.

"Practice makes perfect, and there are plenty of good bodies to try again on," the Veteran said.

The Veteran would make this point in the presence of others. He would say, "If you're smart, you'll stay away from doctors, or you could end up like me." That was his way of getting back at the doctors—and then he would brandish his pus bag.

"The average person today learns very little from reading. The average person learns from others and from watching videos," the Veteran once told me.

"Whoever controls the programs on TV has the greatest influence on the average person's beliefs and behaviors and on consumerism."

The Veteran continued. "When I show a person my repulsive bag, I might make a believer out of him. That's what you call social engineering by the use of fear, which is the most successful method of delivering convincing information in the United States.

"Americans have become homogenized. Television and the Internet and social media command the attention of the population, young and old. They are the main reason that people look alike, act alike, and desire similar things and lifestyles. The constant exposure to advertising promotes corporate consumerism. The media is biased toward the government and ensures standards of behavior that facilitate control of the population.

"The government protects and looks out for the people—but not the ones who attract too much attention by calling out corporate and governmental foul play and corruption. These individuals can wind up in a federal kangaroo court on some erroneous charges. Then they're found guilty by juries of people who aren't technically their peers," the Veteran said.

DOCTORS ARE 008 AGENTS

Doctors require a lot of money for their services, usually so that they can support their materialistic lifestyles. Money is the most popular reason that students choose to attend medical school to start with; that's an indication of the breed of people who are attracted to the profession.

The Veteran told me that the last surgery he had undergone was a new procedure and that the strong pain medication that had previously been given to him had impaired his ability to make a good decision. Many medicated patients make serious surgery decisions while impaired. I suspect some make serious life-threatening mistakes.

The Veteran said that doctors are classified as double-oh-eight agents. I asked what that meant. He said that they're similar to double-oh-seven British spy agents who are licensed to kill bad people. The difference is that double-oh-eight drug-therapy agents have a license to kill anyone they diagnose with health problems in lieu of money. "Got you," the Veteran said, laughing.

The Veteran had had no reason to think that the simple operation would be threatening and had allowed the physician to proceed. He said that this was often the case and that when VA doctors make mistakes, they are rarely questioned.

"Doctors practice medicine—maybe the next time, mine will get it right. If I could do it over, I would not go first."

I chuckled out of fear.

"It's all in a day's exorbitant pay for a doctor," the Veteran said.

AN OBESE NURSE LECTURES LENNY AT STARBUCKS

It was time for coffee, and there was a Starbucks nearby. I parked my scooter and worked my way to the counter. I ordered my coffee. I looked around for a place to position my Apple computer, my iPhone, and my papers. I prefer to stand at the counter in front of the window. All of the spaces were occupied, so I took a seat at a shared table.

Standing is much healthier than sitting, especially for extended periods of time. Furthermore, standing is better for the spine and burns more calories. I have often advised people who have chronic back pain in the small of their backs to cut down on their sitting time.

I built a podium so that I can stand to do my computer work, read, or even watch TV. If no physical problems exist, this is the fix for back pain. Even if there is a physical problem, standing will minimize the pain to some extent over time.

My thoughts quickly returned to the Veteran. Damn, I could feel his pain when he called. His voice had made me shiver. Damn those doctors! The two open seats at the shared table allowed me to see only a green wall and positioned my back to the world. Sitting in that position still creeps me out.

In Vietnam I always sat with my back to the wall and kept my eyes on the entrance or on anyone I didn't recognize. I would drink my beer with one hand and hold my Belgium nine millimeter in the other hand to ensure my survival.

The Veteran said he'd done the same thing, but he had had a thirty-caliber carbine with a fold-up stock, a gun from World War II. Neither one of those weapons had been issued to us by the military. It was a common practice to purchase specialty weapons on the black market.

Because of their lengths, those weapons performed well in close quarters in the event that we had to shoot our way out of situations. Today only a Vietnam combat veteran or a mobster would have had those kinds of experiences.

I was reminded of the cowboy movies I had watched as a kid. The good guys would find trouble in saloons and sometimes have to shoot their way out. I found myself in a similar situation when I became an adult.

Watching many cowboy movies gave me confidence when I went into Vietnamese saloons where we were often attacked by the Viet Cong. I had watched many different bad men attack good cowboys in saloons.

I felt like a professional gunslinger and like no bad man could attack me by surprise.

I had one eye on a beautiful Vietnamese "baby-san." With the other eye, I looked for the bad man's next move. I thought that if the "baby-san" was satisfying, I would consider making a deal and going upstairs for a roll in the hay while my partner stood guard for me. We never moved alone.

What a parallel! How many people can say that they've had old-time Western experiences in modern times? I do get a blast from the past, so to speak, when the Veteran spins his thirty-three-and-a-third Major Lance album on his completely rebuilt forty-year-old record player. His music repositions me in Rose's Bar in Vietnam. The Veteran is much more nostalgic than I. Unlike most men my age, I live in the twenty-first century.

My best days are happening now, not in the past. Because of my lifelong interest in health and hormone supplementations, I am bigger (more muscular with less body fat), stronger, faster, smarter, and more financially secure than ever. The sayings "the good ol' days" and "back when I was" do not apply to me. I am living in the present and have never been as excited about my life as I am now!

I was abruptly woken up from my daydream by the sound of a heavy body crashing into the seat beside me. A middle-aged lady immediately turned to me and loudly said, "That heavy cream you ordered in your coffee will cause you to gain weight, and even worse, it will cause the arteries to harden (arteriosclerosis), and you'll get heart disease."

"Do you know that you could have opted for skim milk? It has no fat," she said with commanding authority.

I wished the Veteran had been there. He was good with rapid screw-you responses to absurd comments. The Veteran loathed obese people. Obese people were like his whipping posts. He was capable of striking an obese person dead with words.

I elected to say nothing. A storyteller is not a verbal fighter; he is a trained listener. I fight in civilization with the written word. At that instance, I recalled that she'd been standing behind me when I had ordered my coffee, and I had noticed how morbidly obese she was. I had not been able to stop staring at her sweet drink, which was piled high with processed whipped cream and chocolate sprinkles.

I observed that the lady's heels were calloused and that her swollen and obese body indicated faulty hormonal signaling and a very sedentary lifestyle. Considering her age, I would've wagered that she had type 2 diabetes.

An idiom that described this distasteful encounter came to my mind: "What's good for the goose is good for the gander." Of course, I kept it to myself.

Encounters of this nature are disturbing. My delayed response was, "What makes you think that?" I was referring to the comment about cream.

Let's stop here for a moment and compare cream to skim milk and, most importantly, discuss why skim milk is more likely to cause weight gain.

Fundamentally speaking, the body takes more time to convert the cream, or fat, to glucose, which gives the body more time to use the glucose for energy. Then less insulin is deposited into the bloodstream to carry sugar into the cells for metabolism, and less glucose is converted to triglycerides, which are stored as fat.

Diabetes is a disease not of blood sugar but of excess insulin. A diet too high in carbohydrates causes excess insulin and leptin, along with other hormonal disruptions.

I was brought back to reality when this lady bellowed out the answer to my question, which I felt I had asked long ago. Drawing attention to herself, she said, "I'm a nurse!"

I guess I was supposed to say, "That's proof enough for me! I will never order heavy cream in my coffee again. Thank you, madam. I will never make that mistake again."

This large woman was the perfect example of what her warning was, obese! I caught myself before I said, "Help me—I'm surrounded by self-righteous idiots who are oblivious to what they are."

At that very moment, a place at the counter became vacant. I felt immediate relief as I fled to the comfortable space at the counter with a view of the window. I'd felt the same solace in Vietnam when I'd been pinned down by heavy enemy fire. I had broken free thanks to a navy jet that had accurately dropped some bombs that had resulted in the fiery napalm death of the enemy before me.

The welcome smell of the enemies' burning flesh returned to me momentarily.

My phone rang! It was Betty. In a whisper, she told me to make sure that I stopped by later, and then she hung up.

I had no doubt that the Veteran was there. How did I know it? I had hung out at Rose's Bar in Bien Hoa, and in 1968 the most popular recording artist in Vietnam had been Major Lance. His hit "The Monkey Time" had been playing in the background when Betty called me. Major Lance had continued to perform until his death in 1994. The Veteran had his entire collection of songs.

It was obvious that Betty did not want the Veteran to know she had called me. My concern reverted to the Veteran's phone call, when he'd asked me to drive him to the hospital for what could be a somber visit. I thought again of how his condition had been deteriorating over the last couple of months.

He had served his country gallantly and had suffered silently for forty-seven years from the mental and physical scars of combat. His pain was many times greater than mine. There was no question that the Veteran was tougher than I was when it came to coping with mental and physical pain. His wounds ran deep!

As I drank my then-cold coffee, I was overwhelmed with memories of my combat experiences—memories that only another combat veteran would understand; I thought of how I had accepted death and then had felt surprised over and over again when I didn't die during my two tours of duty.

This would be at the top of my list of causes of PTSD, or post-traumatic stress disorder. PTSD can also be caused by the shock of being wounded in combat and the shock of being spit on, discriminated against, refused medical attention and employment, harassed and locked up by the police, and denigrated by the media and government after making it home from Vietnam alive.

Vietnam veterans suffered with PTSD for over a decade before becoming eligible for treatment. This anxiety disorder was not recognized until 1980. It was too late for tens of thousands of Vietnam veterans.

■ ■ ■

PLANS TO TAKE THE VETERAN TO THE REGIONAL VA HOSPITAL, AND RUBY RETURNS

I left Starbucks and headed to Betty's house. I had an idea of what was on her mind. I was sure she wanted to go over what was going on with the Veteran and to relay all of her concerns to me. If she thought she could be of any assistance, she would pack her bag and go with me to the VA hospital. But she must have realized her condition and understood that she would have complicated matters.

When I arrived at Betty's house, the door was cracked open, which was Betty's invitation for me to enter. I pushed open the door. Betty was there with her forefinger on her lips and told me in a whisper to be quiet.

My first thought was about how she'd mounted her wheelchair to get to the door. I said nothing. I entered and closed the door, and Betty stopped me from walking any farther into the house. Our location was the farthest point from where the Veteran was sleeping.

Betty noticed my startled look and said, "Lewis is sick—very sick! I dragged myself across the floor to my wheelchair and pulled myself up onto the seat. I had to do this myself. If Lewis had been awake, he would've been too weak to pick me up. I am so worried for him."

She looked at me and said, "What is the plan?" I hesitated, still disconcerted. Betty looked me straight in the eyes and nodded in a demanding way. I had only seen her do that one other time.

Stammering, I replied. "We...We are leaving early tomorrow morning for the regional VA hospital. The Veteran set this up when he called me, Betty. Do you think we should leave now?"

With a solemn look on her face, Betty said, "No. I brought this up to Lewis a couple of hours ago, when he was awake, and he said definitely not.

He wanted to rest and leave early tomorrow morning, Lenny. Now allow me to tell you the other reason I wanted you to stop by."

"OK, Betty. Why? I have no idea."

"Don't worry about me tomorrow. I will be fine," Betty said. "Guess who I had a two-hour phone conversation with earlier today?"

"Please tell me, Betty."

"Ruby, Lenny. I spoke with Ruby!"

"Please explain what's going on, Betty," I said. "How is a telephone call from Ruby relevant?"

"She'll be here midmorning, and I invited her to stay here. She can help me out if the hospital keeps Lewis awhile. I like Ruby. She and I have always enjoyed each other. I can't wait."

"OK, Betty. I got it. I'm glad that someone will be with you. Now don't you worry. I'll keep you posted on the Veteran's condition." Betty had become used to my referring to Lewis as "the Veteran." To me, he was the Veteran, not Lewis.

I closed the door and walked in the direction of my car only to be met by Ruby's dog, who was coming for her evening meal. The next day would be a homecoming for Jojo too. I realized that I should have told Betty to tell Jojo the news. I was sure she would also be excited.

The thought brought a smile to my face, and it felt good. There had not been much to smile about lately. The intense pressure over the last few days had obviously made me feel unsteady.

THE VETERAN TELLS HIS STORY

The very next morning, I drove to the Veteran's home. He was outside close to the curb, awaiting my arrival. I could see Betty watching from the living room's picture window. From the road's edge, I could see the horrid expression on her face. I waved and nodded in an effort to give her a sense of assurance.

The Veteran was carrying a small bag known as an "AWOL bag" and a folder with letters in it. He was leaning on a No Parking sign. The Veteran struggled to enter the car. I quickly circled around the rear of the car to the passenger's side to assist him. However, he managed to seat himself before I could make contact with him. I did help him position his legs.

His condition was much worse than I had imagined. I had just visited the Veteran and Betty less than twelve hours before. I then understood Betty's concern. It looked like all hell had broken loose overnight.

I was overwhelmed with emotions and avoided eye contact so that I could simulate emotional stability. I pretended to pay close attention to the road in front of me so that I could conceal my teary eyes. I did not want to alert him to what we had both seen before in the eyes of young soldiers in Vietnam: the look of death.

After pretending to orient myself in the direction we would be traveling, I asked if I could do anything to make the trip more comfortable. He placed the large accordion file on the seat beside me. Without turning his head, he said. "Hold these records until I return. These documents are evidence of my life. And by the way, if they keep me for a few days, would you check on Betty a couple of times a day?"

It was unnecessary to give me instructions on what to do for Betty. The Veteran knew that I understood her needs. I said yes and nodded several times.

He noticed how nervous I had become. I did not see any advantage to asking him if Betty had told him that Ruby was on her way. I was sure it would have been a surprise to him, and the Veteran did not need surprises at that time.

I thought of *Tarzan*, starring Johnny Weissmuller. In one of the movies, an elephant slowly moves through the jungle, innately heading for the mystical place where elephants go to die. Many men traveled from countries afar to search for the elephant graveyard and the tons of ivory that would make them wealthy.

In my opinion, knowledge, not ivory, was what made people wealthy. Being the custodian of a great man's memorabilia meant more to me than tons of ivory. I trembled from the fear of such a responsibility.

Can a story of a man like the Veteran attract readers, or is it true that readers prefer the conquests of the rich and powerful? I made a decision to tell his story regardless of whom it would appeal to.

His story will not be one of wealth, power, corruption, or beautiful women. This story will fill pages with vital information and with descriptions of the trials and tribulations involved when a common man confronts some powerful entities. Telling his story is telling my story.

During the three-hour ride to the VA hospital I listened as he told me the story of his life. Like my story, his story always drifted back to the time when he'd been the most impressionable—the time he'd spent in Vietnam. I agreed with him when he said that it had set the stage for the rest of his life and had been instrumental in making him the man he'd become.

I thought to myself that Vietnam soldiers were the last of a breed of hand-to-hand-combat warriors. They did what they did for honor and for their country, not for money, like those in the modern professional army. The Veteran continued his narrative, and I listened to him.

"The people of America eventually learned that the Vietnam War was a lie and that the government was guilty of promoting the lie. The lie was that we had to stop communism in Southeast Asia to prevent it from reaching the shores of America—and let's not forget that the call to arms today is to stop the terrorism in the Middle East to prevent it from reaching the shores of America.

"Wow, here they go again. Who will take the blame this time when the money is no longer there, and the rich and powerful stockholders of the Military-Industrial Complex lose interest in the Middle East or discover a richer cash cow?

"When the Vietnam War ended, to save their own corrupt asses, politicians used the power of the government to influence the media and to cast aspersions on the soldiers. Nothing has changed. The same selfish breed of politicians inhabits today's Congress. To this day, the government's disinformation is printed in textbooks that ignore the adverse treatment of Vietnam veterans," the Veteran said.

The Veteran's take on this wrong record of history is simple. According to the Veteran, "He who wins the war writes the history; he who loses the war writes the music." The Veteran said, "The losers were the Veterans and their families, and the winners were the corrupt politicians and special interests that financially profited."

The Veteran said something that stuck in my mind: "Today a person won't stand up for what he believes in for fear of being arrested. Even a minor criminal charge can cost you your life savings. If you're found to be not guilty, the arrest record will remain, and many people will view it as the equivalent of a guilty verdict. It can even disqualify you from many better-paying jobs or from military service."

The Veteran looked over at me and said, "How could any reasonable individual go along with an unfair and corrupt justice system that decides guilt or innocence based on the amount of money that the accused can spend on his or her defense? Take your head out of the hole, people, and look.

"Poor people go to jail, and wealthy people go free. Every disagreement must be settled in a court of law these days—even something as minor as an argument with a neighbor."

The Veteran moaned in pain with his eyes closed and loudly said the following: "Whoever has the money to put on the most convincing show with the best lying lawyer wins money or is found not guilty. Many others who are less privileged go to for-profit prisons."

THE VETERAN, IMPRISONED FOR SOMETHING HE DID NOT DO?

"Did you know I went to prison for two and a half years for something that I didn't do?" the Veteran asked.

That revelation startled me. In the thousands of conversations we'd had, the Veteran had never mentioned anything about prison.

"I had a perfectly legit business," he said. "I fired an employee, and he went to the IRS and told them that I was not paying all of my taxes. When a complaint is made, the normal procedure is to investigate it. The IRS agent who investigated me was a young woman who had recently been hired. She was cohabitating with the head prosecutor for that district. The prosecutor was a man in his late fifties. She was, at the most, twenty-six years old and was working her way up the ladder of success.

"The young female agent entered my business and screamed, 'IRS criminal investigation!' My employees were mortified, and so was I.

"I immediately said, 'Do you have a warrant?' Her loud response was 'No!' I then requested that she leave my building. She ignored me and walked around, observed the premises, and asked my employees their names, and wrote their names down.

"Some employees were scared and thought that they might have been in trouble. I took her arm and led her to the door she had entered through and pushed her out of it. One of her high heels got caught in the coarse industrial doormat, and she stumbled and fell into a holly bush, which resulted in several scratches.

"I then came outside to help her up. I said, 'I'm sorry—I didn't mean for that to happen.' When I took her arm, she said, 'Don't touch me! You will pay for this.' She stood up and hurried to her car.

"I later called her supervisor, who was the head prosecutor, to apologize and to explain what had happened. He said, 'I'm sorry too. You'll be going to prison.' And then he hung up.

"A few days later, a team of IRS agents seized the business records, locked the doors, and charged me with conspiracy to defraud the United States. The charge had first been used during the Nuremberg trials to convict Nazi war criminals when little or no evidence was available. The charge stated my partner and I had been conspiring to not pay taxes.

"The IRS attorneys boasted to a jury of people who were not my peers that the IRS was so thorough that it had caught us before we'd committed the crime. The IRS lawyers had come up with an amount of money that we'd supposedly been planning to take, and they convinced the jury to find me guilty.

"This was the result of a federal prosecutor's personal vendetta against me. He had the power to affect the verdict. The lesson I learned is that if you can't convince the news media to cover the trial, the federal government can contrive the outcome.

"What else did I learn from that experience? If the IRS offers you a deal, take it even if you're not guilty. Never go to trial! The IRS wins ninety-eight percent of their cases. They do occasionally allow a case to be won by a privileged defendant. The prosecution would not appear to be fair if they won one hundred percent of the cases.

"The rule is that if you decide to take a case to trial, you will be sentenced to no less than double the deal you were initially offered. No matter how innocent you are, you cannot win in court if the IRS decides to put you in prison. As unbelievable as it sounds, that's the way it works. The average American has been indoctrinated to believe that the IRS is an honorable agency. People have no idea that the IRS can forge a case from nothing using its unlimited finances to manufacture information, coach witnesses, and sell lies to a jury.

"I promised you a learning experience and a story you would never forget. No wrong has done more damage to me than that wrong has," the Veteran said. The story was devastating to the Veteran. His head fell to his chest. I decided to increase my speed to shorten our arrival time.

THE VA HOSPITAL

Minutes before we arrived at the VA hospital, the Veteran seemed to take a turn for the worse. He awoke from his sleep and began to mumble and to go in and out of consciousness. It was bad enough that I again increased my speed, this time twenty miles per/hour past the speed limit.

"The hell with the corrupt IRS and the entire criminal justice system," the Veteran mumbled. It was the last coherent statement he made.

I sounded the horn as I entered the driveway to the emergency corridor. The Veteran's body had slumped, with his jaw agape. Only the seat belt kept him from falling forward onto the floor of the vehicle.

A team of hospital personnel immediately greeted us. They entered the car before we had come to a complete stop. They dragged the Veteran from the car and placed his limp body onto a stretcher.

I quickly exited the car, caught up with the stretcher, and grabbed his arm to let him know I was there for him. I knew from my combat experience that when a man is in dire straits, he could be comforted by another's touch.

Throughout this calamity, the Veteran continued to incoherently mumble his story. He vanished as the door to the ward quietly shut. I filled out his admission forms and listed myself as his emergency contact.

In awe, I awaited the Veteran's preliminary diagnosis. I ask myself why I tear up when I am reminded of horrid past events. I silently answered my own question: because of post-traumatic stress disorder or pseudobulbar affect (PBA) or both.

My thoughts momentarily jumped back to Vietnam and to one moment when I was holding tight in my arms a young man who'd been mortally wounded. I held him until he bled out and died. When the end drew near, with his last mortal breath, he called out for his mother.

The Veteran had taught me how to deal with this excruciating memory, which I relive from time to time. He said, "Don't try to forget it. It was an honor for you to be there in the end for this young soldier."

From that moment on, I began to experience a warm, euphoric high when I looked back on those few moments. Turning a negative memory into a positive memory was the cure for years of mental torment. That's what a great man does. He helps others live better lives.

I thought time had stood still. Betty called every hour on the hour, and I told her the same thing. "As soon as they tell me how he is doing, I will let you know," I said.

The most interesting call was from Ruby, who said that Betty had told her all about me and that she looked forward to meeting me. I wondered what Betty could have told Ruby about me.

To conclude, she said, "Don't worry about Betty. She's holding up well. Tell Lewis that I'll take care of her if he has to stay a couple of days." She spoke a few other words, but I guess I blocked them out, thinking that they were insignificant.

My focus was on the Veteran. Ruby was definitely different from what I had imagined. Betty had said that her mother had referred to her as a streetwalker, and that was what had stood out in my mind.

She carefully selected her words as though she were an English professor—she was calm and precise. I knew instinctively that my preliminary judgment of Ruby had been far off the mark. Betty's leg twitches the night before had convinced me that sooner or later, she would walk.

THE VETERAN IS DEAD

Three hours later, a doctor appeared and called out my name. He was quick to announce the Veteran's death, and then he hurried away. I was dumbfounded and momentarily paralyzed.

I ignored the flurry of arrangement questions rapidly coming from the hospital's social worker. I looked away, extended my hand, and surrendered the dog tags that I had taken from the Veteran's hand when we'd entered the emergency room.

I quickly turned and marched out of the hospital. Forty-seven years before, I had surrendered other great young men's dog tags.

A disturbing thought entered my mind as I walked to the car: Who would surrender my dog tags, and who would be the last omega man (the last Vietnam veteran) standing?

I fumbled with the keys to my car. I was mentally incapacitated and was having a hard time composing any thoughts. I decided to sit awhile until my ability to think returned.

The phone rang, and fear came over me. I knew who it was. I had no choice but to let it go to voice mail. I needed some time to think of how to break the news to Betty. I wondered whether I should call Ruby. I noticed she had called me on her phone. Then I said to myself, "Why Ruby?"

I reclined the seat and closed my eyes. I returned to the last time I had had a shock of this magnitude.

AMBUSHED

My squad was ambushed on a routine patrol. No Viet Cong had been reported in the area. We were taken by complete surprise. My men were in shock and immediately turned to me for orders. I knew the next decision had to be made quickly—and had to be right.

I gave the signal to stop firing so that I could assess the number of enemy soldiers and the direction they were firing from. I know there must have been an opening. You can't totally surround a unit. If you completely surround a unit, you'll end up shooting at your fellow soldiers.

The sound of the enemy's firing told me where the opening was. The escape route was due south based on my compass. I ordered my men to form one single line; even numbers would suppress the fire to the left, and odd numbers would suppress the fire to the right.

I ordered them to follow me. I ran as fast as I could for a quarter of a click, firing from the left to the right. Then I ordered them to halt, line up abreast, and reload. I knew the VC would come together and chase us. We lay in wait.

The enemy ran up to us, and we completely surprised them, killing twelve and wounding another twenty at point-blank range. The remaining Viet Cong turned and ran in the opposite direction. We sustained no casualties.

I came back to the present with a new sense of hope and started the automobile. I pulled out of the parking area and pointed my car in the direction of home.

■ ■ ■

DEVASTATED

I worked my way through the city traffic to the interstate and proceeded south for the next 145 miles. I didn't care how long it took me to reach Betty's house. It would just be a matter of time before Betty called again.

I was barely driving the speed limit. There was no doubt in my mind that I wasn't ready for what was to come. I needed a distraction from my situation, and there it was: a stranded motorist on the side of the freeway with the hood of his car raised.

I pulled off the freeway and stopped near the rear of the car. I stepped out and moved to the front of the car, where the man was peering under the hood. "What can I do for you?" I asked. He pointed to the engine.

When I bent over to look at the engine, he stuck a knife into my side and said, "Move, and I'll cut you into two pieces."

He then instructed me to hand over my wallet. "I have a cardholder full of credit cards but no money," I said.

"Don't shit me, mister! I'll cut your fucking ass!"

My gut feeling was that he had no intention of letting me walk away, money or not. I slammed my fist into the side of his head, and as he went down, I felt the cold steel of the knife go from one side of my body to the other. I fell backward and rolled down the steep bank on the side of the freeway.

I jumped to my feet, pulled a survey stake from the ground, and picked up a large rock with my other hand. I would use the stake to hold his knife at bay and would use the rock to bash his head in.

I slowly started climbing up the bank. I heard a sloshing sound coming from my shoes. My shoes were full of blood. Aware of what he had done, the man slammed the hood of the car closed and left before I could reach the top.

I slung the large rock toward his car as he sped away. The rock slammed into the rear passenger's side quarter panel, making a large, noticeable dent in it.

CAN LENNY MAKE IT TO THE HOSPITAL BEFORE HE BLEEDS OUT?

I knew I was in trouble. I remembered that not long before, I had passed an exit and that it would be faster to go in the opposite direction for help. I started the car and illegally crossed the median to the other side of the interstate.

I tried to hold the cut together to slow the bleeding, but the cut was so long that I couldn't hold it with one hand and drive with the other hand. I was concerned that I would lose too much blood and pass out. I knew I was in serious trouble. I put the accelerator to the floor.

I could see the exit. I turned and came to a sliding stop at the first service station. I called out to a young man to help me. He came over, looked into the car, and screamed, "Oh, my God!" He backed away from the car and said, "I'll call nine-one-one." He reached for his cell phone in his back pocket.

"No! I'll die before they arrive. Drive me to the VA hospital. It's only a few miles down the interstate. If you drive me, I can apply pressure to the cut with both of my hands to slow the bleeding."

He hesitated. "Come on, man—save my life!" I said. I moved over to the passenger's side, and he opened the door and slid behind the steering wheel. "Go, man! Go!" I yelled.

"I know where the VA hospital is. I work there. Are you a veteran?"

"Yes," I said.

"Me too," he said. I was in luck. It was not my day to die. I held the cut together and could feel my head getting lighter from the blood loss. "Go, man! Go!"

RETURN TO THE EMERGENCY ROOM

We turned into the entrance to the emergency corridor. I told the young man to sound the horn.

"Huh?" he said.

"Just do it!" I screamed. "I've been here before!"

He complied, and emergency personnel were standing by to receive us. I refused the stretcher, accepted support on both sides of my body, and walked in, leaving a trail of blood in the small room.

In less than a minute, a surgeon entered with a couple of nurses. The nurses were quick to cut off my shirt, which was one of my better ones. The doctor instructed the nurses to wipe the excess blood off my skin so that he could see the seriousness of the wound. One of the nurses started injecting a numbing solution into several spots along the cut.

"You're lucky. The cut didn't totally cut through your abdominal muscles. We need to give you a pint of plasma," the doctor said as he looked at my dog tags to determine my blood type. "O positive," he said, and a nurse took heed of his order for blood and left the room.

Another nurse quickly took her place and started cleaning the wound again. "I'm going to begin suturing this cut," the doctor said. "The nurse will give you a shot of an antibiotic to prevent infections. Your nurse will be back shortly to start the blood transfusion." He then started suturing the wound. I felt nothing.

The Veteran and I had determined that his lethal infection had been acquired at the hospital. The overuse of antibiotics has created superbugs that are resistant to them.

The Centers for Disease Control and Prevention (CDC) reports that bugs and infections acquired in hospitals kill approximately one hundred thousand people a year and seriously injure a million more.

The CDC claims that over half of these injuries and deaths are preventable. The report states that hospital personnel should take infection control more seriously, primarily by washing their hands in between patients.

The report further states that hospitals are not the only place where medical consumers can acquire these deadly bugs. People can also acquire infections at outpatient surgical and emergency centers, nursing homes, assisted-living facilities, and even doctors' offices.

There was no doubt in my mind that was what had happened to the Veteran. The nurse returned and hung the bag of blood plasma and proceeded to position the transfusion needle into my arm. She asked me if I was in pain and then said, "I have pain pills if you need them." I lied and said I wasn't in pain.

"I would rather suffer a little now than suffer discomfort later," I said. What I meant was that going up is euphoric, but coming down from drugs is miserable. It's the same with any drug you take—that's part of the reason that people become addicted to them. A high percentage of addicts start with prescription drugs. The drug users refuse to face the coming-down blues.

The physician finished suturing the wound and told me I was going to be fine. He suggested that I stay a couple of days to be sure. The nurse unhooked me and said, "I will help you to a room where you can rest."

When we exited the room, a police detective approached me. He introduced himself and asked if he could accompany me to my room. "The quicker I can start the investigation, the more likely I'll be to find the assailant." I agreed.

DETECTIVE RAY INVESTIGATES THE ATTEMPTED ROBBERY

He started questioning me as he walked beside my gurney. "What can you tell me that will help me locate this suspect? Your friend in the waiting room told me what he knew while I was waiting for the doctor to finish suturing your wound."

"My friend?" I said.

"The young man who drove you here. He'll visit you after I'm done questioning you. He's the one who called us."

"Oh, OK," I said.

"Now what can you tell me?"

"This man was about my height, five-eleven, and one hundred and seventy pounds. He had short black hair, and he was Caucasian. He was wearing a green shirt and white pants and driving a red ninety-five or ninety-six Toyota Corolla. He had a Florida license plate, G-E-R-seven-eight-four-five-three. I threw a large rock and hit the rear passenger's side quarter panel. That made a large dent in it."

He smiled and said, "You're making this easy." He shook his head. "How did you remember those facts with what was going on?"

"I'm a combat veteran—cool under fire, Officer."

"Give me your name, your address, and a telephone number I can reach you at. I'll keep you informed of my progress." He then looked me dead in the eye and said, "Thank you for your service." And then he left. I will always remember that day as a day in hell.

ENTER WILL JOHNSON AND SELMA, ALABAMA, 1965

A young man stuck his head through the doorway and asked if he could come aboard. That told me that he'd been in the navy. "Please do. I have nothing against sailors," I said. Then I smiled.

I told him how much I appreciated what he had done. "Do you realize I would have bled out if you hadn't taken control of the situation?"

I then asked him if he would find my phone and personal belongings. "I'm sure the nurse at the counter would know where they are. I have an obligation to tell my people where I am." They'd taken everything I'd had on, leaving me in an embarrassing gown.

"Oh, forgive me. What's your name?" I asked.

"Will Johnson. Will is short for Willy." He hesitated and then continued. "Willy is not a good name for a black man. It's too ethnic."

"OK, Will. My name is Lenny." I stuck out my hand, and Will shook it.

"I'll be right back," Will said. Will's comment that his birth name was too ethnic for a black man bothered me. "How could people still think that way?" I asked myself.

My mind drifted back to Vietnam. Some of the best soldiers I'd fought with had been black. I thought about Selma, Alabama, on March 7, 1965, also known as "Bloody Sunday." The demonstration consisted of a fifty-four-mile march from Selma, Alabama, to Montgomery to draw attention to black people's constitutional right to vote, which the Southern authorities were denying them. I also thought about the confrontation led by members of the First Baptist Church to colored people (that's what they were called in those days) sitting at the soda counter in my hometown drug store.

A congregation of members from the church armed with rifles and clubs confronted them and demanded they leave or be beaten and jailed. I remember the church deacon saying "niggers" are not allowed to sit at the counter with white people. I was a teenager at that time and thought that they were wrong.

One of the colored men was the father of a kid I played ball with in the field beside my house. His son was one of my best friends. I had been to his house and he had visited my house many times. His family were nice to me and my family always welcomed this kid to our house. I think this situation could be the catalyst for my disdain for religion. My father agreed that the church mob was wrong.

The irony of the civil rights movement was that a disproportional percentage of black people were fighting to win South Vietnam's democracy, while in the United States they were being denied the right to vote. They were also denied the right to be served at lunch counters reserved for whites only throughout the land. Many cities segregated restrooms and waiting rooms into black and white.

The civil rights marchers were confronted by Alabama state troopers. Many marchers were severely beaten; one lady was killed in the police effort to shut down the march. That happened fifty years ago, and we as a nation obviously still have a way to go. Police brutality and indiscriminate killings of African Americans by the police are still problems.

Will returned and handed me a bag with my personal belongings in it. My money and cardholder were bloody. My cell phone, which I always carried in my back pocket, was clean. I noticed numerous calls from Betty and a few from Ruby.

"Will, I told you on the way here about what had happened to me. How much time do you have?"

"What do you mean?"

"I mean do you need to be anywhere?"

"No," Will said.

He told me that he hadn't been here long and that he'd moved by himself from California less than a month before. "I applied for the VA job online and was told that a position in my field was available here. I was allowed to interview for the job in California, and I was hired. I packed my bags the next day and left," Will said.

"What is your field?" I asked.

"Sociology. I have a master's degree from USF—the University of San Francisco."

"Impressive!" I said.

"I have nothing to do. I took off three days to look at another VA facility that I was told needed me more than the one in Tampa. I was told that moving there would increase my pay by one pay scale. I'm still living out of a suitcase in a motel. If I had been permanently situated, the offer probably wouldn't have come up, Lenny."

"Where is the VA that you're considering located?"

"Cape Coral," Will said.

"Holy crap! That's the closest VA clinic to where I live. We need to talk about this. I need your counsel, Will. Allow me to explain my situation, and then you tell me what I should do."

"OK, tell me your situation, Lenny."

I backtracked to that morning and told him the entire story.

"You should get busy on your phone and tell Betty exactly what happened, but I suggest that you call Ruby first. She can stand ready to comfort Betty when you shatter her with the news that Lewis is dead. Make sure you tell Ruby to walk away from Betty when you call, Lenny. Betty shouldn't overhear the conversation before you personally tell her what happened."

I realized my luck was changing. How convenient it was to have a sociologist to advise me.

"Can you hang around while I do this?" I asked.

"I will sit right here," Will said. "Do not choke up when you tell them."

"Thanks, Will. I'll give it my best shot."

RUBY SAVES THE DAY

When Ruby had called me, I'd added her number to my contact list. I dialed her number. She must have done the same thing with my number. "Lenny?" she said.

"Ruby, listen to me very closely before you say anything. If you're near Betty, walk away. If you must, tell Betty that the call is personal."

"I'm at the grocery store, and Betty is home," Ruby said. "Is something wrong? Betty and I have called you numerous times and only got your voice mail. Betty's a nervous wreck."

"Ruby, I need your help."

"Sure, what can I do, Lenny?"

"Listen to me, and don't say a word. Lewis is dead! Then a man tried to rob me on the way home and cut me from one side of my abdomen to the other. I'm in the VA hospital. I would have bled to death if it hadn't been for the assistance of the young man who's still here with me now. I could be here for a couple more days." I waited for Ruby's response; a moment or more passed, but she didn't say anything. I raised my voice. "Damn it, Ruby, are you there?"

"What do you require of me?" Ruby said, her voice strong. It was apparent that she was confused.

"Ruby, will you stand close to Betty when I inform her of Lewis's death? Comfort her with all of the love you can provide. Are you with me, Ruby? Do you understand?"

"Yes, Lenny, I do! What about you?"

"Don't worry about me. Worry about Betty! I'll figure something out."

Will interrupted me and loudly said, "I'll help you get home."

"Did you hear that, Ruby?"

"Yes, I did."

"When you arrive at the house, send me a quick text, and I'll call Betty."

"I'm leaving now. It will take me less than thirty minutes."

"Thank you very much, Ruby." I turned to Will. "How did I do?"

"A perfect ten." Will then stood up and said, "Lenny, I'm going to take off, eat, and go to my motel room. You have the difficult task of telling Betty. Good luck with that. This has been a nerve-racking day for me too. A little quiet and rest would be good for me. I'll return tomorrow, Lenny."

"Thanks again, Will. Oh, I almost forgot. Can I have your number? I want to text you Ruby's number to be safe. You never know. How do you plan to go back to your motel?"

"Taxi."

"No, take my car. You said you'll be coming back, right?"

"I did." I tossed him the keys. "OK, thanks," Will said. "See you tomorrow, Lenny."

I received the text from Ruby. I took a couple of deep breaths and dialed Ruby's number. She answered on the first ring.

"Ruby, are you ready?"

"Yes," she immediately said.

"Ruby, hand your phone to Betty." I had decided that I would not hesitate.

"Betty, Lewis is dead, and I'm in the hospital." I heard a scream and the sound of the phone hitting the floor. It sounded like there was a struggle.

Ruby picked the phone up and said, "I caught her before she fell out of her rocker." I could hear Betty crying in the background as Ruby spoke. "I'll hold her until she regains her composure."

"I'll text you Will's number. Use it if you need help. He's the man who saved my life."

"OK," Ruby said. "I need to go attend to Betty." She hung up. I was on high alert. The last time I'd had so much adrenaline had been during a firefight in Vietnam.

HOW DOES LENNY CARRY ON?

The emotional pain of a loved one's death is something I have never totally learned how to deal with. The death of my wife two decades ago almost took me to my grave. Only the voice of my daughter, Annie, saved me. We talk on the phone on a regular basis. She made a life in Korea. I hope to one day visit her.

I was facing another painful situation with the death of the Veteran. As I was without the comfort of family, I turned to a psychiatrist at the VA named Fox. Over the years, Dr. Fox had proven that his true concern was for my mental well-being.

I realized that the crux of my emotional problems was Vietnam. The Veteran had been a godsend for me. He had lived through similar horrid events and through combat, which had left deep scars. We had come to depend on each other during trying times. His death left a large vacancy in my support system.

The Veteran and I had spent many hours discussing the influence that Vietnam had on us. Our talks included how to cope with the permanent emotional damage caused by killing another human in hand-to-hand combat. The Veteran and I had talked about the impression these up close and personal horrid moments made on us. Their faces are as clear to both of us today in our minds and dreams as they were fifty years ago. The Vietnam warrior was the last American soldier that actually engaged in hand-to-hand combat on a regular basis.

We had identical coping methods. The Veteran and I composed a statement about what we do in difficult times. We referred to this statement as our "golden coping rule." This was our statement: "We will review the tragedies of our pasts to see how we survived; we will gather the coping techniques that pulled us through them, drag them into the present, and put them into play."

I suddenly remembered my condition, and the pain from my knife cut re-emerged. I thought about how amazing the human mind is. My mind had repressed the pain coming from my abdomen and had focused on the greater mental torment of dealing with the death of the Veteran, the greatest friend I'd had.

The cut across my abdomen reminded me of a story that the Veteran had once told me. A man in his platoon had been shot in the abdomen with a high-velocity, small-caliber projectile.

The purpose of that weapon was to maim someone, not to kill him. A man hit by such a weapon would see his intestines pop out of his body as though he were a jack-in-the-box and would go into shock, creating panic and fear among the other soldiers.

A medic would close the wound, gather the man's intestines, stuff them into a shoulder bag, and hang them around the man's neck until a mobile army surgical unit (MASH) physician could disinfect them and reposition them in his abdomen.

This strategy to wound, not kill, compromised three soldiers at once, because two soldiers would need to carry the wounded soldier. We learned this tactic from our enemy.

I would like to quote Dwight D. Eisenhower, a U.S president: "I hate war as only a soldier who has lived it can, only as one who has seen its brutality, its futility, and its stupidity."

THE NEXT MORNING

The first thing I saw the next morning was a nutritionally deficient hospital TV breakfast staring at me. I was hungry but managed to push the poison aside. I'm ashamed to admit that I did not do the same thing with the sleeping pill that was provided to me. My rationale was that there is a time and a place where medication can help, and for me, it was that time and place.

Also, there is a time and a place for a physician—like when I needed one to put my injured body together. However, I decided to pass on other services.

I prefer to prevent or cure diseases and to stay away from legal-drug pushers. I know what you're thinking: "I know a doctor who takes care of patients and doesn't care if they have no money."

In response to that, the Veteran would have said, "Show me one doctor who is not in it for the money, and I will show you a thousand who are."

There was nothing more satisfying than watching and listening to the Veteran express his scorn for a doctor. He even refused to capitalize the *d* in "doctor" when "doctor" was the first word of a sentence.

I agreed with the Veteran. I started to refuse to capitalize the *d* in "doctor." But I made exceptions for doctors who had used their surgical skills to save the lives of injured people. They earned the capital *d*.

The Veteran laughingly said that not capitalizing the *d* was one small way to show disapproval without having to hire a lawyer. "Resistance is futile!" he'd say.

He also said that resisting the acceptance of a popular idea in the good ol' United States could be construed as a crime and could lead to incarceration.

"The federal prisons are full of people who speak their minds. The average American never speaks out. Most people have no idea of the control that the government has over them. A lifetime of conditioning has rendered them obedient. Compare the behavior of older people to that of younger people. Younger people question authority, and older people don't," he said.

Considering what I had gone through the day before, I felt good. I needed to be my best for the day. I knew there would be many obstacles to overcome in the following days. The crisis at hand was just the tip of the iceberg.

The nurse had informed me that the doctor would visit me the first thing in the morning and then release me. The doctor entered and said, "How do you feel?"

"Great! I need to leave here before I catch a superbug and die like my best friend did yesterday."

"I heard about that," the doctor said. "But I insist on doing a few things first. We'll run another blood test to make sure that you don't have any infections in this wound. The nurse can pull the blood and take it straight to the lab. If your white-blood-cell count is in the right range, I will clear you to leave." The doctor left as the nurse prepared to draw my blood.

I checked my phone. I had no calls. However, it was only six-thirty in the morning. That left me time to think over the day's events. I wondered whether I should I call Betty or call Ruby to see how Betty was doing. I realized that it might be best to not call.

I then thought about the newspaper clipping that the Veteran showed me when we stopped for coffee on our drive to the VA hospital. It was a letter to the editor that a man wrote to a newspaper for a Veteran's Day story. He had served in the Veteran's platoon during the Tet Offensive. This is what he wrote about the Veteran:

COMMEMORATING THE VETERAN

It was Vietnam, 1968. The "Vietnam War" fighting was at an all-time high. When I arrived, the soldier they called the Veteran was in the last quarter of his third tour of duty. I was under his command the day he got "shot up" in battle and ordered by his commanding officer to go home. I had no doubt that he would have stayed for the duration of the war if he had not been wounded. Every man that had served under the Veteran had a story to tell about the Veteran's leadership in battle.

The soldiers in the compound avoided him. They said he was insensitive and preferred to be alone. The talk was his behavior was his way of coping with the emotional pain of losing his men in combat.

I overheard him tell a young soldier that tried to befriend him, "I do not want to know your heart or anything about your family, because it hurts more to see you die. I don't give a damn if you don't like me. I do not need gratitude.

"My job is to take men into battle and bring as many of them back alive as possible. If I fail, I feel somewhat guilty for their death. I realize I will see their faces in my mind for the rest of my life." He then told the young soldier, "No soldier under my command dare question my Goddamn orders."

One young soldier did defy his order, and his actions resulted in a soldier's death. The Veteran shot that young soldier in the leg and said, "I am sending you home before you cause the death of another good soldier." The Veteran said in his report, "He was wounded in combat."

When the incident was investigated, every man in the platoon backed the Veteran's story. It was rumored that the inspector general knew what happened and chose to not to make a case, mostly because he knew the Veteran's dedication to his men and country.

When a dangerous mission was ordered, soldiers jostled to be in the Veteran's platoon. No platoon leader in the battalion brought more men home alive than the Veteran. He would call a formation before leaving the compound.

The Veteran would say, "We are warriors, and killing is what we do. I promise you I will leave no man behind. I will bring every brave man home, dead or alive!"

It was whispered that a man that was a coward and died would be left for helicopter evacuation that sometimes took days. By the time a helicopter arrived for the body, the animals would have picked his bones clean.

Another story was a private took a bullet for the Veteran and died. The Veteran carried him on his back ten kilometers to the compound. The private bled out on him and the blood had dried, adhering him to the Veteran. It took a MASH surgeon two hours to cut the private from his body. Some men said they saw tears coming from the Veteran's eyes. Others said no way!

When the Veteran marched his platoon out of the compound and into harm's way, he would lead them in the spirited airborne ranger chant; over the hill, under the hill, round the hill, through the hill, never stop, never quit. Airborne ranger, airborne ranger!

LENNY'S ASSAILANT IS ARRESTED

My phone rang. "This is Detective Ray. Is this Lenny Lewis?"

"Yes, it is."

"Lenny, we have the suspect in custody. The information you gave me checked out, and we picked him up at his house late last night. The blood on his knife and shirt matched your blood type. I managed to recover a sample of blood from the quarter panel of his car—there must have been some on the rock you threw. I went back to the crime scene and took another sample of blood from the ground. Then I took a sample of the blood on the shirt they cut off of you at the hospital. The forensics lab showed that the samples matched one another. I'll be amazed if this man goes to court. The only choice he has is to plea out for a shorter jail sentence. This was an easy arrest. If more victims could remember the details you remembered, my work would be easy. When are you going to be released? You need to identify this man in a lineup, Mr. Lewis."

"I was told I would be released this afternoon, Detective."

"You have my personal number. Will you call me ASAP when you get home? I hope you can identify him before he makes bail, Mr. Lewis."

"I will definitely call you when I'm on my way, Detective Ray."

"By the way, Lenny, my older brother died in Vietnam. The family goes to Washington, D.C., every Memorial Day to place a family wreath under his name on the Vietnam Veteran Memorial wall." The wall lists the names of over fifty-eight thousand men and women who died in Vietnam.

"Lenny, it is my honor to serve you in this investigation."

"Thank you."

Detective Ray hung up.

POLICE OFFICERS ARE THE LAWYERS' AND JUDGES' K9S

Detective Ray really impressed me in a way that no law enforcement officer had ever impressed me before. I had no doubt that the fact that his brother had died in Vietnam had influenced my opinion of him. I believed him to be one of the rare good ones.

The problem is that the "blue wall of silence" has been a part of police culture since the beginning. This code often prevents a police officer from admitting wrongdoing and from reporting another police officer for wrongdoing. It is the nature of the profession.

The culprits are the corrupt and despicable lawyers and judges who create the deviant subculture that influences police officers' behavior. Indirectly, the police work for and reflect the lawyers' and judges' attitudes. The lawyers and judges protect their cash cows (the police) with the public's money.

The police officers gather business for the criminal justice industrial complex. No other country on the planet incarcerates as many people as the United States does—and we disproportionately incarcerate the poor and minorities. A jury's verdict can be influenced by money or privilege.

I decided to send a text to Betty and Ruby. I informed them that I would be there that evening or earlier.

There was a knock on my door. I recognized the face I saw in the door's window. The social worker I'd briefly encountered the day before was there. She was the one I'd handed the Veteran's dog tags to when I'd exited the hospital.

"Enter," I said.

"I heard from other hospital personnel that you were here. I'm very sorry for your loss and for your own misfortunes."

"Thank you for your concern," I said.

She informed me that the Veteran's burial request was on file and then said, "He has been taken care of by the VA. His body will be available for review for seventy-two hours, and then it will be cremated per his request. I brought you the VA paperwork concerning these events. If you have any questions, please don't hesitate to ask me now. If not, these documents should answer all of your questions. There is a twenty-four-hour phone number at the top of these documents. Call it if you or any loved ones need to speak with someone. Do you have any questions?"

"I have no questions," I said. She turned as she had done once before and scurried away. I noticed that her card was attached to the document. Her name was Maria Rodrigo. I had to give this lady kudos. She spent her days roaming around the hospital dealing with people who had just lost loved ones.

I've always had empathy for others. I found it hard to write letters to families announcing their sons' deaths, which was something I did many times in Vietnam. Her job was even harder. She had to talk face to face with them. I felt guilty that I hadn't been nicer to her. I did appreciate her taking the time to deliver the Veteran's final documents.

"Are these documents all that's left of this great man's life?" I said to myself. Everything seemed to have been done by the book. To me, the book about the Veteran was still open. As I'd said before, I hoped I could somehow commemorate the man's life.

My phone rang. "Hello, Will, how's it going?"

"I slept very well. I was drained from all of the drama. How are you doing, Lenny?"

"I'm ready to vacate this place."

"I understand that, Lenny."

"Look, I have a few things I need to do before I come visit. I called an employee I work with, and he said that you're scheduled to be released late this afternoon. If it's OK, I'll use your car to get a few things done and be there before you're released. I would greatly appreciate it."

Without hesitation, I said, "That would be fine with me."

"That is great. And thank you!"

"I'll see you later," I said.

I had an incoming text. I opened the text, and to my astonishment, it was from Betty. It said, "Thank you, Lenny. I love you. Ruby and I are OK. Don't worry. We will see you soon." The text took my breath away. I guessed I had underestimated Betty's resilience. Ruby had showed up at the right time. I wondered about the reason and timing of her arrival.

"That takes a load off of my mind," I thought. We had encountered extreme obstacles in the last twenty-four hours and had met them with solutions. I decided to relax, regain my composure, eat, and prepare for another day of life.

Fifty years ago in Vietnam, "life" would've been replaced with "battle."

CHECKING OUT OF THE HOSPITAL

My phone rang, and I awoke from my daydream. It was Will telling me that he would be there in an hour or so. He asked me if I had been cleared for release. I said that I hadn't yet but that my physician was due any minute.

"See you soon," Will said.

The physician entered with his nurse. He examined my wound and said that it looked good, that my white-blood-cell count was in a good range, and that I had no inflammation beyond what was to be expected during the healing process.

"I'm going to clear you for release. You will need to go into the Cape Coral clinic every other day to change the bandages. Your primary-care physician can take it from here. Your records have already been transferred there. The ward nurse has the release papers that you're required to sign. She'll be here soon. Good luck."

I liked this physician. There was no small talk—only business. The ward nurse entered. She asked me if I had questions. I said no. She explained the aftercare instructions and handed me a pen so that I could sign on the lines marked with Xs.

She handed me my copy and said, "There are people outside waiting to see you. I'll tell them that they can come in on my way out."

■ ■ ■

ENTER WILL, BETTY, GLORIA, AND RUBY

The door opened, and in walked Will. He held the door open from the inside, and Betty entered, pushing a walker. It startled me to see her walking. She came straight to my bedside, positioned her arms around me, and told me she loved me. I had no words, but I had deep feelings of sorrow for that beautiful woman.

Ruby entered. Next came Gloria. I finally gathered my composure and said, "What's going on?"

"Betty called me and asked if I could pick the family up. They wanted everyone to be together for the ride so that they could surprise you," Will said.

"This is a wonderful surprise. Thank you again, Will!"

"How are you doing, Lenny?" Ruby asked.

"I'm OK. It could have been worse if I hadn't had on my new leather jacket. It prevented the blade from completely cutting through my abdominal muscles. My jacket was destroyed. My clothes were cut off at the hospital. I have only this embarrassing paper robe to wear."

"Betty brought you a change of clothes," Ruby said.

Betty looked down and said, "They belonged to Lewis. I hope that's fine with you, Lenny." I nodded.

Ruby handed me the bag of clothes. Betty asked if I was capable of dressing myself. I slowly rolled off the bed.

"I'm sore, but I can manage it. I'll dress in the bathroom. I won't take long."

As I dressed, I thought about what I should say to Betty. I decided to say nothing. I thought it would be best to let her speak first. I was sure she had an agenda. The clothes fit perfectly. The Veteran and I had worn the same size.

I walked out and said, "I suggest that we go to the cafeteria and make our plans." I opened the door and gave Betty a nod to indicate that she should lead the way. Betty moved her walker in the direction of the door. I couldn't help but stare. Betty's strength and agility fascinated me. Her legs were twice the size they'd been six or seven months ago. I wanted to comment on her new mobility. I decided that it was not the right time.

Gloria asked if the police were trying to find the man who had assaulted me.

"The police have already taken a suspect into custody. The detective requested that I go in and identify him in a line-up."

"Did you find out why he tried to rob you?"

"I suppose he needed money, Gloria. Detective Ray did not say why he'd gone to such extremes to acquire money.

"I'm glad they caught the SOB," Gloria said.

I asked Gloria, how she was doing. She said that Ruby's coming home had changed her life for the good.

"Betty, you look good!"

She smiled and said, "I'm growing stronger by the day, Lenny. I stopped breathing when you told me of Lewis's death. I don't know how I would have survived without Ruby and Gloria. I thank God for sending Will to us. What a smart young man he is. His understanding of this situation and his suggestions on the way here convinced me to go on with life."

RUBY TELLS HER STORY TO LENNY

Will led us to the cafeteria. He spoke to the manager, whom he knew. The manager came over and introduced himself to us. He turned to Betty. "You have my condolences. Do not hesitate to mention any special food needs." Betty thanked him. Will had been working at the VA hospital for a month. It appeared that he knew his way around.

We went to the counter to order. Ruby remained seated with Betty. She asked Betty what she would like.

"Green tea only," Betty said.

Ruby then instructed Gloria to pick up a cup of tea and a cup of black coffee. Gloria shook her head and eagerly complied.

We took our seats at the table. Betty was the first to speak. She looked at me and said, "Lenny, you're probably wondering why I'm here. I came to take a last look at Lewis before his body is cremated. Will told me that he would go with me to view his body."

Then she addressed the table and said, "Anyone who wants to accompany me is welcome. If not, I perfectly understand." She used her walker to push herself up. She looked at Will and me and said, "I am ready."

Ruby and I stayed. Ruby looked to be in her late twenties. She was tall and slim, and she had dark hair and perfectly proportioned features. She was dressed very sexily. I had noticed the stares she'd received from men and women on our way to the cafeteria.

I looked at Ruby, and Ruby looked back at me. It was a standoff. Who would speak first? I smiled and said, "Ruby, you came home at the perfect time. You saved the day—and possibly Betty. I don't know how we would have made it through the last couple of days if you hadn't been here, Ruby. I would like to know more about you. I plan to commemorate the Veteran, and you, Ruby, have become the unexpected star of my story."

"Lenny, I feel like I know you. Betty has told me so much about you. Mostly she talked about the diet that you and Lewis devised for her. She claimed that it changed her life. She told me that you and Lewis were very close and that she accepts you as a member of her family. To start with, Lenny, it is wonderful to be home, and I have no plans to ever leave again. I have settled the ongoing dispute with my mother that compelled me to leave.

"I know it would be better for me to not live with my mother. Betty wants me to live with her, and I accepted her invitation. Betty and I have so much in common and always have. Lenny, I grew up next door. We have similar tastes in literature, almost identical political views, and comparable likes and dislikes. Betty is old but is very much living in the twenty-first century. She understands current events.

"Now I would like to tell you my story. Stop me if the story is too much for you. As a young girl, living in my mother's house with the man she married was nothing short of treachery for me.

"He first started raping me when I was twelve. My stepfather's convincing lies discredited my cries for help, especially in the eyes of Gloria, my mother. No one believed me. He continued to rape me until I turned seventeen. When I became strong enough to put up a fight, he used a knife to threaten me.

"He said that if I resisted him, he would cut me and then cut himself and tell the police that I had tried to kill him. Then because I was on probation for smoking pot, I would go straight to jail.

"I knew from past experiences that no one would believe me. I tried to avoid being in the house alone with him. However, sometimes my mother would leave when I was in my room studying, and he would come to me.

"Most of the time, he would hold the knife to my head while I sucked him off. He would then make me open my mouth and show him the sperm and then order me to swallow it.

"On one occasion, he slammed his nasty cock so hard into the back of my throat that it caused a tear. The tear became infected, and Mom had to take me to the doctor for antibiotics. When I was asked what had caused the tear, I lied. I said I did not know.

"After that he insisted that I wash his dirty cock with a solution that was ninety-one percent isopropyl alcohol before he fucked me in my mouth. He forcefully penetrated every orifice of my body. When I knew that my mother would be leaving, I would climb out my window and run to Betty's house.

"One day a thought entered my mind. I thought, 'If I had a gun and knew how to shoot, I would kill this wretched rapist.'"

"Do you think that if you had had access to a gun, you would have actually attempted to kill him, Ruby?"

"Lenny, I would have if it hadn't been for what happened."

"Then tell me what happened, Ruby!"

RUBY PLOTS A MURDER

"I got a boyfriend when I turned seventeen. He was a gangbanger. He made me feel safe. He sometimes carried a handgun.

"One day I asked him if he would teach me how to shoot. I never told him the real reason I wanted to know how to shoot a gun. He assumed I wanted to become a member of his gang.

"He eagerly said he would. He drove me to the country and down a dirt road away from any people. First he taught me how to break the gun down and clean it. He told me that if I took good care of my gun, it would take good care of me.

"I always looked forward to practicing. We had a good time shooting bottles and cans. After much practice, I could shoot all six bullets in the gun into six cans from twenty feet away without missing one.

"He told me that I had to practice quickly going for my gun and rapidly firing it with accuracy. 'The movement to protect yourself should be a natural response,' he said.

"One day he said that it was time for the last step. He went to the trunk of his car and pulled out a poster the size of a man and leaned it up against the side of a tree. I laughed when I saw it. It was a life-sized policeman. He laughed and said that cops are perfect practice targets for minorities.

"He instructed me to sit on a stump and to put the gun on the ground about five feet from the stump. 'When I say go, as fast as you can, reach for the gun, release the safety, and fire at the target,' he said. I did, and I missed. 'See that?' he said. 'Everything changes when you have to move fast and shoot.'

"We practiced the move until I got it down. He then told me to turn around but not to look. He placed the gun in a different place and moved the target. He said, 'When you hear me move, as fast as you can, turn, find your gun, remove the safety, find the target, and shoot. Don't miss.'

"I practiced many different moves over the next few days. One day he asked me if I felt comfortable with a gun. I said, 'It feels like I'm holding the hand of a friend.'

"He gave me a strong hug and said, 'You are ready! Close your eyes, and don't look until I tell you to.' He led me to his car, opened the door, closed the door, and said, 'You can open your eyes now.'

"He placed in my hand a gun just like his—a thirty-eight caliber snub-nose Smith and Wesson. At that time, it was the best present I had ever received."

I couldn't help myself. "Holy shit, Ruby! You were only seventeen. What were you planning on doing with that gun?"

Ruby looked me straight in the eye and said, "I was going to kill that SOB the next time he came to my room to rape me. That SOB had raped me for as long as I could remember, and I had decided that it was way past time for him to die.

"Thank God he died in an automobile accident before I had the chance."

"Ruby, I can't say I disagree with you. I would have felt the same way."

The John Grisham novel *A Time to Kill* came to mind. I could see then how good people in similar situations could end up on death row. "What did you do with the handgun once you didn't need it, Ruby?"

"I returned it to the young man who'd given it to me."

"Were you mentally or physically affected by what you endured for all those years?" I asked.

"I realize the effect that that tragedy has had on my life. The upside is that I'm a damn good shot with a handgun. After my mother saw the lying rapist for what he really was, she apologized, cried, and begged for my forgiveness. Mom accepted what I had been through, and that was enough to expunge our differences. We now have the kind of close mother-daughter relationship that we never had when I was young."

"Ruby, that is a shocking story. Do you mind if I include it in my book?"

"Tell it, Lenny. Tell it just like it happened! If it prevents one little girl from going through what I went through, it will be well worth it. Do you know about the rumors that the SOB constantly spread about me to mask what he was doing to me for most of my younger years? I was portrayed as a lowlife and a whore, and everything I said was regarded as a lie, Lenny."

RUBY, THE STREETWALKER

"I know you've heard horrible things about me, Lenny. Don't sit there and wonder if I'll be offended by your inquiry. This is your opportunity. Man up, Lenny! If you're going to tell this story, ask me those hard questions that you're thinking about. Don't hesitate, Lenny! Do it!"

"OK, Ruby. Allow me a moment to gather my thoughts. I need to recover from the sheer horror of what you told me. Were you a streetwalker, Ruby?"

"What do you mean by that? Are you asking me if I hooked for money? If that's what you're hinting at, my answer is almost. I tried it a couple of times, but I couldn't go through with it. So you can record a no for that question. Next question?"

"Where did you get the money you gave to your mother after her husband had died?"

"I hung out with street performers who did break dancing for tips. They taught me how to perform. They were hardworking dancers. They danced to entertain people, and people showed their appreciation for them by tipping them. I danced too, Lenny. It was fun, and I would make a couple hundred dollars some days. I would give the money to my mother for her house payments. She never asked how I'd earned the money. I knew that dance was what I wanted to study at the university."

RUBY'S BREAK-DANCING PERFORMANCE AT THE UNIVERSITY

Ruby put on a break-dancing demonstration for a couple of her new friends soon after she arrived at the university. The dance drew a large crowd. After the dance exhibition, Ruby became a dance celebrity on campus.

The school's dance department asked Ruby to teach break dancing for fun as a nonaccredited course. Ruby taught break dancing twice a week and maintained a full class schedule throughout her four years there. The student government showed their appreciation for her by awarding her sixty-five dollars a week from the student-services-and-activities fees.

Teaching break dancing let Ruby earn money. All of her other needs were taken care of by her full academic scholarship.

TEACHING DANCE IN FORT MYERS

"However, the real money came when I returned home from the university. I taught dance."

"What?"

"That's right. I taught dance when I returned home from the university."

"Dance companies around the area would call me when their wealthy customers asked for private lessons. They knew that I was the best dancer in southwest Florida, that I was formally trained, and that I was an experienced teacher thanks to my four years of teaching break dancing during school. Would you like to know how I started teaching?"

"Yes, Ruby. I would. How did you go about teaching dance?"

"I dropped my résumé off at some dance studios. A couple of them asked me to demonstrate my abilities. I had choreographed a demonstration that incorporated all of the different kinds of ballroom dances. They were overwhelmed by my talent. Most of them asked me why I was there.

"After the word about my talent got around, I was able to name my price. When the studios would get requests for private lessons, they would call me. I taught private lessons for one hundred dollars per hour, plus travel time. I gave most of the money to my mother until the day she called me a whore. She assumed that I was hooking. She still believed her dead husband's lies about me.

"I fired back harsh words about the old man she was fucking for money. That really pissed her off! She then told me to leave her house."

RUBY GOES TO VEGAS

"I packed a few of my things and took off for Vegas the next day with one of the street performers. I was gone for more than five years before I returned two days ago. Betty informed me that my mom had lost her job about five months before and that the old man who'd been supporting her had died. Betty admitted that she'd told Gloria to leave her alone because her gloom-and-doom attitude had been driving her crazy. After Mom and I had a heart-to-heart talk, I wrote her a check for ten thousand dollars to stop the foreclosure.

"I demanded that she apologize to Betty, and she did. For now, we're all one family again, and it couldn't have come at a better time. We need to all pull together to support Betty during this unexpected tragedy."

"Ruby, you are so right. I want to thank you again for all you've done over the last two days. You definitely saved my ass. What did you do in Vegas to make that kind of money?"

"I auditioned at MGM Grand's Crazy Horse Paris. It's known as the most sophisticated cabaret in Las Vegas. The dancers are beautiful. They're classically trained, and every dance is skillfully choreographed. For my audition, I choreographed a special dance that ended with break dancing. The unique performance earned me a standing ovation from the director and the staff. I signed a contract for one year that very day.

"I agreed to do a minimum of five shows a week. I received twelve hundred dollars per show and was paid biweekly. I furnished my own insurance for the first year and was told that after that, I would be eligible for benefits.

"Ninety days later, the director wrote a solo break dance into the show. The audience was fascinated by my performance. I received another two hundred dollars each show for the solo performance.

"I later danced privately on my days off for a minimum of twelve hundred dollars an hour and earned as much as twenty-five thousand per hour for doing nude dances or performing courtesan services for dignitaries.

"I saved one million five hundred thousand dollars and invested one million of it in the stock market. That's what I accomplished in Vegas. I trust that you'll share this information only with my permission, Lenny."

"You have my word, Ruby."

"The need to establish a relationship with my mother, Gloria, was more important than the money. I had a burning desire to prove that my evil stepfather had been telling lies about me. I have no doubt that my investments will sustain my modest lifestyle for the rest of my life even if I have to take care of mom, Lenny."

RUBY'S FIRST LOVE, JAMES ROGERS

"Ruby, what happened to the street performer you left with?"

"There were too many street performers in Las Vegas. He had stiff competition, which made it difficult for him to earn good money. He left for San Francisco."

"Was that a sad moment for you?"

"Yeah, it was. He'd been my best friend, and I missed him. We have each other's e-mail addresses. Astonishingly, we were never intimate, which is confounding to me. We showered together and slept nude together and were no more than friends."

"On occasion we would rent a porno movie and buy a nice bottle of wine. We were comfortable with each other. We would watch the movie, drink the wine, and masturbate together. I would stare at his hard cock and open up my vagina so that he could stare at it.

"Sometimes I would assume a position on all fours so that he could view me from behind. Then I would reach back and spread open my vagina. That would drive him to ecstasy.

"I enjoyed bringing him pleasure. He would keep himself from ejaculating until I was ready so that we could orgasm together, and I would do the same for him.

"On some occasions, he would wait for me to orgasm first. I would position my face close to his cock—close enough to it that I could smell it and close enough for him to spew his warm sperm onto my face. That would excite me and set off my second orgasm. We never tried to make anything more of these experiences. They simply satisfied our human biological needs.

"When times were hard, we would hold each other tight until we fell asleep. He never tried to penetrate me. He was respectful of my problem with penetration. It was a once-in-a-lifetime friendship.

"He accepted our relationship for what it was. I heard from him often until he found someone he loved in San Francisco. I was happy for him. He'd taught me how to break dance. The break dancing that I added into my MGM audition separated me from the pack, and it was why I got the job.

"I learned from the best. Break dancers referred to him as the king of break dancing. His name was James Rogers. I will always keep a light on for him."

"That's an amazing story, Ruby. I really thank you for sharing it with me."

"I hope it will serve you in some capacity."

"I am sure it will." I had become excited by Ruby's story and was embarrassed by the bulge in my pants.

Ruby giggled and said, "I hope that account will satisfy that need. You should not be embarrassed by your natural reaction to it."

"Thank you, Ruby. Your story is better than I could have ever imagined. Can I ask you a question about the sex scene you described?"

"Of course."

"Did you make the story up?"

Ruby looked at me and said, "That was exactly the way we pleasured ourselves. Maybe one day I'll tell you about my Las Vegas private encounters."

I hesitated for a second and then said, "Wow!"

WILL IS HOME, AND LENNY IS NEVER GOING HOME

"Ruby, would you like another cup of coffee?" I asked. She nodded. I needed time to think. What else did I need to ask Ruby before the family returned from the hospital mortuary?

I needed to know more about her mother, Gloria. "That was a nice thing you did for your mom—giving her ten thousand dollars to stop the foreclosure."

"I think her job interviews will go better now that the pressure is off of her. She might be old, but she does have twenty years of experience as an administrative assistant. It's just a matter of time before she finds a position."

"Ruby, do you know the story of how Will became involved?"

"He picked us up and drove us here. We had four hours to drill him on everything that happened."

"OK, then, tell me what you think."

"What I think about what, Lenny?"

"Will and me."

"That's not a fair question."

"Why not?"

"You have a history with everyone concerned, and so far, everyone has spoken highly of you—especially Betty. As for Will—well, the jury is still out. But he's obviously educated, caring, and, I must say, attractive. My mom spoke to me about offering Will the adjoining apartment to her house after I told her that I would be living with Betty. He said that he's going to take the job at the Cape Coral veterans' clinic. I think he's impressed with our little family and would like to belong to it.

"He did travel across the United States by himself. I really don't believe that he has any family. During the four-hour ride here, he didn't mention anything about his family. I bet he's tired of being alone.

"You know, Lenny, that's the reason I came home. I want to be with my family. Do you have family?"

"No, Ruby. I will never be going home."

∎∎∎

BETTY RETURNS FROM THE HOSPITAL'S MORTUARY

Ruby nudged me to tell me that Betty and Will were coming into the cafeteria. Betty was leading the way. She was moving with her walker at a fast walking pace. It was obvious that the walker would soon be unnecessary.

Betty's face was red and swollen. "I made it, Lenny. I never dreamed I would outlive my child. We won't have to return in three days to collect his ashes. The VA offered to deliver them.

"Lenny, I was hoping that you could take me to pick out an urn tomorrow. We have a great deal to talk about." Without hesitation, I agreed to take her.

Will was holding Betty's hand. Betty then turned to Will and said, "I feel like the Lord sent an angel to guide me through these trying times." Will blushed, but he was noticeably humbled by Betty's words.

Betty took a seat, and Gloria sat down beside her. Betty instructed everyone else to take a seat. Gloria immediately jumped up and said, "How many coffees, and how many teas?" She took requests and scurried off toward the beverage bar.

Gloria returned with the beverages and said that she'd decided to rent the part of her house that she'd converted into a two-bedroom apartment to Will. Will nodded in approval and said that he'd accepted the sociologist position at the Cape Coral VA clinic.

I was first to congratulate him. "Welcome aboard." I thought that was fitting for him, as he'd been a navy man.

Ruby pounded her spoon on the table and said, "Speech! Speech!"

WILL JOHNSON SUGGESTS A SLOGAN FOR THE FAMILY

Will choked up, cleared his throat, and said, "Over the last two days, I've had an awakening. You have showed me the warm feeling that having a family can give a person. You've made me feel needed. I've never felt as comfortable with a group of people as I do with the people seated at this table. I grew up in an orphanage.

"When I was a kid, I read Alexandre Dumas's novel *The Three Musketeers*. There's a saying in it that I like: 'one for all, and all for one.'

"I didn't know that that kind of togetherness existed in real life. I thank all of you for inviting me into your homes and lives." Everyone but Ruby applauded. She rose out of her chair and gave him a hug and a kiss on the cheek.

I then stood and said, "Thank you, Will, for saving my life. I will always be your friend and will always be grateful to you."

Betty remained seated. "We lost my son and gained a great friend. We love you, Willy Johnson."

"It will be a privilege to have an intelligent young man whom all of my friends love and respect living in my apartment," Gloria said.

"Are there any more pertinent announcements? I'm ready to vacate this house of pain. Two days here are about all I can handle," I said.

Ruby stood up. "I have one last announcement. We need to stop by Will's motel room and get his belongings. Since Will doesn't have a car, I'm offering to sell him my Honda Fit at its wholesale value. It has only thirty-five thousand miles on it. He can begin paying me when he's established himself here. He will no longer need to waste money on taxis. Plus, I had already decided to purchase a larger car."

I thought to myself that was what millionaires should do—help people. Ruby received a round of applause. Will teared up.

"Lenny, you can drive," Betty said.

I asked Will to sit in the front seat so that he could direct me to the motel where he had been living. It was only a couple of miles from the VA. When we arrived, I chose to sit in the car with Betty.

Gloria and Ruby went in with Will to help him gather up his clothes and belongings. They were out the door within ten minutes. His belongings barely filled the trunk. Will sat down and said, "Those are all of my worldly possessions." He laughed. "I only had to pay for one extra bag when I flew from San Francisco to Tampa."

WILL ACCEPTS THE POSITION IN CAPE CORAL

We turned onto the interstate ramp and drove south. Not one word was said in the first hour. I think our feelings were mutual. We each needed time to sort out all that had happened over the last three days.

Will was the first one to speak. "The VA gave me two weeks to move and to make adjustments."

"That was good of them," Gloria said. "Are you looking forward to your new position in Cape Coral?"

"I'm excited about the work and about my new living quarters. I didn't like Tampa. It was too large for me. I prefer a small-town atmosphere. Fort Myers is the perfect size. The people at the Cape Coral VA clinic were very nice and told me how happy they were to finally receive the funding for a sociologist."

"I thought you were living in San Francisco before you moved to Tampa," Ruby said.

"I just say San Francisco because everyone knows where it is. Actually, I was living in a small town named Modesto outside of San Francisco with a college friend. I moved there when I graduated from USF. I bought a scooter for transportation. It got eighty miles per gallon. I sold it to acquire the money to fly to Tampa."

STOPPING AT A TRUCK STOP FOR FOOD, FUEL, AND RUBY'S SHOW

There was another period of quiet. I broke the silence by asking if anyone needed to stop. Gloria said, "My bladder would appreciate that." At the next exit, we pulled off and into a Love's truck stop.

"Truck stops are fun," Betty said. "They have so many neat things to look at. I'll go in." I locked the car, and everyone went inside. Betty and Ruby looked at the electronics that truckers use in their homes on wheels, and the truckers looked at Ruby.

One middle-aged trucker approached her and asked her if she was a celebrity. Ruby said that she'd been a Las Vegas showgirl. He then asked if he could take a selfie with her, and she agreed.

"I saw your picture on the MGM Grand's Jumbotron!" another man said. "You're Ruby Ridge. You were the hottest showgirl in Las Vegas."

"Oh, my God! How are we going to get out of here?" Betty said. "Lenny, Will, help Ruby out! She's surrounded by men."

"I'm OK, Betty," Ruby said. "I can do this."

Ruby took charge of the situation and started teasing the men with seductive poses as they took pictures of her. She then entertained the entire store with a short stage dance. She finished with an appreciative curtsy, blew a few kisses, and excused herself. The store occupants cheered and applauded.

I'd never seen a woman tame excited men like Ruby Ridge could. I was witnessing for the first time her unprecedented talent and why Ruby Ridge had been designated the best of Las Vegas five years running. She was beautiful.

We gathered our selections, paid, and entered the car in silence. Gloria had two handfuls of fresh fruit. Will had purchased a ham-and-cheese sandwich. Ruby had bought a Bose wireless headset for Betty. I'd grabbed a couple of bananas.

My appetite had not totally recovered from the events of the last three days. "Lenny, is that all you're eating?" Betty asked. I repeated to Betty what I had just said to myself. Her face showed concern, but she didn't say anything for a moment. She then said, "I brought my food. I intend to stay on the eating regimen that you and Lewis designed for me. It's worked miracles for my health." Gloria shared her fruit with Ruby. I refueled the car. Ruby insisted on paying. I again turned onto the south ramp of Interstate 75. The only noise was the crunch of food.

Silence always puts me into my world of dreams.

MY RUBY DAYDREAM

I silently reviewed Ruby's truck-stop performance. Ruby attracted attention from men and women. Her lifetime of dance had perfectly sculpted her body from head to toe. She had a vivacious personality. Her facial features were unexcelled; her skin was almost gold and without blemishes; her eyes were bright blue; and her hair was short, thick, and light brown. She was tall and agile with perfectly fitting breasts, and she was extremely leggy.

It was obvious to me why she'd earned a million dollars in Las Vegas. The combination of her intelligence, beauty, and dance skills had commanded the highest rewards from directors and from the super-rich customers she'd done private dances for.

THE THEORY OF IGNORANCE

By the time the average American reaches thirty years of age, he or she will be ignorant and will continue to become more ignorant each year thereafter.

The Veteran and I had many discussions on this topic. We had wondered why that happens to the great majority of adults. Why does their knowledge lag behind the times? Why are they so resistant to inevitable changes?

I decided to reveal in this book the Veteran's theory on the slippery slope to ignorance. He believed that the period between one's birth and one's high school graduation was the period of learning, experimentation, and change.

In school, young people study different disciplines on a daily basis. After school, the young participate in many different events and go from one interest to another. Every day they have new and varied experiences.

Once a young man or woman's education has been completed, he or she will be expected to assume a conventional life. That means securing a job, finding the right mate, marrying, and starting a family.

With his or her partner, that person will purchase a home, enter into a thirty-year mortgage, and raise kids. Typically, both the wife and the husband will work, so they'll need two cars. Their long-term financial obligations will become their main focuses. Very little information will penetrate the work or home environment. The Veteran called this situation "a closed-mind system without oxygen."

That is what the great majority of American people do. They have routines; they come home tired from work, eat, watch television, work on their computers, talk on their cell phones, and then go to bed.

Even in gyms, people engaged in resistance training mindlessly listen to music through their earbuds. A benefit of resistance training is focusing on coordinating the mind with the muscles being worked. If you are focused on music, how can you improve your mind-muscle coordination?

Beware of routines!

When the same thing happens every day, the brain is not exercised. As a result, the brain becomes lethargic. Nothing goes into it, so nothing comes out of it. The formula for this idea is $0 = 0$.

The Veteran used to laugh and say that every day was the same. His routine kept repeating, just like in the movie *Groundhog Day*, with Bill Murray. When the human brain doesn't receive any new stimulation, atrophy prevails.

More years go by, and nothing changes, and nothing new is learned. In some instances, the knowledge that one gained in his earlier years fades or vanishes. Ignorance grows with each passing year.

The Veteran called this process the "adult dumbing-down process." This process can be evidenced by the beliefs and actions of older people. Their morals remain the same even though much has changed over the years. They wear the same kinds of attire, have the same likes and dislikes, and still listen to the same music they enjoyed in their youth.

They constantly talk about the good old days and surround themselves with old people and old ideas. The truth of the matter is that they have no idea of how things presently are. A fifty-year-old can be as many as twenty-five years behind the trends.

The Veteran said that explained the generation gap and why the old men and women in Congress could seem out of touch with the times. He believed that they needed to listen to Bob Dylan, a man of their day, and to his song "The Times, They Are A-Changing."

"Lenny, are you feeling OK? Are you OK?"

"Um, yeah, Betty. I'm good. I was in a daydream."

"Lenny, I can drive. Your midsection must be bothering you. I can't believe you chose not to take the pain pills that the doctor offered you," Will said.

"Will, driving and daydreaming are distracting me from the pain."

"How many stitches did you end up with?" Will asked.

"I think the nurse said one hundred thirty-five."

"Holy shit! I had no idea," Ruby said.

"Lenny, Ruby and I will take care of you. You should stay with us for a few days or for as long as you'd like," Betty said. "And you and I need to look for an urn tomorrow. We can do that first thing and then go to the police station to identify the man who assaulted you."

"I need to go to the bank to sign the papers for my new loan. It looks like everyone but Will and Ruby have things to do tomorrow," Gloria said.

"I would like to relax," Will said.

"Me too," said Ruby.

"Meeting adjourned," I said.

■ ■ ■

BREEZY MEETS JOJO

We entered Betty's yard. I informed Betty that I was going to go to my apartment to grab a few things and to pick up my dog, Breezy. "My dog, Jojo, needs a friend," Ruby said. "Who keeps your dog when you're gone?"

"Breezy stays with my neighbor when I'm gone," I said.

"Don't be gone long," Betty said.

"I called Detective Ray and told him that I could make it in tomorrow, Betty. He asked how I was doing, and I thanked him for his concern."

I arrived at Betty's house at about eight at night. I released Breezy, and he found Jojo right away. It looked like Jojo was giving Breezy a tour of the yard. Jojo introduced him to the dog door and to the kitchen, where the food was kept. The fact that Breezy wasn't alone anymore made me feel warm inside. I told Betty that I was tired and would like to lie down. She suggested that I take the Veteran's room and said goodnight.

I was woken up by someone banging on the door. It was Betty. "Lenny, breakfast is ready! We need to be going. We have a list of things to do."

It was six-thirty in the morning. After dressing, I dragged myself down the stairs. Ruby and Betty were sitting at the table. I sat where Betty told me to sit. Ruby served me eggs and bacon. She informed me that they were antibiotic-free. The eggs were free range, and the pigs had been fed only natural foods with no pesticides and no synthetic hormones, and they'd been slaughtered in a humane manner. "I like knowing that, Ruby. Thank you."

Ruby announced that she was going to buy a Honda Odyssey. She had done her research online. She wanted a lot of space, and this car would satisfy that need. Will was going to go with her and would take possession of her old car when she purchased the Odyssey.

"Lenny, after we select an urn, I want to go with you to the police department to look at the SOB that cut you," Betty said.

GLORIA GOES TO THE BANK TO STOP HER FORECLOSURE

Gloria was waiting to see her banker. Her appointment time had passed thirty minutes before. She decided to confront the receptionist.

"I'm here to see a mortgage specialist about my home loan. My appointment was more than thirty minutes ago. Can you help me with this matter?"

"I'm so sorry. Please give me a minute to check on this matter," the receptionist said, and then she left the room. She was quick to return. "Your mortgage agent is otherwise occupied. The president of the bank will meet with you. Follow me, and I'll escort you to his office."

"Thank you," Gloria said.

GLORIA REUNITES WITH HER FIRST LOVE, BOB RICHBURG

The receptionist glanced down at the appointment list and said, "Mr. Richburg, this is Gloria Ridge." Gloria's eyes grew wide, and Mr. Richburg's did the same.

"My God! Gloria Ridge, how have you been? Sit down, please!"

"I'm well, Bob. Where have you been all these years?"

"After school I married a woman from Iowa and moved there. Her father got me involved in banking. She died of cancer three years ago. I decided to move back to Florida in search of a fresh start. What about you, Gloria? You're still beautiful."

"Thank you! My husband died in a car accident. He left me in a lot of debt. My daughter, Ruby, returned home very wealthy. She's the reason I'm here. I want to stop my foreclosure. If you tell me the amount I need to pay, I'll give you a check. I was previously told that it would take ten thousand dollars."

"I have your file on my desk. Can I have my secretary serve you a cup of coffee while I go over the figures?"

"Sure," Gloria said.

"Our policy does not allow her to serve me coffee, but it does allow her to serve coffee to our clients."

"Thank you very much, Bob."

Gloria thought back to when she and Bob had gone steady in high school. He'd been her first love. Bob had gone off to college and hadn't returned to Fort Myers. He had caused Gloria's first heartbreak.

"All right, Gloria. The figures are in order."

"This has been a nightmare for me, Bob."

"Do you have the check ready?"

"Here it is."

"Thank you. Now sign these documents, and that will be it. But I would advise you to refinance your home. Your interest rate is very high, but interest rates have never been so low. You could cut your payments in half. I'd advise you to bring your daughter in and to add her to the refinance application."

"Are you serious, Bob? My payments would be one half of what they are currently?"

"Yes, that's about right."

"That would be great."

"I will be back with you."

"Can I work with you, Bob?"

"Gloria, it would be my pleasure. This is not too professional of me, but I have to ask you something. Will you have dinner with me? We could talk about the old times."

Gloria showed no hesitation and said, "I would love that, Bob."

"When would be a good time for you?"

"This coming Friday?"

"Perfect. I'll pick you up at eight."

Gloria left with her high school smile on her face.

BETTY SELECTS A SCATTERING URN FOR LEWIS'S ASHES

"I'm ready when you are," Betty said. "I don't care to carry the walker. I'd rather hold on to your arm. I want to end my dependency on my walker, Lenny."

Betty's walking on her own was nothing short of a miracle. I threw my arm out, and Betty grabbed it. We left the house, and to my amazement, she was holding on to my arm only for balance. I walked her to the passenger's side of the car and opened the door, and she helped herself in. She winked at me and said, "I want my driver's license back too, Lenny."

It was eight in the morning when we turned south onto Highway 41 to Naples. I never grew tired of beautiful Florida mornings. "Lenny, Gloria wanted to come with us. I explained to her that I felt comfortable with you. She realized that this was a personal situation for you and me. I reminded her that she had an appointment with her banker. She left immediately to go get dressed. Gloria is a totally different person now that Ruby is back."

"I'm glad you're friends again. I don't believe anyone can have too many friends."

"I agree, Lenny. Ruby and I looked at many urns online. I just couldn't imagine making this decision by looking at pictures on a screen. The parlor that we're going to has a large assortment of urns that I can place my hands on. That will help me make a decision."

"I support you, Betty. Is this the street?"

"Yes. Turn left, and park in the first spot you see."

"I'll come around and assist you out of the car, Betty."

"All I need is your arm. I intend to donate my walker to Goodwill."

We went into the parlor.

"Lenny, which urn do you like? There are so many to pick from. Show me what you would choose. I insist!"

"OK, Betty, this is how I feel. Don't be disturbed by my answer."

"I promise I won't."

"I remember the Veteran's saying that he wanted his ashes to be scattered. That being said, I would select a scattering urn."

"Thank you for reminding me of that. You're right. I like the one with the ocean scene. Lewis wanted to be scattered in the ocean on a cool morning. It's only fifty-nine dollars. Let me pay for the urn so that we can leave soon, Lenny. What if the VA tries to deliver his ashes, but we're not home?"

"The VA will call before delivering Lewis's ashes. Did you bring your meal?"

"Yes."

"I'm going to stop at this Dunkin' Donuts for a cup of coffee. We can rehydrate in the car before going to the police department."

"That sounds fine."

"I'll leave the car running so that you'll be cool. I'll be right back."

I went into Dunkin' Donuts for my coffee and then returned to the car.

"That was quick."

"There was no line."

"Lenny, I know how close you and Lewis were. I hope you'll still come around now that he is gone."

"Betty, I'll be around more now, if that's OK with you."

"I would like that. I'll give you my extra key so that you can make yourself at home."

BETTY REVEALS RUBY'S INTEREST IN LENNY

"Can you keep quiet about a personal matter, Lenny?"

"Of course I can."

"I need your word that you won't disclose to anyone what I'm about to say."

"You have my solemn word, Betty."

"Ruby has a romantic interest in you."

"Damn! That comes as a surprise."

"Why?"

"I'm much older than she is, and she can have any man she desires."

"Spending five years as a lead Las Vegas showgirl is the equivalent of aging twenty years, Lenny. Ruby told me her clients were your age. Not many young men can afford twenty-five thousand dollars an hour for her company. That's what she is used to. Money is of no concern to her now. She's looking for something else."

"I know it is not money if she's looking my way."

"Ruby's impressed by your physical condition at your age, and by the knowledge you possess—especially your knowledge of psychotherapy. Ruby thinks there's something that only you can provide."

"What could that be?"

"She has money, beauty, and intelligence. My guess is that that something is very personal, Lenny, and I think you know what I'm referring to.

"Her position in Vegas exposed her to some of the world's richest and most powerful men. You'd better believe that she knows powerful men. She told me that she doesn't want kids and that she'd prefer a mature, intelligent man who can spend time with her."

"Even in my younger days, I never had a woman as dashing as Ruby. She becomes the center of attention in every room she enters. I don't know what to say."

"Then say nothing, and see where it goes."

"You're right, Betty. Thanks."

WILL IS THE MAN AT STARBUCKS

Ruby dialed Will's number, and Will was obviously half asleep when he answered.

"Hello?" he said.

"Rise and shine!" Ruby said. "I'll be outside in ten minutes."

"I need coffee!" Will said.

"We can stop at Starbucks and have coffee."

Ruby beeped the horn, and Will staggered out the front door.

As he entered the car, Ruby offered him a loud "good morning."

"How can you feel so chipper so early in the morning?"

Ruby's response was a girlish giggle. She was wearing a very small diaphanous black halter top with small, thin, clingy diaphanous shorts and emerald-colored high heels. Will looked at Ruby.

"Are those earrings and that pendant made of real emeralds?" he asked.

"They are of the finest quality. They were gifts from a super-wealthy German industrialist."

"Wow. What are they worth?"

"They were appraised at one hundred and fifty thousand dollars," Ruby calmly said. "Next stop is Starbucks!"

The place was packed. Will ordered hot coffee with steamed heavy cream. Ruby ordered a hot green tea.

"Let's sit and enjoy our beverages," Ruby said. "Why are you so shy, Will Johnson?"

"You really want the truth?"

"Of course," Ruby said.

"I have never been in the presence of a woman as beautiful and as sexy as you. Everyone stares at you because you're perfect. People can't take their eyes off of you. They look at me and wonder what I possess and why I have you by my side. I don't know how to deal with this kind of attention. This is new to me, Ruby."

"I have danced nude for kings and presidents. I charged them as much as fifty thousand dollars per hour. I have thousands of dollars' worth of sexy apparel, and I'm comfortable wearing it. I like being in the spotlight on center stage.

"I break danced on the streets for quarters when I was a child. I grew up being stared at. Men and women salivated over me. I have experienced all of the forbidden sexual behaviors that men and women truly enjoy but publicly claim to detest. I catered to taboo sexual desires for five years in Las Vegas, and I accumulated a fortune while doing it. None of this is new to me.

"You and Lenny are the new arrivals in the family. Betty took care of me and provided me with a sanctuary where I could escape my stepfather, who raped me. She's dear to me. Betty's son is dead, and I'm so sorry that I didn't make it home in time to get to know Lewis. But Betty told me that if I could understand Lenny, I could understand her son. Betty is the wisest woman I have ever known.

"I will not tolerate one more minute of your lack of confidence, Will. I have seen your heart, and it is chock-full of good, and that is why I respect you. I am humbled to be in your presence. You are family."

"It is time to man up. Start now, Will! I know what men think. I make believe what they want to believe. They can tell by looking at you that you're not rich. That leaves only one other possibility. It's show time, Will. So hold your head high as though you have the biggest cock in town, and walk out of here with your hand rubbing my ass."

"Really, Ruby?"

"You're Goddamn right."

Will opened the door for Ruby with one hand, knowing that all eyes were on his other hand. When they reached the car but were still in full view of the people in Starbucks, Ruby wrapped one of her incredibly long legs around his thigh, grabbed his ass with both of her hands, and pulled him tight into a kiss.

Will then ambled around the car and placed himself confidently into the passenger's seat.

"Ruby, I have never before aroused the envy of others. Thank you for giving me that incredible, euphoric experience," Will said.

"OK, Big Cock," Ruby said, and then they laughed together.

RUBY AND WILL BECOME BEST FRIENDS

Ruby turned to Will. "Let's go pick up my car. I made the purchase online. I bought a Honda Odyssey Touring Elite with every option available. I'm excited, Will. I've never bought a car before without worrying about the cost. I never could've imagined being able to do this.

"Will, I have something to say just between you and me, OK?"

"Of course."

"I want us to be friends. I have to deal with onslaughts of sexually hungry men whenever I'm not with a man. I realize that there is a time to play and a time to work. Can you be my friend without us becoming intimately involved?

"I will remind you of a business rule that has stood the test of time: Do not mix business with pleasure. I never played around with my producers or directors or with anyone affiliated with the shows I was in. The best way to destroy a friendship is to make the mistake of having sex, Will. Can you comply with this rule?"

"Of course."

"Will, I want you to be perfectly honest with me. Can we do things together? Can we go to Red Sox games? I love baseball games."

"Ruby, our trip to Starbucks was fun. I can be that man for you if you'll teach me how to ballroom dance."

"Deal," Ruby said.

"Betty is looking into securing a bank charter. If things don't go your way at the VA, you could work with the family. It will be a while before that becomes possible. By that time, you'll know the direction you want to go in.

"I'm going to pull over and move to the backseat to change my clothes. I need to concentrate on the business at hand. We have no time for small talk from every man with a hard, swinging dick. I have a baggy sweat suit. I'll put it on. That will take some of the pressure off of you too. Twice in one day could be too much for you."

"You might be right." Will grinned. "I'm still running a little hot." Ruby laughed. "I had a lot fun in Starbucks, Ruby. Are all showgirls like you?"

"No. I was the lead showgirl for five years. I won't be modest. I was billed as the best dancer in Vegas for five years running and as the best woman break dancer of all time. I turned down movie offers."

"Why did you turn down Hollywood?"

"I'd completed the goal I'd set when I'd gone to Vegas. I wanted to go home, reconcile with my mother, and have a regular life. No one has beaten my head-spin record."

"What is that?"

"Twenty-eight full spins on my head."

"What? You mean you spun around on your head without any other support?"

"That's right, Will."

"Holy crap!"

"It would bring the audience members to their feet. I'd do it during my solo, which was the last dance of the show. Spins and twisting flips were my best moves."

"Will you give me a demo one day?"

"I would love to. I have DVDs you can watch."

"Are you nude in any of them? I'm just joking."

"I do have nude ones, Will. I was the highest-paid private dancer in Vegas."

"How much did you charge, and did you really dance nude?"

"This goes no further than here, Will. Promise?"

"I promise!"

"I danced nude for kings and one president for fifty thousand dollars."

"Maybe later I'll let you watch one. Will you trust me for now?"

"I trust you, Ruby!"

"We'll just have to wait and see, my friend. I'm dressed, so let's move."

RUBY PURCHASES A HONDA ODYSSEY AND SELLS WILL HER HONDA FIT

"This is the Honda dealership. Will, turn here, and park in the front. Let's go in and see the sales manager. His name is Ralf."

"You work here, mister? I'm looking for Ralf," Ruby said.

"I will find him. Wait here, please."

"This shouldn't take long, Will."

"My name is Ralf. You must be Ms. Ridge," Ralf said. "We have your car ready. Let's see if everything is to your satisfaction. If it is, we'll return to my office to sign the deal."

"Ralf, let's go over the options to ensure none of them were left out. I will read them out and you point out that particular feature. If I have a question I will stop and ask. I doubt that I will stop you, Ralf. I studied everything about these features on line. Ralf, it looks like everything I wanted is on the vehicle. Your service department has done a great job. "I love it, Ralf! I'm ready to sign the final paperwork."

They returned to Ralf's office.

"Sit here. I'll pull the documents up. Did you bring the cashier's check in the amount of forty thousand dollars?" Ruby handed the check to Ralf. "You paid the rest of the amount with your credit card?"

"Yes, Ralf."

"This car has every optional feature offered. Your operator's manual will explain how to operate these features if you forget. If you have any questions, you can return to the service department. They will help you."

"Thank you very much, Ralf. I do have a question. How quickly can you do a full service on my Honda Fit? I'll be turning that car over to this man, and I want it to be in top condition."

"I can arrange that for you," Ralf said.

"When can we have the car back?" Ruby asked.

"If you leave it now, I will make it a priority, and you can have it back by six tonight."

"Great, give Ralf the keys, Will."

"Thank you for your business, Ms. Ridge."

"I'm going to take the long way home. We can go north on Interstate 75 and exit at Palm Avenue to McGregor and drive in that way."

"Go for it, Ruby."

"Guess what, Will? I forgot to get the wholesale value of the Fit. I'm going to call Ralf." She called him. "This is Ruby Ridge. I need to speak to Ralf."

"Hello, Ruby. What can I do for you?"

"I need to know the wholesale value of my Honda Fit, less twenty percent. It has a navigation function and thirty-five thousand miles on it. It's two years old, and I never had any problems."

"That comes to fifteen thousand dollars."

"Thank you, Ralf."

"That's what you can pay me when you have the money, Will."

"Thank you."

"No problem. We're home. Look, Will. I see that Gloria is here."

IDENTIFYING LENNY'S ASSAILANT

Betty and I pulled into the police department. I went to the side of the car where Betty was seated. Betty had already pushed the door open.

"I don't need any help," she said. "All I need is for you to lend me an arm for balance. Soon I won't need an arm. You can bet your last dollar on that, Lenny. Like I said before, I will soon walk on my own and secure a driver's license."

"Betty, I have no doubt that you will succeed with that kind of determination," I said. "I'm here to see Detective Ray. He's expecting me. My name is Lenny."

"I've got this, Officer," Detective Ray said to another officer. "Good to see you, Lenny. Thanks for coming down."

"This is Betty, the mother of the Vietnam veteran I told you about—the one who died on the day I was assaulted."

"You have my condolences, Betty."

"Lenny told me you lost a brother in Vietnam. You have my condolences, Detective Ray."

"Thank you, Betty. You are right on time, Lenny. The lineup should be ready.

"Lenny, can you identify one of these men as your assailant? Don't be afraid, Betty. They cannot see us."

"Yes, I can. The third man from the left is the man who assaulted me."

"Do you have any doubt that he's the right man?"

"No, Detective Ray. No doubts whatsoever."

"Then we're through here. Lenny, when this investigation is complete, will you join me for a beer?"

"I would enjoy that."

"OK, Lenny. I'll give you a call."

"I'll be looking forward to it, Detective Ray. Betty, let's go home—mission accomplished."

"Betty, your house looks like town hall. Everyone is here," I said when we arrived at her house.

Betty smiled and said, "Lenny, I like it this way. It feels like I have a family."

"I would have to agree—and the family is growing."

Betty laughed and said, "Let's go and see what everyone is doing."

"I forgot a few things. I'm going to run back to my apartment to pick them up. I'll be back shortly."

"Don't be gone too long—everyone is here."

"I won't be."

It delighted me to see Breezy and Jojo playing in the yard. Breezy had always gotten along with other dogs. Like people, dogs prefer not to be alone. I know Breezy well. I have never seen him so content. Breezy and I were always together. I found Ruby, and Breezy found Jojo. Neither one was left alone. The timing could not have been better. Life likes life, and that seems to hold true with the canine species too.

RAINING ROCKETS

When I drove away alone, my mind flashed back to Vietnam. I thought about the Tet Offensive, when my platoon was assigned to patrol the outer perimeter of the Bien Hoa air base.

Our objective was to seek out and destroy the Viet Cong, who were lobbing mortars and rockets into the air base in an attempt to kill and psychologically harass personnel and to destroy our aircraft.

I could not escape the thought that I could be the next unlucky soldier who disintegrated in a ball of fire. Everyone would eventually adopt the attitude that if it was time to go, going in your sleep might be the best way. Then at least you could sleep. However, it would take a few months or longer for us to arrive at that way of thinking.

You could always tell whether a soldier was on his second or third tour. The seasoned soldier would sit outside the bunker in a lawn chair, drinking rocket repellent, a drink made with beer and vodka. His attitude was "Fuck it, might as well enjoy the fireworks show. Why worry? If it's my time, it's my time!"

When new arrivals would ask that soldier about his attitude, his reply might be something like, "Running or hiding won't help if it's your time, Soldier."

The enemy was difficult to locate. They would come out at night; fire their destructive weapons into the base, killing or wounding a few American soldiers; and quickly disappear.

There was one particular event that I will never forget. An eighteen-year-old man from Alabama arrived in camp by helicopter at around six at night. The VC fired the first rocket at around six-thirty, and it was a direct hit on him. Only a few chunks of flesh scattered over a large area were found. That was unlucky!

The talk was that he'd finished his twelve-month tour of duty in thirty minutes.

His name was Edward. From then on, the first thing said to an arriving soldier was "Keep your head down for the first thirty minutes—you don't want to become a dead Ed." Edward had been assigned to my platoon. I had to write a letter to his parents to notify them of his death. I hadn't met the kid. I will never forget the letter. I finally decided that I had to tell it the way it was. I gave them the information that I mentioned above, but I left out the "dead Ed" remark that we'd make to new arrivals.

By day the enemy would withdraw to tunnels deep in the earth. They had intentionally made the tunnels small, which prevented the average American soldier from entering them. The smallest Americans became "tunnel rats," as we called them. The life expectancy of such soldiers was unfortunately short.

OK, back to reality. I needed to get Breezy's food, a pair of jeans, and a couple of polos. Then I'd get out of there!

ENTER ADOLF, THE GERMAN INDUSTRIALIST

I entered the driveway to Betty's house. The first thing that caught my eye was a Mercedes limousine in the front yard. Two men were standing guard outside it. The windows were tinted, which prevented me from seeing inside.

I parked the car, removed my bag of clothes, and proceeded to the front door of the house. The door opened for me. Gloria seemed very nervous.

"Gloria, what's going on?" I said.

"A boyfriend of Ruby's from Germany is here," she said. "He flew in to Fort Myers in his private jet. He asked Ruby to marry him and to go back to Germany. Lenny, his family manufactures cars. They are one of the most prominent families in Germany. He proposed to her at the front door. Then they decided to go to his car to talk privately. They've been out there for almost an hour. Lenny, I'm going nuts.

"I just got my daughter back, and now she could be leaving for Germany. This was totally unexpected. He showed up at the door and caught all of us by surprise."

"Well, Gloria, why don't we wait and see what Ruby decides to do? I brought back a bottle of twelve-year-old Glenlivet single malt scotch. In the meantime, can I pour you a stiff drink?"

"Damn right, Lenny. Pour me a very stiff one."

"Hi, Betty, what's up with you?" I asked when I saw Betty.

"I feel the same way that Gloria does. I just got my best young female friend back. I'm hoping she won't leave with him."

"Ruby is a millionaire, Betty. I don't think that the money will lure her away. She told me about many things that went on in Las Vegas, but she never mentioned him. You know what they say: Everything that happens in Vegas stays in Vegas."

"This is not the time for that statement, Lenny."

"Sorry, ladies!"

"Thanks for the drink, Lenny. Gloria, how did the appointment at the bank go?"

"Great. I have a date with the president this coming Friday. He was my first boyfriend in high school. He was gone for years and recently returned. His wife died of cancer."

"Things are looking up, Gloria!"

"I don't want to end this streak of luck by losing my daughter."

"You do realize that she's a grown woman and plenty capable of making the decision that's best for her, don't you?" I said.

"You're right, Lenny. It's hard for me to accept that she's not my little girl anymore."

"Gloria, all parents are faced with the same heartbreaking thoughts. Kids do grow up. My daughter is living in Korea. I didn't like that decision, but I had to learn to accept it. It was what she wanted to do," I said.

Betty was standing at the window. "Ruby is getting out of the limo!" she said. "She's headed for the door, and the limo is pulling away."

Ruby entered the house. She appeared to have been crying. Betty, who was without her walker, confronted her. "Darling, are you OK?"

Ruby hesitated and then said, "Yes, but it hurts."

"What hurts so much, Ruby?" Gloria asked.

"He was there for me for many years. We had, from time to time, a very intimate relationship. He would fly often from Berlin to see me. At first he was one of my best clients. It later turned into more than a client relationship. I have strong feelings for him, but I don't feel love for him, and I'm not devoted to him. He loves me very much, and I'm sad that I had to turn his offer of marriage down and hurt him. I need time to digest what I just did to that wonderful man.

"He's very powerful. I don't think he's used to not getting what he wants. He cried when I told him that I would not be going back with him."

"Did you give him back those emeralds, Ruby?" Will asked.

"I offered to, and he said that he wanted me to keep them. He said that the moment that he gave me those emeralds was one of the better moments of his life. He said he would contact me from time to time with the hope that I would reconsider his proposal or accept an invitation to visit Germany."

"Ruby, I'm so glad that you're not leaving," Gloria said. "I'm so thankful you've come home, and so are the others here." Gloria held on to Ruby awhile. Everyone remained silent.

RUBY ASKS LENNY OUT

"Lenny, would you take me to dinner?" Ruby asked me. "We can drop Will off at the Honda dealership so that he can pick up his Honda Fit, which is being serviced there."

I had difficulty replying. I was in shock. "Sure, Ruby. I would like that." Everyone but Betty was startled. She had told me that Ruby had her eye on me. "What should I wear?"

Ruby smiled. "Something casual but classy. Now excuse me—I'm going to bathe and dress."

"Betty, Gloria, I see that you're huddled up. Will you tell me what you two are secretly up to?"

"We had nothing to do with Ruby asking you to take her to dinner, Lenny. She told us that she was going to ask you out, but we were as shocked as you were when she did. So run along, and get dressed. You can use my bathroom to shower," Betty said, grinning.

"At least with you, Lenny, we're keeping Ruby in the family, which is more satisfying than seeing her jet off to Germany. That's what we were rudely whispering about," Gloria said. "So now that we've come clean about what we were thinking; we would enjoy hearing your thoughts."

"OK, I don't have any thoughts. No, I take that back—I'm scared shitless. To make myself clear, I cannot understand why a woman like Ruby, who turned down the hand of one of the most powerful men in Germany, would have an interest in me."

"Be logical and not so emotional, Lenny," Betty said. "Ruby has money, and she has no desire for power. Ruby is emotionally free and solution oriented. You should realize that maybe Ruby knows what she needs and sees that you, Lenny, could deliver it. The German was obviously unable to give her something that she must have.

"Ruby informed us that she was very impressed by your ability to comprehend complicated personal matters. There has to be something that Ruby feels that you can help her with. If any man has the intellectual ability to work her through a sensitive personal issue, it's you, Lenny. Besides, Ruby's intuition sensed this about you. But Betty and I did tell her about your thesis in psychotherapy on sexual dysfunction."

"I have an idea of what's at stake here," I said.

"Then tell us, Lenny," Gloria said.

"It wouldn't be good to say something that I'm not sure is true at this time. We could end up having only a friendship."

"Lenny, Ruby lived a fast-paced life in Vegas. She's wise for her age," Gloria said.

"She has her own plans. Ruby might be the girl to guide you to the peace you're looking for," Betty said.

"OK, I see what you ladies are up to. I appreciate your concern. Excuse me. I should get ready."

RUBY'S SEXUAL DYSFUNCTION IS EXPOSED

After showering I put on a pressed pair of designer jeans, a pressed polo shirt, and a pair of deck shoes. "Has Ruby finished dressing, Betty?"

"No, she hasn't come out. It didn't take you long," Gloria said. "I must tell you what I know. Ruby told me that she developed a serious issue because of my late husband.

"We had a heart-to-heart discussion that convinced me that my late husband had sexually abused her throughout her teenage years. My accepting the truth was enough to cause Ruby to forgive me."

"Gloria, Ruby did tell me that your late husband raped her for many years and that she contemplated murdering him. Before she could carry out her plan, he died in a car accident. She obviously still has sexual issues that originate from the sexual abuse."

"I know she does, Lenny. She told me she did," Gloria said. "Lenny, you should not speak a word of this to Ruby."

"I swear that this conversation will go no further, Gloria."

Ruby entered the room. "Wow, Ruby, you look fantastic! Am I underdressed?"

"Lenny, you look fine. Are you ready to go? We can take my new Honda Odyssey. I'll drive. Our first stop is to drop Will off at the Honda dealership. You can drive us home."

"Will went to his apartment."

"We can pick him up."

Ruby entered the driveway, and out of the house popped Will. He entered the car. A few minutes later, Ruby drove into the Honda service bay, turned to Will, and said, "Will, you don't have to concern yourself with the service bill. I already took care of it. If you have any problems, ask for Ralf. He knows the situation.

"See you later."

"Thanks, Ruby. You guys have a fun time."

"Will is such a nice guy. He saved my life, Ruby."

"He is precious. A little naïve, but he has plenty going on."

"Ruby, I'm a little bit nervous. I haven't been on a date in years."

"Relax, Lenny. My instincts tell me that we have a lot in common."

"Thank you for that, Ruby."

"I would suggest a little restaurant that serves nothing but organic foods and grass-fed and grass-finished beef. What do you think?"

"That's what I was hoping you would suggest. I want to learn more about food, Lenny."

A NICE, CLEAN-EATING RESTAURANT

"Ruby, I must warn you that this place is nothing like a Vegas restaurant."

"Damn it, I should hope not, Lenny. I'm looking forward to dining at a quaint, healthy, down-to-earth eatery."

"Honestly, I need time to adjust to being with a woman who possesses unequaled beauty and class."

"Thank you, Lenny. I want us to feel comfortable with each other."

RUBY AND LENNY DISCUSS WHY THEY DON'T HAVE PARTNERS

"Ruby, women are like parking spaces. The good ones are always taken. The ones who are left are handicapped. Do you realize how rare it is to find an available, intelligent woman who is over twenty-five but not obese? I take good care of myself, and I expect to be with a similarly fit woman. I will not tolerate a fat woman. Enough said, Ruby?"

"I never really thought about it like that, Lenny. I don't think you're asking too much. I understand now why you don't have a girlfriend. Your choice is to be alone or to be unsatisfied and get only a portion of what you want. Am I right?"

"You're dead on. What about you, Ruby?"

"I've had plenty of boyfriends. I attract them like flies to sugar. They're all attracted to me sexually. I've never been comfortable enough with a man to reveal my flaw to him. I'm damaged freight. You know what I'm referring to, Lenny. Do you understand what I'm saying?"

"I do, Ruby. The talk we had in the hospital's cafeteria revealed plenty about you. The erotic story you told me about your sexual encounters with James Rogers revealed an absence of penetration in your lovemaking. When you're ready, Ruby, we can open the past and reinterpret the horrid experiences of your youth. You'll have to relive your experiences and learn to see them in a positive way. We can conquer the fear that's preventing you from experiencing true intimacy. To be specific, I'm talking about your teenage years, when your stepfather abused you. Your experience is not unique.

"Thousands of young girls are sexually abused every day. Most never recover from it. Your willingness to discuss this dysfunction is the first step to recovery. The second step is to make the decision to take action. What do you want me to do for you, Ruby? I hope you can respect my candor."

"Lenny, I'm impressed. You're the first person who's suggested that relief for my chronic sexual dysfunction is possible."

"We can cross all of those prohibited bridges you have set for yourself, Ruby. Your therapy will be built on honesty, trust, and intimacy.

"Betty told me that you would be easy to talk to. I can recognize your intellect. Your accomplishments are evidence of your brilliance. I must confess that I am impressed with your perfect intrinsic and extrinsic characteristics."

"I still have to check my animal instincts when I'm in your presence. We do have common ground. Ruby, let's set this perplexing issue aside and see if we can enjoy our first meal together."

"I can't wait to see the menu."

The restaurant's maître d' asked if we had a seating preference.

"Could you show us our choices?" Ruby asked.

"Follow me, please. Do you prefer a private booth, a table by a window, or a table in the garden?"

"The garden," Ruby said. "Is that OK with you, Lenny?"

"Perfect. I can smell the plants and hear the waterfall. This is nice. It's sure not Vegas, Ruby."

"It's better. It has a natural look and smell, and best of all, there are no slot machines clattering in the background."

"What are you hungry for? I know what I want. Before my choice influences yours, why don't you read the menu? If I may, I'll order a bottle of wine. Do you favor red or white?"

"I'll go with your choice."

"I would prefer a bottle of California Bonterra Cabernet Sauvignon."

"Thank you, Lenny."

"Greg, forgive me. I did not expect the owner of the restaurant to wait on us. How are you doing?"

"Business is good, Lenny. I had to come over to meet the lovely woman you're with."

"Greg, this is Ruby Ridge. Ruby, this is Greg Sams, the owner."

"Glad to make your acquaintance," Ruby said.

"I'll send your wine right out, folks. Don't hesitate to ask if you need anything. Good to see you, Lenny," Greg said.

"I read the menu, Lenny. You can now tell me what you want to eat."

"How about after we have a glass of wine?"

"That's fine with me, Lenny."

"Ruby, what would you like to discuss?"

"Lenny, reveal your troubles to me."

"If I had to name one, I'd say that I do get lonely from time to time. But I don't like to talk about my troubles while they're happening. I would rather talk about them when they have passed. But I have no major troubles at this time, Ruby. However, there could be a tornado brewing. It is said that a man should make his own way. I agree with that to a certain extent, but there's something missing in that saying: luck! The reason that I'm here with you must be luck."

"Lenny, it's not because of luck. I'll remind you that I asked you to go to dinner with me. That is not luck. It was my desire to spend this evening with you. You're the first man I've asked out. If luck is involved, it's mine, not yours."

"I'm sorry, Ruby. I live a very esoteric life. When it comes to women…. Well, I don't know. With you, I'm reaching up for the first time. I have nothing but my military compensation, Ruby."

"Lenny, you chose to invest in knowledge instead of wealth. I have wealth. I would rather have your knowledge. Together, we are wealthy in both ways, I suppose."

"I'm ready to eat. You can tell me what you're going to order."

"I'm a meat eater, and with that said, I will have the Chateaubriand steak. It is excellent!"

"Lenny, I too am a meat eater. I'll have the same. When I was dancing in five shows or more each week, meat was the only food that could satisfy my energy requirement. The showgirl life is demanding. I was always looking for a way of creating more energy. Try dancing sixty to seventy hours a week. Most normal people are exhausted sitting on their butts in an office forty hours a week. When we were not dancing in the show we were practicing. Then four or five nights I would dance privately into the early morning."

"Damn, Ruby, I never imagined anything like that. You worked your pretty butt off for that the one and a half million dollars."

"Indeed, I did."

THE GUT MICROBIOME

"This Chateaubriand is grass fed and finished, Ruby."

"Lenny, what exactly does that mean?"

"It means that this animal was never fed grains. Animals don't naturally eat grains. Corporate farms feed their livestock grains because they're cheap, and they fatten the livestock. The animal we're eating lived outside in the sunlight and grazed on grass that hadn't been grown with chemical fertilizers or treated with pesticides. The animal was never given antibiotics or synthetic growth hormones.

"The antibiotics in meat can wreak havoc on the microbiomes in our guts. The microbiomes manufacture vitamins and have the ability to dismantle carbohydrate polysaccharides, the starches we call dietary fiber. We don't carry many genes for carbohydrate-active enzymes. It was only 10,000 years ago when the agriculture revolution began, that humans begin consuming carbohydrates. This means that much of the digestion of carbohydrates depends on our microbiome to function as a metabolic organ extracting and processing nutrients from food.

"Recent research has shown that these microbiomes heavily influence our immune systems. They defend us from diseases. The habitat of these all-important bacteria, the gut-associated lymphatic tissue—also known as the GALT—makes up seventy to eighty percent of the body's total immune system."

"I never heard anything about that, Lenny."

"Here is the most amazing fact: Do you realize that the longest cranial nerve in the body, the vagus nerve, runs from the gut to the central nervous system? The trillions of bacteria in one's gut directly affect this nerve. Those bacteria regulate the heart rate and control digestion. These bacteria release chemicals that are similar to neurons and can directly talk to your brain. This subject is definitely a new frontier in health, Ruby."

"Is this the topic that you write and lecture about—the one no one wants to learn about, Lenny?"

"That's right, Ruby! Spy and romance novels make up sixty percent of what Americans read. That explains why the US population is known to be the most ignorant among the populations of the affluent nations of the world. I had an idea. I'm writing a novel that will trick the average citizen into learning more about his or her environment. Now you know why I'm writing my first novel, Ruby."

THE CHEMICALS IN OUR MEATS

"Ruby, it is my opinion that many of the chemicals that are injected into and fed to livestock are hostile to our microbiomes and are somewhat responsible for many of the diseases that are so prevalent in today's society.

"More diseases require more medical treatments, which result in more profits for the powerful industries that have financial interest in diseases. Am I boring you, Ruby?"

"No, Lenny. Not at all!"

"Food becomes more and more important to our health as we age. I want to age gracefully and avoid diseases if possible."

"So do I!"

"Lewis and I enjoyed discussing the environment's effect on our health and our food. You are one of the few women I've talked to who don't think this subject is boring—outside of women in this field of study, of course."

"Chateaubriand for the very beautiful lady and Chateaubriand for the gentleman. Allow me, my lady, to cut the first piece for you to taste. How does it taste, my lady?"

"This is really excellent," Ruby said.

"How does yours taste, sir?"

"Perfect, as always!"

"Can I serve you anything else?"

"Thank you, but we're good for now. Ruby, this is one of only three restaurants that I'll eat at. I prefer purchasing quality foods to be prepared at home."

"I'm not trying to be patronizing on our first date. I agree with your position on food. I realize how important it is to select the right foods. I can't wait to begin reading about this."

"And you can begin teaching me how to dance and how to have fun once again."

"Lenny, I know I can loosen you up. I know what men run on."

Ruby laughed and said, "Lenny, don't you think it's unusual that we were living together before we had our first date? This is Betty's fault."

"She is a wise lady, Ruby."

"Excuse me," Ruby said as she got up. I watched the other patrons' eyes grope Ruby as she walked away.

Greg suddenly appeared. "My God, where did you find that trophy?"

"Las Vegas."

"How long will she be in town?"

"She lives here now, with me."

"Sorry, Lenny!"

"No harm done, Greg. The meal was fantastic."

"Thanks, Lenny, for coming in. You remind me of the captain of my university's football team. He dated the hottest girls on the campus and was the envy of every male student."

"Are you through with your dinner?" I asked Ruby. "I will request the check."

"Don't bother, Lenny. I took care of the check while I was up."

"You drove me to dinner and paid the bill too? What can I do?"

"Lenny, I invited you to dinner. It seemed reasonable for me to pay. I have plenty of money. That's no secret."

"Thank you, Ruby!"

"What would you like to do next? We still have time to get to the beach for the sunset."

"How long has it been since you've seen a good ol' Fort Myers Beach sunset?"

"Almost six years."

"Well, let's go now before we miss it."

"You drive, Lenny. I doubt I'd remember the way."

RUBY EXPLAINS HER RELATIONSHIP WITH ADOLF

"This Honda Odyssey is nice, Ruby. There's enough room to live in here."

"I like to have plenty of room for my passengers."

"Have you figured all of the features out?"

"It will take me a while. I ordered every feature available."

"I'll help you with them."

"I would welcome the help."

"Ruby, would it be too intrusive to ask you about the German?"

"I have no problem with telling you anything. I trust that our secrets will stay between us."

"You have my word, Ruby."

"Other than James Rogers, Adolf was the only man I had an intimate relationship with. The relationship lasted the entire time I was in Vegas. We never lived together, but I stayed with him when he was in town.

"At first it was all business. After a considerable amount of time, I developed something short of love for him. Realistically, Lenny, I knew it would be impossible for me to live with Adolf or with any man who regularly required penetrative sex.

"My sexual dysfunction is the reason I'm single. He would fly in at least once a month for two or three days, and every now and then, he'd fly in twice a month."

"In the beginning, he was married but in the process of a divorce. He settled with his wife out of court for three hundred million dollars. If children had been involved, the settlement would have been at least twice as much. The amount he paid made virtually no dent in his family's wealth.

"OK, Lenny, please really think about what I'm about to say. I dreaded having sex with him. I would fake orgasms. I had to work at not hating him. I connect penetration with my memories of my stepfather ruthlessly raping me in all of my orifices.

"Because of those tragic events in my life, I will never have a normal relationship. That's the reason I'm single and will remain single. I am permanently damaged, Lenny."

A POSSIBLE CURE FOR RUBY'S SEXUAL DYSFUNCTION

"James Rogers accepted my dysfunction and accommodated my sexual needs in ways that avoided penetration. Being penetrated traumatizes me.

The German never would have understood that. I knew he would not accept my problem.

"I became a master of deception. I would always find a way to avoid sexual penetration. Adolf thought of me as the hottest woman in Vegas. That was the way the MGM Grand marketed me. Lenny, I will always be sexually dysfunctional."

"You are repairable, Ruby! Your condition is not unique."

"Please don't say things to make me feel better."

"I would never play games with your mental health, Ruby. I would like nothing better than to see you as a sexually complete woman. Let me make one thing perfectly clear: You have no obligation to me, Ruby. Is that understood?"

"Yes, Lenny!"

"What led you to believe that I would be capable of devising a form of therapy that could eradicate your fear of penetration?"

"Betty said that she knew simply by talking to Lewis that you were astute and that you understood psychological problems. She told me that your first degree was a criminology degree with a focus on rehabilitation. In plain English, you studied psychotherapy, and you wrote your thesis on sexual dysfunction."

"I will disclose to you my secret, Ruby. I was fucked up mentally when I came back from Vietnam. I chose to study psychotherapy so that I could solve my own problems. Studying human behavior and the use of psychotherapy did help me cope with my confusion.

"I had no desire to practice the profession. I went on to study my real interest, which was evolutionary biology."

"Incredible, Lenny. James Rogers was the first person I told my secret to, Lenny. I told my mother about my dysfunction during our heart-to-heart talk after I came home from Vegas. Betty surmised that I had a sexual problem. When she confronted me about it, I admitted to it. It was then that she informed me of your knowledge on the subject matter. Lenny, you are the third person who knows about this. I trust you will be discreet."

"Ruby, not even a peep will come out of this mouth. I would be a fool to lose your interest in me."

WATCHING THE SUNSET

"Perfect timing, Ruby. We have approximately thirty minutes before sunset. We can park and be on the beach in twenty minutes."

"This brings back memories, Lenny. James Rogers and I used to break dance in Times Square for tips. On some holidays, we made several hundred dollars. The snowbirds sometimes gave us big tips. I'll never forget that James and I made six hundred dollars on one Fourth of July."

"Do you have anything against sitting on the sandy beach?"

"I prefer to sit on the beach, Lenny. I did so many times when I was a teenager. Thank you, Lenny. I can't think of anything more pleasurable to do. The sunset is going to be beautiful. Look at that fantastic orange-marmalade sky. I'm going to put my sunglasses on so that I can see that huge, magnificent glowing ball descend to the other side of the earth with my eyes wide open."

"You could have been a poet, Ruby."

"I never cared for Vegas. For me, it was all about the money, and as soon as I reached my financial goals, I wasted no time, and I left. Lenny, this is my kind of life—I like small-time Fort Myers and having you as company."

"Most people live and work in cities. Many never witness a sunset over the ocean. While I was in Las Vegas, from time to time, I thought about the saying about the beach in Fort Myers: 'Another Day in Paradise.' Lenny, I don't want to leave here ever again. I have the financial means to do what I want to do. I want to do some good.

"Las Vegas was all about taking. I want to give happiness to as many people as I can—and especially to children from needy families. That's my mission, Lenny."

"That's an admirable goal."

"Tell me what you did when you first settled in Fort Myers Beach, Lenny."

"Not long before, I had lost my wife. She'd been struck by lightning. I was at the lowest point in my life. Every day for a week, I came to the beach to see the sun set over the Gulf of Mexico. It was like medicine for me. I could not get enough of nature's therapy.

"One day while I was watching the sunset, I thought about how beautiful the sunrise must have been. I had to see the sun come up over the Atlantic Ocean. That gave me an idea. One evening I drove across Florida to Jupiter Beach and checked into a motel. I arose while it was still dark and made my way to the beach. I watched the sun come up over the Atlantic Ocean.

"I then drove back to Fort Myers and watched it go down over the Gulf of Mexico on the same day. It was a day to remember. What do you think, Ruby?"

"I know what I think. I want to do that someday."

"Here's the rest of the story."

"There's more?"

"Yes, Ruby. There's the grand finale. I watched the sun come up over the Atlantic Ocean on the beach in Fort Lauderdale. I then drove to the airport in Fort Lauderdale and flew to Los Angeles, where I rented a car, drove to Manhattan Beach, and watched the sun set over the Pacific Ocean on the same day."

"Lenny how many people have ever thought about doing something like that, much less actually done it? I would love to make that trip too some day."

REHABBING RUBY'S SEXUAL DYSFUNCTION

"Ruby, your stepfather began sexually abusing you when you were eleven years old and continued until you were seventeen, right? Many years have passed since you were seventeen. Fear and anger have become imprinted in your nature.

"Allow me to explain why sexual-dysfunction therapy success rates are so low. No two people's fingerprints and DNA are alike, just as no two people's psyches are alike. Most therapists make the mistake of thinking that one kind of therapy fits all.

"The form of therapy that we will use will be unique to your constitution and will hopefully eliminate the symptom, which is your fear of penetration, and the cause, which was forced penetration.

"Ruby, you will discard your negative experiences of penetration and replace them with positive experiences of penetration. You will need to experience your first orgasm caused by penetration in order to successfully overcome your fear.

"The foundation of this therapy is trust. You must consider me to be your trusted partner, not your therapist. Ruby, can you totally trust me?"

"Yes, Lenny—totally and without doubts."

"Why?"

"I trust Betty's advice. I now know you well enough to know that you have no ulterior motives. You just want to help me."

"Ruby, we will start immediately."

"Are you ready?"

"Yes, I'm ready."

"I will remind you once again that you must trust me completely. Are you absolutely certain that you're ready, Ruby?"

"Yes, I am."

"Where are we going?"

"Back to my place down the street.

"This is my apartment, Ruby. It really seems strange to open the door and to not see Breezy here."

"I can relate, Lenny. I was grateful to see Jojo when I returned home. She even remembered me. It was so nice of Betty to take care of her while I was gone."

"Ruby, are you ready to begin?"

"Yes, Lenny."

"Come close to me. I will continue to remind you that you must trust me and that nothing bad is going to happen. You can stop what is happening at any time, Ruby.

"Put your arms around me, and hold me tight. Now relax, and familiarize yourself with my body. You may touch it. Stop if you feel uncomfortable. Are you OK, Ruby?"

"Yes."

"Now remove your clothes. Take them all off. You're doing well, Ruby. Do you feel uncomfortable?"

"No. I feel comfortable without clothes. I was a showgirl."

"I will remind you that nothing bad is going to happen. You can stop what we're doing at any time. I'm going to remove my clothes, Ruby. If at any time you feel uncomfortable, stop. You are to force nothing. You are in total control and can stop at any time.

"Are you still comfortable with what's happening?"

"Yes, I feel comfortable."

"Ruby, look at all of me. I'm going to look at all of you. Nothing will happen unless you want something to happen. I have an erection. You can look at my erection if you'd like, but don't touch it. This is not the time."

"I'm getting really aroused."

"That's OK, Ruby. But you are not to touch yourself. This is not the time for touching. Come close to me, and press your body up against mine. Since I can maintain control, I expect you to do the same. How do you feel?"

"I feel very aroused."

"Do you trust me?"

"I trust you."

"Remember that nothing bad is going to happen. You can stop what we're doing if it disagrees with you or if you feel uncomfortable.

"There are no more physical mysteries between us. No one will impose his or her sexual will on you ever again. Does being nude or touching me make you uncomfortable?"

"I'm comfortable, Lenny."

"Ruby, can I touch you?"

"Yes, you can touch me!"

"Ruby, you are in control. Remember to stop if you feel uncomfortable. Can I fondle your breasts?"

"Yes, Lenny."

"Now you can rub my cock while I rub your pussy. How do you feel?"

"I'm extremely excited."

"Do you trust me?"

"Yes, Lenny!"

"Then we must stop. We need to both calm down."

"OK!"

"Do you trust me?"

"I don't think I have ever trusted a man more than I trust you."

"Did you experience fear or negative thoughts?"

"No. I was in a euphoric state of mind."

"We have finished our first session, Ruby. Here's a towel. Let's relax in the hot tub."

"What will we do next?"

"I'll show you on the way home."

"Lenny, this hot tub feels great."

"I have a personal question. Can I ask you it?"

"You can ask me anything, Lenny."

"Ruby, your pubic area and vulva are perfect. Were they perfect when you were born?"

"Top showgirls get nonsurgical pubic lifts using the latest technology. These surgeries use radiofrequencies and lasers, so you don't need to take any time off afterward. A total makeover of the vulva, including a vaginal-tightening procedure. The procedure revitalizes the skin's sensitivity and elasticity by stimulating blood flow and collagen production. That gives the vulva a youthful look and makes it look almost like a perfectly formed bun. That drives men crazy. Many showgirls get laser treatments to permanently remove their pubic hair. That prevents razor burn and ugly ingrown hairs. The result is a mons pubis that is as smooth as silk. As a matter of fact, all of my body hair has been removed. That's the reason my skin is so smooth.

"We were billed as the most beautiful, talented, sexy women in the world. Very wealthy men demand the best, and they'd pay tens of thousands of dollars to perform oral sex on beautifully sculpted female genitalia. Some impotent older billionaires would pay upward of fifty thousand dollars. I made that practice my specialty because of my inability to have penetrative sex. That's how I accumulated so much money in five years. Lenny, I'm telling you things I've never told anybody. I will follow the protocol of this therapy. Lenny, I trust you!"

THE THERAPY IS ON
"Ruby, will you drive?"

"No, Lenny. I'm still trying to remember how to get around. You said that we weren't through, right?"

"I'm going to take you to an adult toy store, Ruby. We can do some shopping."

"That sounds interesting."

"Do you own any sexual aids or adult toys?"

"No, I don't."

"Tell me why not."

"You know that I have a problem with penetration. I have no need to torment myself with any type of penetration. Wouldn't that be a self-defeating prophecy? But I do use my fingers to stimulate my clitoris when I masturbate, and I do like to watch porn on occasion. It helps me become aroused."

"Is there any kind of porn that brings out anger or fear in you?"

"This might sound weird, but I love to watch other women experience penetration."

"Do you find it strange that we're talking about very personal matters even though we've known each other for only a few days?"

"You're right about the time frame, but it seems to me that we've been together for years. If anything is strange, then that particular thought is strange. I can talk to you without inhibitions. That was how I felt with James Rogers. We just accepted my dysfunction and worked around it.

"It never occurred to me that my sexual dysfunction could be cured. More than anything, I want to become sexually complete. You can rest assured that I will put a great amount of effort into therapy."

RUBY'S SEXUAL-DYSFUNCTION THERAPY CONTINUES AT THE ADULT TOY STORE

"The idea is to supersede bad experiences with good experiences, Ruby."

"How do you accomplish that?"

"You will stop talking and thinking about what caused the dysfunction. You must find a partner to focus on you trust. You said you trust me.

"Adult toy stores offer a forum for positive conversations about sexual toys that provide pleasurable sexual experiences.

"The sales lady will explain the functions of the toys used for sexual penetration. It is perfectly common for a customer to ask questions and discuss the sexual pleasures provided by the toy. We will replace your forced negative sexual experiences with consenting positive sexual experiences.

"Are you with me, Ruby?"

"I think so."

"Do you have any reservations about going in?"

"I would if I weren't with you. However, being with you excites me. I want to see what our next step will be."

We entered the store.

"Good evening. How can I help you?"

"We would like to look at popular adult toys used for female penetration."

"Follow me, please. My name is Nancy. This is my store. All of the items in this display case can produce pleasurable female penetration. On the left side of the display case are the most popular sellers. The items on the right side of the case are for more advanced couples.

"They are all priced according to movement, texture, and quality. The more complex a toy is, the higher the cost will be. I will tell you that in terms of satisfaction and quality, you truly get what you pay for in the world of adult toys.

"The basic companion of the woman is the dildo. As you can see, they come in all sizes and different colors. You have ones that vibrate, ones that twist, and ones with adjustable speeds that do both. You'll have to feel them to determine their textures. Which one would you prefer to hold first?"

"I have demo products that you can observe."

"Ruby, are you fine with this?"

"I'm a little edgy. Miss, can we have a minute alone?"

"Of course. Call me when you're ready."

"I'm pleased that you came forth with your objection, Ruby. Tell me what's going on. Would you like to leave?"

"I had a moment, but it passed. Will you tell me what you have in mind, Lenny?"

"I want you to become familiar with these toys. The environment and conversation is therapeutic. We are talking positively about your fear. You will not be expected to use them for penetration right away or even ever if you decide not to. We'll move forward only when you're comfortable."

"I'm OK with that. I'm ready to check them out now."

"Ruby, which one would you like to see?"

"I told you that my vagina was surgically tightened. The idea was to accommodate the average man's cock, not some freak cock. The girls with surgically tightened pussies were instructed to not have penetrative sex with men whose cocks were above the average size. The surgery itself produced the same full sensation with the average-sized cock. I want to keep my vagina tight, Lenny, so I would prefer an average-sized one.

"Those are about the size of your cock. Was that the reason you wanted me to see your cock at your place?"

"No, not at all, Ruby. However, that did prove to be useful."

"The big ones would tear me. Don't you like a tight vagina, Lenny?"

"Yes, Ruby, I do! I'll ask the lady to tell us more about them, Ruby. Are you still OK?"

"I think this store has aroused my curiosity. I have no fears when I'm with you."

"Good. I'll call the lady over, and you can ask her questions and decide which one you'd like to own."

"OK, Lenny. I'm ready for that."

"I'll call her over. Do not imagine any of them penetrating you at this time. Imagine that you're watching a porn flick. The one that offers the woman in the imaginary movie the most pleasure is the one you want."

"That's a good idea, Lenny. Watching a woman experience penetration without becoming angry or fearful excites me. I'll use my imagination."

"Miss, we are ready."

"Which one would you like to hold?"

Ruby seemed comfortable and said, "I want to hold the best model with all of the features. I would prefer that one. The color of it is familiar to me."

"That's a size seven. That's a seven-inch dildo, Ruby."

"What color do you prefer?"

"A flesh-colored one," Ruby said, giggling.

"I'll have to take one out of the inventory in the storage room. I will be right back."

Ruby grabbed my arm, pulled my ear close to her mouth, and whispered, "It arouses me because it looks like yours." Then she giggled and laughed out loud when she noticed that had embarrassed me. She smiled beautifully and gave me a kiss on the cheek.

"Here it is, folks! Give me a moment to open it and to install the batteries. How do you like the way it feels?"

"My God, it feels real, Lenny."

"That's what you can expect when you purchase a top-of-the-line dildo," Nancy said. "It is pricey, but it's the best that money can buy. Allow me to run through the controls for you."

"Wow," Ruby said. "I had no idea that they could do all of that. I will take it."

"Can I show you the anal plugs we have?"

"Please do," Ruby said.

"If you're unpracticed, I would recommend one of these. They increase in size. If you look closely, you'll see that the levels graduate from small to larger.

"That allows you to learn to relax and to use the width that you're comfortable with. The deeper the anal plug penetrates you, the greater pleasure you'll feel. The ridges will keep it in place if you want to keep it in while dancing or posing. The anal plug will cause erotic sensations in all of the parts of your body. The more expensive one can be adjusted and can vibrate and twist.

"An anal plug will also enhance your pleasure when you're performing other sexual acts. It will give a full feeling that only double penetration can provide. You might want to wear it during the entire time you're together or until you're ready for anal sex. When you remove the plug, your anus will be open, and you'll be ready for deep penetration."

"It does take a while for some to practice this, but some claim that the sensations are superior to those caused by vaginal penetration. In the beginning, it helps to have a partner to assist you. He/she must be gentle each time the depth is increased. Here is the top-of-the-line anal plug."

"That is exactly the way my Vegas cohorts described anal, Lenny."

"It too has all of the features that the dildo you selected has."

"It feels like real flesh, Lenny!"

"I will take this anal plug in the flesh color too."

"If you're not practiced, I would suggest a lubrication specifically formulated for anal sex. These lubricants are approved for human consumption. What is your favorite fruit, sir?"

I blushed and said, "Bananas."

Ruby once again giggled and kissed me. "We have the banana flavor."

"We will take it."

"How will you pay?"

"American Express," Ruby said.

"Do you want me to wrap these items or to place them in a generic bag for privacy reasons?"

"A bag will be fine."

"Thank you for your purchases, Ruby and Lenny!"

"Let's go home, Lenny."

"Ruby, are we moving too fast? I never would have thought that we would go this far in one day. Tell me what you think."

"I don't know what to say, Lenny, except that this has been one of the most fascinating days of my life. I don't feel that we're moving too fast. I'm having fun."

"We need to go home and check to see if Betty is all right. You and I can then find a nice hotel suite on the beach and continue."

"I'm willing to take what we've been doing a step further. I have no apprehensions, Lenny."

"If you're sure and if Betty is OK, I'm ready. My testicles ache like never before."

"If you want, I'll give you head while you drive."

"Not so fast, Ruby! We cannot take that chance."

"I've never been so at ease while talking about sex. With you, Lenny, I'm comfortable discussing my wildest sexual fantasies."

"Ruby, that indicates that we are making progress. You need to calm down before I come in my pants."

Ruby giggled. "My panties are wet! I'm going to wipe my wet pussy and legs. Do you want to pull the car over and watch?"

"Can I ejaculate while I watch?"

"I would like that, Lenny. I will give you a show."

"Oh, my God, Ruby, that is the most beautiful thing I have ever witnessed. I'm coming…. I'm coming, Ruby!"

"I'm coming too, Lenny. That was extreme pleasure!"

"James Rogers didn't have it so bad, Ruby.

"You are exactly right, Lenny. What do you have to say about that?"

"Have we lost our minds?"

"I didn't realize that losing my mind could feel so right, Ruby."

"I agree. I have zero sexual inhibitions with you, Lenny."

"Gloria is with Betty. I'm relieved that someone is with her. She is so dear to my heart."

"I love Betty too. Can you ask your mother if she can stay with Betty tonight? I would feel more comfortable if she were not alone."

"I will convince her to stay with Betty."

"This evening means the world to me, Lenny."

Betty met us at the door. "Did you two have a fun day?"

"Most definitely!" Ruby said. "Betty, what's with the cane?"

"Gloria drove me to Goodwill. I donated my walker. It's history, Lenny."

"That is good news, Betty."

"Mom, I have something to ask of you."

"Fire away, Ruby."

"Mom, can you stay with Betty tonight? Lenny and I are going to go out for the night.

"If the wine is fine, we might elect to rent a room somewhere. Neither one of us wants to drive under the influence.

"You can sleep in my room, Mom."

"That sounds like a plan to me, Ruby. Betty and I never run out of things to do or talk about."

"Thank you, Gloria," I said.

"Lenny, I'm going to pack a few things, and then we'll leave," Ruby said.

"I'll do the same. Betty, it's time that we change your diet to include more solid foods. The diet's purpose was to direct most of the energy used for the digestion of solid foods to the process of healing and rebuilding your body. Now you can use some of your energy on digesting nutritional solid foods. We will supplement protein with hydrochloric acid and fats and carbohydrates with digestive enzymes.

"That means that you can indulge your love of cooking again. If you'd like, you can cook a meal for you and Gloria tonight. Gloria, do you think you and Betty could go to Ada's and buy organic chemical-free food? Betty is well versed in the selection of unprocessed foods."

"That would be fun. I need to know more about healthy food choices," Gloria said.

"Betty can show you, Gloria."

"You might want to cook Bob a healthy meal. You know what they say: The way to a man's heart is through his stomach."

"Ha-ha, I will keep that in mind, Lenny, although I know that you're teasing me."

"Got to go, Gloria."

"We love you."

PHYSICAL-DYSFUNCTION THERAPY AT THE PINK SHELL

"You and Ruby have fun, and be safe," Betty said.

"Lenny, I've gathered a few items that we can use. Are you ready to go?"

"Give me a moment. I will be right back, Ruby."

Betty smiled and said, "Gloria and I were hoping you two would come together, Ruby."

"We had so much fun today, Betty."

"You ready, Ruby?"

"Yes, Lenny. I brought my laptop and a few high-definition DVDs of my choreographed dances. Stop outside of Starbucks to see if we can pick up Wi-Fi. I'll see which hotel has the best suite. I want the nicest room on the beach, Lenny. This will be a landmark event in my life—I just know it!"

"This is the closest parking spot to Starbucks. Are we close enough?"

"I have Wi-Fi."

"Ruby, try the Pink Shell, Diamond Head, and the Hilton for starters."

"I'm going to look at the presidential and honeymoon suites, Lenny. It looks like the best room is the honeymoon suite in the Pink Shell, and it's available. It has three large, open rooms, a huge round bed surrounded by mirrors, a fifty-five-inch flat-screen TV with a DVD player, and a large hot tub. What do you think?"

"That sounds fantastic!"

"I'm going to reserve it. I'm waiting on a confirmation. It's ours for the night, Lenny! I'm excited."

"You are not alone with your enthusiasm. I'm literally shaking with anticipation."

"Is this what they call mixing therapy with pleasure?" Ruby said, giggling. "Lenny, you are in for the best, most sexually arousing show of your life. This performance will not be for money. It will come straight from my heart. I could have the greatest epiphany of my life tonight.

"I had given up on the possibility of ever experiencing the rapturous sensations of penetration, Lenny. My Vegas cohorts used to say, every orifice stimulated produces a different sensation. I want to experience those sensual pleasures."

"Ruby, the true test is still to come. Remember that nothing bad is going to happen. You can stop at any time that you feel uncomfortable. We won't go too fast or too slow."

"I understand that we have the night, Lenny."

■ ■ ■

GLORIA'S FIRST DATE WITH BOB

"Friday is here, Betty. I had a manicure and a pedicure, and I got my hair highlighted. I had the sexiest dress I own dry cleaned, and I bought a new pair of heels. I'm really excited. This is my first date since my husband died," Gloria said. "Betty, he is so handsome, and he's the bank's president.

"I even got up early and exercised."

"Gloria, you should calm down. You don't want to appear to be too excited. I thought you and Bob had a high school romance."

"We did, Betty, but that was long ago. I started restricting my food intake the very moment I walked out of his office. I've lost five pounds."

"Don't try to be more than what you are, Gloria," Betty said. "That way, you will not have to dig yourself out of a hole later. You know what I mean. He must like you the way you are. You can't force a relationship. If it's right, it will happen on its own."

"You are so right. Thank you for setting me straight. I'm so happy to have you back in my life. You're the best friend I've ever had."

"Now run along and get ready. I'll be fine by myself for a little while. I have my telephone in case anything goes awry."

"The door is open. That was quick, Gloria."

"How do I look?"

"You look fantastic," Betty said.

"I asked Bob to pick me up at your house. I can't wait for you to meet him, Betty."

"That was nice of you."

"You never know when you might need a banker."

"Will told me to tell you that he's going to come over for a visit."

"We haven't had time to talk lately. I look forward to his visit."

"Gloria, how is Will doing?"

"He loves his apartment and the car that Ruby sold him with terms that he couldn't refuse. Will is on cloud nine. He told me that he loves his new job."

"I love to hear stories like Will's," Betty said, smiling. "I have been blessed with new people in my life. I don't know how I would have survived Lewis's death without all of you. Someone is knocking on the door. It should be Will. Will you open the door, Gloria? Remind him that he can knock and then let himself in."

"Come in, Will!"

"Betty says that you should knock and then come in next time. Going to the door every time a family member knocks is a strain on her."

"I'll remember to do that next time, Gloria."

"How are you doing, Will?" Betty asked.

"Everything is like a wonderful dream. The apartment is nice, and I have a beautiful live yard."

"What do you mean, Will?"

"I always lived in apartments with paved yards. But here I can have a garden, Betty. I can't thank everybody enough."

"You have thanked us already. You were there when we needed you. You don't owe us anything."

"Gloria, you look nice."

"Thank you, Will. I'm waiting for my date. He should be here any minute. I can't wait to introduce him to you."

"Tell me about your job," Betty said.

"The job is more than I imagined it could be. I have the opportunity to do plenty of good. The first day I started, I had five clients. I was a little lost, but the people working around me came to my aid. They all treated me as though I were special. Their actions made me feel welcome."

WILL MEETS BAILEY AT WORK

"I made friends with the lady who gave me a tour of the clinic. We had lunch and discovered that we have many similar interests. I like that she's sort of a clown. She's lighthearted, she tells funny jokes, and she laughs a lot. Her presence calms me.

"And I have never owned a car before. I worked my way through school with a motor scooter for transportation. The car that I own now—thanks to Ruby—has already opened up new horizons. I asked the funny girl out. We're going to an improv-comedy show tomorrow night.

"The VA increased my salary. For the first time in my life, I have enough money to take a date out for the evening. You guys made it all happen. I will be forever grateful for your family, Betty."

Someone knocked on the door twice. "Gloria, you know who that is." Gloria took a fast look in the living room mirror and pushed her hair back. She opened the door. Bob presented Gloria with a beautiful bouquet of wildflowers. Gloria gasped.

"Bob, they are beautiful! Please come in, and allow me to introduce you. You know that my house is next door. This is Will. He's my tenant. This is Betty. She is the lady of the house and the head of the family."

"Gloria, would you like me to put those lovely flowers into a vase?"

"That would be nice, Betty."

"Did Gloria tell you that she was my first girlfriend?" Bob asked.

"Bob was my first boyfriend," Gloria said.

"It was great meeting you, folks," Bob said. He motioned for Gloria to lead the way. Bob opened the front door for Gloria, and they walked out holding hands.

"Betty, are you ready to go grocery shopping?"

"Will, we'll only need a couple of hours at the most. I'm ready. I can't wait to start cooking food again."

BETTY INTRODUCES WILL TO HEALTHY FOODS AT WHOLE FOODS

"There have been drastic changes in my food preferences, Will. No more sugar or processed foods. I eat organic vegetables below fifty on the glycemic-index chart and antibiotic- and hormone-free meat. I have graduated from using a wheelchair to walking with a cane in ten months. When I donate this cane to Goodwill, it will be time to renew my driver's license. Soon I'll be totally independent, Will. I appreciate your taking me food shopping."

"It will be a learning experience for me. I've heard Bailey talk about Whole Foods."

"Does Bailey eat clean?"

"She eats food from Whole Foods too. Will you teach me the fundamentals of eating healthy food?"

"I would love to pass on what I've learned. Lewis and Lenny spent many days showing me the ins and outs of food.

"The average person has no idea what is being done to food before it arrives at the grocery store. Many food additives are made from petroleum or coal tar. One category of additives is glutamates.

"These chemicals trick the brain into believing that foods that actually don't taste that good taste great. The new foods that are being created by food manufacturers are known as 'the foods of commerce.' These foods cannot satisfy the body's nutritional needs, which results in nutritional deficiencies, obesity, and diseases.

"Will, food companies are pretty sly. They know that the public is becoming aware of the preservatives and other toxic chemicals added to food. Food processors hide the most toxic additives by declaring that they're trade secrets. That's perfectly legal, according to the FDA.

"That means that those additives don't need to be included on nutrition labels. A brief investigation into a company's history and reputation will reveal important information. Once you find a company with integrity, you can normally trust its food products.

"Keeping records on the food companies that you regularly use will pay off in the future."

"Why do they add questionable additives if the consumers don't want them to, Betty?"

"Profits, not the health of consumers, dictate which ingredients are used.

"Preservatives keep a food item fresh and prolong its shelf life. Other chemicals affect a food's texture, taste, and looks."

"I thought government agencies were created to assure the consumers that the foods being sold were safe."

"That was the idea. However, these government agencies have been corrupted by corporate money. That means that the agencies care more about the corporations' interests than the consumers. This collusion between businesses and the government is called 'crony capitalism.'

"Look how fresh these fruits and vegetables look. I'm only interested in the organic ones. Whole Foods carries conventional fruits and vegetables too.

"Will, when it comes to fruit, stay away from juice."

"What? I thought fresh-squeezed orange juice was healthy."

"When the pulp is removed, fruit becomes a junk food. Without the fiber in the fruit, sugar enters the bloodstream too fast. In many cases, that causes the pancreas to secrete too much insulin. Over time, the consumption of large amounts of sugar without the restriction of fiber contributes to insulin resistance and to type two diabetes, Will.

"More times than not, the darker a leafy green is, the higher its nutritional content will be. Ounce for ounce, watercress is the most nutritious vegetable you can eat. As a rule, you can't go wrong with selecting brightly colored green, red, yellow, and orange vegetables. Vegetables lose nutrients when they're cooked. Whenever possible, eat them raw. But here's a warning: Eat fruits and vegetables in moderation. More is not necessarily better.

"If shakes are your pleasure, blend your vegetables. Do not juice them, though, for the same reason that you shouldn't juice fruits. Now let's look at nuts."

"Wow! I've never seen so many different nuts and seeds."

"Nuts are chock-full of nutrition, but you don't want to overindulge in them if you're concerned about gaining weight. They are very high in calories. Fourteen walnut halves will provide you with two times more alpha-linolenic acid than you need in one day.

"This omega-three fatty acid is responsible for memory and coordination. I prefer the taste of almonds, walnuts, and pecans. I normally buy a pound of each. I'm not supposed to eat grains at this time unless they were sprouted before they were milled. The grain's cell wall is cracked by the birth of the grain's sprout. This allows the digestive system to easily extract the nutrients.

"Around seventy-five percent of phytonutrients are destroyed when whole grains are turned into the breads that you buy at the grocer. About one percent of Americans suffer from celiac disease, which is an aversion to gluten.

"Here is where it becomes expensive. The meat department is important. No matter what you might have heard, there is no better source of protein than meat. Beef is the only sustainable source of B12. An ample amount of B12 is necessary to produce healthy red blood cells.

"Red blood cells' major responsibilities are transporting oxygen to the body's cells and removing carbon dioxide from those same cells. Bone broth is extremely rich in collagen and is chock-full of muscle-building nutrients. Organ meats contain more nutrients than meat from muscles.

"Many nutritional authorities have demonized beef because of its high saturated-fat content. I'm sure you've heard their accusations many times. However, saturated fat from beef raised chemical-free, grass-fed, grass-finished has not been proven to cause heart disease or any other related diseases

"Most Americans have a deficiency of vitamin E. A three-ounce serving of sardines provides more than one hundred percent of the daily requirement of vitamin E.

"Pork should be nutritious and free of chemicals. Fowl needs to be cage-free and chemical-free. All meat should be free of antibiotics. Meat retains and releases its nutrients better when it's slowly cooked.

"Is this too much too fast, Will?"

"Not at all, Betty. It's interesting."

"Frozen food is good too, but nothing beats fresh food. I'm getting worn down, Will. Let's go home. I have everything I came for. The problem with good food is that it costs a great deal more than junk food. That makes it unavailable to the general population. That breaks my heart, Will!"

BETTY AND WILL BOND OVER A BOTTLE OF CHAMPAGNE

"Betty, do you object to stopping at a wine store on the way home? I've never before had money beyond what I needed to pay for my financial obligations, so I've never purchased a bottle of fine wine. Tomorrow is Saturday. I have a date with the funny girl I met at the VA.

"Tonight I would like to celebrate my good fortunes with you, Betty. It would be my honor to share the wine with you. I've never tasted a fine wine before."

"I shared a bottle of wine with Harold, my last boyfriend, many years ago in Michigan. I accept your invitation."

"There's one thing, though. I don't know much about wine. Could you suggest a wine?"

"Since this is a celebration, wouldn't champagne be more appropriate?"

"Yes, I agree."

"How about a bottle of White Star champagne?"

"Coming right up, Betty. Is this the right bottle?

"That is it, Will."

"Betty, I have been meaning to ask Lenny why I have a reaction to milk. I get an upset stomach, no matter if I drink whole milk or low-fat. Would you know why?"

"I think I can handle that question, Will. The human diet changed from hunting and gathering to agriculture and dairy farming around

10,000 years ago. Before that time humans never drank domesticated animal milk and were devoid of the gene that produces the enzyme lactose necessary to digest milk sugar.

"People of northern European descent were compelled to drink milk to survive the cold winters. Evidence suggest that around 4,000 years ago a gene mutation occurred. Another cattle-herding tribe in East Africa also drank milk. Other gene mutations soon followed in other parts of the globe as dairy farming spread. Obviously Will, your lineage did not evolve from a dairy-farming area and did not acquire the gene for producing the lactose enzyme, necessary for digesting milk sugar in milk."

"That is so interesting, Betty. She said that Lenny would know. I can't wait to tell her that you told me why."

"I asked Lenny the same question. He gave me the answer I just gave you."

"We are home. Take my key and open the door."

"Will, fetch the champagne cooler from the freezer."

"What does it look like?"

"It has a flat cover."

"Is this it?"

"Yes. It'll cool the champagne in about five minutes."

"Where do you buy something like this?"

"I really don't know. Lewis bought it one New Year's Eve."

"It's a unique device. I had no idea that something like this existed. Betty, I've noticed that everyone consults you on important personal matters. What I'm trying to say is that you're like everyone's mom. They tell me that you've read almost everything in the library."

Betty laughed. "Will, I was a librarian for thirty years. I tried to read as many books as I could in order to serve the members of the library. They would always ask me what I thought about certain books that they were thinking about reading.

"To say that I've read everything in the library would be a giant stretch. The Library of Congress was started in 1800 to help the members of the U.S. Congress to do their research. At that time the library contained a little over six thousand books. The Library of Congress was moved from Philadelphia to the White House, in Washington, D.C.

"The British burned the White House in the War of 1812. At the time, it housed Thomas Jefferson's personal library. Many of his books were lost. It caught fire and burned a second time in 1851. Most of the books were restored. Today the Library of Congress has its own building and contains over sixteen million books. Realistically, Will, there's no way I could have read all of the books in the library. However, I will take your statement as a compliment.

"I love to read. I still read four to six books on varied subjects every month. Recently I have been deeply involved in reading books on health. Lenny got Lewis involved, and together they laid out a diet-and-exercise program that rescued me from death.

"I have gone from using a wheelchair to a walker and then to using a cane. I plan to donate this cane and to walk on my own. I'm determined to apply for a driver's license. I have studied the driver's license book online. The first chance I get, I intend to go down to the department of motor vehicles, take the written driver's test, and secure my learner's permit."

"I would love to take you down during my next day off."

"I would be most appreciative of that, Will."

"Then it's a done deal."

"Will, if you want, I can give you the books I read on health. I would like to bring back the kinds of discussions that we used to have on a regular basis. We haven't had any intellectual group discussions since Lewis died. I would like to involve you, Gloria, and Ruby in them.

"You can't go wrong when it comes to caring for your health, especially when you become my age. I am a living example of a comeback, and it's all thanks to the knowledge that Lewis and Lenny carefully introduced to me.

"After many hours of reading about and discussing the topic of health, Lewis, Lenny, and I wrote a condensed version of our combined findings. We assembled our thoughts, and I was elected to be the editor and to process the information. We call it 'The Health Manifesto.' We think of it as an eye-opening introduction to health for anyone who wants to identify the source of his or her health issues and learn how to heal them, how to maintain or improve his or her health, or how to prevent premature death.

"We hope that the family will become involved in this discussion sooner rather that later. I think that common interests seal friendships. What better interest could we share than an interest in health, which is the most important thing in life?"

"I agree one hundred percent, Betty."

"I have a copy for you in the desk drawer over by the window, Will."

"Don't bother to stand. I'll fetch it, Betty."

■ ■ ■

THE HEALTH MANIFESTO

This manifesto is based on the education and experiences of Lenny, Lewis, and Betty. We define "health" as a state of complete mental, physical, and social well-being.

Additional information has been gathered from government agencies, universities' research, medical journals, and varied authorities on health. We believe that this manifesto will cast serious doubts on the information that you have been given and told to never question.

A health system that treats only the symptoms without regard to their causes is basically flawed and immoral. It is the opinion of these authors that people and corporations who amass great profits from inducing human misery should be prosecuted for crimes against humanity. Furthermore, claims of ignorance should not be seen as acceptable excuses.

To comply with a federal law that we do not agree with, we must inform the readers of the following: By no means do we intend to suggest that the information contained within this manifesto will answer all of your questions about health.

The authors' intention is to highlight what could be considered genocide of the ignorant and elderly populations of the United States, the motive of which is money.

The authors must recommend that the readers consult with their personal physicians before engaging in the therapies explained in this manifesto.

The unofficial law of this land (the United States) supports the American Medical Association and the pharmaceutical corporations' drug-therapy cartel by suppressing information and thus keeping the public ignorant of the prevention and causes of diseases.

The average citizen does not realize that he or she is not going to be cured of diseases by his or her doctor; nor does he or she understand that the toxic drugs that doctors prescribe mask the symptoms of diseases and, in many cases, can cause even more severe diseases in the long run.

Legal-drug addicts don't know that they're addicts. That's the nature of addiction, people. "Addiction" is synonymous with "impairment." The only difference between a legal-drug addict and an illegal-drug addict is prison.

The rapid change in the environment called cultural evolution began with the agricultural and Industrial revolutions. Cultural evolution's effect on gene expression produced what scientists refer to as "mismatched diseases. These illnesses are the result of our ancient bodies' design not being adapted to the drastic changes in our modern environment.

Duke University researched the causes of these new diseases. The findings of the university's research were in contrast with the pharmaceutical industry's claims.

The perpetual treatment of a disease provides steady money for a physician throughout the lifetime of his or her client. Curing a disease is a one-time event that generates a lower profit than treating that disease for years. For detailed information on mismatched diseases, we recommend *The Story of the Human Body: Evolution, Health, and Disease*, by Daniel Lieberman, Ph.D., an evolutionary biologist and professor at Harvard University.

The authors researched the pharmaceutical corporations' shenanigans. The following are a few of the many shenanigans they found: The drug companies sponsor most drug research. The research is considered the intellectual property of the drug company that sponsors it. That means that the results belong to the sponsor. The drug companies decide which universities will do the research.

In many cases, the research results are controlled by the sponsor's strict research criteria. Once the research is complete, the sponsor can decide whether the results should be published. Often the research is flawed, the drug's benefits are grossly exaggerated, and the drug's side effects minimized. The drug company will publish only the favorable findings. Unfavorable results will be trashed.

When a patent expires, a drug manufacturer can create what is called a "new molecule entity." Although the new molecule entity may not be significantly better than the original drug, the drug company can patent it as a new drug and raise its price. Between 1990 and 2004, the FDA approved 1,100 new molecular entities. Of that 1,100, only 183 were actually new, and in recent years, even fewer were new.

The drug industry employs over one hundred thousand attractive salespeople. Their jobs are to call on doctors, hospitals, and care facilities for the elderly. They offer many rewards to the physicians responsible for dispensing drugs, including gifts, football tickets, vacations, elegant dinners, and invitations to VIP parties.

The best description of the atrocities of conventional medicine comes from Gary Null's book *Death by Medicine*: "The number of people who die each day because of medical errors, physician mistakes, hospital-related illness, and reactions to FDA-approved medications is the equivalent of six jumbo jets falling out of the sky." He continues: "More Americans are dying each year at the hands of medicine than all American casualties in WWI and the Civil War combined."

The pharmaceutical corporations who make up the U.S. drug cartel are corrupting our legislature and the mainstream news media with large sums of money in exchange for their keeping the truth from the public.

The United States legal drug cartel targets not only healthy people but also children, sacrificing their health for profits. During the last part of the twentieth century, the powerful drug lobby persuaded Congress to create and pass a bill allowing drug advertisements on television.

Repeatedly advertising drugs conditions people to ignore the signals from their bodies that tell them that changes are needed. Instead, starting at a young age, we are told to ask our doctors about our symptoms and to do what they tell us to do without questions. This conditioning technique ensures our complete obedience and, in many cases, causes us to avoid seeking other opinions. This often results in unnecessary, debilitating drug therapy, unnecessary surgeries, and death.

It is well known that drugs cannot heal the human body. For example, there are no pharmaceuticals or surgical procedures that are capable of curing type 2 diabetes, cancer, arthritis, osteoporosis, or heart disease. Drugs only mask the symptoms, and surgeries only prolong the inevitable. Licensed medical physicians by law can prescribe only FDA-approved drugs; thus, no cures are possible.

Physicians who practice therapies not authorized by the FDA can be prosecuted, lose their licenses, and be fined. Hypothetically, if a physician cured someone using a therapy other than an FDA-approved pharmaceutical drug, he or she could be legally prosecuted, lose his or her license, or be imprisoned.

The United States and New Zealand are the only countries that allow drug companies to directly advertise to people. Advertising increased drug profits threefold by the early part of the twenty-first century. The cost of drugs also increased threefold. The drug companies claim that the increases in drug prices are due to research and development expenses. The truth is that the drug companies spend more money on advertising their drugs than on research and development.

The FDA relies mostly on the safety testing supplied by the chemical and food industries, which give the FDA the go-ahead to market products. The average consumer assumes that the FDA performs safety tests on all chemicals added to foods and on other personal products. Sadly, that is not the case. In most cases, the FDA relies on the manufacturers' safety research.

The Environmental Protection Agency (EPA) has become nothing more than a yes-man for national and international conglomerates. Without true restraints on their power, these corporations continually abuse the environment with toxic pesticides and fertilizers, destroying the soil and contaminating the water table.

Our modern lifestyles exist outside the natural ecosystem that we became accustomed to over tens of thousands of years. Our minds are constantly in disarray because of never-ending, mind-boggling everyday stresses. Our bodies cannot achieve homeostasis, which is a necessary component of health.

The synthetic and highly processed foods advertised on TV have become integral parts of our diets. These new foods created by men are known as the "foods of commerce." Food advertisers have only one thing in mind: conditioning the viewers to eat foods that earn them the greatest profits regardless of their effects on viewers' health.

Food manufacturers add thousands of toxic chemicals to foods without the consumers' knowledge. The most common ones are preservatives, bleaching agents, emulsifiers, flavor enhancers, humectants, texturizers, color agents, smell enhancers, and ripening agents like ethylene gas, which is used on bananas.

Our lives and environment have drastically changed, and not for the better. One-third of the US adult population is overweight, and another one-third is obese; these figures are steadily increasing.

Why is it that 90 percent of the people who lose weight are unable to permanently keep it off? Furthermore, 70 percent of Americans will develop heart disease, and more than half will die from it. The number of diabetics has increased from seven million to thirty million in the last twenty-five years.

Chronic fatigue, anxiety, and depression affect 50 percent of the U.S. population. More than four hundred thousand people die from the direct or indirect effects of high blood pressure annually. So why does the unsuccessful treatment of these symptoms with drugs continue?

The United States spends over two trillion dollars a year on health care—that's more money than any other nation spends on health care. It is estimated that up to 75 percent of the illnesses that we treat are preventable. Why? Because our bodies have not adapted to inactivity; toxic food; and the comfortable, clean, modern, stressful everyday lifestyles that so many people have.

The United States remains the most diseased affluent country on earth. Furthermore, the United States has the highest medical mortality rate. How is it that this failing health-care system can continue to exist regardless of how unsuccessful it is? It is the belief of a growing number of experts that conventional drug therapies are nothing more than a holocaust for profit.

In conclusion, when a person's mind and body function in complete harmony with the environment, he or she will begin to experience wellness. Only the body can heal the body. If the body's needs are met without unnatural interferences, the result will be health and wellness. The body needs complete, unadulterated nutritional support; an appropriate amount of exercise; as little internal and external exposure to toxins as possible; and as little stress and anxiety as possible.

■ ■ ■

BACK TO THE STORY

"Betty, I never knew this vital information about health."

"That is the way it is, Will. The information you're looking at is just not accessible by the average individual. People are too busy with their lives to think the information that they receive about health might be wrong. The average person doesn't consider his health until he develops a disease. Then he/she goes to a doctor, and the pill therapy begins. Not one thought is given to why he/she became ill in the first place. The health-care system treats the symptoms of diseases without regard for the causes, which is definitely not how it should operate. Will, believe me—there is so much more to know. Our health manifesto is only a brief introduction to what you need to know. The idea is to supply the readers with information and to generate in them an interest in health. Too much information will overwhelm a person. People interested in health will take the next step. That's why our manifesto is only the tip of the iceberg, Will."

"Betty, you keep topping my glass off with the champagne. I may be consuming the better part of the bottle."

"One glass is plenty for me, Will. You need to remember that I am a feeble old woman. One glass is a satisfying amount. The champagne adds fuel to my old burner. I truly enjoy the buzz, and most of all, I enjoy sharing these precious moments with you."

"If there's anything I can do, don't hesitate to ask."

"I do have a request of you, Will. I want you to walk with me around the block. I'll just need to hold on to you for balance from time to time. I'm on a mission to cure my dependency on this cane as soon as possible. Do you know why, Will?"

"I know that you want to obtain a driver's license."

"You're right—and I want to buy a new automobile."

"You walked at a good pace, Betty," Will said when their walk was over.

"Thanks for taking me around the block, Will. Bring your new girlfriend to Sunday brunch. Gloria is bringing her new boyfriend, Bob."

"OK, Betty, see you on Sunday!"

BETTY TAKES CHARGE OF SUNDAY BRUNCH

"Good morning, Lenny. Thanks for getting up early," Betty said. "We need to get started in the kitchen. I'm glad to see that Sunday brunch back. Gloria is bringing her new boyfriend, and Will is bringing his new girlfriend."

"Ruby should be up and about shortly. She was up for the better part of last night, talking with Adolf, the German industrialist," I said. "He will not give up on bringing her to Germany."

"That's a conversation for another time, Lenny."

"Ruby bought smoked salmon and bagels. She started slow cooking some kind of a casserole early this morning during her conversation with Adolf. Ruby also bought fresh, organic, grain-free dog food for Jojo and Breezy.

"Will and I picked up a grass-fed and grass-finished chemical-free roast and organic vegetables from Whole Foods yesterday. The roast has been in the slow cooker since last night. It's smothered in onions and carrots. Gloria and Bob are going to bring over fresh gulf shrimp that they bought straight off of a shrimp boat."

"I need a cup of coffee, Betty. I'm going to put on a pot."

"There is organic coffee in the cupboard, Lenny."

"I know, Betty. I even know where the heavy cream is," I said, laughing.

"I forgot for a moment that you're living here," Betty said. "Don't you need to remove the champagne from your car and put it on ice?"

"Damn, I almost forgot! I will come back to the sweet potatoes after I take care of the champagne. Good morning, Ruby."

"I did not plan to be up for most of the night, but Adolf and I had plenty to talk about. I don't know what I think about him now. He was my best male friend the entire time I was in Vegas. We spent time together. I thought he lived in his jet. He flew from Germany to be with me sometimes a couple of times a month. I know he loves me. I'm sorry to say that I don't love him enough to take off to Germany and to give up on my dream of living with you and the family. I need for you to understand where I am on this matter, Lenny."

"I appreciate that, Ruby. I realize that you have some tough decisions to make and that your decision concerning Adolf is a major one. I don't want you to feel like I'm suffocating you."

"Lenny, I wish you would suffocate me more. I like you close."

"Come on, you two—unlock your lips, and get busy. You've been acting like two teenagers in love ever since you stayed out all night," Betty said.

"You're right Betty—that's how we feel! I will never forget the first night we spent together at the Pink Shell. That night was the pinnacle of my life. I was broken, and Lenny fixed me. We were destined for each other."

I have a habit of drifting off into a dream world. Sometimes that's good, and sometimes that's bad. I was happily married for nineteen years to a wonderful woman named Mary Gibson. I have had two relationships since then. When I look back on those relationships, I see that they had several problems in common. I loved those women more than they loved me. I gave them much more than they gave me. I lost ground, and they gained ground. I stayed too long. What am I trying to admit to? After my first marriage, I made bad choices when it came to relationships. So why is this one so different? Because I did not choose Ruby—Ruby chose me. Maybe that's why this is so perfect.

I awoke from my dream to find Ruby looking me in the eye. "Ruby, is that a green-bean casserole I smell?"

"It is."

"Lenny, I made coffee. Would you like me to pour you a cup with heavy cream?"

"Please do, Ruby."

"Where is Mom, Betty?"

"She's on her way. Will went to pick up his new girlfriend."

"He found a girlfriend quickly, didn't he?"

"I'm not surprised, Lenny. He's a nice-looking young man," Ruby said. "He said he would be here by twelve-thirty. Bob, Gloria's boyfriend, said he would make it by one."

"Hi, Gloria," Betty said when Gloria arrived.

"How is everyone?" Gloria asked.

"We are all doing great—especially our two resident lovebirds, Ruby and Lenny," Betty said. "Would Bob have something to do with the new smile you're wearing, Gloria?"

"We can't wait to meet Bob," I said.

"Mom, where's the shrimp? I haven't had gulf shrimp since I left. I can't wait to have a few."

"They're in the ice chest in my car."

"Would you bring the chest in, Lenny?" Ruby asked.

"I sure will."

"Ruby, don't touch the shrimp until everyone is here."

"OK, Mom."

"Look who just rolled up in a good-looking Honda Fit! It's Will and Bailey," Ruby said. "She's a beauty, Lenny. Come look."

"You're right, Ruby. She is a looker. I hear that she's well educated and that she has a master's degree from the University of Florida."

"Do you know what her master's degree is in?"

"Will told me that he met her during orientation. She works in the administration department, on the fourth floor. Her degree is in finance."

"That's interesting—that makes them academic neighbors. She and Bob will probably have a lot in common. You know, Bob's master's degree is in banking."

"We have a lot of knowledge in our growing ranks. I have the best-looking and smartest boss in existence. I'm referring to none other than Ruby Ridge," I said.

"Will you two get a room?" Gloria said. "My God! You can't keep your mouths off of each other long enough to eat brunch."

"OK, Mom. We will try—but no promises."

"Can you believe them, Betty? We have two love-crazy teenagers in our family."

BAILEY AND BOB MEET BETTY'S FAMILY

"Hello, folks. Allow me to introduce Bailey. Bailey, this is Betty, the lady of the house and the head of the family. Over there by the window are Ruby and Lenny. This is Gloria, my landlord and the mother of Ruby."

"Will has told me about all of you and about how you treat him as though he were family. I'm honored to meet you."

"Make yourself at home, Bailey. Brunch is coming. We're waiting on one last guest, Gloria's boyfriend. He is due any minute, and then we will have brunch."

"Would you like champagne, Bailey?"

"Thank you, Ruby. I would."

"Bob is pulling into the driveway, Gloria. You can meet him at the door."

"Thanks, Lenny. I'm a little nervous. I'm sure Bob is too, especially because he doesn't know anyone."

"Don't worry, Gloria. It will be fine. He's a banker—he's used to meeting new people."

"Yeah, that makes sense, Lenny. Hi, Bob. Thanks for coming! Allow me to introduce you to everyone. But first, would you like a beverage? We have tea, coffee, beer, and champagne, but no sodas. I'm having champagne."

"Then I will too."

"Let me serve you, Bob. Now you've met the family—that's what we call the group present here today."

"That is very interesting, Gloria."

"What do you think?"

"I don't know. I'm impressed by the amount of education that all of your friends have."

"After brunch, we have a discussion. Recently, the topic has been health. Lenny and Betty are the leaders of these discussions.

"Betty has a Ph.D. in library science. She has been reading for seventy years. Some say that she has read everything. Of course, that's not exactly true. However, she does know something about everything. Lenny has a service-related disability from Vietnam. He is first an evolutionary biologist, and like Betty, he is a master of many disciplines. His studies encompass psychotherapy, nutrition, exercise, paleontology, physiology, and epigenetics with an emphasis on mismatched diseases. He is a writer and a serious lifetime scholar."

"Holy cow, Gloria! Those two have an amazing amount of knowledge."

"You are welcome to join in on the discussion after brunch, Bob. The discussion will be on the perils of conventional health care."

"My daughter, Ruby, has a master's degree in dance," Gloria said. "Ruby stayed with Betty for most of her young life because I worked all the time. Betty was Ruby's mentor. She instilled in Ruby a drive to be the best. She received a dance scholarship from USC. She became the lead dancer and choreographer at the MGM Grand in Las Vegas and made herself a millionaire in five years.

"Her goal is to teach dance. Will works for the VA and has a master's degree in sociology. His girlfriend also works for the VA and has a master's degree in finance. Your master's degree in banking fits in well here, Bob. And you know that I'm an unemployed administrative assistant with a master's degree."

"Gloria, with your experience, I doubt that you will remain unemployed for long," Bob said.

"You may hear the name Lewis, who was also known as 'the Veteran,' as Lenny called him. Lewis is Betty's late son. That's a story for another time, Bob. Now there's one final business matter, Bob. Will you prepare the documents I'll need to refinance my house?" Gloria asked. "Ruby said that she'll open a savings account at your bank, put two hundred thousand dollars in it, and sign my refinance loan with me."

"I'll do that on Monday, and I'll let you know when you and your daughter should come in to sign the documents."

"Thanks, Bob."

"Thank you, Gloria."

"That's enough, Bob. Let's enjoy the moment."

"I'm totally flabbergasted, Gloria."

"What's wrong?"

"I never imagined that your friends would be so intellectual. In high school you were just a nice, pretty average girl."

"Bob, it's not like that was my plan. I live next door to Betty, and she's a magnet for intellectuals. Her son, Lewis, was sort of a genius.

"Like many other veterans, he caught a superbug and died at the VA hospital. Betty and Lenny refer to the VA clinic as the 'veterans' death clinic' and believe that it's run by incompetent and corrupt political hacks.

"Will saved Lenny's life when he was cut with a knife during an attempted robbery. He's become a loyal friend to Lenny. He has a little bit of genius in him too. He attended USF on a full academic scholarship and graduated with a degree in sociology at the top of his class. A VA representative attended his graduation to recruit him.

"Bob, do you feel trivialized by my friends? I can't believe you're feeling that way. Don't compare your knowledge to theirs. You are the president of a bank, and you have a master's degree in banking. That's an amazing accomplishment in itself."

"I'm sorry, Gloria. You are absolutely right. I was momentarily intimidated by their brilliance."

"Thanks for setting me straight and for giving me the opportunity to meet these talented individuals. You are a remarkable woman, Gloria!"

BETTY WELCOMES NEW FAMILY MEMBERS

"Come with me, Will," I said. "I must see what's happening with Betty and Bailey. They're embracing each other and crying. Ruby, what is going on?"

"Betty and Bailey discovered that they had a similar horrid experience. They both lost their husbands to wars when they were young. They were both pregnant, and their husbands died before they knew that they were pregnant. Betty's husband was a marine. They were together for only thirty days before he shipped out to fight the Japanese in the Pacific during the Second World War. He died during the battle of Iwo Jima. He never knew that Betty was pregnant with Lewis, who just recently died.

"Bailey married her husband while he was on a thirty-day leave. He was killed in Afghanistan and never knew that Bailey was pregnant with Joni."

"I'm sure that Betty can help her."

"Betty is a wise, strong woman," Ruby said.

"I want everyone here to recognize what this beautiful young lady is going through," Betty said. "I was never quite the same after Bill, my husband, was killed. Then I suffered another blow, the unexpected death of my son, Lewis.

"But the wonderful people around me gave me the will to continue. I truly know the pain that this young lady is living with every day. I hope that our home will become her Shangri-la and that everyone here today will provide her with the comfort that she deserves.

"Things have changed. Life today is more complicated. We must give one another a hand in order to accomplish our individual goals. I think it would be fitting to evoke a phrase that has been used since biblical times: 'United we stand, and divided we fall.'

"I am humbled that so many people care about me. Before I was alone, and I am an orphan, like Will. I have never had the support of a family. Will told me when we met that he felt like he had become a part of a family for the first time in his life.

"I asked him several times to describe that feeling to me. I now know firsthand what he was feeling. I thank all of you."

"I moved here on my own. I am alone. I would like to be recognized as a member of this family," said Bob Richburg.

"Gloria has told me about you and about the magnanimous people you surround yourself with, and today, I met them."

"We would be honored to have you, Bob. Great strength is found in exceptional people," Betty said.

"I am fascinated by Betty, Lenny."

"Bob, you are not alone in that. She is the kindest and most sagacious person I have ever encountered. She is pure goodness, Bob. Any decision she makes is without incoming influence.

"Betty would not be bringing so much talent together if she didn't have a plan."

"Is Betty financially secure, Lenny?"

"I don't think there's any harm in answering your question. Betty is worth tens of millions of dollars."

"My God, Lenny. I never would have guessed that."

"Time to eat, everyone. There's no seating arrangement. Pick a seat, and dig in," Gloria said.

"What a fantastic-looking setting, Will," Bailey said.

"I agree."

"Go ahead—help yourself, people. Everything is within reach. No one serves the food here."

"Ruby, you know the food is good when the room becomes quiet," I said. "You can't talk with a mouthful of delicious food."

"Bob, how did your date with Gloria go?" Ruby asked.

"This might sound strange, but we just took up where we had left off. It was almost like we never were apart. We're both the same people we were in high school. I guess we're sweethearts again," Bob said, laughing.

"We will clear the table and resume our weekly discussion," Betty said. "Every Sunday we talk about subjects that could be helpful to the family. If any member has a question or needs help with any matter, he or she may bring it to the table.

"The idea is to help one another and to provide solutions to one another's problems by drawing from the combined knowledge of the family members.

"The family's motto is 'one for all, and all for one.' Attendance is not mandatory, but participation is encouraged. You may ask questions or make comments. I am normally available for conferences. On the wall to our left is a library of books on every aspect of health, history, finance, psychology, evolution, government, and politics. I have to mention that the library includes two books and numerous articles written by our own Lenny Lewis. Over seven hundred and fifty books are available for you to borrow. I ask that you sign the book labeled 'checkout' when you borrow a book.

"If you have questions about a book, Lenny and I can answer them. Since both of us are retired, one of us will always be available twenty-four-seven. Lenny and I believe that learning is a lifelong activity."

■ ■ ■

THE PERILS OF CONVENTIONAL HEALTH CARE

"I would like to invite you to share useful information with the family. Please let one of us know when you would like to present your discussion," Betty said. "Lenny and my son started this discussion group. Lewis became interested in health because of my deteriorating condition.

"Everyone knows what happened to me. I was nothing but a gold mine for the pharmaceutical companies. I went from using a wheelchair to enjoying a full recovery thanks to the health plan that Lewis and Lenny laid out for me.

"Reading every book about health on this wall has led me to conclude that the conventional health-care system has little regard for an individual's health. It cares only about his or her money.

"Today, Lenny and I would like to point out what is really going on behind the scenes in conventional health care. If you know how to avoid the perils of conventional health care, you can avoid diseases, sustain your youthful vitality, and increase your longevity.

"The problem begins with the medical schools that educate the doctors. To start with, I would like you to understand how the practice of treating only symptoms and not diseases evolved."

"Betty, what exactly do you mean by 'treating only symptoms'?" Bailey asked.

"Answer this question, Bailey. If a farmer sells all of the apples he grew this season, will more grow during the following season?"

"Of course," Bailey said.

"That is what treating the symptoms is all about. The symptoms are cured for the time being."

"Does that mean that the disease wasn't cured and that the symptoms temporarily disappeared?"

"That's right, Bailey. The disease is alive and well and waiting for another treatment. And the doctor is waiting for more money."

"I get it, Betty."

"Big pharma was quick to realize that by utilizing its financial power, it could influence what was being taught to impressionable young medical students. In 1910 the American Medical Association (the AMA) founded the Council of Medical Education (the CME) and was given the power by Congress to oversee the academic protocol and accreditation of all medical schools in the United States and its territories."

"Similarly, the banking industry is controlled by government regulators," Bob said.

"And as if that were not enough, under the strong influence of big pharma, in 1972 the AMA founded the Professional Standards Review Organization (PSRO) to force doctors to use only drug therapy to treat patients. Congress gave the PSRO the authority to enter any doctor's private practice and to revoke any doctor's license to practice without even a hearing."

"I had no idea that doctors were bound by the rules of that organization," Gloria said.

"The constant fear of losing their licenses keeps even knowledgeable doctors from promoting prevention or natural therapies when they would be helpful to their clients. 'Crimes' like those can be considered felonies, and the PSRO can request the assistance of the federal Food and Drug Administration, whose SWAT teams can forcefully enter private practices to arrest disobedient doctors who continue to prescribe treatments other than FDA-approved drugs."

"How could that be, Lenny?"

"Think money's influence, Bailey. Think about how it is and not how it is supposed to be."

"I thought the FDA was supposed to protect the American people from harmful substances."

"That was the original idea, Bailey. However, I am sorry to inform you that the FDA favors the interest of the multinational corporations. Studies concerning how the environment affects the human body received no government financial support and were canceled by the FDA. Biochemistry, the discipline concerned with food and how it fulfills the biological needs of the body, was pushed aside in medical schools in favor of the new science of pharmacology—and drug therapy's offer of limitless profits.

"In order to gain accreditation and to receive congressional funding, a medical school must demonstrate complete compliance to the CME's academic protocol. Schools that refused to comply with it were forced to close."

"Wow, I just assumed that the drugs prescribed by doctors were the only things that could cure sicknesses," Bailey said. "You're telling me that drugs can't cure sicknesses?"

"That's what I'm saying, Bailey. Only the body can cure sicknesses. Most Americans learn by watching TV. Television networks are responsible to their advertisers, not to their viewers. Television programs won't say anything that disagrees with the views of their sponsors."

"Are we blind to what's really going on?"

"To some extent, we are, Bailey. I'm afraid that we are a nation of ignorant people. Corporations use repetitive advertising tactics, mostly on TV, to make consumers buy their food products.

"The idea here is that food advertisers promote the foods of commerce. These are cheap foods that are nutritionally deficient but earn the manufacturers the most money. The foods of commerce are devastating to one's health. It's basic capitalism, Bailey—buyer beware!"

"I never imagined that the health-care system could be controlled by the corporations that invest in health care."

"That's like the fox watching the henhouse," Bob said. "The banking industry is controlled in the same way."

"Ruby will now be teaching dance. Is anyone interested in that? Lenny and Bob are clearing the living room to make space. How many want to learn ballroom dancing?"

"Everybody wants to learn it, Ruby."

"Let's get started, people! We have plenty of beverages in the icebox."

"Looks like we're having a party, Betty."

■ ■ ■

THE VA DELIVERS THE VETERAN'S ASHES

"Ruby, Lenny, can you get up and meet me at the breakfast table? I wouldn't bother you if it weren't important," Betty said.

"Let's go, Ruby. Something is wrong." I could hear it in Betty's voice. "Throw on your bathrobe, Ruby."

"OK, I'm ready. What's wrong, Betty? Are you in pain? Stop crying, and talk to us. Dry your eyes with this towel."

"The VA came early and presented me with Lewis's ashes, a thank-you letter, and an American flag. It was just too much for me. His ashes are on the mantel in the living room, Lenny. Oh, Lord, give me strength!"

"Betty, I'm going to fix you a cup of green tea. Please try to calm down."

"Thank you, Ruby."

"I know how difficult this is for you. I hurt too. Would you like to go spread his ashes?"

"Yes, Lenny! Can we do it now? It's still morning. We can honor his wish for his ashes to be scattered in the ocean during the early morning. Ruby, get dressed—and please hurry. We need to go to the ocean now!"

"It will only take me a minute to dress," Ruby said.

"Finish your tea while we wait for Ruby."

"I'm better, Lenny. Can you fetch my pink windbreaker from my closet? Lewis said he favored that jacket."

"I'll do it now, Betty. I'll also fill Jojo's and Breezy's food and water bowls and lock the dog door. We can leave them inside the house."

"Are we ready to go?" Ruby asked. "We can take my Odyssey, and you can drive, Lenny. I'll sit with Betty. Where are we going, Lenny?"

"Bowditch Point Park in Fort Myers Beach, Ruby. Betty, are you strong enough to walk to the island point?"

"I will make it, Lenny. I love you two."

"We love you too, Betty," Ruby said.

"Betty, the walk through the sand will require us to be on both sides of you just in case you need us for balance."

"I will attempt to make it on my own. Let's go! This is a lovely morning—exactly what Lewis wanted. Where are Lewis's ashes?"

"I have the urn," I said.

"You can hand it to me when I get in position," Betty said.

"I have a few words to say before I release his ashes."

"Betty, this is a place I visited many times with the Veteran. One day he said to me that when the world was closing in on me, I would come here, and the world would release me from its grip. I lost him, but I gained you, Betty."

"The Lord took Lewis and gave me you and Ruby. That's a two-for-one deal," Betty said. "I can live with that! You and Lewis revived me and gave me a new reason to live. Now we have a family full of talented people, and it is growing. With all of these wonderful people entering our lives, we can do wonders. Lenny, would you hand me the urn? Thank you."

BETTY'S EULOGY

"I would like to cast a few words into this wind to fly along with Lewis's ashes."

"Go ahead, Betty."

"Lord, I lost a young, handsome warrior in the Second Word War, but before that, he impregnated me with a beautiful child. You now have taken him and given me a large family. I trust that has a purpose because you designed it. I accept the exchange. You sent me Ruby and Lenny and a mission. I will not let them down. I will use all of my wisdom to serve them. I have no misgivings. I will stand tall to meet the challenge you have blessed me with. You have shown me your greatness, and I now cast my loving son into your wind."

"My God, Lenny! I can't take this."

"I know, Ruby."

"Hold me, Lenny! Don't let me go!"

"I will never let you go."

There was total silence in the car. In the rearview mirror, I could see Betty wrapped up in Ruby's arms. Both of them were sound asleep. I thought to myself that everything changes when you succumb to love and family. Your thoughts are on the people you love, and there is not much time for abstract thoughts. I thought that maybe that's why the smartest people are loners or sometimes judged to be insane. In today's world there is a fine line between sanity and insanity. I opine that every person at some time has questioned his or her own sanity. How often you question yourself might tell you which one you are.

RUBY'S INFLUENCE ON LENNY

I drift into incredibly deep thoughts when I spend days by myself. I have noticed that my writing is the best during those times. Furthermore, I've noticed that when I return to reality, I feel awkward. I eventually find my way back to talking about the weather and engaging in simple, brainless social conversations, including conversations about the daily news and politics.

Ruby rescued me from my conundrum, worried about what others thought. I no longer felt compelled to care. Ruby was secure in her convictions and did not give a rat's ass about social positions or acceptance into what she called the "look-what-I-have crowd."

"I don't need those materialistic morons, and I won't waste one minute of my time thinking that I need anything that they have to offer," she would say.

I agreed with her when she called them "morons." We thought so much alike that it frightened me. Betty knew that. And that was the reason that she thought we should spend time getting to know each other. Betty was undoubtedly the wisest woman I have ever known. Betty had a "transparent eyeball," which is a philosophical metaphor originated by Ralph Waldo Emerson, the nineteenth century American essayist, lecturer, and poet.

"Lenny, are we almost home?"

"Five more minutes, Ruby."

"Betty needs to be laid down. She is out cold. The stress drained her."

"I'm so grateful to have you at my side during these trying times, Ruby. The Veteran was the best friend I ever had. It took all of my strength to not burst out crying while I was listening to Betty's eulogy. He was the brother I never had."

"Lenny, I can't express in words what you have done for my life."

"Stay where you are, Ruby. I will come around and get Betty. I've got her, Ruby. Can you gather up everything that needs to go in? I'll carry Betty to her bedroom. Ruby, turn the sheets down. She needs a good nap."

"I will lie with her until I know that she's sound asleep. Don't go, Lenny. Open the top dresser drawer and hand me her light-blue nightgown."

"Is this it, Ruby?"

"Yes, bring it to me, and then you can leave."

"I will be in the den reading *Brain Maker*."

BETTY INFORMS RUBY OF HAROLD AND HER PLANS

"Ruby, I am sorry to be such a burden to you and Lenny. Scattering Lewis's ashes took everything out of me. I thought I would be stronger. "I love you and Lenny. I do have a plan to reward the both of you."

"Betty, don't you think you need to rest?"

"I must tell you what I'm doing. Now is the right time. Ruby, you know about my friend Harold."

"Yes, Betty—from previous conversations."

"We were friends for thirty years during the time I ran a public library in Michigan. He'll be coming in the next couple of months. We have been talking on the phone since Lewis's death. He is a wealthy retired lawyer. His vicious attacks on the government and corporations earned him a reputation among other lawyers in his day. They called him the 'Michigan Wolverine.' When he filed a lawsuit, the defense would usually insist on settling out of court. He was a master at charming juries, and they very rarely denied him guilty verdicts.

"He has maintained his license to practice and has filed a wrongful death lawsuit against the VA for Lewis's death. The VA has already admitted that it was at fault and has offered me five million dollars to settle out of court. We filed a twenty-five-million-dollar lawsuit, Ruby."

"So that's the reason you've been working so hard to lose the cane."

"Yes, Ruby, and that's why I need to obtain my driver's license and buy a nice car. Harold is healthy and thirteen years younger than I am. I want to be my best for him.

"I dream of building a new home large enough to have a ballroom for dancing, a private movie theater, and a huge meeting room. The house would have a library capable of accommodating thousands of books and be equipped with several iMac computers for research.

"You and Lenny would have stylish accommodations with a separate entrance, a professional-style kitchen, a beautiful floral garden, a Hydro Spa, and climate-controlled garage parking for three cars. For now, I plan to build a totally smart annex to this house for Harold. I'm alive again, Ruby!"

"You continue to amaze me, Betty. Lenny and I love you and will always be here for you. Now take a nap. When you wake up, you can tell Lenny yourself what's going on."

"What do you think about David Perlmutter's book, Lenny?"

"It confirms what I already expected. Intestinal microbiomes play a larger part in health than was previously expected. The surprise is the impact of the bacteria on the brain, which is much greater than I'd originally thought. The possibility that gut bacteria could control the brain is difficult to even imagine. However, more and more research is supporting that hypothesis. Is Betty all right?"

"She is exhausted. She will be fine after a nap. I need to call Will and exchange cars with him for tomorrow."

BETTY WANTS A DRIVER'S LICENSE

"Betty wants her driver's license back. She allowed it to expire when she became confined to a wheelchair. She is determined to purchase her own car. I said I'd give her some driving practice," Ruby said.

"Why does she want it back?"

"She wants to become independent again, Lenny. Her boyfriend of sixty years is coming down to visit her. I need to call Will."

She called Will to make the preparations to take Betty driving.

"Will, I want to ask if we could swap cars. The small Honda Fit will make it easier for Betty to pass the driver's test. I will let her practice driving before you take her down to the Department of Motor Vehicles. If you can, Will, bring the Fit to me, and pick up my Odyssey."

Will said, "I'll bring the car over."

"Thanks, Will, for coming."

"Ruby, I thought Betty was going to get a learner's permit first."

"She drove for years. I'm going to check her out as she drives. If she's maintained her driving skills, she can go straight to the test."

"Good idea, Ruby. I will be styling in your Odyssey," Will said, laughing. "I'll call you tomorrow. I'm going to pick up Bailey now. See you later!"

DINING WITH DETECTIVE RAY AND HIS WIFE

"Ruby, while you were in the bedroom with Betty, Detective Ray called. He wanted to know if we might join him and his wife for dinner later this evening. I told him I would call him back when you were available. He apologized for the short notice and said he would understand if we could not make it. Is he the detective who tracked down the man who almost killed you?"

"Yes."

"We should respectfully accept his invitation. I'm going to start my bath."

"I'll call Detective Ray back and let him know."

"Ask him where we're going so that I will know how to dress."

"Good idea. Can you hear me, Ruby?" I called him and then told Ruby the plan. "Detective Ray said that we'll be going to a Japanese sushi restaurant in Coconut Point."

"That sounds good, Lenny."

"The review said that the restaurant doesn't add monosodium glutamate or chemicals to the food. We won't have to be concerned about eating toxic food. Wow! You look fantastic, Ruby. The emerald necklace and earrings with the black silk dress are stunning. God, I am a lucky man. Why me?"

"Lenny, you have every quality that I desire. Your personal financial worth is of no importance to me."

"I never thought of you as earnings, Ruby."

"Your payment for restoring my sexuality is my love. No amount of money could have done more for me. I am the luckiest woman on the planet—it's pure love, Lenny. I hope you don't mind driving the Fit."

"We are early, Ruby. Let's check in with the hostess." I turned to the hostess. "Hello, we are meeting the Ray party."

"Yes, would you like to be seated?"

"Is there a waiting area? We would prefer to be seated with the rest of the party."

"I understand, sir. May I escort you to our Asian garden? When the rest of the party arrives, we will come for you. You will receive a complimentary beverage of your choice while you wait."

"Thank you."

"Follow me, please."

"This garden looks very culturally accurate, Lenny. It looks similar to a Japanese eatery in Las Vegas that is owned by Japanese people and was built by Japanese people."

"May I take your beverage order?"

"Ruby, what would you like?"

"I will have sake."

"Me too."

"Look, Lenny, a couple is dancing."

"Would you like to dance, Ruby?"

"I would, Lenny."

"Ruby, Detective Ray and his wife are here. The hostess is motioning for us. Let's go, Ruby."

"Lenny, how are you doing?"

"My wounds have healed, and everything is on the upswing for me, Detective Ray."

"Lenny, please call me Art. Meet my wife, Barbara."

"Art and Barbara, this is my girlfriend Ruby Ridge."

"Let us be seated. Lenny, I served in the military, but as you know, I missed Vietnam."

"Art, I just lost my dearest friend. He served with me in Vietnam."

"I'm sorry, Lenny."

"Ruby, did you know that Art lost his brother in Vietnam?"

"I didn't, Barbara."

"I know what Lenny went through. I'm sorry for your family."

"Ruby, that is the most beautiful necklace I have ever seen. Are those emeralds?"

"Yes, Barbara."

"Ruby is a dance instructor."

"What dances do you teach?"

"Well, ballroom dancing and actually all kinds of dances, Barbara."

"Art and I have been talking about taking dance lessons. We thought it would be fun and also an enjoyable form of exercise."

"Art, what was the final verdict on the man who cut me?"

"He pleaded guilty and received a two-year jail sentence with seven years of probation. It was his first felony, and he had a supportive family. He also expressed remorse for what he had done. That impressed the judge."

"Congratulations on your promotion, Art."

"Thanks, Lenny."

"My salary did not increase as much as my responsibilities did. Some of the officers think that my promotion was political. They refuse to respect me. In some cases, that causes insubordination, making my job even harder. I am slowly earning their respect.

"I graduated from Florida State University with a degree in criminology and joined the Lee County sheriff's department. I thought I could make some needed changes right away. I soon found out that the process of making changes is a very slow, uphill struggle.

"I admit that the department has come a long way, but to be totally honest, law enforcement still has a long way to go. It's an institution, and institutions are known to resist change. The recent killings of black people by white policemen have expedited the changes. My promotion put me in charge of community relations.

"I focus mostly on the minority populations of the county. But we really need better education for students and more jobs, and those are in the hands of the state legislature. I'm also in charge of updating the officers' training and starting sensitivity training. I'm sure you've watched on the news a few of the many demonstrations going on around the country.

"We have a good and wise sheriff. Some of the older police officers will not accept the mandatory changes concerning how we handle demonstrations and engage suspects.

"The sheriff has also charged the personnel department with hiring more minorities. He said that the officers' race should reflect the demographics of the population. Furthermore, the sheriff realizes that he must initiate changes that will prevent similar problems from happening in Lee County.

"I advocated for getting the deputies out of cars and among the people. Furthermore, deputies should live in the communities that they are policing."

"Is he taking your advice seriously?"

"He is listening."

"It sounds like the sheriff is trying to do the right thing."

"I think so too, Lenny, but he too realizes that change is difficult. Sheriff Leonard is nearing retirement age, Lenny. He suggested that I run for sheriff when he retires. He told me he would support me. Barbara and I have decided that I will run for sheriff when the time comes. I have always wanted to be involved in a political campaign."

"Give me a call when the time comes, Art."

"Thank you, Lenny. I will make note of your offer. You can't have enough supporters or campaign funds."

"Barbara, do you work?" Ruby asked.

"When Art received his promotion, he asked me to give up my job or to work part time. He wanted me to become involved with underprivileged kids in the neighborhood. That's what I've always talked about doing."

"I would like to work with the local Boys and Girls Club of America, Barbara."

"Do you have a hobby, Lenny?" Art asked.

"I lecture, write, and advise people on diets, exercise, wellness, and mismatched disease. My passion is evolutionary biology. I'm always available to do whatever I can to help a veteran."

"Ruby and Lenny, are you ready to order?"

"Thank you, Art. Ruby, will you order for us? Ruby is an expert on sushi. She always orders for both of us."

"You know each other that well?"

"We never disagree."

"We will take the sushi-and-sashimi combo for two with the ten-piece spider roll, nine pieces of sushi wrapped in seaweed, the nine-piece assortment of sashimi, and two seaweed salads. And bring Lenny a Sapporo beer and me a green tea."

"Barbara, what do you think we should have?"

"I think we should order the same thing."

"The softshell crab and the spider roll sound delicious. Bring us the same thing, please."

"Do you want to try a Sapporo beer, Art? The Japanese built a brewery in La Crosse, Wisconsin. That's how I justify buying Sapporo. The company is supplying jobs to Americans."

"That convinces me, Lenny. I'll have a Sapporo. Barbara?"

"I will take tea."

"Thank you, madam. Will there be anything else?"

"No, thank you."

"Ruby, would you like to finish our dance?"

"Yes, Lenny! The three-piece band plays romantic music that's perfect for slow dancing. Art, will you and Barbara join us?"

"Why not, Ruby? Barbara, will you, please?"

"I accept, Art."

"That was nice. Thanks, Ruby, for reminding us that there is more to life than working, solving crimes, and making money. Barbara and I have not danced in years. We noticed how well you and Ruby move together."

"Ruby has been working on my moves for a while, Art. I see that our food is here. What do you think about that Sapporo beer Art?"

"I am impressed Lenny. It has a taste like no other beer I've had. I would have never guessed this beer was brewed in the U.S."

"This spider role is unbelievable. I could eat a second helping if I was not concerned with my weight," said Barbara.

"Do you work out Barbara?" ask Ruby.

"Now that I don't work, I plan to start. Art wants to join Anytime Fitness. That would allow us to work out no matter what shift he might be working at the department. Since I want be working, we could work out together anytime, night or day. Anytime Fitness is perfect for police officers and others that have a work schedule different from the traditional nine-to-five job. "

"Barbara, I like the twenty-four-seven concept. Lenny, maybe we need to look into a membership at Anytime Fitness," said Ruby.

"Give us a call if you do," said Barbara.

"If we made a decision to join, we would definitely let you know," said Lenny.

"It's that time, people. I had a long day, and it's time to go home and relax," said Art.

"Thank you for inviting us, and thanks for suggesting this place. Good night, you guys."

I turned to Ruby. "What did you think?"

"The food was excellent."

"Should we have invited Art and Barbara to Sunday brunch?"

"Don't you think we should talk it over with Betty, Lenny?"

"I'm sure Betty would approve of adding a soon-to-be-sheriff to the family."

"Still, we should run it by Betty first."

"I agree, Ruby."

"We need to hurry home, Lenny. I called Betty from the restroom. She said that my mom was on her way over. Betty is going to look over her résumé. She's going in for a job interview at Hertz's headquarters next week. Afterward I will go to the bank with her to refinance her home."

"I see that Gloria is still here with Betty, Ruby."

"Hi, Betty, I see that you two are busy. I'm going to bed early. Good night, everyone. Are you coming, Lenny?"

"I will be there soon. I have some reading to do."

"OK, Lenny, but don't forget that we're going to the gym early in the morning. Don't stay up too late. Wake me up when you come to bed."

"I will."

"I was just leaving. Good night, everyone," Gloria said.

BETTY EXPLAINS TO LENNY WHY RUBY CHOSE HIM

"Betty, for so many years, it was just Breezy and I. When I went to bed, Breezy was with me. It did not take even a month for Breezy to decide to sleep with Ruby. Jojo too. They go to bed with Ruby. Betty, what do you have to say about that?"

"I have nothing to say to your nothing questions, Lenny! Am I detecting a little insecurity about your relationship with Ruby? Why do I have to listen to this jabber, Lenny? Will you say what's really on your mind? It's not like you to be confused. You and I have responsibilities to the others in this family. Should I cut to the chase and say what you won't say? What will it be, Lenny?

"I insist that we move quickly. Be specific! We have a growing family, and everyone relies on us, Lenny."

"I have a small studio apartment at the beach. It will not do for Ruby and me. I am living with Ruby in your house. Ruby is wealthy, and I live off of my VA disability. What should be my next move?"

"I will tell you what I see, Lenny. Then I'll expect you to take action immediately and to overcome this insignificant distraction. We have a demanding agenda. You should dump your apartment at the beach. Living here is the right thing to do at this time because Ruby would prefer to live here. Ruby chose you, Lenny. She'll let you know if it's time for you two to change your relationship.

"Ruby doesn't care about your financial situation. She cares about you personally. She is in love with you. So end this now, Lenny! You have a talented and beautiful woman. You won her with your intelligence and your deed. You gave her what she thought she would never have."

"Do you know about the rehab, Betty?"

"Yes, I know about everything that happened at the Pink Shell, right down to every orifice that you penetrated and every orgasm that Ruby experienced that night."

"God, Betty. Are you serious?"

"Lenny, I am the one who told Ruby that you—and maybe only you—had the ability to cure her sexual dysfunction. Ruby and I talk, Lenny. You earned her. You made her a complete woman. She is yours, and, Lenny, you deserve every beautiful part of her."

"I never imagined that you and Ruby would share so much personal information with each other, Betty."

"Well, now you know. You did a beautiful thing. I am proud of you. Are we done with this matter?"

"Yes, Betty. For sure."

"Now go to bed. Ruby is waiting for you, and tomorrow she is going to take me out to practice driving."

RUBY TAKES BETTY DRIVING, AND LENNY VACATES HIS APARTMENT

"Lenny, rise and shine. I have a big day ahead of me. After working out, I plan to spend the rest of the day with Betty. If she has retained her driving skills, her next stop will be the DMV with Will. What do you have scheduled?"

"After our workout, I'm going down to the beach to vacate my apartment."

"I was going to suggest that you do that. There is absolutely no need for it."

"You are right, Ruby."

"Don't keep anything that you have there. We'll purchase everything you need, and that includes clothes. We will go shopping and buy you a new wardrobe. Good morning, Betty. Lenny and I are going to the gym for a workout. When we come back, you and I are going to test your driving skills. We will return in about two hours."

"Lenny, you look stressed. Is there something going on that we should talk about?"

"Ruby, you are getting to know me. Yes, I am experiencing stress."

"Then I insist that you let me in on the cause, if you know it."

"I do."

"I'm all ears."

"My stress is normal, given my situation. Ruby, I am doing three things on the list of the top-ten most stressful things: I'm moving into a new home,

I am in love and cohabitating with a woman for the first time in nineteen years, and I'm still dealing with the death of the Veteran."

"Can I help you with those things? I thought the cause of your stress would be something unusual."

"No, Ruby, a good workout will help. I will move through this. These are not nearly as bad as the other stresses I have experienced in my life. I am appalled by the fact that my stress was so noticeable. You caught me in that moment."

"Don't worry about it, Lenny. We are going to be better together. I'm going to the aerobic room to do my break-dancing routine. It's my full-body workout."

"I'm going to work on my shoulders."

"See you in a couple of hours, Lenny."

"OK."

■■■

ESTABLISHING A LIFELONG HABIT OF EXERCISING

"Hey, Lenny, can I work out with you?"

"Sure, Ed."

"What body part are you working today?"

"I'm doing shoulders."

"What's so great about shoulders?"

"The shoulders work magic when it comes to a person's physique. When one's shoulders are broad, his waist appears to be small. Damn, what's going on? The whole gym is walking toward the aerobic room."

"Ruby is doing a break-dancing work out. She's the unbelievable hottie who does flips and spins and does unbelievable acrobatics. I heard she was a famous Las Vegas showgirl."

"Ed, she is my girlfriend."

"I'm sorry. I had no idea, Lenny."

"It's OK. People always say that, and they're always shocked when they find out that she's my girl."

"She's a dance celebrity, right?"

"Yes. Ed, do you want to do this shoulder workout?"

"Yes, let's get started."

"Ed, what do you want to accomplish with your workouts?"

"I never thought about it. I want to look better!"

"OK. When you look in the mirror, what don't you like?"

"I want to be stronger and more proportional."

"To accomplish your goal, we will start with the overhead-press machine. Sit down, Ed, and keep your back straight. Adjust the seat until your elbows are even with your shoulders. Inhale and extend your arms vertically to the end of the movement. Now exhale. Do this movement twelve times. If you cannot complete the twelfth one, it will tell us how much weight we need to subtract. Good job, Ed. I see you knew what weight you needed to start with. My turn now. That felt good. Add weight to your next set.

"You want to fail to complete the motion before you reach twelve repetitions. Failing around the ninth repetition would be perfect. You did ten repetitions, Ed. That's good. My turn. Back to you, Ed. Add more weight. Push, Ed—you can make that eighth repetition. My turn."

"Push harder, Lenny."

"That's all I can do. How many repetitions was that, Ed?"

"Seven."

"I'll live with that. This will be our final set, Ed. Add weight, and go. You can make it, Ed—push! Push! You did five, Ed. Rest while I do my last set. I barely got to the fourth rep. I'm happy with that.

"This exercise can be done seated with dumbbells, Ed. This exercise focuses on the three deltoid muscles. The greatest stress is on the anterior deltoid muscle. The clavicular head of the pectoralis major, the triceps brachii, the trapezius, and the serratus anterior and, deeper in, the supraspinatus, are all stressed. For our second shoulder exercise, we will do lateral dumbbell raises. Take a dumbbell in each hand, and stand with your legs slightly spread and your arms hanging on each side of your body.

"With your elbows slightly bent, raise your arms horizontally. Do the same number of sets and reps that we did with the overhead press. This movement stresses the middle deltoid as well as the anterior and posterior deltoids. If you raise your arms above horizontal to the ground, the upper and middle portions of the trapezius will be isolated and overstressed. How are you doing, Ed?"

"So far I feel good."

"Let's go to our final exercise, high-cable lateral extensions. The cable on each side is adjusted to the top-of-your-head position. Extend your arms to the front and grip the handle on the left side with your right hand. Then grip the right handle on your right side with your left hand. With the cables crossed, extend your arms to the side and back and exhale. This exercise stresses the posterior deltoid, the infraspinatus, the teres minor, the trapezius, and the rhomboids.

"Do the same number of sets and repetitions that we did with the lateral dumbbell raises. That's it for the shoulders, Ed."

"Thanks a lot, Lenny. Do you have any further advice for me?"

"Sure, Ed. Read, read, and read some more. Start with *Grain Brain* by Perlmutter."

Ed was a good example of a person who was interested enough in health to go to the gym. That's more than you can say for most people. I thought that if he went for long enough, he could possibly take a serious interest in exercise and make it a lifelong habit.

To arrive at this milestone, one must make an investment. Once an individual has invested a great deal of time and energy into something, he comes to the conclusion that he has invested too much into it to quit. That becomes a motivating factor. That commitment leads to noticeable physical and mental results, and because he fears losing his cherished rewards, the practice becomes habitual. He may eventually start investigating food, avoiding environmental hazards, and controlling the stresses in his life.

Anytime I see a man or a woman with Ed's attitude, I encourage him or her. I hoped Ed would find his way through all of the disinformation and misinformation from the AMA, the pharmaceutical corporations, the food processors, and the corrupt government officials. Don't forget that the medical industrial complex generates billions of dollars in profits by preying on the ignorant!

AN UNFORTUNATE GYM EXPERIENCE

Ed was smart enough to realize that I'm an authority in the world of exercise. After all, I have several related degrees and fifty years of experience. That told me he was smart enough to take advantage of others to achieve his desires.

I will tell you a story of another man who failed to figure out what Ed did. One day while training in the gym, I noticed a new man. He immediately caught my attention because of the way he was dressed. I was totally confused. This man was definitely a blast from the past. I found out his schedule by asking a friendly employee. I watched him each day he attended. His clothes were straight from the sixties. He was wearing tube socks and short silk shorts. His clothes were similar in color and appearance to those of the LA Lakers in the sixties. I also recognized that his workout routine was from that time. We've learned much about the body since his day.

After forty years or so, he'd returned to the gym wearing the same clothes he'd worn when he was young and doing the same workout routine his body had responded to when he was young. He did not last long. He disappeared after only a couple of months. Again I relied on the employee for an answer. After a couple of months of hard work, he had become discouraged. He virtually had nothing to show for his hard work. He said that he did not feel better and that he actually felt worse. Every body is different. The greatest difference of all is between the young body and the old body.

He confessed to the desk attendant who canceled his membership that he had become too old to recapture the youthful vitality that he had once possessed. He simply gave up! Before he gave up, he did solicit help from the club. A personal trainer who could have easily been his grandson was assigned to assist him. This young trainer said that he should work harder and eat less to accomplish his fitness goals and that he should sign a six-month contract for five hours of training a week at sixty dollars an hour. That suggestion sent him packing.

To this day I regret not approaching that man of my generation and enlightening him on what new science could offer him. Most trainers are young and ignorant of the needs of older bodies. Personal trainers and fitness instructors advocate for the same exercise program for the young and the old and for males and females.

Some gyms hire and train their instructors in their way in only a few hours. Many personal trainers receive certifications on Internet websites in a few days. Every body is unique and different. Exercise programs affect each body differently. An individual's history, level of fitness, age, gender, past and present health conditions, and needs should be considered before an exercise program is assigned to him or her.

"Hello, Ruby. You finished your workout."

"I did, Lenny. And you?"

"I had an interesting workout. I possibly did a good deed too!"

"How did that come about?"

"I helped Ed. He's new to finding his health. I think he might stay with it. I showed him a few things and suggested some reading for him."

"Ed who, Lenny?"

"Damn if I know, Ruby. He's most likely another one of those individuals who was hit in the head, woke up, and realized too late in life that he should begin doing something about his failing health."

"That's as good of an explanation as any, Lenny," Ruby said, laughing.

EVERYBODY KNOWS HOW TO EXERCISE

"Lenny, I warned you about trying to help the average gym member. More times than not, you will be disappointed with the result of your effort. You cannot tell the average Joe anything that he doesn't already know about exercise and health. My question is, how did he obtain his information? One answer to this mystery is that he was born knowing it. The worst answer is that his doctor told him. Doctors aren't trained in fitness."

"Thanks, Ruby, for reminding me of that dilemma. Did you have a good workout?"

"I had one of my best workouts."

"You had an audience."

"I usually do. The larger the audience, the harder I dance. You know that entertainment has been my life, Lenny."

"I am beginning to savor the attention I receive with you on my arm—even the sighs, moans, and groans that you elicit from people, Ruby. Your extraordinary intellectual prowess, talent, and beauty dazzle me. You are my fantasy come true! Let's continue this great day, Ruby."

"Lenny, you vacate your apartment, and I will take Betty driving."

RUBY'S DANCE CAREER, AND CHANNEL SIX NEWS

"Excuse me, madam. Are you Ruby Ridge?"

"Yes, I am, and who are you?"

"My name is Sarah Hart. I'm with the channel six news team. I was wondering if we might interview you and film your next workout for a story on the local news channel.

"I do feature stories on celebrities living in Fort Myers. We know that you were the lead dancer for five years running at the world-famous MGM Grand Crazy Horse Cabaret in Las Vegas. You were featured several times in the *Las Vegas Review-Journal,* in the 'Best Of Las Vegas Section.' The community would enjoy hearing your story and watching you dance.

"You were born in Fort Myers, Ms. Ridge, right?"

"What do you think, Lenny?"

"I think you should, Ruby."

"Can I ask who you are, sir?"

"Lenny is my boyfriend, Sarah."

"Ms. Ridge, we can do the interview now and come back with the film crew for your next workout. We have already obtained permission from the gym to film you anywhere in the gym."

"OK, Sarah. Can we sit at the trainers' table? I'm exhausted from my workout."

"Sure, Ms. Ridge."

"Please call me Ruby, Sarah. Yes, I was born in Fort Myers."

"What high school did you attend?"

"I went to Cypress High."

"How did you first become involved in dancing?"

"I started out as a skateboarder. I met a boy named James Rogers one day while skating. He became my first boyfriend. He was known as the best break dancer in Fort Myers. James had no family and survived as a street performer. He break danced for tips on the street. He taught me how to perform. I practiced all day; every day for months and soon began to perform myself.

"We even choreographed a dance together that earned us so much money that we were able to acquire a fairly nice apartment. I stayed with him sometimes but mostly lived at home with my mother and stepfather. James kept me focused. My mother worked long hours. James encouraged me to be a good student and looked after me.

"I was a straight-A student. A school counselor took interest in me and suggested that I join the school's dance team. I joined and did well with conventional dances. He convinced me to take a battery of tests and to fill out an application to UCLA for dance. He later informed me that I had been offered a full scholarship to UCLA's school of dance.

"I completed my undergraduate work with a perfect grade-point average and was offered a grant for graduate school. I have a master's degree in dance. I left Fort Myers for Las Vegas with James Rogers. When I found out how much money the MGM Grand paid its dancers, I choreographed a dance.

"My audition was a pretty normal routine. However, I added a two-and-a-half-minute break-dancing routine at the end of it. The producer and the director were blown away. They offered me a contract on the spot. Later, for the first time in Las Vegas's history, a solo break-dancing performance was added to the conclusion of a show. It brought me instant fame as a Las Vegas showgirl."

"Ruby, I have never interviewed someone with a story as interesting as yours. You rose from the streets of Fort Myers and became the top showgirl in Las Vegas. Can I ask you why you quit and returned home?"

"I made a great deal of money in the five years I worked there. I worked during the weekends and holidays. I returned to Fort Myers to fulfill a dream of mine."

"What was that dream Ruby?"

"I have a burning desire to open a social club for kids or to be the strongest supporter of the Boys and Girls Club of America in Lee County."

"The most exciting experience I've had since returning was meeting the love of my life, Lenny."

"My interview with you has left me breathless. I can't wait to observe your dance workout. What day should we have the film crew come in, Ruby?"

"Lenny, do you think the day after tomorrow would be all right?"

"I see no reason why. Thursday wouldn't work."

"Ruby, would ten in the morning work?"

"Sounds good, Sarah."

"Thank you so much, Lenny and Ruby."

"Lenny, don't you think that the interview and video will be a good thing? A little publicity can't hurt, especially since I'm planning on doing charitable work."

"I agree, Ruby. A little fame is helpful when you're building support for a cause."

"I did not include you in my plans, Lenny."

"You are scaring me, Ruby. What does that mean?"

"I want to have time to share with you. I don't want to surrender so much time to my cause that it becomes an obsession. For the first time in my life, I am happy, and it's because of you, Lenny. My priority is sharing my time with you.

"I have seen too many relationships destroyed by the toils of business. I will not jeopardize our relationship with the stress that comes with a business—and besides, we don't need the money. My other concern is Betty. Since Lewis died, we have an obligation to Betty. Betty's desire is to purchase a huge house or to enlarge her house such that it will accommodate our expanded family.

"Also, we need to be available to help at the bank if we're asked to."

"I completely agree with you, Ruby."

"Do we ever disagree, Lenny? Do you believe always agreeing is healthy for a relationship?"

"I do, Ruby. Our connection is by no means average. Do you remember the song 'I Can't Get Enough of Your Love,' by Barry White? When I look at you, it plays in my mind. What are we going to do, Ruby?"

"You and I should enjoy every moment together for the rest of our lives, Lenny."

"I could not have said it any better myself!"

■ ■ ■

LENNY LEAVES HIS APARTMENT AND MOVES INTO BETTY'S HOUSE

"We are home, Betty."

"Did you and Ruby have nice workouts?"

"We had very good workouts, Betty. I'm going to vacate my apartment, Betty, while you and Ruby go driving. I will need to make several trips to Goodwill. I'm going to donate my worldly possessions. My books are the only possessions I care about. They will fill the van."

"Lenny, the books will be a wonderful addition to our library," Betty said.

"I will have only the clothes on my back when I return."

"Poor little Lenny," Ruby said, laughing.

"Damn, Ruby. Don't be so cold!"

"Lenny, I'm going to restyle you with some more fashionable twenty-first-century apparel. You are going to enjoy a total makeover."

"Now I'm frightened, Ruby!"

"Oh, Betty, do you want me to pick up some fresh shrimp while I'm at the beach? The shrimp fleet is in. I can buy it straight from the boat. You can't get any that's fresher!"

"That would make a great dinner, Lenny. Pick up ten pounds. Bob and Gloria will be here by the time you are back. What we don't eat, we can freeze."

"I love you two beautiful women. Bye-bye!"

I'm on my way to finish another chapter of my life. This will be the last time I go to the place where I started over without Mary Gibson.

There were many esoteric experiences in my life. Some were good, and some were not so good. Each experience represents a change in my life's direction. Add together all of these experiences, and you'll have the man that I have become.

I was sleeping here when Ruby Ridge rode into town and chose me. Her charm reset my mind and showed me the positive side of life. Before she appeared, I was running low on hope.

My journey ended at the end of an imaginary rainbow in Fort Myers. I thank Abraham Maslow, a developmental psychologist, for his hierarchy of needs pyramid, which I've used for guidance.

LENNY'S LYRICAL

Every item I donated to Goodwill represented a place or a time in my life. One memory led to another. When the Veteran died, I lost the only person who could relate to every event of my life. We had similar experiences from our births to his death. I've always had a problem communicating with the average person.

The Veteran was no average, run-of-the-mill person. The Veteran and I experienced events in our lives that only one in one million people could ever imagine. We relied on each other when bothersome thoughts revealed themselves to us unexpectedly—especially when those thoughts were about our horrid experiences in Vietnam.

Our in-depth conversations over the years provided us some relief from the ingrained pain of combat. Thoughts of killing others and of young bodies torn apart would return to us over and over, usually late at night when we were all alone.

The challenge was to learn how to live in a never-ending horror movie. I was not doing a good job of coping before the Veteran appeared.

He applied a bandage to my mental wounds, and his consoling words helped me face the rest of my life.

He confessed that what he'd done for me had also worked for him. When the Veteran died, I was concerned about whether I could continue to cope without his presence. The first few nights were scary. I felt victimized.

I felt like a child who had lost his comfort blanket.

I was barely surviving. Much of my energy was focused on keeping myself mentally healthy. During that period, I accomplished nothing. I spent a lot of time thinking of new distractions for the coming days. I was continuously analyzing myself.

I knew that if I could just hang on, time would become my savior. I sometimes imagined that I had a broken leg and that it was just a matter of time before it would heal and I would soon be running again. I eventually realized that my living performance hadn't exceeded 50 percent of my capability since my wife, Mary Gibson, died a horrible death. I rationalized by thinking that no one operates at 100 percent of their capability and that most people don't even know they're capable of doing more. Ignorance does not know what you don't know.

I sometimes thought, in my lowest moments, that ignorance was a desirable virtue, and I would wish for it. I would later celebrate the fact that my wish had not come true. I must admit that during those moments, I was close to the edge. This up-and-down lifestyle stayed with me for an amount of time that I would not feel comfortable revealing. Everyone has heard someone say that things have a way of working out.

That's exactly what happened when Ruby Ridge chose me. My function ability immediately became 100 percent. I wonder what the Veteran would have said about me running at full throttle? We once promised each other that whoever arrived to where we were going first would save the seat beside him for the other.

I decided that I wanted to change that seating arrangement. I wanted to ask him to save three seats: one for Betty, one for me, and one for Ruby.

"Rest in peace," I said.

WHAT IS GOING ON WITH BETTY, RUBY, GLORIA, BOB, HAROLD, AND LENNY?

"Betty, you ready to practice driving?"

"I can't wait to start, Ruby."

"I know where a large industrial parking lot is. Several of the larger businesses moved out, so there's open space that we can practice in before we hit the open highway. It's not far away, Betty."

"That sounds good."

"I will park here and change seats with you. Let's go over all of the car's features. Ask me questions if you don't fully understand the features after I demonstrate them. Betty, if you know what the features do, start the car. Move forward and stop, and then move the car in reverse and stop. Then drive around in the parking lot and find a space to park in.

"Parallel park in one of those marked parking spaces. That's not quite right, Betty. Do it a few times to get the hang of it. That's it. You nailed it, Betty. I don't think you've forgotten anything. Let's hit the downtown area and then the freeway. You are ready, Betty."

"I did drive for sixty years. It's hard to forget after that many years, Ruby."

"Drive us home, Betty."

"Thank you, Ruby. Can we have tea and talk?"

"We can. I noticed that you didn't use your cane."

"My legs are as strong as they have ever been. I'm doing two hundred squats a day. Now that I have recovered my balance, I'm as good as new."

"When is Will going to take you down to the DMV?"

"The day after tomorrow."

"Then we will go driving again tomorrow, Betty. It will help to do a few more hours of driving before the test. I'll give Will a call to let him know that we'll be keeping the Fit. Betty, do you remember Detective Ray?"

"I certainly do."

"Lenny and I had dinner with him and his wife, Barbara. They are a nice couple. He plans to run for sheriff in the near future, Betty. I was thinking about inviting them to our family gathering. What do you think?"

"Lenny and I spent time with Detective Ray when we went to the police station to identify Lenny's assailant. I was impressed by his professionalism. He can count me in for a campaign contributor. My instincts tell me he is an honorable public servant. We need more good people to become involved in running for offices in all areas of government."

"Then I will extend an invitation to him."

"I agree, Ruby. Now tell me how you and Lenny are doing."

"It is magical, Betty. We're both having trouble focusing on other matters of importance when we're together. All we care to do is entertain each other. Thank you, Betty, for matching us up. Lenny literally brought me back from the brink of giving up on my sexuality. Please try to understand this confession: My first sexual experience with Lenny was my first sexual experience that was motivated by love."

"He gave you what you thought you would never have, right, Ruby?"

"It is my opinion that he performed a miracle on me, and he expects nothing in return."

"That's Lenny's nature."

"How did you know we would gel?"

"I know both of you so well that it's like you're my own kids. When it came to behavior, Lewis and Lenny were one and the same. I saw that you two were made for each other the first time I saw you together."

"Now it's my turn to ask you a question about your love life, Betty. What is going on with you and Harold? Tell me more about him."

"Harold was my best friend—or that was the way I preferred to see him. He was always there for Lewis and me. I knew he felt differently toward me. It took a lifetime for me to get over the loss of my husband, Bill.

"When Lewis died, I realized that we all need somebody. That realization motivated me to start corresponding with Harold in a more passionate way. When I felt sure I was going to recover, I invited him down. He had already started preparing my case against the VA. I finally acknowledged that Harold loved me. He had never given up on me.

"I saw you and Lenny together. Your happiness convinced me to share my remaining time with Harold if he would still have me."

"Wow, Betty. I am so happy for you!"

"Good afternoon, Bob and Gloria. I thought that you two would be stopping in. Lenny is picking up ten pounds of fresh gulf shrimp at the beach. We're going to have a shrimp fest, and you are invited. Good to see you, Bob. How are you and Gloria doing?"

"Quite well, Betty. Gloria and I have been enjoying each other ever since we met."

"Betty and Ruby, we have an announcement. We are engaged! Look at the ring I received from Bob."

"Very nice. Congratulations! I took Betty out today to practice driving."

"How did you do, Betty?" Bob asked.

"It felt great. It's like riding a bicycle—you never forget."

"When are you planning to take the test, Betty?"

"Will is taking me down on his day off, the day after tomorrow."

"If you buy a car, you know that my bank would love to do the financing."

"Thank you, Bob. But this time around, I plan to pay cash."

"By the way, Bob, when can Mom and I come down to refinance her home?" Ruby asked.

"I will be in a meeting most of the day tomorrow, so how about the next day? Does that sound OK for you and your mom?"

"Sure, Bob."

"Call me when you're coming, and I'll have everything ready."

"I will call you tomorrow for sure, Bob," Ruby said.

BETTY UPDATES BOB ON THE COMMUNITY-BANK CHARTER

"Bob, have you looked into the syndicate of investors that approached you about chartering a bank?"

"Yes, I did, Betty."

"What did they say to you?"

"They asked me for more details, Betty."

"What details do you need?"

"They want to know how much money they will need to prepare the charter. They want to know the amount of start-up money required to satisfy the demands of Florida's banking regulatory agency."

"There is much more to qualifying for a charter than money, Bob. The family has already created a limited liability corporation to handle these matters. Once I have the mailing addresses of your investors, a packet containing the state's requirements and the details of the partnership will be delivered through certified mail to them. Every detail is outlined and explained therein. When can you supply me with their addresses?"

"I have their address in my briefcase, which is in the car. I will fetch my briefcase now."

"You may tell these investors that they will need a minimum of twelve million dollars. Of course, the details are explained in the packet. Harold, the family's lawyer, will be here in the next thirty days or so. He will be available twenty-four-seven for any further questions that the investors may have. He will handle the legal concerns and represent the charter before the state authorities.

"We will discuss sharing the dividends when we have letters of intent, meaning that they have to show us the money that they intend to invest. The family's LLC will be responsible for satisfying the state's requirements, including, if necessary, our attorney will speak to the state charter-approving committee on the bank's behalf. We will supply legal information about all of these concerns.

"We will contribute the majority of the money. At this time, I will not tell you the amount of the family's financial contribution. If you are asked about the amount of money that the family intends to contribute, your answer— 'I do not know'—will be the truth. I will be the chairman of the board."

"The family's LLC will be the majority stockholder. You will be the bank's president. Gloria will be the CFO. If anything happens to me, Lenny will sit in my seat with all of the privileges of the chairman of the board.

"Bob, the family is one for all, and all for one! You do your part, Bob, and the family will take care of you. Do you have any further questions?"

"No, Betty, everything is quite clear."

"Then let's be social! Gloria, you are familiar with everything. Will you please fix Bob a drink? Let's celebrate your engagement."

"Ruby, play some music, please, and give Will and Bailey a call and ask them to come over. Oh, I see that Bailey's car is in the yard."

BOB IS ENLIGHTENED ABOUT BETTY AND HAROLD'S FINANCES

"Sorry it took so long, Betty. The traffic was heavy going over the bridge to the beach. I was successful in purchasing twelve pounds of fresh gulf shrimp."

"Bob, we are running late. Will you assist Lenny with the butane burner and the large pot? Thank you, Bob. That would be appreciated," Betty said.

"Lenny, I just had the shock of my life."

"What was that with, Bob?"

"Betty told me about her bank plan."

"Don't tell me, Bob—let me guess. You were fascinated by Betty's knowledge on the matter."

"She does her research thoroughly."

"Get used to it, Bob. Betty knows everything! That's why she's the head of the family. Did she provide you with the answers you were looking for?"

"She had it perfectly laid out. I was flabbergasted by the financial knowledge she has."

"She alone could supply the money for the bank, Bob."

"Betty does not appear to be financially well off. She lives an average-looking lifestyle."

"Bob, Betty has invested wisely over the last sixty years with her boyfriend, Harold. I do not know how much they're worth, but I can assure you that their combined wealth is astonishing. Betty did mention Harold, didn't she?"

"No, she did not."

"Harold is her lifelong boyfriend. Harold filed a wrongful death suit for twenty-five million dollars against the VA. Lewis, her son, was a veteran and acquired a deadly infection while in the VA hospital.

"The Centers for Disease Control and Prevention states that at least one hundred thousand patients die each year and that at least fifty percent of these deaths could be prevented in hospitals. Another two million patients are seriously harmed in hospitals throughout the United States.

"The VA's internal investigation found that the deadly strain of bacteria that killed the Veteran was endemic in the operating room. Hospital personnel not washing their hands or properly disinfecting equipment primarily cause bacteria infections.

"The VA defense team has already admitted fault and has offered a five-million-dollar out-of-court settlement. It won't be long before an acceptable settlement will be reached. The VA will not go to court. Its reputation for veteran care is at an all-time low.

"The community-bank plans were already in motion. They came to an abrupt halt when Lewis, her son, unexpectedly died. It appears that she put the plans in high gear after his death."

"I sure was lucky when Gloria strolled into my office, Lenny. I have found the love of my life and a once-in-a-lifetime opportunity all in a matter of a couple of weeks."

"Things happen when you are associated with Betty Anderson, Bob."

BOB AND LENNY TALK PERSONAL MATTERS
"Lenny, can I ask you a personal question?"

"It depends on the question, but either way, I won't be offended."

"What is it like to have a girlfriend like Ruby? I mean, is it difficult socially to be with a woman who attracts so much attention? She is stunningly beautiful!"

"I am asked that question on a regular basis, Bob. It does not bother me in the least to answer it. I know how sexy Ruby is. It is her nature to flaunt her sexuality. I have learned to enjoy her exhibitionism. I feel lucky that she picked me to be her hanger-on.

"In the beginning, I couldn't believe she'd chosen me. And as if that were not enough, Bob, she turned out to be the most intelligent women I have ever known, with the exception of Betty and my late wife, Mary Gibson.

"Betty was responsible for Ruby's intellectual development. Gloria worked long hours when she was young. Ruby stayed with Betty for most of her younger years. You could say that Betty was Ruby's mentor. I don't question the relationship now. I'm just thankful for every day that Ruby is at my side."

"Thanks, Lenny, for accommodating my discourteous question. I do apologize."

"No apology needed, Bob. I would like to congratulate you. I have never seen Gloria as happy as she has been since you entered her life. I don't believe she will disappoint you. She is very content with the relationship."

"We both feel that our relationship picked up where it left off in high school. Gloria said to me soon after we met that I'm the same now as I was then. I felt the same with her. We have been in love since we first met."

"You never had any children?"

"I was working my way up in banking, and my wife was a high school teacher. We were career oriented. When we decided to try for a family, we were not successful.

"After spending months with different doctors, we found that she was in the later part of perimenopause. The doctors recommended using fertility drugs. During her fertility examination, they discovered that she had cervical cancer and that it had metastasized throughout her body. After her death, I longed for a fresh start. I took the bank-president position here in Fort Myers."

"We all have good things going on now in our lives. Think about it, Bob. You will not only be the president of a bank but also own a considerable amount of stock in it. Welcome to Betty's family, Bob! Let's get this shrimp boiling and celebrate our good fortune."

"I agree with that, Lenny."

BETTY MEETS BAILEY AND JONI

"Hey, everybody, look who decided to join us—Will and Bailey," Gloria said.

"Bailey, give me a hug," Betty said. "Is this Joni? She is beautiful. Joni, my name is Betty. Can I be your friend? You can play with Breezy and Jojo. They love small people."

"I like puppies," Joni said. "Mommy, can I play with the puppies?"

"Go ahead, but you must stay in the house."

"Tell me what you three have been doing."

"When Joni is not in school, we go sightseeing and explore southwest Florida. We have been visiting preserves, museums, beaches, and landmarks. We want to become more knowledgeable about the environment we're living in."

"You are becoming a Floridian, Bailey."

"We love it here."

"Will, do you have any good news?"

"I have fantastic news, Betty. Bailey and I have decided to move in together at my place. The timing is perfect. Bailey's lease is up this month. We both love being a part of a neighborhood rather than an apartment complex.

"We can save money by eliminating one rent payment and one grocery bill and by riding to work together."

"Most of all, we'll be close to the family," Bailey said.

"You two have me really excited now! When both of you are next door, we'll have more quality time together too. I would love to babysit Joni."

"That would be so appreciated, Betty."

"You know, Ruby stayed with me for most of her younger years. We spent much of our time reading and playing games."

"I bet that was the reason she excelled in school and received many college scholarships," Will said.

"Ruby was a good student," Betty said.

"Betty, is it true that the family is looking into establishing a community bank?"

"We are in the process of doing that."

"I'm impressed, Betty."

"I suppose that you have heard about my boyfriend, Harold?"

"Yes, we have, Betty. I speak with Ruby daily," Bailey said. "We have become best friends."

"I am so happy for you kids!"

"Will informed me of the family's motto, 'one for all, and all for one.' Will and I share a commonality. We are both orphans. Having a family is new to us, Betty. Will is so grateful that he met you and became a member of your family."

THE FAMILY DINNER

"The shrimp is ready. Everyone take a seat at the table. We have a new couple to introduce. Please welcome Art and Barbara Ray. Art is with the sheriff's department. His investigation led to the arrest of Lenny's assailant. Art plans to run for sheriff in the near future.

"As is our custom, I've put the shrimp in the center of the table on brown paper. Clean the shrimp before you eat it. If you've never popped the head, shucked the scales, and cleaned the intestinal tract, then speak up. An experienced Florida shrimp eater will be glad to show you the procedure," Betty said.

"When we're done eating, we'll roll up the remains in the brown paper and dispose of them. Everyone is responsible for his or her drink." People, let's get busy eating," Betty said.

"After brunch, I plan to teach ballroom dancing," Ruby said. "What dance would you prefer to learn, Bailey?"

"The dance you see kings and queens doing in the movies."

"That would be a smooth ballroom dance, Bailey."

"Count Barbara and me in on this session, Ruby."

"Examples of that kind of dancing include the fox-trot, the waltz, the tango, the Viennese waltz, and the quickstep. The partners stay together and gracefully move in a counterclockwise direction over the entire dance floor."

"I have always wanted to know how to dance that way, Ruby. Will would love to dance in that fashion too."

"Then that's what we'll do, Bailey!"

"When you're ready, I will teach you and Will the waltz. It is a dance that exemplifies formality. It is our favorite dance.

"Even Betty has been practicing the waltz. She wants to master the foxtrot, the hustle, and the tango before Harold arrives. Those are dances that allow you to mostly stay in one place and to dance separately from your partner. They are energetic, sexy, and exciting. When Will is ready, you let me know, Bailey."

"Betty, Barbara and I want you to know how much we enjoyed the food and Ruby's dance lessons. Thank you for inviting us."

"The family looks forward to financially supporting your bid for sheriff," Betty said.

■ ■ ■

WELCOME HOME FROM VIETNAM (1969)

I will never forget the day I arrived home from Vietnam, forty-seven years ago. Angry protesters lined both sides of the entrance to the terminal. I exited the aircraft and used a *Sports Illustrated* magazine to shield myself from the protesters who were spitting at me. I had no family to meet me at the gate and no home to go to like the other men had. I had been somebody in Vietnam, but then I was just something to spit on.

I did not have a girlfriend when I left. I did receive letters from Mary Gibson from time to time. She was an unusual friend I'd made in Atlanta, Georgia, a month and a half before I'd entered the army. I would show pictures of her when other men shared their pictures of their girlfriends or wives. I did not want any of the other men to know that I didn't have anyone waiting for me.

I had been on my own since the age of seventeen. Being alone seemed perfectly normal to me. Vietnam veterans were branded as drug addicts, baby killers, and losers. Someone had to be blamed for losing the war.

The establishment decided to make the soldiers the sacrificial lambs. Of course, the politicians and the fat cats making all of the money claimed that they'd had nothing to do with keeping the war going instead of winning it. The government-influenced media portrayed us as losers to shield the corrupt politicians.

One of the worst tragedies of the Vietnam War was when a lieutenant named William Calley Jr. ordered his men to massacre between three hundred and five hundred unarmed Vietnamese citizens. The dead included men, women, children, and infants. It was called the My Lai Massacre, and the story was widely reported all over the United States.

This event happened in March 1968 and was solely responsible for the belief that Vietnam soldiers were baby killers. Indeed, one bad apple spoils the bunch! Many businesses and educational institutions were discriminating against Vietnam veterans. Even some VA clinics did not welcome Vietnam veterans when they requested help.

In some areas of the United States, the police were known to harass and lock up Vietnam veterans for frivolous charges. The prisons were full, many veterans were homeless, and a disproportionate number of them were unemployed.

At all times during the Vietnam conflict, there were 37 million males between the ages of eighteen and thirty-five. Of this group, approximately 2.6 million males served in Vietnam. From the beginning of the war to the present it has been estimated that one hundred and fifty-two thousand Vietnam veterans have committed suicide.

No official statistics were recorded for suicides for any prior wars the United States were involved in until recently. The use of Agent Orange and experimental biological warfare by the Central Intelligent Agency (CIA) was highly classified in Vietnam and was denied for decades. It was years later that the alarming suicide rate of Vietnam veterans were noticed when mental health clinics were expanded at the VA to treat specifically Vietnam veterans who had been exposed to various unknown chemicals.

Even to this day the CIA denies the arial spraying of experimental mind-altering chemicals in Vietnam, with one exception, Agent Orange. Of course, these statistics were compiled retrospectively and unofficially by various concerned persons and organizations without the CIA's cooperation. The CIA contends that these accusations are only conspiracy theories. Like always and to be expected, clandestine government organization hide their wrongdoings by classifying their horrid actions under the disguise of top secret.

It is my opinion that these above-noted statistics are low. Furthermore, it is reasonable to assume we will never know the truth nor the harm these many secret organizations do. When they do report publicly, history has proven that what they report is only propaganda that serves their best interest.

IN SEARCH OF A HOME

After processing out of the army, I decided that my destination would be Florida. I intended to use the GI Bill to return to school. Getting a quality education would be a good way to start the rest of my life. Furthermore, it would give me time to do a postmortem on my nightmare problem.

One of the most difficult decisions I had to make was whether to reveal or not to reveal in this story the events that caused my nightmares and the confusion I experienced in my young mind soon after returning from Vietnam. I do know it is the most personal experience I have ever lived through. No matter what you tell yourself, the doubts creep in, usually late at night when you are alone. The thought that you might have to pay a price for the life you took in battle will not leave you alone.

I must inform you that the Vietnam veteran was the last American soldier to kill up close. I'm talking about hand-to-hand combat. You can't get more personal than looking a man in the eye screaming while you are ramming a knife in and out of his body as fast as you can to kill him before he kills you. You take that face to bed with you for the rest of your life. Imagine going through an experience like that over and over. If it does not bother you, you would have to be insane!

How many times has the average person accepted that he was going to die, made his peace, and surprisingly survived? Have this experience a couple of times and I promise you afterward you want be the same person you were. Since my Vietnam experience I find it hard to kill a fly in my house.

I managed to hitch a jet from Vietnam to California, where I processed out of the Army. I wanted to see what was going on. I decided the best way to do this was to hitchhike my way to Florida. In the late sixties and the seventies, hitchhiking was a popular way for young people to travel and to see the country. I caught a ride with a trucker who had turned north outside of Sierra Vista, Arizona. I was going straight east, so I thanked him for the ride.

As I climbed out of the truck, I remembered that at the discharge orientation, we'd been told to travel in civilian clothes and in pairs. I was alone and wearing bell-bottom jeans, a tank top, and combat boots. What I had on was all that I owned. At the processing center, everybody had been talking about the movie *Easy Rider*. I thought I'd stop at one of the towns I was planning to go through and see it.

VIETNAM VETERANS HAVE THEIR REASONS FOR DISLIKING AUTHORITY

Many minorities and poor people do not like cops. Most police departments target the indigent and minority populations and charge them with petty fines as a way to earn money to serve the criminal justice system, which is run by corrupt lawyers and judges.

These citizens are found guilty because they have little money, and the criminal justice system requires one to spend large sums of money to prove his innocence. That was what I heard from minorities, especially black soldiers, with whom I served in Vietnam. I agreed with them.

The modern civil rights movement began on December 1, 1955, when an Afro-American woman named Rosa Parks was arrested for refusing to move to the back of a public bus in Montgomery, Alabama.

Could this feeling of disrespect for authority be connected to how minorities and poor people are treated by society in general and by its criminal justice system in particular? These same cops and the same criminal justice system treated Vietnam veterans very similarly when they returned home.

The police arrested them on frivolous charges and beat them, and in many cases, the courts gave them longer-than-normal prison sentences. The VA refused them health care, and businesses refused them jobs. The public blindly believed the lies of the government-influenced media, and many turned their heads.

Even today many Vietnam veterans still have no respect for authority because of the way they were abused when they returned home from Vietnam. Personally, I need no help understanding why people spit on me when I returned home from Vietnam. I am told to forgive them because they did not know the news media had lied to them to protect the elite. Ignorance is not an acceptable excuse. I hold the average American, the police, the courts, the VA, the mainstream media, and the government in contempt and always will.

When I see people of that age that did not go to Vietnam, I think about spitting on them. Of course, I would never do to them what they did to me. I am better than that. That is only a figment of my imagination. However, I do believe that the U.S. Congress should apologize and pass a bill to pay reparations to all Vietnam veterans, especially to the families of the more than fifty-eight thousand people who died needlessly. No other veterans in U.S. history were as mistreated as the Vietnam veterans.

CAUGHT BY A COP BEING A VIETNAM VETERAN (1969)

I had saved $7,000 while in Vietnam so that I could start my life. For security reasons, I kept my money coiled around the inside of my combat boots. I only kept a few dollars in my pocket in case I was robbed.

I pointed my thumb east. The first car to pull over was a police car. A large middle-aged policeman with a potbelly demanded to know where I was going.

"I was just passing through on my way to school in Florida."

He said nothing and just looked me over. Then he said, "Are you a Vietnam veteran?"

"I am."

"You have any weapons or drugs on you?"

"No, Officer. No weapons or drugs."

"Are you here to purchase drugs?"

"No way," I said.

"Then you are a vagrant."

"I don't intend to hang around. I will leave in the first car that stops, Officer."

"If you don't have fifty dollars in cash on you, then according to one of this city's ordinances, you are a vagrant."

"I have money." He then told me that if I didn't show it to him, he would arrest me for vagrancy.

I reached into my pocket and pulled out my money. He ordered me to count out $50 in full view. I counted out $41. He then said, "Forty-one is not fifty. Turn around, and put your hands behind you. You are under arrest."

"No, Officer, I have more money!"

"You've got one minute to show me the rest of the fifty dollars. Keep your hands where I can see them."

I bent over and unlaced one of my boots. I reached in with my forefinger and thumb to take out one bill. When I pulled on it, several one-hundred-dollar bills fell to the ground. His eyes widened, and he said, "How much money do you have in your boots?"

"I have about seven thousand dollars. I saved it while I was in Vietnam so that I could start my life as a student."

"Bullshit. If you are a Vietnam veteran, you're a drug dealer." He repeated his order for me to turn around and to put my hands behind my back. He handcuffed me. He then called our physical address in, and he was told to stand fast.

GOONS FROM THE UNITED STATES TREASURY DEPARTMENT (1969)

A few minutes later, men who were dressed like hippies but carrying automatic weapons surrounded me.

"United States Treasury Department agents! Get your ass flat on the ground!" they said.

The road was burning me. I lifted my face to keep it from burning. One of the agents pushed the barrel of his weapon into my temple and forced the side of my face against the hot concrete. I could smell the pavement cooking the side of my face.

"How does that feel, you chickenshit baby killer?" he said.

They handcuffed my hands and ankles and rolled me over. I felt the skin on my cheek rip from my face. They removed my boots and gathered the money. Then three of them stood me up, dragged me over to a car, and threw me into its backseat.

They told the local policeman that they would take it from there and come back to take care of him. I knew when I heard that I would be lucky to ever see my money again.

"You can't arrest me. You haven't charged me with a crime," I said. Both of them laughed. "I need my face to be taken care of. I have no skin on my cheek," I said. I was told that if I didn't shut up, I would not have any skin left on the other cheek. "Where are you taking me?" I asked.

The man in the passenger's seat told the driver to pull over. They opened both doors, grabbed me on both sides, turned me onto my head, and stuffed me upside down between the back of the front and the rear seat. The man in the passenger seat said, "Did you know that President Johnson declared a war on drugs and martial law? Do you know what that means? I will tell you. Constitutional rights are suspended within twenty miles of the Mexican border. We can do anything we want to your sorry Vietnam baby–killing ass without being questioned.

"We are taking you out to a remote place in the desert. There we will give you one last chance to tell us whom you were going to buy drugs from." I was beginning to feel like I had in combat when I'd accepted that I was going to die. I said to myself that I would die with honor.

"Hey, you pieces of shit!" I said. "I'll tell you what! Unshackle me, and I'll kick both of your draft-dodging asses. You are badasses when I'm cuffed, but I think both of you are chickenshit draft dodgers. Your daddies got you jobs with the government so that you wouldn't have to go to Vietnam.

"You want to play 'who's your daddy?' My daddy is a hardworking, patriotic man. I would bet your daddies are corrupt politicians or ass-kissing political hacks with influence. I killed better men than you in combat. At least they faced me and died like men. Do you think I'm scared to die? Fuck you."

"Drive off the road a mile or so into the desert," the man in the passenger's seat said. "We're going to let you dig your own grave."

"Fuck you!" I said. "You'll have to shoot me, you chickenshit 4-F." The car came to a stop. The driver turned the engine off, and they both got out. They left the window closest to me cracked open.

"How long do you think it will take the desert heat to kill him?" one of them said.

"I bet he won't last thirty minutes in this heat with the windows rolled up." He then put his mouth up against the small crack in the window and said, "You ready to tell us from whom and where you were going to buy drugs?"

I knew I couldn't last much longer in the heat. As I had a few times in combat, I made peace with myself and prepared to die. I then said what I thought would be my last words: "Fuck you, you bastards! I'll kill you in hell!"

I have to remind you here that this really happened. That's how your government operated then, and sadly, it's even worse now!

LIVING IN A BOX FOR THIRTY DAYS (1969)

I woke up strapped down to a table and guarded in a hospital. I asked myself how many times I could cheat death. The doctor entered and asked how I was feeling.

"Alive!" I said.

I was shackled and transferred to a temporary lockup run by the United States Treasury Department. My cell was a small tank with no lights or windows. At the back of the tank, there was a small trapdoor. It opened, and sitting just outside of it were three containers.

"Reach out, and pull them inside," someone said. I did, and the door shut. The tall container contained water, the wide bowl contained what looked like a beef stew with a whole carrot in it, and the larger container was for excretions. There was no toilet paper. I did not drink all of my water. I used it to clean my butt with my hand after defecating.

The door opened again, and the voice said, "Push the containers out." It closed again and later opened again. The voice said, "Pull the containers in." Then the door closed. That happened twice a day. Twenty-nine days and thirty nights went by.

I was never allowed out of the tank. Early in the morning of the thirtieth day, a voice said. "Move away from the door to the back wall." The door opened, and I was handcuffed.

I was taken to a room, my handcuffs were removed, and I was locked inside the room. The room contained a shower, a complete change of clothes, and a pair of tennis shoes that were my size. After I had showered and dressed, a man came to the window in the door and told me to face the wall with my hands behind my back. I was handcuffed again.

Two men took me outside the perimeter fence and removed my handcuffs. They said I could go. I asked where my money was. I was told that I didn't have any money and that if I didn't leave, I'd be put back into the tank for another thirty days. I knew there was no chance of recovering my money, so I walked away.

I had avoided dying or being captured while fighting in a war for my country, but I could not avoid being arrested, incarcerated, and ridiculed by the US government and its citizens simply because I had fought in that war.

WHO DIES AND FOR WHAT?

Why is it always the lower-and middle-class young men who make the ultimate sacrifice? This was the Veteran's take on war: The old men who benefit financially from the decision to plunder sovereign countries for money should occasionally lose their lives too.

Additionally, it should be mandatory for their sons and daughters to go first. You know, just like in the old movies, the rich should lead the charge. I'm talking to you, Congress! Oh, and let's not forget the stockholders of the factories who support the military industrial complex, and that includes the gluttonous women who invest in war-manufacturing products, which are major propellants of wars. Shame on them!

∎∎∎

BETTY SECURES HER DRIVER'S LICENSE, AND THE FAMILY COMES TOGETHER (PRESENTLY)

Will took Betty to the Florida DMV for her appointment. She passed the eye test with no problem and received a perfect score on the driving test.

Betty had mostly been concerned about the eye test. The diet-and-exercise program that Lewis and I had devised had obviously improved her vision too. Betty deserved most of the credit, as she had stuck to a rigorous diet-and-exercise regimen for a year. Betty was actually cured, which would have been impossible if she'd used drug therapies.

The person who examined her eyes was amazed that she got a perfect score without the use of glasses. She said that Betty was the first woman of her age to get a perfect score since she'd begun giving eye examinations.

Ruby deposited two hundred thousand dollars into Bob's bank for collateral and cosigned a refinance note with Gloria on her home. The lower interest rate cut her monthly payments in half. Gloria was jubilant! Her doom-and-gloom attitude of the last few months had passed. She had her daughter home, she was engaged to be married, she had a serious job with Hertz, and she could make easy-to-live-with payments on her home. "Life is good," Gloria said.

Ruby and I had been so busy over the last few days with our different schedules that we had not had time to say good morning or good night to each other. For the first time in my life, I feared being alone. I was not alone in thought. Ruby had set her phone up to text me the same message every other hour: "I love you and miss you!"

I said, "It feels so good?"

"Hi, Betty, and hello, Gloria. What have you ladies been doing?"

"Lenny, Gloria and I have been looking at cars all day."

"What do you like, Betty?"

"I would prefer something large. I feel safe when I am surrounded by plenty of steel. A larger car is safer. I like the large Buick SUV. I do live in Florida, so white or silver will be cooler. There's too much sun to buy a dark color."

"When do you plan to purchase it, Betty?"

"I told the salesperson I would call him when I was ready."

"Betty, where's Ruby?"

"She went to the grocery store, Lenny. She said the butcher told her that today their supplier would be delivering fresh grass-fed and grass-finished rib-eye steaks."

"Your mentioning that makes me salivate, Betty."

"Bailey and Will will be dining with us this evening."

"Joni is having fun playing with Breezy and Jojo. Lenny, that's all she talks about—going to see Breezy and Jojo," Bailey said.

"Will had a few errands to run. He won't be long."

"I'm sure he'll enjoy watching the NBA finals with Ruby and me."

"Lenny, I like basketball too," Bailey said.

"Wow, then we will have a foursome. Gloria, are you going to hang around for the game?"

"Bob will be here soon. I'll let you know. Bob will be working with me on the bank-charter application."

"Will and Bob are here," Bailey said.

"Hi, everyone," Will said.

"Will, was Bob outside when you came in?"

"Yeah, he was on the phone."

"OK," Gloria said.

"What took you so long, Bob?"

"Today was a very busy day for the bank. I had many clients. Betty, I'm really sorry. Did you receive the financial data you needed from my investors?"

"Yes, I did, Bob."

"Oh, good. How does it look, Betty?"

"So far, so good! Pull up a seat," Betty said.

"Ruby, do you need help?"

"There are more bags in the car, Lenny."

"I'll bring the rest of them in. You can start getting the steaks ready to throw on the fire."

"I will help too," Bailey said.

"Hello, everyone. The local news station is doing a lifestyle feature on Ruby's workout after this advertisement. A representative from the station recorded Ruby's workout routine at the gym. She does a thirty-minute break-dancing routine for exercise four days a week and does weight training for her upper body two days a week. If you have not seen this routine, you should take a look."

"Lenny, you are embarrassing me," Ruby said.

"I want to see this," Betty said.

"I think we all do!" Bob said.

The food was delicious, the Cavaliers lost to the Warriors, and everyone was amazed by Ruby's dance on the local evening news.

■ ■ ■

THE RISE OF CIVILIZATION AND THE AGRICULTURAL AND INDUSTRIAL REVOLUTIONS

"Lenny, I'm starting an organic garden in the back yard," Bailey said. "Gloria said that that would be OK with her. I obtained information from the library on how to garden and located a store where I could purchase my seeds. I have a question for you, Lenny."

"What is your question?"

"I have really been getting into gardening. I'm curious about how farming began. Will told me that you would know the answer. I'm just curious, Lenny."

"Bailey, farming developed slowly over a long period of time. This period of development is referred to as the 'agricultural revolution.' I will give you the short version. The last ice age ended around twelve thousand years ago.

"The weather became warm, consistent, and seasonal. It is thought that around this time, hunter-gatherers began to experiment with gathering seeds and planting crops. Hunter-gatherers discovered that certain plants could be cultivated and eventually cross-pollinated with other plants. These hybrid versions were larger and tastier. Certain animals were captured, domesticated, and prepared for human consumption.

"Once plants had been cultivated and wild animals had been domesticated, they became dependent on men for survival, which created the farmer. Farming made hunting and gathering unnecessary. Consequently, the warm weather and the available food caused a population explosion.

"The agricultural revolution spawned trade, jobs, and the growth of villages. However, many new infectious diseases developed. People lived in close contact with animals, and numerous people would all live together in unsanitary conditions. New diseases spread and sometimes resulted in plagues that killed tens of thousands of urban residents."

"I cannot imagine carnage of that scale. Are you saying that we caught diseases like chicken pox and measles from animals?"

"Indeed, Bailey."

"I never knew that so much was caused by the agricultural revolution. Is it solely responsible for our way of life?"

"No, Bailey. It is not. The Industrial Revolution started in the early eighteenth century and lasted until the mid-nineteenth century. It first began in Great Britain. The process of manufacturing things by hand was replaced by the process of manufacturing things with machines. Factory workers began to earn hourly wages.

"Assembly lines in factories were responsible for the concept of eating three meals a day. In the beginning, workers would eat when they were hungry. This practice stopped production lines, costing time and money.

"To eliminate this problem, factory supervisors mandated that workers eat prior to working. They would be given a midday break to eat lunch, and they'd eat their last meal of the day when their work was completed.

"No longer were assembly lines held up so that people could eat. Thus, eating breakfast, lunch, and dinner became customary in our industrial economy.

"The new foods, like vegetables, fruits, and grains, that were developed by farmers through hybridism and cross-pollination are not well accepted by our primeval biology, which has slowly evolved over tens of thousands of years. These new foods cannot survive on their own in the wild, which makes them unnatural. They are in conflict with our bodies. That is not known by any of the food experts I've ever spoken with.

"Vegetables and fruits can be toxic to the human body. The United States is currently experiencing an obesity and diabetes epidemic. Never has the human species consumed these hybrid vegetables and fruits in such large amounts. They are low in fiber and rapidly become sugar, which causes the oversecretion of insulin into the bloodstream.

"The overconsumption of vegetables and fruits is a prelude to obesity. Obesity causes many diseases. The wild vegetables and fruits that humans consumed for hundreds of thousands of years contained more fiber and many times less sugar but were available for only three to four months out of the year at the most.

"Now we can consume these new, slightly toxic vegetables and fruits throughout the year. But eventually the chemicals used to protect and stimulate the growth of these vegetables and fruits accumulate in the body and cause diseases.

"The year-round availability of these unnatural domestic vegetables and fruits was made possible by the development of refrigeration and transportation during the Industrial Revolution. Vegetables and fruits grown in a favorable climate can be transported to areas that they cannot be grown in. *The overconsumption of domesticated vegetables and fruits is one of the many causes of diseases.*

"My advice is to eat quality organic vegetables and fruits in moderation. Of course, my advice would not be well received by agricultural experts. Their vested interest in the industry causes them to advocate for eating as many vegetables and fruits as you want. They would agree with the following because vegetables and fruits are not identified as sources of sugar.

"The consumption of too much sugar, especially high-fructose corn syrup, and too many starches play a significant role in the cause of obesity. The rapid environmental changes brought on by the combined effects of the agriculture and Industrial revolutions are called 'cultural evolution.'

"The science of epigenetics tells us that our genes express themselves in response to the environment. These sudden environmental changes have caused new medical conditions, including type 2 diabetes, heart disease, flat feet, smallpox, autoimmune diseases, cancer, and so on. These conditions are called 'mismatched diseases,' meaning that they don't match our current evolutionary design and are in conflict with our genes."

RUBY TEACHES THE FAMILY MEMBERS TO DANCE

"I'm sorry for the sermon, Bailey. This subject is so complicated. Short explanations are impossible."

"I enjoyed the sermon," Bailey said, laughing. "Health is important to everyone. The world of finance is quite boring."

"So is the banking world," Bob said. "I need to do more for my health. Gloria and I are planning on joining the gym."

"OK, everybody, it's time to practice the mambo and the rumba," Ruby said. "The mambo is Latin American, and the rumba is the Cuban version of it.

"They are both considered to be ballroom dances. Betty, you and Lenny will alternate as my partner. Everyone follow my steps. We will start slow, and as you become more practiced, we will increase the speed until we come to the proper rhythm.

"The first dance will be the mambo. Betty, you are getting good."

"Ruby, I have to be good. Harold has been taking ballroom-dancing classes for more than a year. When he comes, I want to be able to dance all night.

"We have a lot of time to make up for. He told me that he's waited a long time for me to come around. I lived in the past for too long, Ruby. I now am living in the present. Thanks mostly to Lewis, Lenny, and you, we have quite a family now."

"Thanks to you, Betty, I found happiness," Ruby said.

"Not one of you beautiful young people should ever worry. Harold and I will lead all of you to where you have dreamed of going, Ruby. That's the purpose of our family. We have assembled a team of knowledgeable people chock-full of varied experiences.... And knowledge is power, Ruby! Make no mistake about it—I mean that it gives you the power to do good."

"Betty, you gave excitement and hope to a group of not-so-sure people."

"Purpose is what I was referring to, Ruby. The family gives me purpose and great strength. My only regret is that Lewis is not a physical part of this family."

"Now, scram, Ruby, and take care of Lenny! You should be proud. You brought heaven to Lenny's hell!"

■ ■ ■

RELEASED FROM WRONGFUL INCARCERATION (1969)

The gate closed behind me, and I watched the Treasury Department agents disappear into the windowless building. The thoughts racing through my mind were pure evil. To remain free, I would have to reluctantly abandon any thoughts of retaliatory action and get on with my life. I won't deny my hate for the government because of this event.

These are the kind of happenings you keep to yourself for the rest of your life. Why? Well, so few people witness these types of events that to speak out about them would only bring you more harm. This discrete and out-of-the-way government compound had definitely been set up to use torture to extract information from accused drug smugglers,

The United States Treasury Department agents I encountered had the same attitude that the United States Central Intelligence Agency agents who tortured prisoners in Vietnam had had. There is no shortage of sociopaths in government.

THE FIRST CATEGORY OF SOCIOPATHS

We are taught that sometimes, a malevolent attitude toward people is caused by horrid events in one's childhood that one failed to cope with. This explanation is sometimes true for the second category of sociopaths. Nothing could be further from the truth for the first category of evil sociopaths.

Pure evil is natural for our species, and evil people walk among us. Less civilized countries hunt them down and kill them. Some, like Adolf Hitler, become leaders of countries and do great evil. They are the serial killers and mass murderers who are eventually arrested, given capital punishment, or incarcerated for life.

THE SECOND CATEGORY OF SOCIOPATHS

The luckier dangerous sociopaths are hired by intelligence agencies in governments throughout the world. Their jobs include secretly spying on, killing, or torturing people to satisfy various governments' needs. There is a double standard for government-employed sociopaths.

These sociopathic killers are admired because they kill people for righteous governments. This idea can be seen in a movie in which sociopaths are released from prison to kill for the U.S. Army. The movie is *The Dirty Dozen*. No one knows how many murders are covered up by governments or the exact amount of money that these clandestine government agencies spend.

Unbeknownst to the average citizen, the U.S. government's records show that these agencies spend around $100 billion annually. Realistically, there is no way of knowing what is actually spent. The United States has more intelligence agencies than any other country in the world. These major intelligence agencies include the CIA, the NSA, the USSS, the FBI, the DOT, the DEA, and more.

THE THIRD CATEGORY OF SOCIOPATHS

People with milder sociopathic personalities are sought by federal, state, and local law-enforcement agencies. They are rarely dangerous. These people are inconsiderate of the feelings of others. For example, when police officers set up seat-belt checks or speed traps to rob citizens and to meet their departments' financial quotas, they feel no remorse. Law enforcement's original creed, "to protect and serve," has recently become "stop and fleece people for their money"; they behave like the sheriff of Nottingham in the tales of Robin Hood and his merry men. Sociopaths have no place in government agencies or in any positions of authority in a democracy.

The covert facility that robbed me and never charged me with a crime was in the desert and fell under the jurisdiction of the Department of the Treasury. Constitutional rights are a hoax when it comes to the covert government agencies that no one knows about. They have no place in a democracy.

There was no name on this building, and it was surrounded by a chain-link fence and obviously staffed with the second category of sociopaths and with blind government loyalists. Clandestine investigating agencies fall into this category.

Furthermore, the parking lot contained normal-looking cars of different makes and different colors. The compound appeared to be some sort of private facility. I walked down the only dirt road leading away from the compound. "Now what?" I thought.

LENNY MEETS ERIC, A NAÏVE AND GULLIBLE GOVERNMENT LOYALIST (1969)

After walking for maybe ten minutes with still no end to the road in sight, a car from the compound pulled up close behind me. "Lenny, stop!" a voice said. No one had called me by name in the last thirty days. I stopped, and the car pulled up alongside of me.

"Lenny, get in. I will drive you out of here. You still have a couple of miles to the paved road."

I thought to myself that I had nothing more to lose, which reminded me that I had also been robbed of the watch I'd bought duty free overseas. It had been a Bulova Astronaut, a watch designed specifically by Bulova for the first astronauts. Forty years later, it became a priceless collectors' piece.

I got into the car and said nothing. The driver told me that his name was Eric and that he worked as a private contractor for the United States Treasury Department as a payroll clerk. "The money is very good," he said. He then apologized, saying that private contractors do not know and cannot ask about what goes on at the facility. "Most of the complex is off limits to me," Eric said.

He offered to drive me to the next county, which was outside of the twenty-mile waiver zone. "Why are you doing this for me?" I asked.

"My brother is in Vietnam."

He pulled over at a Big Boy restaurant and said, "I will buy you a meal if you'll answer a few questions about Vietnam. My family is very worried about my brother."

I agreed.

I looked up at the Big Boy holding the burger and started salivating. I had eaten only stews for the last thirty days. I ordered two Big Boy hamburgers and a large order of French fries. I will never forget how good that unhealthy food tasted.

"Lenny, how long were you in Vietnam for?"

"I did two tours."

"Did you get injured?"

"I got shot once during my second tour. I had a flesh wound. The bullet went straight through my leg, missing the bone."

"My brother is with the Ninth Infantry Division, in Bearcat."

"I was there several times, Eric. It's outside of Saigon."

"Is it a safe place?"

"Honestly, there are no places that are safe from the enemy's rockets. But it is one of the safer bases. Bearcat is heavily fortified."

"His letters tell us that rocket attacks come every night."

"They do. The bunkers protect the men from the rockets. Casualties happen only when men are caught outside of their bunkers. What is his MOS, Eric?"

"You mean his job?"

"Yes, Eric."

"He's a company clerk."

"Then tell your family that he is safe."

"Why is that?"

"He's in a double-sandbagged bunker with the CO—the commanding officer. The CO is very protected. He's like the king in chess—often the last one to go!"

"God, I can't wait to tell that to my mom. She's a nervous wreck. What about your family, Lenny?"

"I have none."

"I'm sorry."

"Don't be. It has its advantages. I don't have to worry about a family worrying about me." Eric laughed. "Do you know about my money, Eric?"

"What money?"

"The seven thousand I saved in Vietnam so that I could start my life."

"I'm a secretary confined to an office, Lenny. I never know what they're doing. I was told that you were a Vietnam veteran, that you hadn't committed a crime, and that you were being released."

"Well, the people you work for stole my money and watch."

"They are sworn federal agents, Lenny."

"Get your head out of your ass. They're thieves too."

"How are you going to make it to wherever you're going without money?"

"I'm on my way to Florida to attend school on the GI bill. Getting there is for me to worry about, not you. I appreciate all that you have done. I will leave you with a few words of wisdom: The average American is conditioned to see only what the government tells him to see. Try using your own observation skills to determine what's going on in your immediate environment.

"Nice people worked for Al Capone even though they knew he was a murderer. The truth is that people generally don't care whom they work for or what the evil their employer is doing as long as they can spend the money that they earn. It's the same with you, Eric.

"Wealthy and powerful people exploit the poor, have good getaway plans, and don't get caught, because they have privilege, influence, inside information, and connections. Good luck, Eric!"

I'm sorry to say that when I removed myself from the presence of that naïve piece of crap, I had the first good feeling I'd had since being released. He was so typical of the average American and dumb to the bone. How could anyone be in a pool of evil for eight hours a day, five days a week and not notice what was going on?

Day after day, I heard the screams and cries of people being tortured, most of whom were Spanish-speaking people. It reminded me of battle and of young men who'd been mortally wounded crying out for their mothers or their gods.

People who have no understanding of the pure evil going on around them disgust me. How could Eric not have heard their screams of pain? I waited every day for my time to be tortured. I guess that I was lucky or that after the desert situation, they realized I was not going to beg for my life.

The United States has a history of using torture to extract confessions from foreign and domestic adversaries. The government tells the people that we don't torture anyone, and Americans believe it. The Veteran said Americans were concerned about more important things, like trying to figure out who would be the next *American Idol* or who would win *Dancing with the Stars*.

The government proclaims that torture is never used, the media reports on what the government says, and the naive citizens do not notice that there is no opposing opinion being offered.

THE EVIL THE CIA DOES

I saw enough in Vietnam at a very young age to lead me to believe that the United States may be one of the top offenders when it comes to cruel and unusual punishments and crimes against humanity. During Vietnam, the devil in sheep's clothing was the CIA.

The CIA would pick our prisoners up and take them to secret locations for torture. As they drank at the base's club and waited to be picked up by their units, the CIA agents would brag about torturing the prisoners.

The story they told the most involved throwing prisoners out of a helicopter that was hovering at five hundred feet. They threw them out one at a time and said the last one would always talk. After he talked, they would still throw him out. They were category-two sociopaths.

I realized how angry and resentful I was. I couldn't think of a reason not to feel that way. I knew I had to be careful to not take those feelings out on anybody. I was back in civilization, and the act of touching someone could be construed as a physical assault. Even the act of shouting at somebody could be construed as a verbal assault and land me in prison, especially because I was a Vietnam veteran.

I was sick of Sierra Vista, Arizona. I could see Interstate 10 and the truck stop at the foot of the entrance ramp. I decided to hitch a ride there.

■ ■ ■

FINDING CALLIE, A VIETNAM VETERAN, AT A TRUCK STOP (1969)

I was not so sure I wanted to stick out my thumb. It had recently caused mayhem. I decided I would walk to the truck stop. That would give me twenty or so minutes to think about how to feed myself and find a ride. The two Big Boys in my stomach, which had been empty for thirty days, did not satisfy me for long. I wondered whether I should beg, rob someone, or find something I could do to earn a meal.

I decided to walk over to the truck stop and to see if any ideas came to mind. No one offered to give me anything. I didn't have it in me to steal. I didn't want to rob someone. I guessed I would have to ask for help. The first order of business was food. Many Vietnam veterans found themselves in my situation. When they reached out for help, they were denied it. Then, out of panic or even anger, they made bad decisions and stole things or robbed people and ended up in prison. Thousands committed suicide, and in that day, no official records of those suicides were kept.

I decided to begin in the cafeteria. It looked like it was just opening.

"Hello, miss," I said. "I was recently discharged from the army in California and was robbed by federal agents on my way to Florida. I am hungry. Is there something I could do to earn some food?"

"What is your name, young man?"

"My name is Lenny."

"Lenny, help yourself to a cup of coffee, and sit down at that table. Pour me a cup of black coffee, Lenny. As soon as I set up the cash register for the employee, I will join you."

"OK, thank you." Coffee—how long had it been since I'd had coffee? The only addiction I've ever had is my addiction to coffee.

"Lenny, are you down on your luck? My name is Callie. Call me Cal for short. It is not a good time to be a soldier, especially one who was in Vietnam, but you came to the right girl. I was discharged from the army a little over a year ago."

"No shit, Callie!"

CALLIE'S VIETNAM TOUR

"I did a tour at the main military hospital in Saigon. I flew over two hundred fifty helicopter medical-evacuation missions in and out of many hot landing zones. My job was to try to keep the wounded alive until we arrived at the hospital trauma center in Saigon.

"I know the feeling you get when munitions whiz by your head. I held many dying young men in my arms. It still makes me sick to my stomach when I think of all of the beautiful young men who lost their lives for nothing and for the hundreds of thousands of wounded. I still become angry when I think of the politicians who were looking out for the financial interests of their rich donors, many of whom manufactured war materials."

Noeleen Heyzer, the director of the United Nations Development Fund for Women, said, "Presently we have so many wars at the local, national, and international levels because we have invested in the commodities of war. Not everyone wants peace; some people benefit economically from instability, insecurity, and warfare. Until we dismantle that and get to the root causes of why we have violent conflicts, we will not achieve peace."

"I don't remember seeing you come through, Lenny."

"They patched me up at the twenty-fourth evacuation hospital."

"What did you last eat?"

"A couple of Big Boy hamburgers. Before that, I hadn't eaten much for thirty days."

"Go to the first cashier and point to me. Fill your plate up, and sit back down."

"Wow, Cal! Excuse me while I focus on my food."

"Go ahead, Lenny. I will watch," Cal said, laughing. "Tell me your story, Lenny…. That's quite a story."

CALLIE EDUCATES LENNY ON THE SLANDER OF VIETNAM VETERANS (1969)

"I manage the cafeteria, Lenny. I live in a trailer parked behind the truck stop. I have a roommate. She left for a couple of weeks to visit her family in Washington state. You are welcome to stay with me. I have the next two days off. That will give me time to familiarize you with the area."

"Thank you very much, Cal. I don't know how I could repay you."

"Think no more about it. We army guys stick together, right? Especially, when the government, police, media, and such a large part of the population are demonizing the Vietnam veterans."

By the year 1988, one-third of the Vietnam veterans were in prison, and half had served time in jail.

"Your mistakes, Lenny, were your jungle boots and short hair. Those two items identified you as a Vietnam veteran. You were persecuted by law-enforcement officers who had been misled by politicians and the government-influenced media. Our systems of democracy, capitalism, and corporate commerce depend on ignorance. A vast majority of Americans do not read. They depend on television for information.

"Slick-talking establishment wordsmiths manipulate the people. No one fact-checks the advertisers, the mainstream news media, and the government's pundits' claims. The TV viewer has no other creditable information choice but to believe what's said on TV is correct.

"Network news reports favor advertisers and the people who have the power to affect the network's welfare—mainly the government, Lenny."

"What do you mean when you say 'establishment,' Cal?"

"The establishment is the elite group of people who control the president and the congressional representatives who make our laws."

"Who are those people?"

"They are the owners of corporations and the wealthy donors who supply millions of dollars to the politicians' campaigns."

"Cal, I have some anger about Vietnam that I don't understand. How did you come to think this way?"

"I realized that something was not right with what I saw and with how those same events were reported by the military Stars and Stripes radio news when I was in Vietnam.

"Lenny, a great majority of television viewers have never been involved in the military, government, or politics. They've never witnessed for themselves how biased and dishonest the mainstream news media can be when reporting.

"I find it hard to accept the fact that I know what the establishment is doing but can't do anything to stop them, Lenny. The masses have become hopelessly oblivious to the truth. Even skeptical citizens have too many distractions and daily obligations to challenge the establishment's information control of the institutions we learn from and what certain clandestine government agencies are doing."

I must confess that Cal opened my mind to the false information and ideology spread by institutions and government. Political correctness is a major threat to "free will." If we fear the right to choose, "freedom" will become only a figment of our imagination.

The Veteran would have said that this is social engineering at its best. Most people do not apprehend that if they lose their "free will," the precursor to "freedom," they will eventually lose their "freedom." The analogy he would use to explain how "free will" and "freedom" are lost is like dying in your sleep. You never realized it was happening.

CALLIE'S TRUCK-STOP STORY (1969)

"Are you ready to see my humble abode, Lenny?"

"OK, Cal. Can I ask you how you ended up here? You are obviously not from here."

"I am from Texas. My boyfriend and I were on our way to make a life in Las Vegas. We had an argument while dining. He hit me and drove away, leaving me here, in this cafeteria. I was lucky that I had my pocketbook and money with me. Like you, Lenny, I saved over ten thousand dollars in Vietnam. I walked to the motel down the street and rented a room.

"The next day I came to the cafeteria to eat and noticed the Help Wanted sign. I applied for the job and was hired on the spot. That evening I made a deal with the owner of the motel and paid a month's rent up front. I told him that I was not just passing through and that I had a job at the truck stop. He offered me a very good deal on one of the better rooms.

"Before the month's end, the owner of the truck stop offered me a job as the cafeteria's manager. I got good pay and full benefits. It was an offer I could not refuse. The second month, he gave me the trailer in the back of the truck stop, which he had first lived in, free of charge. Most of all, he thanked me for the job I was doing. There you have it, Lenny!"

"Great story, Cal. Did you miss your boyfriend?"

"No, Lenny, not at all! He hit me so hard in the stomach that I thought I was going to suffocate before my breath returned. After that, I didn't ever want to see him again. I called his brother and told him to let him know that if he came around me again, I would call the police and press charges.

"Three people who worked here saw him strike me in the stomach. I got statements from all three of them in case they decided to move away before the police could talk to them. Let's have a drink and have a Vietnam veterans' reunion. What do you think, Lenny?"

I thought to myself that this was the first benefit of being a Vietnam veteran that I'd experienced. The girl was tough. She had restarted in a new environment totally on her own. I couldn't wait to spend some time with her. She was the first round-eyed woman I'd spoken with in over two years. (In Vietnam, we used the term "round eye" to describe Caucasians.)

In Vietnam, men fantasized out loud about returning home and getting round-eye pussy from their girlfriends or wives.

SAIGON TEA AND AN AMERICAN ATROCITY

It was nice to get a lady's attention without having to buy a Saigon tea. You readers who are not familiar with Saigon tea should know that it was similar to Kool-Aid. You had to purchase the tea before you could sit with a lady in Vietnam. The bar provided the ladies and profited by charging men two dollars for a couple of ounces of colored sugar water and a chat with a lady.

Some spoke English well enough to have conversations. The bars were similar to strip bars in the United States, except the girls were nicer and not nearly as greedy. A young man needs a woman's attention—that's biology. Without affection, he will become weary, especially when he is exposed daily to life-or-death combat situations.

American soldiers sired tens of thousands of children with these women. They were known as "Amerasians." The children were left behind when the North Vietnam soldiers chased the U.S. soldiers out of the country. The new Vietnamese government requested that the United States take them or care for them.

The U.S. government refused. The Vietnamese people rejected them. Some escaped to neighboring countries, many were killed, and some died in the streets. Many soldiers made requests to bring their children home. Their requests were denied. The Amerasian atrocity of tens of thousands of children was never reported by the mainstream news networks, which instead cooperated with the US government to not reveal this reprehensible genocide of American-spawned children.

When mainstream news networks elect not to report on an atrocity, that atrocity becomes only a rumor.

THE VETERANS' DILEMMA

Aggressive behavior is a part of the natural evolution of the human male. Man's aggressive instincts were necessary for survival for hundreds of thousands of years. Females are no longer dependent on males' aggressive nature for protection. Today's society provides males and females with a public protector: the police.

For most of our time on this earth the male chose and controlled the male/female relationship by any means he deemed necessary, to include violent physical force. Today in modern society the female chooses the male, and the male can lose his freedom, based on society's laws, if he attempts to use force to control the relationship.

Like it or not, this norm is in conflict with hundreds of thousands of years of male evolutionary behavior. It is total stupidity to think that a law can immediately change innate male heritage. This could explain why millions of American males have acted out their heritage and ended up in prison for behavior that was perfectly normal for hundreds of thousands of years.

Only a few months before, I'd been in a hostile environment where aggressive behavior was necessary to survive. After arriving in the United States, my inherent aggressive behavior that the military had encouraged me to rediscover and hone was interpreted as morally wrong or criminal.

Very few combat veterans make the total transition from warriors to citizens without some mental confusion. Most internalize this confusion, which caused many of the mental problems that combat veterans are known to have when returning from war. Many combat veterans fail to successfully adopt coping strategies; then they end up on the streets, commit suicide, act out, or end up in prison.

People who have never witnessed combat cannot comprehend the warrior's mentality. If the government insists on converting young domesticated male and female citizens into warriors to kill other humans, it must accommodate their mental and physical issues once their service is over. To this day, the Veterans Affairs' politically appointed hacks still do not get that or possibly don't care.

In Vietnam, Cal had witnessed this warrior behavior. It was comforting to be in the company of a female who truly understood veterans and what they needed when they returned to a docile society.

CALLIE AND LENNY CONNECT (1969)

"Lenny, before we purchase a bottle of champagne, can we dance?"

The beverage store was in the quaint little truck stop's bar. The music was perfect for a slow dance. I was excited and said yes.

I was honest with Cal. I told her the way I truly felt. "Cal, I have not been in close quarters with a beautiful round-eye woman in a couple of years. Please try to understand my excitement."

"Lenny, I have seen nothing but truck drivers for a year. I have not been with a man in over a year. I am as excited as you are! I have no interest in men who haven't experienced Vietnam, Lenny. This dance has been a long time coming."

"Cal, why did you take a chance on me?"

"I knew you were good, Lenny. Besides, you are cute, and your timing was perfect. I was at my wits' end. My hormones are raging, Lenny. People who have looked death in the eyes don't have to pretend. We are open with our feelings, especially because for a time, we didn't know whether we'd live to see another day. I know that you are just like me in that regard.

"Because of our Vietnam experience we gained a different perspective on life. We don't play games."

"I could not have said it better, Cal."

"Let's live tonight as though we were still in Vietnam. Let's pretend that tomorrow might never come," she said. At that instant, I grabbed her by the hair and pulled her close.

With my eyes wide open, I covered her lips with mine. I kissed her. She responded by thrusting her lower torso into mine. I smelled her tantalizing feminine aroma. I caressed her body with extreme passion. She moaned in euphoric acceptance of my touch.

I continued to dance with her and to hold her tight.

"Welcome home, soldier!" she softly said. She then took my hand and led me to the bar. "Please pour us double shots of cinnamon Fireball, John, and put them on my tab. This is Lenny. He is a Vietnam veteran and a friend of mine."

We devoured three more shots each and finished our last dance. She wrapped her arms around me, blew her warm breath into my ear, and whispered, "How about some round-eye pussy tonight, Lenny?" I trembled with gratitude. I nodded my head eagerly. Holding each other tight, we strolled to her place.

In just a few hours, Cal had changed my downtrodden attitude. I could not thank her enough. My desire was to reward her with the greatest pleasure of her life. I unleashed everything I had learned from Mary Gibson and from the art of Asian lovemaking I learned in Vietnam. I licked, sucked, and fucked every orifice of that beautiful woman. The year was 1969; we were young and alive!

■ ■ ■

BETTY GOES CAR SHOPPING (PRESENTLY)

Betty and Bailey were on their way to the Cadillac dealer. Betty had decided to purchase a Cadillac Escalade. She and Harold had talked extensively about cars, and after doing her research, Betty had made the decision to go with the Escalade.

Bailey and Betty had developed a mother-daughter relationship over the last few months. When she was not with Will, she was with Betty.

Will had taken an interest in the yard. He had never lived in a house with a yard. He loved planting plants, cutting grass, and all of the worldly rewards of gardening. The yard had come alive since he and Bailey had moved in. It had really deteriorated during Gloria's period of financial difficulties. Gloria gave the couple a substantial discount on rent in exchange for their work on restoring and maintaining the yard.

Betty and Bailey turned into the dealership. The white Escalade and a young lady were waiting for her in front of the dealership. She led Betty and Bailey to the sales manager's office, where Betty presented him with a bank draft. He opened the envelope, read over the document, and presented Betty with the keys. He thanked Betty for her purchase.

He then smiled at Betty and said, "It was a pleasure doing business with you, Ms. Anderson. Do you have any questions?"

"I appreciated your mailing me all of the facts about this car ahead of time. I've done my homework and will keep you in mind if I have further questions. Thank you for your concern," Betty said.

He shook her hand and instructed the young saleslady to escort them back to the car and if needed, explain the car's features to them.

Betty handed the Honda Fit keys to the young saleslady and instructed her to drop the car off at her home.

Betty passed on the feature instructions offered by the young saleslady and climbed into the Escalade. Bailey climbed into the passenger's seat, and off they went.

BETTY AND BAILEY DRIVE THE NEW ESCALADE TO BOWDITCH PARK

Betty told Bailey to buckle up.

"How did you get the dealership to drop the Honda off at your house, Betty?"

"When you spend eighty thousand dollars, they will do whatever you ask."

Bailey looked at Betty and laughed. "This car is beautiful and very large. You think you can drive it, Betty?"

"Aren't I doing that now? The last car I owned was actually larger than this Escalade. It was a 1988 Continental. It was huge, Bailey. Would you like to ride down to the beach on our maiden voyage?"

Bailey smiled and said. "That would be great!"

"Bailey, if you want, we can park and take a walk on the beach. It is a beautiful day."

"I would enjoy that, Betty. Can we go to Bowditch Park? I read in the newspaper that a family of tortoises lives there. The park borders the beach. The paper reported that a couple of them weigh more than a hundred pounds. I have my phone. I can take pictures of them.

"Will likes tortoises. He thinks they are one of the most fascinating land animals. He told me that in a zoo in San Francisco, he saw some that were large enough for children to ride."

"Next stop is Bowditch Park, Bailey. Do you know Bob?"

"Yes, Betty."

"I've been working with Bob on a community-bank charter, Bailey. I know you have a master's degree in finance. My question is, does your financial knowledge encompass banking?"

"Yes, Betty. I do know about banking."

"Bailey, we will require your help in the near future."

"I would love to be a part of your team if that is what you are asking."

"It is. I will keep you informed of our progress."

"Thank you, Betty."

"Betty, can I ask you a personal question?"

"Bailey, you can confer with me on anything."

"You have been a leader your whole life. I would like to know, as a woman, do you need to do anything different from a man to acquire the necessary respect to succeed in a leadership position. I noticed that it is rare for a woman to be a CEO of a large corporation or institution."

"Wow…. That is a huge question, Bailey. The answer is yes. For you to see this quandary tells me that you are a natural leader. I have a book at the house that will address your question. The book describes how powerful women leaders blend traits common to both male and female minds. This skill is called psychological androgyny. I think it would be a good idea for you to read this book."

"Thank you, Betty. I had no idea. I can't wait to read this book."

BAILEY'S FASCINATION WITH WATER

"Bailey, Will told me that your interest is water. He said that you are fascinated by the importance of water to our planet and to all life."

"Betty, I know that sounds a little strange, but that is true. I don't concern myself with politics. I only concern myself with how it affects life on this planet.

"Water is important for every bodily function. It is vital to cleansing the body of toxins, the metabolism, energy, the process of carrying nutrients into the cells, the removal of waste products from the body, and the regulation of the body's temperature. Water is even responsible for communication between clusters of cells.

"Betty, believe it or not, water has the geometrical structure of a tetrahedron. The question I am asked the most is, what is the best water to drink? The best drinking water comes from Fiji, in the South Pacific.

"The water comes from an aquifer that predates the Industrial Revolution. This natural rainwater is totally free of pollutants. Fiji is located in the dead center of the most energetic power-point location on the earth's natural energy grid-network.

"For hundreds of years, the water has been subjected to the earth's natural resonant frequencies. Over time the water has developed its full energy potential. No other water on earth can come close to offering what water from Fiji can offer the human body. This magnificent water has recently become available in the United States.

"A person should drink at least half an ounce of water per one and a half pounds of his weight. If a person drinks enough water, his body will eliminate toxins more completely."

"The U.S. agricultural industry uses over seven thousand pesticides, herbicides, and fungicides. These chemicals eventually end up in our drinking water. Water-treatment plants claim that they successfully remove these contaminants. Plain reason should tell us that something is wrong with those claims.

"The very same water used in home appliances eventually clogs the filters, and the filters must be cleaned before they can perform as they should. That is what happens in our bodies. The body's filter systems become clogged, which results in serious health problems, like arterial heart diseases.

"Betty, I am sure that you realize that the first resemblance of life is believed to be stromatolites, which developed three-and-a-half-billion years ago. Over the next few billion years, atoms became molecules, molecules became cells, cells became tissues, tissues became organs, organs became systems, and systems became complex organisms.

"Water is essential for human development. On the day of conception, the embryo begins its journey through every developmental stage. At five weeks, gills appear for a short period of time, and then they disappear. I can't help but read articles and books about water. Water mesmerizes me!"

"That makes you intellectually unique," Betty said. "I would love to hear your entire exposition on water, Bailey."

"Betty, I had an enjoyable discussion with Lenny on this subject. He was shocked that I was knowledgeable in the area of his favorite study, evolutionary biology. I think I earned his respect with my knowledge."

"You sure did, Bailey. Lenny told me about the conversation you and he had. He was impressed."

"Betty, what was Lenny's profession before he retired? He exhibits an amazing amount of knowledge in so many different disciplines. Ruby, a woman of less than half his age, who is without question one of the most beautiful and talented women I have ever known, adores him. Why is that?"

"Bailey, Lenny has never worked in a profession. He is unique. He has spent his entire life learning. His first wife was an accomplished superintendent of schools. She had a six-figure income and preferred for him to continue his education and homeschool their child. He has spent more than twenty years in universities studying many different disciplines.

"One of his notable accomplishments was a thesis in psychotherapy on sexual dysfunction. He performed a therapeutic miracle on Ruby, earning her respect and love. I will leave the rest of this conversation to your imagination. I trust that this information remains private, Bailey."

"That is totally amazing, Betty. I promise this will remain a family secret. Betty, I love you. Darling, I love you too."

"There's a parking place near the front entrance of the park."

"But, Betty, you will have to parallel park!"

"Let's see how I do, Bailey."

"Damn, Betty! You got it on the first try."

Betty high-fived Bailey and smiled. "I'm back!" she said.

"How are you and Will doing?"

"Betty, we are so much alike that we sometimes say the same thing to each other at the same time. Will said to me in the beginning that was scary. He then asked me if I could read his thoughts sometimes. I assured him that was stretching it.

"We are really enjoying each other, Betty. Do you believe that people who live together for a long time begin to look alike?"

"I do, Bailey. Over time, similar environments produce similar-looking species. The environment dictates the physical and mental development as well as the health and longevity of all life, Bailey.

"At first I did not see the significance of that fact. On second thought, I did see how understanding that information could be considered necessary to understanding how to manage one's health. Furthermore, a knowledgeable patient could prevent an unscrupulous physician from suggesting unnecessary surgeries or expensive long-term treatment by using the hereditary and familial disease fear tactics, Bailey."

"Physicians are still being taught that all gene expression is predetermined. Physicians' ignorance can result in the loss of life and the unnecessary removal of breasts and organs."

"Bailey, it was my ignorance that allowed my physician to prescribe unnecessary prescription drugs to me. If Lewis and Lenny had not intervened, I would have died."

"Betty, how well do you understand mismatched diseases?"

THE ORIGIN OF MISMATCHED DISEASES

"I first heard about the concept of mismatched diseases from Lenny. He said that the environment is basically responsible for gene expression. He contends that the primary environmental trigger of gene expression is food.

"Epigenetics has shown that a large number of a human's genes are nonimprinted genes. These genes can be modified within one generation or immediately influenced by environmental factors that don't alter DNA sequences.

"The human body evolved over millions of years. During that time, humans ate wild vegetation, fish, fowl, eggs, mammals, reptiles, rodents, and insects. The environment was devoid of toxins and contaminated water.

"But humans now consume nutritionally different domestic plants, animals grown with chemicals of one sort or the other, and processed foods;

breathe toxic air; have sedentary lifestyles; and drink contaminated water, and all of that promotes mismatched diseases we listed earlier.

"These conditions did not result from natural evolution over tens of thousands of years. The rapid change in the environment was caused by cultural evolution. Cultural evolution began with the discovery of agriculture somewhere between twelve thousand B.C. and ten thousand B.C.

"Cultural evolution gained speed exponentially when the agricultural revolution met up with the Industrial Revolution in the late eighteenth century. These two events instantly changed the environment.

"Most authorities on the subject believe that our transition from hunting and gathering to farming made urban life possible, which led to a downward slide to crime, strife, diseases, and misery for the human species."

BETTY AND BAILEY DISCOVER A TORTOISE FAMILY

"Look, Bailey! There are the tortoises. Two big ones and three little ones are coming toward us."

"Should we run, Betty?"

"I don't think so, Bailey. They may think we have food for them. I'm sure they won't bother us. Many people come to this park. See there—they stopped. Now they are looking up at us. This would be a good time to take pictures."

"The small tortoises are cute! Will is going to love these pictures. His favorite land animal is the Aldabra giant tortoise."

"Do you mind if I hold on to your arm while we're walking in this sand, Bailey?"

"Of course not. The beach is so nice on this part of the island. Taste the salt air, and smell the ocean. Look at those beautiful long-legged egrets. How do they stay so white, Betty? Why are they so plentiful on this part of the beach?"

"Could it be because few people come to this side of the island? I bet Lenny would know."

"People need nature, but nature does not need people, Bailey"

BETTY CONFESSES TO BAILEY, NOT MARRYING HAROLD WAS A MISTAKE

"Betty, I can't wait to meet Harold. When do you expect him?"

"It will be soon, Bailey."

"You and Harold have spent time together?"

"We've been together for almost thirty years. I should have married him. To this day, I don't understand why I pushed him away. It was a mistake.

"He's stayed with me for all of these years. I owe him for staying with me. You will love him. He loves kids. I worked seven days a week. He more or less raised Lewis. He was a master at not bringing his work home with him. When he'd leave his law office or a courtroom, his workday would be done."

"Was he a successful lawyer, Betty?"

"Indeed he was. He is also handling my lawsuit against the VA for Lewis's death. Between you and me, Harold won tens of millions of dollars in lawsuits. His money wasn't the reason I liked him, maybe because I had earned plenty of money from my own investments. When people meet him, they never think that he is worth millions."

"My God, Betty. He is that wealthy?"

"Yes, he is, Bailey. We decided to reinvest our money together in a community bank. Promise me that you won't tell anyone how wealthy he is."

"OK, Betty. I promise."

BETTY'S ADVICE ON WILLY JOHNSON

"The ocean is so beautiful. Take your shoes off, and wade into the water with me, Bailey."

"Hold my hand, Betty. How far out do you want to go?"

"Maybe up to our knees, Bailey, and then we will go around to the point where I scattered Lewis's ashes for a moment. This is exactly where I was standing when I released Lewis's ashes into the wind and the surf, Bailey. Lord…. It seems like yesterday. Thank you, Bailey. We can head back now. How is Joni doing with Will?"

"They hit it off from the beginning. She calls Will 'Dad.' She wants to go everywhere with him. She's like his shadow. She was beside him digging in the garden when I left."

"That is good, Bailey."

"Betty, I have a question."

"What is your question?"

"Will is good to my child and to me. So why do I continue to think of my husband, who died in Afghanistan? He was killed over three years ago. Every time I look at Joni, I feel sorry for her and think about him."

"I think your reaction is normal, Bailey. That is exactly the way I felt for a long time after my husband died in the war. I allowed it go on for too long. Like I said before, I neglected Harold. I hope you can learn from my mistake, Bailey.

"Will is a good man. If you love him, and I know you do, don't lose him over a ghost."

"I do love him, and I want Joni to grow up with a father. Neither Will nor I had a family. You gave us our first taste of a family. Will thinks of you as his mother, and I guess I do too, Betty."

"Well, Bailey, that's an honor that I hope I can live up to."

"I love you, Betty."

"I love you too, Bailey. Let's go now!"

BETTY AND BAILEY SHOP AT NEIMAN MARCUS

"Bailey, I would like to stop by Neiman Marcus to purchase a new outfit. Looking my best for Harold is one of my priorities. Will you help me pick out an outfit, Bailey? You can show me today's fashions. I have no idea of what is in style."

"OK, that will be fun, Betty. I've heard about Neiman Marcus, but I've never been able to afford to shop there. Do you know where the store is, Betty?"

"The store is in Coconut Point. It is not far from where we are."

"This will be exciting, Betty."

"What do you think?"

"There is someone pulling out of a parking space, Betty."

"I'm on it, Bailey."

"This is a beautiful store, Betty. Look at these clothes! You would look fabulous in this dress and in this one and in this one."

"I can't make up my mind. Which one, Bailey?"

"I like them all."

"Then I will take them all."

"Wow, Betty, that's going to cost you a pretty penny!"

"That's OK. It would please me if you would pick out a dress for yourself."

"I can't afford these clothes, Betty."

"It's on me. Any one you want."

Bailey screamed and grabbed a royal-blue strapless dress and ran off to the dressing room. She soon emerged from it and did a twirl in front of Betty.

Bailey was small breasted, thin, and taller than the average woman—maybe five foot eleven. She had freckles, short red hair, and light-green eyes. Her facial features were most unusual; she had very large eyes, a large brow, a large nose, and a large jaw. The consensus was that she had a unique kind of beauty. Most of all, she was always energetic and cheerful. Betty adored her and claimed that she was her own daughter.

"How do I look, Betty?"

"You look gorgeous. Now we can go to the shoe department and find a pair of matching heels."

"Betty, how many pairs of shoes do you intend to buy?"

"I bought three dresses, and I will buy three pairs of shoes. Bailey, did you decide on a pair?"

"I love these royal-blue heels, but the price is prohibitive."

"Those heels perfectly match the beautiful dress you selected."

"Betty, they cost four hundred dollars."

"Don't think about the price. I insist that you have them. Tell the clerk that we are ready to pay."

"OK, Betty."

"How would you like to pay, miss?" the clerk asked.

"Credit card."

"You qualify for a five percent discount with your Neiman Marcus credit card. Thank you for shopping with us, Ms. Anderson."

"You have a Neiman Marcus credit card?"

"Yes, I do. I applied for it when I found out that Harold was coming."

"Thank you very much, Betty. I have never owned a dress this nice."

"You looked so beautiful in that dress Bailey. I would enjoy hearing what Will's reaction is when he sees you in that dress."

"I will make it a point to tell you about it, Betty."

"You drive. I want to play with the radio and the other gadgets."

"My God, Betty. I can't drive this car! What if something happens?"

"Bailey, I have good insurance. Start the car!"

"Here—take my phone. The camera is set up. Shoot a few pictures and a short video of me behind the wheel to show Will."

"OK, start driving, and I'll take the pictures. My goodness. Next week is Bob and Gloria's wedding. That would be a great time to show off that beautiful royal-blue dress, Bailey."

"Oh, yeah—that would be a perfect time! I can't believe you bought a dress and heels for me."

"Why not? You are my favorite gal. I don't want to hear anything else about it."

"This car drives like a dream. It glides down the road, Betty."

THE BURNING CAR

"Look, Betty! One of the cars that passed us slammed into the back of the truck that's stopped at the red light! I noticed when it passed us that a young lady was driving and that the backseat had several kids in it."

"My God, Bailey. It's smoking and looks like it might be about to catch fire."

"What should we do, Betty? No one got out of it."

"Stop the car, Bailey. I will go to the driver's side, open the door, and unlock all of the doors. I will attempt to assist the driver. Bailey, you open the opposite side's rear door and drag those kids to the sidewalk and away from the car. Hurry, Bailey!"

"Betty, don't you try to run! You might injure yourself."

"I know what I can do. Now go!" The driver's door was locked. Betty noticed that the front windshield had shattered. She quickly reached through it and pushed the button on the top of the armrest to unlock the doors. She then opened the driver's door.

The airbag's explosion had dazed the young lady. She took off the lady's seat belt and screamed for her to get out. She pulled on her with all of her strength. The young lady rolled out of the car and fell to the ground. A man ran up to them, grabbed the lady's arms, and dragged her away from the burning car.

Betty moved away from the car to locate Bailey. Bailey had positioned herself on the far sidewalk near a bus stop. She was holding in her arms three screaming young kids. Flames consumed the car. Betty moved slowly to the side of the street to be with Bailey and the kids. Bailey hugged Betty. "Are you all right?" she asked.

The five of them sat huddled together on the sidewalk. A news truck arrived, and onlookers pointed to them and explained what the two ladies had done. Soon the news team's cameras were rolling, and questions were being asked. Betty and Bailey held on to the children until the fire department's emergency medical team arrived.

They released the children to the EMT and answered the news team's questions. Betty informed the EMT personnel that she was exhausted. The EMT demanded that Betty go with the lady involved in the accident and the three kids to the hospital to be examined. Bailey kissed Betty and told her that she would follow her to the hospital. The EMT transported Betty comfortably on a stretcher.

THE EMT CREW INSISTS THAT BETTY GO TO THE HOSPITAL

When the crew raised Betty's stretcher, the crowd began clapping and cheering. Betty smiled and waved to the crowd as she was loaded into the ambulance. By that time, three local news teams were broadcasting the story live.

Bailey turned the Escalade in the direction of the hospital and called Will. She told Will to stay with Joni and to call Ruby, Gloria, and me. "Tell them to meet me at Lee Memorial Hospital," she said. The hospital employee at the information desk told Bailey that Betty was being examined and that if she checked out, she would be released.

"Bailey, have you seen Betty?" I asked.

"She is still in the examination room. I told Gloria when she called that it was not necessary for her to take off from work."

"Lenny and I came as soon as we could. Tell me what you know about Betty," Ruby said.

"Betty has no physical injuries. She complained of exhaustion. The EMT insisted that she be examined just to be safe."

"Did they give you any timeline, Bailey?"

"What do you mean, Ruby?"

"How long will the examination take?"

"The nurse said it would not take long."

"I'll see what I can find out. I'll be right back," Ruby said.

"What did you find out?" I asked.

"I was told that the attending physician wants to keep her under observation until her heart rate has decreased. The physician said that the excitement caused her to secrete an inordinate amount of adrenaline, which raised her heart rate and increased her energy."

"Ruby, epinephrine and norepinephrine are known as the 'fight-or-flight' hormones. When a human's life is threatened, these adrenalines are secreted to give extra strength and stamina to escape from or fend off hostile attackers or historically a large predator. This evolutionary adaptation was necessary for the survival of our species."

"Lenny, I never thought that something like adrenaline could be a survival adaptation," said Bailey.

"I like it better than an exoskeleton that insect species developed for protection."

"I agree the adrenaline adaptation is a more practical evolution, Lenny."

"I'm not so sure. Insects have stood the test of time."

"Some adrenaline responses are considered to be natural. However, the everyday stresses of our modern unnatural lifestyles promote the continuous secretion of adrenaline. Some evolutionary biologists believe that continuous secretions of adrenaline are unnatural and negatively affect the body.

"Betty's secretion of adrenaline fits the definition of natural and could be considered a heart-healthy exercise.

"I heard the story on the local radio station on the way here, Bailey. The reporter said that you and Betty saved four people's lives, three of whom were children.

"The news reporter said that moments after a mother-and-daughter team removed the occupants of the car, the car was engulfed by flames. He also said that all four of the occupants of the car and the elderly lady responsible for the rescue were taken to Lee Memorial for a medical evaluation."

"Lenny, the mother-and-daughter remark is an honor to me and will bring a smile to Betty's face. You wait here. I will find coffee for the three of us."

"Thanks, Bailey. That sounds good," Ruby said.

"The coffee is perfect," I said.

"I knew you'd want heavy cream, Lenny."

"Thank you very much."

"You and Betty make quite a team," Ruby said.

"We are like two bugs in a rug. We have fun together. Betty is so good to me. I never knew my mother. She is the mother I never had."

"Bailey, go ask when we can see Betty," I said.

"I'm on it, Lenny!" she said. When she came back, she said, "Lenny, I had to sign a guest list. There are six people ahead of us, and only three people can go in at a time. What do you think is going on, Lenny?"

"I have no idea. I will see what I can find out. Excuse me, I'm trying to see Betty Anderson, and the lady with me was told that there's a waiting list. Do you know why?"

"Yes, sir, she is the elderly lady who saved those people from burning in that terrible car crash. The family members of the children she pulled out of the car are visiting her to thank her. She's today's hero. Haven't you heard the news today? The west wing's conference room is packed with reporters waiting for the mayor and the fire marshal's press conference."

"Bailey, we need to go around to the west wing's conference room. Betty will be going there to meet with the mayor and the fire marshal. You need to join Betty for the press conference."

BETTY, BAILEY, AND SEÑOR GONZALES, HOLD A PRESS CONFERENCE

"Sir, I'm sorry, but the conference room is full."

"I have with me the lady who assisted Betty Anderson. This is Bailey Darby."

"Wait here. I will let the mayor's assistant know."

"Ms. Darby, we were wondering where you were. Please come in. The mayor and the fire marshal would love to meet you. They are on their way. Betty Anderson is due out any minute. You will want to join her. Ladies and gentleman, Bailey Darby is here. We ask everyone to refrain from asking questions until Betty, Bailey, the mayor, and the fire marshal are all here together.

"Bailey, Betty is entering the room. Go to her! The mayor and the fire marshal are coming in through the other door."

"Ladies and gentlemen, thank you for coming. The fire marshal and I are here to present an award to Betty Anderson and Bailey Darby for the bravery they exhibited today.

"On behalf of the citizens of Fort Myers, the mayor of the city of Fort Myers and the fire marshal of Lee County are honored to present to Betty Anderson and Bailey Darby the Fort Myers Outstanding Citizen Award for their brave actions while rescuing four citizens, three of whom were children."

"Would you like to comment, Ms. Anderson?"

"Bailey and I thank the good people of Fort Myers for this distinguished award. Bailey and I will answer a few questions. We are exhausted from all of the excitement. We will then ask you to excuse us so that we can return to our homes for the evening. It has been a long day."

"Ms. Anderson, there had to have been ten other people who were closer to the accident than you and Ms. Darby. Those ten people were at the bus stop directly in front of the accident, and not one of them reacted to it. Why do you think they didn't help?"

"That is not exactly true," Betty said. "One of them dragged the lady away after I took her out of the car. Can that man please step forward if he is here? Sir, what is your name?"

"No speak English."

"Is there someone here who speaks Spanish?"

"Yes, I speak Spanish."

"Will you ask this gentleman why he assisted me when no one else did?"

"He said that the people were in danger and that he felt it was his duty to help you save their lives."

"What is your name, señor?"

"His name is Jesus Gonzales."

"Will you tell him that the people of this community are grateful for his brave act and we would also like to reward him equally?" the mayor said.

"I will, sir!"

"Señor Gonzales said he is very thankful to the people of Fort Myers for such an award."

"Ms. Darby, what made you react so decisively?"

"Betty and I made a quick plan, and we carried through with it. There was no way I could have allowed those children to perish. Betty and I are hungry and very tired. May we be excused?" Bailey said. She grabbed Betty's arm and led her to the car. Ruby and I were quick to follow them.

I couldn't help but think about what Señor Gonzales had said when he'd been asked why he'd helped rescue those people. He'd said that he'd felt it was his duty to help save their lives. But why had he been the only one to help? Why hadn't all of the people at the bus stop helped?

The answer could've been the subject of a study. I believed that Señor Gonzales was a leader. Betty was a leader. That's how leaders react to these situations. Betty instantly formulated a plan and instructed Bailey on what to do.

The rest of the people at the bus stop exhibited no concern or desire to help. Their mind-sets were more typical; they didn't think it was their job to help, they didn't think there was anything in it for them, they didn't want to become involved, and they expected someone else to take action.

"What has this world come to?" I asked.

BETTY RETURNS HOME AFTER THE RESCUE AND NEWS INTERVIEW

"Bob and I came over to see how Betty is doing. The burning car was all over the news," Gloria said. "The news said that Betty had been released from the hospital. Is she all right?"

"She is resting. Bailey is watching her in her bedroom."

"Everyone at the bank was talking about the story," Bob said. "We kept up with it on the radio. The award ceremony was covered live on all three local news stations. Betty and Bailey are very popular women in this town. Hi, Bailey, is Betty up now?"

"She's sound asleep, Bob."

"Gloria and I will be next door if you need anything."

"We will keep you posted," Ruby said.

"Bailey, Will and Joni are here."

"Have a seat, Will. Hey, Joni. Breezy and Jojo are in the kitchen," Ruby said.

"Bailey is a local celebrity, Will."

"I followed it on the portable radio as it happened. Joni and I were in the garden. Bailey and I will watch it on the news together tonight."

"You and Joni made your yard look like a tropical flower garden, Will."

"It is the best form of stress relief that I have ever known. When I'm gardening, Lenny, I am totally without one thought of the many everyday problems that I encounter at the VA."

"I found my sanctuary, and Joni loves playing in the dirt. Joni and I are a team, Lenny."

"Good for you!"

"When Joni and Will are working in the garden, I have time for my favorite hobby," Bailey said.

"What is that?"

"I love to read, Lenny."

"Bob and Gloria want to use the garden for their wedding and then have a pool party afterward. Bob has done a great deal of work on the pool. He says it would be a good way to get to know the neighbors. Gloria and Bob suggested that Bailey and I join them and that we make it a double wedding."

"Wow, Will! What did you tell them?" Ruby asked.

"We said that we would consider it."

"I think it would be great," Ruby said.

"Excuse me. I'm going to check on Betty," Bailey said.

"Joni collects the bugs she finds when she's digging in the dirt, Lenny. She gives them names."

"That is so cute," Ruby said.

"At the day's end, she says good-bye and puts them back in the ground," Will said. "Her favorite critters are the huge Florida earthworms and white grubs. She has a special container that she keeps them in. I suggested that she hold on to them so that we could use them for bait when we go fishing. Then I told her about how to place one on a hook. She said that she didn't want to put her friends on hooks. She then said that they would live happily ever after in the ground.

"I did tell her that the white grub worm is a larva that would soon turn into a scarab beetle.

"She said, "When, Daddy?

"We ended up putting a few in a jar with their dirt to wait for them to turn into beetles. The jar is now sitting on the dining room table."

"Will, do you remember when we first spoke?" Ruby asked.

"I sure do, Ruby."

"I called you early that morning and asked if you would come to Fort Myers to pick us up and drive us to the regional VA hospital. I told you we all wanted to go to support Betty as she viewed her son for the last time. Furthermore, we wanted to surprise Lenny."

"I will never forget the phone call, Ruby."

"I believe that you and Bailey appeared for a reason."

"Bailey never had a relationship with her mother. She never knew her mother. She adores Betty."

"You and Bailey were destined to add your sum and substance to our evolving family. There is so much yet to come. 'Everything happens for a reason' is my personal mantra. I believe we will understand the reason at the right time. One for all, and all for one! Will, you were the first one to say that about the family, and it stuck," said Ruby. "Hi, Betty, the world is waiting for you. How do you feel?"

"I'm ready to resume my life. I demonstrated what can happen to an individual when she secretes too much adrenaline and overexerts herself. God, I'm pleased that Bailey and I were successful. The extreme exhaustion I experienced was well worth it. How long have I been out for?"

"Twelve hours if we include your time at the hospital," Bailey said.

"That's more than I would have guessed. This definitely put me behind on my work on the bank charter. I have a deadline. Bailey, thanks for looking after me. You run along. You guys need to spend your precious weekend together."

"If you need us, don't hesitate to call," said Bailey.

"I have a strong need to nourish myself. I am back to my normal self, and I need some time alone. I will call you if I need to."

HAROLD'S RESIDENCE'S FURNISHINGS

"Ruby, have you packed everything you'll need for a week?"

"I put my clothing in two large suitcases and packed Betty's clothes. The suitcases are ready to be loaded into the Odyssey."

"When do we need to be out of here by?"

"We need to be gone early tomorrow morning. The contractor told us that most of the materials would be delivered tomorrow, before noon, Lenny.

Betty and I met with him last week. He has tripled his labor manpower and will be working twenty-four-seven to finish this renovation in fourteen days.

"No expenses have been spared on Harold's accommodations, Lenny. The self-contained smart home amenities can be remotely controlled from anywhere. The kitchen counters will be all granite, and there will be hand-finished mahogany cabinets and Sub-Zero and Wolf kitchen appliances.

"The bedroom will be enlarged, the ceilings will be vaulted, and custom ceiling fans and programmable LED lighting will be installed. A complete collection of Salvador Dali's signed prints will decorate the walls. The bathroom will be huge and all granite with dual lavatories, dry and wet saunas, a whirlpool tub, and a large shower with duel showerheads.

"The bedroom will adjoin a very spacious entertainment room. Next to it there will be a beautiful all-mahogany study equipped with a full set of Florida law books, which is due to arrive the following week.

"The annex will have its own AC and heating units, its own entrance, a fenced-in redwood porch with a therapeutic Hydro Spa, outdoor cooking accommodations, and remote-controlled night vision observation cameras."

"Betty told me that Harold is paying for most of it. Where will we be staying, Lenny?" Ruby asked.

"Betty rented a huge three-bedroom waterfront condo in downtown Fort Myers for eighteen days in case there is a delay of some sort."

"That will be like a honeymoon for you and me, Lenny."

"Ruby, every day is a honeymoon with you!"

"There are so many things to explore downtown, Lenny. It will be educational and fun. Betty said that she is excited about investigating the historic downtown area."

■ ■ ■

AT THE TRUCK STOP WITH CALLIE (1969)
"Wake up, Lenny! I made breakfast, and you can eat with me before I leave for the cafeteria."

"Thanks for waking me up. The bed was unbelievably comfortable. For the last thirty days, I slept on a concrete slab in a U.S. Treasury Department lock-up facility.

"That reinforced my distrust of authority figures and the government. I must admit that you came to my rescue. I was at the point of not giving a shit about anything. What can I do to demonstrate my appreciation?"

"That question is easy to answer, Lenny. I want you to stay here with me. I need your companionship and love.

"This truck stop is in the middle of nowhere. Last night was special. I could not have maintained my faculties for much longer. I was tired of being alone. I must go and open the cafeteria. Come to the cafeteria at around two, Lenny. We will talk more. Between now and then, make yourself comfortable. Your sexual performance was magnificent last night. Bye."

It was time for a real shower. I figured I'd be able to find something to wear. I decided to wear Cal's jeans. I was sure she would not mind. I'd lost weight during my thirty days in that government shithole. Then I had to find a clean shirt. Her extra-large sleep shirt and her athletic socks fit me.

I decided to take another walk around the truck stop and to think about my next move. The place was huge. I had never seen so many transfer trucks in one place.

The truck stop had its own security, a clothing store, a gym, RV hookups, a bar, a grocery store, and many other amenities meant to attract truckers and travelers. I noticed a Now Hiring sign on the window of the security building. "Why not fill out an application? They can call the military hotline if they need more information about me," I thought.

"Can I help you, sir?"

"I am inquiring about the job opening."

"Are you Lenny?"

"How did you know my name?"

"The owner and Callie stopped in to let us know that you would be coming. The big boss said to hire you. That's all we need, except your full name and Social Security number. We know you are a Vietnam veteran.

"Every man here is a Vietnam veteran, Lenny. We're all the boss will hire. You will be replacing Jimmy. He served with the First Cavalry Division. Three months ago Jimmy responded to a call from the bar. A drunken trucker was throwing tables and chairs around. Jimmy told the man he would have to leave. The trucker pulled a pistol out and shot Jimmy in the head. By the time the ambulance arrived, Jimmy was long gone.

"The trucker immediately surrendered his pistol to the sheriff. He was charged with murder and is awaiting trial. The tragedy of this situation is that Jimmy lost a kidney when he was shot in Vietnam. He came home to his wife and his kid, and life was good for them until that pathetic redneck trucker took his life. He was practicing to become a stand-up comedian. He was damn good at it and most likely would have made it.

"On the wall there's a plaque commemorating Jimmy. After that altercation Randy applied for a license for the security officers to carry weapons. You will be issued a nine-millimeter Colt to be used as a last resort. I'm sure you know how to use it.

"When would you like to get your weapon and uniforms?"

I didn't think I should say anything further until I understood what was going on.

"I'm scheduled to meet with Callie at two. I will come back later. Thank you." He had caught me by total surprise.

I had no idea of what Cal had in mind. I was sure she had a plan. Our lunch would definitely be informative. I decided that I wouldn't say much when we met. I would listen before speaking. I was sure there was more to this story. It was two, so it was time for me to head over to the cafeteria.

"Hey, Lenny, find us a private place in the corner by the window. Then go ahead and fix yourself a plate. You need to add some meat to those bones."

"Roger that, Cal!"

"I will close out this cash register in about five minutes. You were right on time. You clean up well! Wow, Lenny, this has been a very revealing day. Randy, the owner, came to me this morning and informed me that my roommate is not coming back. She decided to stay in Seattle. She met a guy and found love. She is going to stay with him.

"Randy asked me about you, and I told him your story. Did I tell you he was in Vietnam? His father built this truck stop. He retired and handed the business over to Randy. He did a tour in Vietnam a year before you arrived, Lenny.

"I told him that we'd immediately hit it off and that I'd suggested that you stay in the trailer with me. He agreed and said it was perfect timing. He then told me that the security department was short one person. The department employs thirteen people, Lenny. That's how many are needed for a round-the-clock security detail for a place this size.

"He told me to walk with him to the station. That's when he told the supervisor to hire you. I hope that you are not upset with our decision. It happened so quickly, Lenny. I did not want to jeopardize the deal. I thought that if you disagreed, you could always refuse the job.

"He is willing to pay you ten dollars per hour and to give you benefits. That's gainful pay. With the free housing, you can save a lot of money for school. Lenny, please say yes and stay!"

"How could I say no to a deal that pays well and comes with a beautiful round eye who is smarter than I am?"

"That is typical talk for a Vietnam vet. At least you don't have to buy me a Saigon tea to talk to me," Cal said, laughing.

"Thank you very much, Cal."

"Oh, I didn't mention the last benefit, Lenny. I have a company car, and Randy said he would add you to his insurance. That means that you won't need to concern yourself with transportation, which is another plus."

"Why is he so generous?"

"Randy believes in paying his people high wages. This truck stop is a gold mine. It has made Randy very wealthy. Last but not least, he takes care of Vietnam vets. He said to take as long as you need to recoup and to report to the security office for duty when you're ready."

"I am so excited, Lenny. That's all the business for now. There were at least three carloads worth of hippies in the cafeteria today.

"They were all headed to a town in upstate New York called Woodstock. They were talking about a music festival where popular bands will play night and day for three days. They predicted that hundreds of thousands of people were going to attend. I wish we could go, Lenny."

"That would be fun, Cal. However, it's not possible at this time."

"Maybe another time, Lenny?"

"Yeah, next time."

"I see you found some clothes of mine that fit you, Lenny. Are you wearing my panties too?"

"No, Cal. I don't have any underwear on."

"That is sexy, Lenny!"

"Shut your mouth, Cal!"

"On the first day I have off, we will go to town and purchase you new clothes."

"If you're done talking, Cal, I'd like to say something."

"I'm sorry. Please do, Lenny!"

"You are the best thing that's happened to me since I was discharged. I am appreciative of all you've done. Can we seal this deal with a handshake?"

"Of course," Cal said, laughing.

"I will see you later, Lenny."

"What time do you finish work, Cal? I will meet you and walk you home."

"That would be nice! If you'd like, I can show you the gym and the outside basketball courts. Meet me at six, Lenny."

I decided to return to the trailer I then called home. I had been thinking about the social-engineering tactics used by powerful entities and the government that Cal had informed me of. I noticed that her bookshelves were loaded with books on the topic. Cal was definitely brilliant.

I wondered whether the authorities considered the books to be subversive. I personally did not care. I wanted to explore Cal's library. I had almost three hours before I'd have to meet her. I would use the time to acquaint myself with the interesting subject of social engineering.

The library included quite a collection of books about radical ideas. A few of her books were on the subject of what was then being called "conventional medical treatment," or "drug therapy," which treated the symptoms of diseases only, totally disregarding the diseases' cures.

I learned that one known radical physiologist believed that of all the allopathic medications prescribed, not one could heal illnesses.

I could not think of a reason that those medications would be used if they could not eliminate diseases. Then I read his statement:

"There is no money in curing diseases. Once a disease is cured, the money stops coming in. The practice of treating a disease's symptoms can provide the doctor with a continuous flow of money throughout the life of the victim."

I noticed that the author used the word "victim" instead of "patient." There was another book that I found particularly interesting. The book concerned a conspiracy by the American Medical Association and its new treatment partner, the pharmaceutical industry. Their objective was to influence Congress to give the Professional Standards Review Organization the authority to prevent practicing physicians from teaching about health, disease prevention, and other natural cures.

This association formed a committee that was responsible for distributing disinformation to the public as a way to discredit other treatments of diseases. Drug therapy became the only curriculum taught in medical schools in the United States and its territories. The goal was to create a drug treatment-only monopoly. Once a monopoly was formed, information and prices could be controlled.

I couldn't wait to question Cal about these subjects. I had much learning to do to catch up with her. Time flew by. I needed to hurry to meet Cal on time.

"I'm sorry I'm late, Cal."

"I will be about ten minutes longer. We broke records today, Lenny. We had two busloads of tourists for dinner—that meant one hundred sixty additional people to feed. The kitchen is running low on food!"

"Cal, cool it. I will give you a massage when we get home."

"God, that sounds so good! Where have you been for the last year of my life?"

"Duh, I was in Vietnam, Cal."

"I forgot that I'm robbing the cradle."

"Come on, Cal. You are only a little more than four years older than I am."

"Closer to five years, Lenny. I completed a four-year nursing program before I joined the army."

"If it means anything, Cal, I like older women."

"Sit down, Lenny, and shut up! I need to finish up here."

"I love you, Cal."

"I can't finish up here when you're playing games, Lenny. How will I be able to focus if you continue to excite me with statements that arouse me? I will wear your young ass out when I get you home!"

"I doubt it, Cal."

"I already know your sexual weakness. Go, Lenny, and find us a table! Git, Lenny! Go now, and pour us two cups of black coffee. I will be right there."

"I spent the entire afternoon in your library. Your books on the distribution of information really captured my attention. I want you to know that I reviewed your talking points you wrote inside your books. I apologize if you consider them to be personal. I am fascinated by this area of thought.

"I have a burning desire to know more about the ways disinformation is distributed to the masses for the benefit of the government, the corporations, and the rich and powerful. I'd never heard of social engineering or of the psychological manipulation of the masses before.

"I'm also curious about drug therapy's assault on the elderly and the covert collusions between the government, the American Medical Association, and the pharmaceutical corporations. These ideas crossed my mind before, but I never knew that methods of persuasion could be considered sciences."

"Lenny, don't take what I'm about to say personally. If you want to study these matters, you'll need an education. A formal education gives one an edge. I have four years of college on you, Lenny. I am not saying that I am smarter than you. It only means that I am more literate. Listen to me closely, Lenny! I really like you for who you are."

"I won't be illiterate for long, Cal. In a matter of a couple days, I have learned so much, Cal. I will catch up with you. These subjects are so interesting. I will devour your library in a few months. My goal is to know everything, Cal."

"Lenny, let me make this perfectly clear. I do not want to assume the role of a mentor. I'd prefer to talk about the differences in our levels of education later. I'd rather enjoy and emphasize our common interests, like Vietnam, sports, reading, and our sexual attraction.

"You and I have been alone for too long. For now, we must focus on our immediate needs. We have good jobs for this time in our lives. You and I are a team, Lenny. I could not work as a nurse after Vietnam. I saw enough blood and guts to last me a lifetime. It still angers me that the war benefited the rich at the expense of the lower- and middle-class young men."

"I see that you highlighted a quote by Eugene Victor Debs: 'The master class has always declared the wars; the subject class has always fought the battles. The master class has had all the gain and nothing to lose, while the subject class has had nothing to gain and all to lose, especially their lives.'

"I refuse to work in a profession that reminds me of the horrid sights I witnessed while working at the hospital in Vietnam."

"Your experience in Vietnam ruined your nursing career, Cal. The government should compensate you for your mental damage."

"Now you are beginning to see things, Lenny."

"You open my eyes to injustices, Cal. There's one more thing. I want to discuss the talking points I read in your notes."

"Which ones, Lenny?"

"I want to know more about the use of technobabble to impress or deceive the ignorant and the policy to teach only what's in textbooks, which is being enforced at a growing number of our higher-learning institutions."

"Without a doubt, that is a sly attempt by the government and the special-interest groups to impose their interests and beliefs on the masses. OK,

Lenny. After you read the book you found containing my talking points, we will have a detailed discussion."

CAL INTRODUCES LENNY TO THE GYM (1969)

"For now, let's go home and change into clothing suitable for working out in the gym, Lenny. I exercise to help me manage the everyday stresses at work. I now have an additional goal."

"What is that, Cal?"

"I want to look hot for you, Lenny."

"I think you are hot now!"

"I have sweats that will fit you, Lenny."

"These sweats are really baggy."

"I like them baggy on you. I don't want other women looking at you," Cal said, laughing.

"If something is good with you, it will be good with me, Cal. I never had an older girlfriend before or one who is as independent as you."

"What do you mean?"

"The last girlfriend I had before I served in the army was in high school, and she lived with her parents."

"Did you have sex with her?"

"No, I did not."

"I learned everything about sex in Atlanta, Georgia, six weeks before entering the army from a woman named Mary Gibson and her daughter, Lori. In Vietnam, I always went to the same whorehouse. I knew that the mama-san kept her girls clean and free of diseases. She gave me her own daughter, and she taught me how to please an Asian woman."

"She taught you well, Lenny. You are the best fuck I have ever had!"

"Thanks, Cal, it makes me feel good to know that I pleased you in bed. I was concerned that you'd think I was inexperienced with lovemaking since I'm so much younger than you. I was beginning to think I had nothing to offer you."

"Let's go, Lenny."

"How late does the gym stay open?"

"It is open twenty-four hours if you have a key. All employees have keys. Visitors pay for a pass. The normal hours are from six in the morning to midnight. Have you ever worked out?"

"Not in a real gym, Cal."

"I will show you how to use the equipment and teach you a routine that will work different muscle groups. What would you like to accomplish?"

"What do you mean?"

"Do you want to gain muscle, lose weight, or just improve your cardio?"

"Cardio, Cal? What's that?"

"Your wind power, Lenny!"

"OK, I get it. I don't know. What do you think I should do?"

"Well, you are a little skinny."

"I lost weight in Vietnam.

"On missions, we'd walk between ten and fifteen miles a day and carry sixty-five pounds of munitions and supplies. The thirty-day soup-and-water routine in the facility didn't help either."

"Your cardio is good because of your age and combat activity. Do you want to put some muscle on?"

"Sure. Will you show me how to do that?"

"No problem. It might take a week to go through a full-body workout. As we go, I'll explain to you the proper ways to do these exercises in order to get the most out of them.

"There's a book that I suggest you read in the meantime."

"OK. I want to learn as much as I can. I did not know a woman could know so much about building muscle."

"Lenny, I read. It will be good for you to develop a reading habit."

"I love reading, and I will read more, Cal. I want to be as smart as you."

"Well, I wasn't smart enough to avoid wasting six years of my life with a bum who punched me and left me here at this godforsaken truck stop. I don't know how much longer I could have gone if you hadn't showed up. I was at my wits' end."

"Damn, Cal. Sometimes bad things happen for good reasons. You have my support. I think you are one of the finest women I have ever met. I will do my best to make you happy. I will work hard to build my body and to strengthen my mind. You are my inspiration, Cal."

"Lenny, you never stop amazing me. I like you the way you are. You are a good man, and you have been a gentleman to me.

"Best of all, you are a survivor of Vietnam. Let's get busy with our workout, Lenny."

"This is why you are so hard and defined for your age, right?"

"Lenny, stop referring to me as old. I'm only twenty-six."

"Most girls your age are soft and smooth. You can tell by looking at them. You are hard as a rock and have a lot of muscle definition, Cal."

"I began working out in this gym the first week I started working here. I found that it relieved the stress caused by being dumped. I ordered a book on bodybuilding by Joe and Betty Weider. His nickname was the 'Master Blaster' because of the amazing physique he created by lifting weights.

"With his brother, Ben, he created the International Federation of Bodybuilders in 1935. Some call him the father of bodybuilding. I studied his training techniques. My body is tighter now than it was when I was eighteen. I have more up-to-date books in my library about bodybuilding. You should familiarize yourself with the muscular system and the exercises that can enhance specific muscle groups. Knowing a little anatomy is a must, Lenny."

"I definitely will take the time to study your anatomy books."

"Today I intend to introduce you to different exercises. You can watch me do the exercise first. Pay close attention to my strict form and to how I use full range of motion for each repetition. These principles are very important for proper muscular development and for avoiding injury.

"I will allow you to do a few repetitions with light weights for practice. I don't want you to do too much and become sore, which is a mistake that most people make when they begin. The training manual will teach you how to select the proper weight for each exercise as well as how to increase the amount of weight you use in order to continue gaining muscle size and strength.

"I will ask you about that important procedure the next time we work out. I will also expect you to read the bodybuilding-training manual and to put together a workout routine. You and I will review the routine before your next workout the day after tomorrow.

"Lenny, before we move on I would like to emphasize what is more important than looking good. When you combine good food and exercise you have insured that you have increased your chance of avoiding disease and a long robust life."

"Cal, you are suggesting I study up on food too?"

"That is exactly what I am saying, Lenny. I have a few books on nutrition you might take a look at. I have given you the basics. The rest is up to you, Lenny."

"OK, Cal. I will read them. Can we go home and shower together? I will wash your back."

"I can't think of a better way to end a hard working day. By the way, tomorrow is my day off. Let's go, Lenny."

■ ■ ■

THE REMODELING IS COMPLETE, AND BETTY AND THE FAMILY RETURN HOME (PRESENTLY)

Ruby was riding with Betty. I decided to go ahead in Ruby's car and to make sure that the house was in good order and that the AC was on. The contractor had assured Betty that the yard would be free of scrap materials, and it was. I called Betty and Ruby, who had stopped at the grocery store.

"Ruby, the place looks great! I am going to start unpacking. Is there anything I can do for you or Betty?"

"I don't believe so, Lenny. If something comes to mind, I will call you. We will be another thirty minutes or so. We are picking up perishables we disposed of before we left."

BETTY AND HAROLD REINVEST THEIR MONEY

Betty spent a lot of money to make Ruby and me comfortable. That was just the kind of person Betty was. Ruby and I accepted her hospitality because we knew that that was what she truly desired. With Betty, you couldn't take the money she'd spent to make you comfortable into consideration. She enjoyed taking care of the people she cared about. It was a large part of what made Betty who she was.

She had invested money with Harold for over sixty years and had amassed a fortune. No expense was spared during the construction of Harold's living space. The money she spent on the elaborate temporary accommodations for us was like nothing to her. Besides, Harold and Betty's desire to charter a bank proved that they had a great amount of wealth.

Betty revealed their reason for investing in the military industrial complex. Harold had defended a powerful Washington, D.C., lobbyist. The man had represented one of the largest military aircraft builders. He'd said that the Military-Industrial Complex had spent millions to support and elect members of Congress who would favor military intervention in South Vietnam to stop the spread of Communism.

He'd advised Harold to buy stock in companies that manufactured war materials. Betty had invested with Harold in war-manufacturing materials, pharmaceuticals, chemicals, and petroleum, and they'd made tens of millions of dollars.

They both later regretted their involvement in crony capitalism. Crony capitalism is the idea that one's success in business depends on close relationships with powerful government representatives or employees. Betty admitted that they'd kept the fortune they'd made. She'd rationalized that choice by saying that they would use the money to do good. I was impressed by Betty's admission of guilt.

Most billionaires don't give a damn about the damage they are doing to the earth or to other people's health. They get their way by buying politicians and convincing them to pass laws that will promote or protect their financial interests. Furthermore, their massive advertising budgets influence the media, which convince the ignorant masses to agree with the corporations' views. The best example is the defeat of the California GMO bill. Big-money advertising convinced the voters that they didn't need to know what was being put into their food. The thought of that happening is enough to cause me to lose faith with people in general.

Betty also said that she and Harold had eventually recognized their moral crime against humanity—investing in the military industrial complex—and how the military was contributing to the senseless destruction of the earth and the needless sacrifice of life over conquest. So they'd withdrawn their money and invested it into sustainable food and clean-energy production and bought stock in a new grocery supplier called Whole Foods. The store caught on and expanded quickly across the United States selling organic foods. Betty and Harold made more millions.

Betty was aware of her age and had decided to make a last push to leave something behind for the people she loved and cared for. I was of the opinion that when Lewis died, Betty opened her treasure chest. She then decided to place her money in a brick-and-mortar investment; a community bank that would employ and provide for her loved ones for generations to come.

I would have to wait and see about Harold. I was willing to wager that he was similar to Betty. I couldn't wait to study the highly successful, intelligent lawyer and investor who had generated great wealth.

BETTY, RUBY, AND LENNY, LEAVE DOWNTOWN FORT MYERS AND GO HOME

My phone rang. Gloria was calling to notify me that she and Bob would be over later. She said they were happy we were home. The doorbell rang.

"It is open!" I said.

In walked Will and Bailey.

"Where is Betty?" Bailey asked.

"They are at the grocery store and will be here shortly."

"How is Betty doing? Is she well, Lenny?"

"She is fine, Bailey." I was aware of how close Bailey and Betty had become since the accident.

"I'm going to call Betty. Betty, this is Bailey. When will you be home? OK, Betty. I love you too. She says she and Ruby will be here in about ten minutes, Lenny."

"Hey, everybody. I have cold beer and champagne. What will it be, Bob?"

"I will have a beer, Lenny."

"Me too," Will said.

"Gloria, I will open a bottle of champagne for you."

"Lenny, give me the corkscrew. I will open the champagne for you while you finish putting those bags away."

"Thanks, Bob."

"Betty is here, everybody," Bailey yelled. She then ran to the door to greet her. "Hi, Betty. I'm glad you are home." Betty hugged her and gave her a kiss.

"I missed you, darling," Betty said.

"Where is Lenny?" Ruby asked.

"He is in the bedroom unpacking," Bob said.

"Will, can you help me with the groceries?"

"Sure, Ruby. And how have you been?"

"All I can say is that it is great to be home, Will. Betty, tell me about the downtown district."

"Bailey, I finally saw Thomas Edison's and Henry Ford's homes. It took two days to see it all. I'd place them at the top of my list of interesting historic sites for you and Will to see."

INSPECTING HAROLD'S ADDITION

"Betty, I have heard so much about the addition," Bob said. "Can you show it to us?"

"I would be glad to. I have not seen it myself. I would welcome some help with evaluating the workmanship. I intend to try out every amenity before Harold arrives. I don't need any workers coming back to do minor repairs once he's moved in. I would like Lenny and Ruby to occupy the suite and to test everything."

"The interior decorators were the last ones in. There shouldn't be anything left to do. The beds should be made, and the bathroom stocked with towels and personal things."

"That kind of preparation is unheard of to me, Betty."

"All he needs to do is bring his clothes. He'll need only a couple of changes of clothes. We plan to purchase him a new wardrobe. His clothes are meant for Michigan's climate. We decided that attire suited for Florida would be more appropriate. Harold considers this move to be his official retirement."

"Wow, that's a celebration within itself. May I suggest a retirement party for Harold, Betty?"

"Thanks, Bob. I will take that suggestion into consideration. OK, if you would like to look at Harold's new suite, let's go now," Betty said.

"This place is unbelievable," Gloria said.

"The entire residence is constructed of marble and granite," Betty said.

"Is it totally smart, Betty?"

"Yes, Gloria."

"All of the electric amenities—even the electric blinds and sunroof—can be controlled remotely by a cell phone or a computer from any location on the earth."

"One hundred percent of the power is supplied by the solar panels on the roof, Bob."

"Does that include the power for the pool and Hydro Spa?"

"Yes, Bob. Everything is run off of solar energy. In case anyone is wondering, Harold paid for everything. I don't feel comfortable divulging how much this addition cost. I suggest that you ask Harold that."

"The pool is small," Gloria said. "This is a pool for swimming."

"The current can be adjusted to whatever speed you prefer, Gloria. Harold is a swimmer. Swimming is a great way to exercise at home."

"If this pool were at my house, I would be in great shape," Bob said.

"Lenny is in the process of packing up our things to move over now. I'm going to leave you and go help him organize them. See you people later," Ruby said.

BETTY GIVES BAILEY A BLUE TOPAZ NECKLACE

"Bailey, have you worn that beautiful blue dress and those heels?"

"I tried them on for Will, Betty."

"I have a beautiful blue topaz necklace that I want you to have. It will match them perfectly. I insist that you accept it."

"Oh, Betty. What can I say? Thank you."

"Bailey, it is perfect for you. We both have birthdays in December. You said that you love to read and that you wanted to write one day. The blue topaz is known as the writers' stone. It helps with writers' block and promotes creativity. Did you know that, Bailey?"

"I hadn't heard that, Betty."

"Will, how did you think she looked in her new dress?"

"She was beautiful, Betty. Nothing but class. She plans to wear the dress to Bob and Gloria's wedding. Gloria has not decided on a date. I told Bailey we would dine and go dancing afterward. I want her to enjoy the dress, Betty."

"She is a lovely young woman, Will, with a heart of gold. You two will have a memorable time."

"I can't wait, Betty," Bailey said.

HAROLD'S SUPERCONDO AND THE STATE OF THE FAMILY

"The addition was a real production, Lenny. Do you know what Harold spent?"

"Betty told me. Between you and me, Harold spent one and a half million. Do you think Betty will live there with him, Ruby?"

"I don't think so. They have lived by themselves for too long. Their idea is to be close."

"Do you think Betty is planning to have me work in the bank?"

"Oh, no, Lenny! She realizes that you and I will do our thing together. She has plans for the family members who need work. She asked Bailey if she would be willing to take a couple of courses specific to banking. She already knows about finances and accounting. Those are her responsibilities at the VA."

"Bailey and her assistant will manage the tellers. Bailey will also assist Bob and his assistant with lending clients' money."

"Betty and Harold will be the cochairpersons of the board of directors. The other members of the board will be the two investors and Bob. Betty said that she and Harold would maintain the majority ownership and control of the bank. Betty says that Bailey will be her greatest asset."

"That comes as a surprise to me, Ruby."

"Betty is all about finances, Lenny. That is why Bailey will be Betty's greatest asset."

"That does make sense, Ruby."

"Furthermore, they have a mother-daughter relationship. Bailey never knew her mother. There's no way Betty would leave her out of the bank. Betty will definitely take care of her financially."

"Does that worry you, Ruby?"

"If you are insinuating that I am jealous of Bailey, you are dead wrong, Lenny."

"That's what Betty and Harold have in mind, Lenny. Betty plans to use us as advisors. She expects us to serve as silent members of the board."

"How does that work, Ruby?"

"We will advise only her and Harold."

THE FAMILY'S INTELLIGENCE

"Lenny, you and I are immediate family. Betty knows that our feelings about her wouldn't change if she didn't have money. She knows our love for her has nothing to do with money. We are her family, Lenny. If something happened to Betty, you would become a very wealthy man."

"Would that make you feel better about me, Ruby?"

"That's insulting, Lenny. I like your mind most of all. You are rich with intelligence. Money can't buy intelligence, Lenny. That is what I admire in a man. Between you and Betty, we have no need for encyclopedias in this house. When Harold comes, we can open the first living library."

"What do you mean, Ruby?"

"Betty claims that Harold is the most intelligent person she has ever known. I'm saying that between you three, there will be no need for reference books. Anything that someone could need to know is contained in one of your brains. Best of all, one of those big brains belongs to my man," laughed Ruby. "That makes me wealthy by association and very content!

"Didn't you once say that we are all a product of our environments? I have money. Now all I need are brains. I don't think I could find a more intellectually stimulating environment to live in. Every conversation in this house is over the top, so to speak. The credit goes to Betty. She attracts brilliance. It will just be a matter of time before some of the incredible brainpower that I'm surrounded by wears off on me."

"How the hell did you come up with that analysis, Ruby?"

"It is true, Lenny. When we have guests, they notice the phenomenon. Don't you remember the first time Bob was over? He said he was astounded by the amount of intelligent people present. He's a bank president who is often in the presence of many intelligent people, so he should know."

"I will say something now, Ruby. It must be working for you. That is a very astute observation and a little boastful."

RUBY SIZES LENNY UP

"The first time I met an intelligent woman was about forty-five days before I joined the army. She became my peculiar lover and later, my wife. When I first came back from Vietnam, I met another older woman. She helped me adjust to civilian life and introduced me to reading. Ruby, I didn't know anything! She inspired my lifetime pursuit of knowledge.

"She was five years older than I, a skeptic, and had a degree in nursing. She was a Vietnam veteran and had seen a lot of combat flying helicopter evacuations of wounded and dead American soldiers in and out of dangerous landing zones. Her name was Callie. Someday, when there is time, I would love to tell you her story."

"Lenny, I'm really not interested in it. Let me clarify my statement, Lenny. The only thing that concerns me is what you and I are doing."

"I will accept that explanation, and it does make sense, Ruby. I turned the Hydro Spa on. Would you like to try it out?"

"I would rather do some swimming first. I need the exercise."

"I agree, Ruby."

"Lenny, why do you always agree with me?"

"We think alike. Ruby. Sometimes I say something, and you see it differently, and then I say that you are right. Is that what you're talking about, Ruby? For instance, when I asked you if you would like to relax in the Hydro Spa and you said you wanted to swim, I agreed."

"Yeah, that's what I'm talking about, Lenny."

"I said the first thing that came to my mind, and when you voiced your preference for swimming, it struck me as a better idea. That's all. I listen to you, Ruby. If your idea is better than mine, I go with it. It does not bother me at all when you correct me or even suggest something different."

"Damn, Lenny—that's intelligent. That's what I love about you. And I see the kind heart that Betty spoke of. You are the first man I have met who does not allow his ego to control his decision-making process when he's dealing with women. You truly treat me as an equal. I can't believe some woman didn't grab you before I came along."

"I have a reply to that statement, Ruby. Most women know only about chronological age. Very few have ever heard of biological age, which is where I excel. Biologically, I am fourteen years younger than my chronological age. Every woman who came before you looked at my face and decided I was not 'Hollywood handsome.'

"You looked at my entire package and decided that I was desirable. You accepted my shabby face, I guess. No other woman seemed to care about my intellect or my physical condition. If you covered my face with a mask, I would look like I was in my forties. You do not have any flaws that I need to accept. I have never known a woman so perfect.

"I thought women like you were reserved for Hollywood celebrities or the rich and famous. Very few women who are six feet tall are perfectly proportionate, but you are. Damn, Ruby, your legs reach my waist. When we go out, I read people's minds. They're thinking, 'What is she doing with that ugly man?' I try to dress better when I'm with you. I'd prefer to have ignorant people think that I'm with you because I'm rich, not because I have a big cock.

"When you told me what people think doesn't bother you, it was a relief. I'm sure you could have gone to Hollywood if you had chosen to, Ruby. I know you could have married a multibillionaire German industrialist. However, you chose to be with me. I gave up on trying to figure out how you came to me or why you are with me. I am one lucky SOB."

"Everything about you is real, Lenny. I love you."

■ ■ ■

RUBY AND LENNY GO TO THE BEACH AT SUNSET

"Ruby, would you like to go to the beach for the sunset? We can take the scooter. I am mentally congested. The salt air and the sunset will revitalize me."

"I could use some beach therapy too. Let's go! I understand now why you love to ride the scooter."

"What brought that up, Ruby?"

"The other day when you went to the gym to work out with Ed, I went for a ride. I liked the feeling of the wind in my face. It is hard to explain. I had a ball while I was rolling down the highway."

"That comes as a surprise to me, Ruby. It never crossed my mind that you would take off like that. You never cease to amaze me, Ruby Ridge.

"If you would like to ride on your own, we could stop into a dealership and look at scooters.

"Before we go out looking at scooters, I'd prefer to do a little research on the Internet. I need a vacation with just you and me. Ruby, hop on the scooter, and hold on. Next stop will be the beach!"

"Lenny, we are lucky. There won't be clouds in the way of the sunset."

"I don't need to rekindle my feelings toward you, Ruby. They grow stronger every day."

"Lenny, most people give things to others in order to receive things. Of course, they openly deny their reason for giving; consider a billionaire who gives large sums of money to a politician's campaign and acts as if he expects nothing in return. I find it sad how many Americans do not see the connection between money and politics."

"That's the reason that corruption is alive and well in our country, Ruby."

"Betty gives without any expectation of receiving something in return. It comes naturally for her. You can't question Betty's methods of selecting friends. She is a master at choosing talented, giving people to be her friends. She surrounds herself with extremely talented people, and they follow her lead without preconceived monetary expectations."

"Lenny, do you think older people are more giving? I do. I don't believe it is a trait that was brought on by aging. I think people in general were more considerate of others in the past. It seems like each generation is becoming more selfish. I hear people refer to the millennial generation as the "me" generation. I'm a millennial, and I agree. I don't understand my own generation. My occupation exposed me to older gentlemen. I have never been around many men my age. The few times I was around youger men, I judged their behavior, to a certain degree, to be juvenile. What do you think, Lenny?"

"Wow, Ruby, I would need some time to digest what you just revealed to me. As of this moment, I would tend to agree with you. You have obviously put more thought into this behavior than me. If it is a matter of importance to you, I will think about it and give you a better or more complete answer later."

"Lenny, don't bother to waste any time on this thought. It means nothing to me. One of the girls I worked with in Vegas used to call thoughts of no relevance 'brain farts.'"

"Ruby, I think I understand."

"You and I have no suspicions about Betty's objectives. We do our part with enthusiasm, and so does everyone else in the family. Why? Because we have mutual respect for one another and know that we are better together.

The motto Will gave us, 'one for all, and all for one,' fits us and makes damn good sense. You can't go it alone in this complex, modern world."

RUBY AND LENNY ARE PRIVILEGED

"Lenny, do you agree that the pier is approximately a hundred meters from where we are?"

"Looks about right to me."

"Ruby, you say when to go."

"Get ready, get set, and…go!"

"Damn, you beat me by at least five lengths. I'm not getting any closer to beating you. Your stride equals two of mine. I guess I need to dance more."

"Don't take losing to heart, Lenny. You know you will never outrun me. We can have a beer on the beach at the Lani Kai. We can sit with our feet in the surf and enjoy another day in paradise. Lenny, we are fortunate."

"How so, Ruby?"

"We don't have to work eight or ten hours a day to provide for our basic needs. This allows more time to accumulate knowledge and to observe the world around us. We see more than the average working American does, Lenny. Did you ever think about that?"

"I have, Ruby."

"When I worked seven days a week in Las Vegas, I had no idea of what was going on. Within a few months of not working and being with you and Betty, I became aware of my environment and developed incredible observational skills. Lenny, my understanding of my environment has grown exponentially. I see what is going on outside my space."

"The average American spends time concentrating on work, kids, or acquiring material needs to support their chosen lifestyle. This leaves little time to focus on crucial mental and physical needs. I think that health and happiness are more important than accumulating excess money and assets, Lenny."

"We do agree on the more important things."

"The mind is a wonderful thing, Lenny."

"In general, people who have free time, ample resources, and live less stressful lives are much happier, experience fewer chronic diseases, and live longer, Ruby."

"Americans work longer hours and have more mental and social problems than people in any other affluent nation. They spend what little time they have after work playing games, listening to music, or watching mindless television programs. How could these people ever become aware of the political or environmental issues that affect their health and lives, Lenny?"

"I have a question, Ruby. Why is it that the finest-looking women, you being the exception, always end up with the wealthiest men?"

"That's something that everybody knows is true, but no one will dare acknowledge, Lenny."

"Does that mean that women have privilege?"

"Yes, it does seem to suggest that, Lenny. If you spoke about women in that manner publicly, you would probably be branded a misogynist, Lenny."

"That reminds me of how fortunate I am to be with you, Ruby. Political correctness keeps all of us from saying what we want to say. What good does that do for any of us?"

"None, Lenny! OK, Lenny, back to simple reality. You lost the race. You can buy the beer, rub my back, and whisper sweet things in my ear."

"I knew you would rub it in!"

THE CT SCAN OF LENNY'S HEART

"The other day when you left the condo, you were gone for almost three hours. You didn't say anything when you returned. A couple of days later, I noticed a receipt from a radiology clinic on the floor of the car. I knew it was yours. It scared the shit out of me, Lenny.

"What is going on with you? The mystery is driving me crazy. When we returned home, I checked the mail. There was a letter from the radiology clinic. I took it, Lenny, thinking that I would present it to you at the right time. As a matter of fact, I put it in the back pocket of my cutoffs when we decided to go to the beach for the sunset. Here it is."

"Are you crying, Ruby?"

"Yes. I just found you, and I fear that you may be seriously sick. Do you have a terminal illness? Why else would you be so secretive about something like this? I know what radiology is. It usually involves a CT scan for tumors and heart disease."

"Ruby, I did the scan for no reason other than prevention. I had a heart scan to determine whether I had the beginnings of blockages in the primary arteries of my heart. If you catch a blockage early, you'll have time to eradicate the problem."

"Is this letter about the result of the scan?"

"Yes, Ruby, it is."

"Hold my hand, and tell me the results."

"I will if you stop crying. Here, wipe your eyes with my T-shirt, and calm yourself."

"Are you upset with me for taking the letter?"

"No, I know now that I was wrong to not let you know about it from the beginning. I am sorry that I caused you to worry. Ruby, my initial thought was that I shouldn't alarm you. I see now how wrong I was."

"Lenny, I don't care what that letter says. We will not allow it to take away what we both waited a lifetime for: each other. Here we go!"

We read the letter. This is what it said:

The scan showed that the calcification score for each artery is proportional to the amount of calcium in the coronary vessel wall.

(1) Left main coronary artery 0
(2) Left anterior descending coronary artery 5.76
(3) Left circumflex coronary artery 0
(4) Right coronary artery.. 0

The total coronary artery calcification score is 5.76. The score indicates a minimal amount of identifiable calcified plaque.

"Ruby, getting this scan is something that anyone can do for less than a hundred dollars. If you visited your doctor and asked for a scan, he would send you to the same clinic, and the clinic would send him the bill, and the doctor's office would add hundreds of dollars to it.

"You can do blood tests in the same way. The point is that you don't have to have a doctor order the tests, and you don't have to have a doctor interpret the tests. You need only go online to learn how to interpret your own test or scan. In that way, you can take control of your own health.

"Furthermore, you don't need expensive drugs with dangerous side effects. Those drugs do nothing more than treat the symptoms of illnesses and allow doctors to make profits. You may only need to change your diet or adjust your environment. Again, the Internet will provide you with information on the causes of illnesses and with suggestions for remedies.

"Sometimes administering one drug will cause a side effect, and another drug will be needed to counter it. Before long, you'll be taking numerous pills.

"Once you unknowingly become an addict, your health will spiral downward. Ruby, no other country in the world kills more of its people by overprescribing drugs or prescribing unnecessary drugs than the United States does. The sicker the patient is; the more money his doctor will earn.

"No other doctors make as much money as doctors in America do."

IT IS TIME FOR THE BEACH

"Promise me that you will never do anything like this again, Lenny. I have been fearful since I found the radiology receipt in the car. I might have overreacted, but you must understand that my unequivocal love for you and your secrecy led me to fear that you were hiding a serious problem. I could not bear the thought of losing you. I feel as if a heavy weight has been lifted from my chest."

"Ruby, again, I am sorry! It has been a long time since anyone has worried about my welfare. For that reason, your concern never came to my mind."

"I want us to spend quality time together, Lenny. I suggest that we obtain a room at the Pink Shell and spend the entire day on the beach tomorrow. I am due for some fun in the sun. It is the off-season. We will have no problem booking a room."

"We can purchase a couple of bathing suits here at the beach. It will be like a re-creation of the first night we were totally intimate."

"I will reserve the same room, Lenny."

"Do it!"

"I will make our reservation."

"First thing in the morning, we can do a workout on the beach. Then we can rent a couple of Jet Skis and look for dolphins or manatees, or maybe we can go kayaking."

"What about Betty, Ruby?"

"She does not need to be alone. I will call Mom and suggest that she and Bob stay in Harold's place. They will jump at the opportunity."

"Make it happen, Ruby."

"Betty laughed when I suggested the arrangement. She will agree to anything that brings you and me closer together, Lenny. I love that woman, Lenny. Guess what Betty wants me to bring her from the beach?"

"I could not guess in a thousand years, Ruby."

"She wants a 'spring break' T-shirt."

"That is funny. Harold's coming is turning her into a teenager."

"Good for her!"

SHOPPING FOR A SWIMSUIT FOR RUBY

"Shall we shop for a swimsuit, Lenny? You can find the best and hottest swimsuits at the beach. The downside is that you have to pay tourist prices. The stores at the beach have the latest fashions because they are in the business of selling swimsuits throughout the year.

"In cold climates, swimsuits are in demand only for a few months of the year. You must have a swimsuit if you come to the beach. Most people bring their swimsuits with them. A surprising number of them will purchase new swimsuits when they see that theirs are out of style.

"Once you are on the beach, you will find yourself surrounded by beautiful people wearing the latest styles. Swimsuit styles change often. People who regularly frequent the beach can own as many as half a dozen suits that will be fashionable for only one year. The thrift stores close to the beach are loaded with expensive swimsuits that were stylish one year ago."

"I'm sure, Ruby, that you know the shop with the latest styles."

"I sure do. Give me an idea of the type of swimsuit that you would feel comfortable with me wearing."

"When you say 'type,' Ruby, are you referring to the size? Or are you asking whether I'd prefer that you wear a one-piece swimsuit or a bikini?"

"I am asking what you would prefer me to wear, Lenny."

"You should already know the answer. I'd prefer that you wear what you want to wear, Ruby. Knowing you, the smaller and the more erotic a swimsuit is, the more you will like it."

"You know me well, Lenny. I am comfortable with nothing but heels on. As a showgirl for five years, I danced in front of hundreds of thousands of people wearing small pasties. Often I was totally nude. I will wear something that is barely legal, Lenny. You know that I am an exhibitionist. Your acceptance of me is one of the many reasons that I love you."

"Ruby, any woman who had a body like yours would do the same thing. Enjoy it while you have it, Ruby."

"I am! I know where to find the tiny designer suits. Would you like to help me choose one?"

"How would I do that?"

"You sit there and judge them. I will pick out three and model them for you. You can make the final decision about which one to purchase."

"This is going to be exciting."

"I will begin my search. I like these three, Lenny. They are diaphanous, thin, clingy, bright, and my style. Hand me my beach bag, Lenny. I don't like to try on sexy swimsuits without heels on. Pink is a popular color."

RUBY'S UNOFFICIAL SWIMSUIT FASHION SHOW

"It's show time, Lenny. I will walk to the end of the shop and back. What do you think?"

"I need time to regain my composure, Ruby, and so do the employees."

"Well, keep this one in mind while I slip into the next suit. It is more like me. It's very clingy and revealing, especially around my private area. I owe my thanks to the MGM Grand and to its artistic surgeon. I like this one, Lenny. It gives me a familiar feeling. The material is the same as the material of my favorite Las Vegas costume. Tell me what you think of it while I walk."

"God, Ruby, you are drawing a crowd."

"Come on, Lenny, you are used to it."

"I said it was show time! Wait until you see this last suit. I will put an extra kick in my walk. Here goes, Lenny."

"My God, Ruby. The place is packed. People think the store is putting on a swimsuit fashion show. You never cease to amaze me. I like the third suit, Ruby. I based my decision on the crowd's responses."

"I really miss entertaining. I appreciate your putting up with me."

"That's what makes you special, Ruby. I find it hard to believe that something this small could cost one hundred eighty-five dollars."

"I have seen bathing suits go for more, Lenny. Most suits in this price range are handmade. The market for them is limited. Only a few women have the bodies to wear such revealing swimsuits, and young girls cannot afford them."

"Excuse me, miss. I'm Robert Porter, one of the owners of Windy Beach Stores. Would you be willing to model suits for our stores? I was impressed by your modeling skills. The crowd you drew gave me an idea. Maybe Windy Beach Stores could sponsor a swimsuit fashion show. We own and operate twelve stores in South Florida. Swimsuits form the bulk of our revenue. No store in Florida sells more swimsuits than Windy Beach."

"Your performance is on our security camera. If you agree, I will use the recording to present my idea at the next board meeting in Miami."

"My name is Ruby Ridge. I am a local resident. I danced professionally at the MGM Grand in Las Vegas. I was billed as the top showgirl in Las Vegas for five years running."

"Believe me, Ms. Ridge, no one would doubt your accomplishments after seeing your modeling performance."

"I definitely have an interest in doing a show. Mr. Porter, you should know that I am qualified to direct the show and to choreograph the girls' movements to ensure that all of the shows are identical. I have a master's degree in dance. I would insist that all proceeds go to charity."

"Ms. Ridge, that is a fantastic idea. You will hear from me next week. Here are two cards. Please write your number and name on the back of one of them for me. Thank you very much, Ms. Ridge. The swimsuit is on us."

"Thank you, Mr. Porter!"

WHAT LENNY KNOWS ABOUT RUBY

Ruby's conversation with Mr. Porter was obviously perplexing to the onlookers. I had been with Ruby long enough to know what a unique operator she was. The conversation had seemed typical to me. She had forged her life on her own.

She was not a modest woman. She was a perfectionist, she knew her talents, and she was quick to share her successes with others. She had no inhibitions when performing, and she never lacked confidence. She was offensive to certain persuasions, mainly because of her overt sexual conduct and the profession she'd chosen earlier in her life.

When she was confronting others or informing them of something, which she did so well, it was obvious that she'd been a Las Vegas showgirl. She was the most overall-beautiful woman I had ever known. She knew the power of her beauty and talents and used them to achieve her goals. Her character and performance had dominated the arena she'd worked in. I had never known a woman who'd been more comfortable in her skin or a woman I'd admired more than Ruby Ridge.

RETURN TO THE PINK SHELL'S HONEYMOON SUITE

"Let's sit on this bench in Times Square and sort out our next move, Lenny. When did Times Square start having bands? It's too loud. What do you think, Lenny?"

"I prefer the screeches of seabirds to screaming guitar music played by old potbellied ex-hippies stuck in the sixties. It is time to go, Ruby. The music is pissing me off. We can take the scooter to the Pink Shell to check out the available lodging."

"Step back, Lenny, I can handle this. What do you have for two adults for tonight?"

"We can accommodate you on any level. Do you have a certain request?"

"Is there a honeymoon suite with a view available?"

"Yes, it has a direct ocean view and comes with a complimentary bottle of pink champagne."

"We will take it. Here we go again, Lenny. Don't you like doing things on the spur of the moment?"

"It is exciting, Ruby."

"Lenny, why does a nice hotel room inspire romance?"

"My guess is that it represents relief from the romance-inhibiting toils of everyday life. Why are you laughing, Ruby?"

"I did not expect a definitive answer. Take your clothes off, and get in the hot tub with me. When we get out, I will manicure you from head to toe."

"You continue to spoil me, Ruby."

"Removing your body hair is too time consuming, Lenny. I insist that we make you an appointment with a laser technician. I will do that in the next day or so if you will assure me that you will go."

"I don't know, Ruby."

THE CAUSE OF RUBY'S SEXUAL BEHAVIOR

"Lenny, do you think I'm a nymphomaniac?"

"No, absolutely not. That's my answer, Ruby. I think a definitive answer is appropriate this time. A nymphomaniac is a woman who can only control her sexual desires if she is restrained. That is definitely not you. Your present sexual appetite can be explained by Freudian psychology.

"If an individual experiences negative events and doesn't deal with them correctly, that individual will repress those events and bury them deep in her subconscious. Unbeknownst to the individual, that repression will invariably affect her behavior.

"In your case, you were well aware of the cause of your sexual dysfunction, although you had no concept of how to cure your fear of penetration. You held on to that sexual dysfunction. Your sexual needs were pent up for ten or more years.

"You defeated the dysfunction, but you'd been without the emotional benefits of consensual sex for ten years. In time you will psychologically satisfy that need. Once you've achieved balance, the can't-have-enough-sex feeling will subside. In the meantime, explore your deepest sexual fantasies during your journey to recovery. Don't deny any sexual desires."

"You are a man's living fantasy!"

"I will aspire to satisfy all of your needs. Ruby, you bring a song to my mind: 'You Light Up My Life,' by Debby Boone."

"Lenny, you are the highlight of my life. You bring a song to my mind: 'Light My Fire,' by José Feliciano."

"I will open that complimentary bottle of champagne now. We will toast to the new lease on life that we both have found."

"I will drink to that, Lenny."

THE SUPERAPHRODISIAC COMBINATION AT THE PINK SHELL

"What is on the lovemaking menu, Ruby?"

"Take twenty milligrams of the amino acid arginine, which is a vasodilator, every hour as needed for nitric-oxide production. Then take two hundred milligrams, a double dose, of sildenafil citrate while we drink a few glasses of champagne. Combined with five hundred milligrams of testosterone cypionate and two milligrams of IGF-1, you should easily be able to sustain a four-hour rock-hard erection, Lenny. You can add another four hours if needed. I packed an injection of Caverject."

"What made you think of bringing the ultimate hardener, Ruby?"

"When I loaded my beach bag, I said, 'What the hell!' You know me. I can't get enough of you."

"I see that you have been doing research, Ruby."

"I have."

"Good thing I brought a bottle of Gatorade to replace the electrolytes I'll lose, Ruby. I suggest that we do the 'around the body,' the penetration technique we devised to effectively induce an orgasm in each orifice, in four hours."

"I worked with women in Vegas who had achieved ultimate orgasmic development. I know it is possible, Lenny. Let's get busy. Practice makes perfect!"

RUBY'S SEXUAL-DYSFUNCTION THERAPY

I would like to pause this story for a moment, to think back tens of thousands of years ago, and ask whether the concept of rape existed then. Everyone has seen a cartoon of a caveman hitting a female over the head with a club and dragging her back to his cave for intercourse and to make her his wife. Was this violent action accepted as a common mating ritual that produced the same results as a wedding today?

I hypothesize that consent and rape is solely a creation of civilized society and the mental-health disorders resulting from rape are learned behaviors. The severity and type of behavioral disorder are dictated by the values of the rape victim, the family, and the community the rape victim resides in, thus environment.

In this regard, rape, as it has been defined recently, began with cultural evolution's agriculture revolution (approximately 10,000 B.C.) that gave birth to civilized society. Mental disorder caused by rape should be considered a mismatched mental disorder (mental disorders caused by conflict of our ancient genes with modern environment) inflicted on a person by environmental influences.

There are many sexual dysfunctions. Victims react differently to different rape situations. Successful therapy requires an understanding of interdisciplinary studies and a holistic approach to therapy. Ruby's case of rape produced a fear of penetration and resulted in sexual dysfunction.

The success of any type of therapy depends on the right combination of therapy techniques. In Ruby's therapy, a combination of psychological and physical therapy techniques was needed to eliminate her sexual dysfunction.

I will not elaborate on the many other mental dysfunctions that result from rape, since our narrative is concerned with Ruby's specific sexual dysfunction. The functional therapy techniques used to eliminate Ruby's sexual dysfunction are not referenced because no two rapes produce the same identical dysfunction. Sexual dysfunctions in both genders almost always go unmentioned and untreated in today's society.

In Ruby's own words, her sexual dysfunction was a secret. She admitted to Betty that she had permanently accepted her dysfunction. When Betty alluded to Lenny's thesis on sexual dysfunction, a "light bulb went on" in Ruby's head.

Conventional treatments advocate psychotherapy or drug therapy or a combination of the two. It is noteworthy that conventional therapy was originally meant to be a treatment, not necessarily a cure. Success in conventional therapy might be acknowledged when the victim learns how to cope with a dysfunction but is not cured.

Conventional treatment is expensive, unfortunately, and often produces questionable results.

Ruby's therapy cost no money, had no side effects, and was exceptionally pleasurable.

Furthermore, it would be impossible to find identical test subjects with the identical environmental influences that produced Ruby's sexual dysfunction. Identical conditions would be mandatory to satisfy the scientific-method testing standards.

Thus, Ruby's complete recovery from her sexual dysfunction can be explained only in the context of fiction or a miracle.

THE MORNING AFTER

"Good morning, Lenny. I woke up early and ordered a pint of pure cream. I knew that when you woke up, you would panic if you didn't have coffee with heavy cream. I will brew you a cup of coffee. I'll be right back."

"Thank you, Ruby. I slept well. Last night we had the best sex ever. It was the first time I caught my second wind. What do you think, Ruby?"

"Your performance was exemplary. I still have a way to go."

"What do you mean, Ruby?"

"I achieved multiple orgasms in two of the three. The orifice I failed was to orgasm from penetration of the one orifice that I haven't had any problems with. I was close, but close doesn't count."

"What was that, Ruby?"

"Believe it or not, my vagina."

"Next time we will try rotating the orifices being penetrated more often. Would you say this is the closest we have come to perfection?"

"I would."

"Damn, Ruby, give it time. Very few American women even know that different orifices produce different-feeling orgasms."

"You are right, Lenny. We will get there."

"Ruby, modern lifestyles keep the masses focused on many irrelevant forms of entertainment. We tend to forget the main reason we are here on the earth. We are here to reproduce. That being said, nothing is more compelling than the act of copulation. The healthier the person is, the stronger his or her drive will be. That explains why younger people are more driven by sex. It's Mother Nature's way of producing healthy offspring.

"However, there is a concerning difference between males and females. Women's ability to procreate ends with menopause. A healthy man is capable of producing sperm for life."

"Lenny, do you think Mother Nature made a mistake with women?"

"I would prefer not to theorize about that point, Ruby. Any answer a man would give to that question could label him as a misogynist. You know very well what is going on today with political correctness. If the truth offends certain people, then the truth should not be spoken.

"I will say that women losing their sex hormones at menopause will decrease their biological sex drive. The woman's loss of interest sometimes frustrates a healthy husband's increased sexual drive, and in many situations he resorts to infidelity. This is one of many reasons why a lifetime monogamist relationship is considered by many to not be a natural reunion.

"The pleasure caused by sexual intercourse is nature's finest gift to us. Without her gift, we would perish."

"Shower time, Lenny! I will scrub the sweat from last night's wicked sex escapade off of you."

"Come on, Ruby, you were dripping in sweat too."

"I like to smell you on me," Ruby said, smiling. "I guess you're not giving me a choice, are you, Lenny?

"All right. Let's scrub that sweet lovemaking smell off of each other," Ruby said, sighing. "We can start with the spa, Lenny. Then we can wash the chlorine off of us in the shower. Lenny, we are living our dream in paradise!

"Roll your clothes into a tight bundle, Lenny. I will stuff them in my beach bag."

"Not necessary, Ruby. I can put them in the compartment under the scooter's seat. It will hold yours too. All we need are our swimsuits."

CHECKING OUT OF THE HOTEL AND THE PHOTO SHOOT

"How do I look, Lenny?"

"You will draw a crowd, Ruby, like always. The swimsuit you bought is not a string-thong swimsuit. The thong is made of monofilament thread."

"I feel at home wearing it, Lenny. It is very similar to the costume I danced in, and you know that the attention excites me."

"You are red hot, Ruby!"

"You do truly understand my needs, Lenny, and the very reason I chose to do burlesque in Vegas. That's one more reason I love you, Lenny."

"I find it astounding that I am cohabitating with a woman like you even though I don't have a huge cock or a lot of money."

"Lenny, I am going to insist that you don't bring that cliché up again. I will explain why. The surgery I underwent to remove the exterior skin from my vagina and to tighten it was meant to make my vagina more beautiful and to allow it to accommodate an average-sized cock. The average cock is five to six inches in length with a maximum circumference of five inches.

"Remember that I insisted on measuring your cock after we had had sex a few times. Your cock is seven inches in length and six inches in circumference. That is as large a cock as I can receive, and, Lenny, that took some getting used to.

"So…Are we through with this irritating-to-me 'man thing,' Lenny?"

"You should admit, Ruby, that your thinking is the exception to the rule."

"I will play your game. You are right. Most women would never admit that they are attracted to wealthy men or men with large cocks more than they are attracted to men with other attributes. Are you satisfied?"

"Yes, you will not hear that cliché from me ever again, Ruby."

"Thank you, Lenny. Now we can focus on the task at hand.

"OK, Lenny. Get in the best position to take pictures of me turning heads at the checkout counter. I'll put them in my photo album. One day when I'm old and not hot, I will have something to look back on.

"You would not believe how many aged women have admitted to me that they wish they had enjoyed their sexuality more when they were young, sexy, and beautiful. Even Betty admitted that she wished she had been more sexual in her prime, Lenny."

REVISITING THE MANATEES

"How long do you want to rent the Jet Skis for, Ruby?"

"A half of a day will be fine. Lenny, we need to go to the south side of the island. I would like to look for the family of manatees that my friends and I swam with when we were kids. I know where the backwater estuaries they lived in are"

"You think they will still be there after all these years, Ruby?"

"The manatee is a descendant of the elephant. They live for sixty or more years and have memories similar to those of elephants. We spent many days swimming with them. They always looked forward to seeing us. They allowed us to ride them.

"Then one day a wildlife officer showed up and said we could no longer swim with them. We would slip back to play with them on occasion. Then a couple of kids were caught with them, and their parents had to pay fines."

"Go ahead, Ruby. I will follow you. That will be fun as long as we don't get caught."

"You need to loosen up, Lenny. Part of the excitement is getting away with violating a stupid law.

"This is the place they used to come to. Cut your motor, Lenny. I will whistle the way I did years ago to see if they are here. Their ears aren't apparent, but they hear very well."

"How long will you whistle for?"

"We will give it a few minutes. They knew us kids by our different whistles."

"Holy manatee, Ruby. Look behind you."

"There they are, Lenny!"

"How do you know, Ruby?"

"The father always led the way."

"He is huge, Ruby."

"I am sure that I'm right, Lenny. I recognize the propeller scar on the top of his head. His family has grown."

"What do we do now?"

"Lenny, hold the rope attached to my Jet Ski. I'm going into the water to see if he will give me a ride. I think he remembered my whistle."

"Be careful, Ruby! Can they be dangerous?"

"None of the kids were ever attacked. They are very pliant creatures. The bull is rising up. That is his way of letting me know that I can mount him.

"Hurry! Take the phone out of the plastic bag, and shoot a video. Are you ready? Here I go! He remembers me, Lenny. Isn't this amazing?

"This is so cool, Lenny. Manatees have powerful rear fins that move them through the water."

"Can you guide him, Ruby?"

"I think so."

"Here we go, Lenny. I am going to see if I can circle you by pressing on the left side of his head. It is working. He is turning left. If I keep the pressure on the left side of his head, he will continue to move left in a circle.

"That's what he is doing."

"How will you get off, Ruby?"

"I'll remove my hand from his head and whistle. He will bring me back to where we started. That's what he is doing."

"Ruby, what an amazing animal!"

"I sure wish I had a head of cabbage to give him. We used to bring them several heads of cabbage and play for hours."

"What about the others?"

"The only other one I am sure of is the larger female. Do you want to ride her?"

"I don't think so. Maybe another time."

"Let's get out of here, Lenny."

"Where are we going?"

"To the shrimp boats.

"I noticed a couple of them coming to dock. We can pick up some baitfish from them."

"Why would we do that, Ruby?"

"We will use the unsellable fish caught in their nets for bait. We can feed the dolphins with them.

"When the dolphins see that you have fish, they will come to you. I'm not sure whether dolphins do that with sight or smell. When we were kids, we'd feed them to bring them close—sometimes close enough to us that we could pet them and swim with them. I would also like to make a video with the dolphins."

RUBY'S SHRIMP-BOAT PHOTO SHOOT

"Lenny, do you have ten dollars?"

"Here is twenty. I don't have a ten."

"Hey, sailor, we will pay ten dollars for a bag of baitfish."

"Miss, I'm the captain. If you come aboard and pose for our shrimp-boat calendar, you can have all of the baitfish you want."

"Captain, I will do that. I prefer earning the fish instead of paying for them. This will be another interesting addition to my photo album, Lenny."

"Take my hand. I will pull you up. One of our crewmembers is an amateur photographer. His name is Phil."

"Hello, Phil! My name is Ruby Ridge."

"The captain and I have been looking for a model for our shrimp-boat calendar. We have not had a lot of success."

"How long will it take?"

"I can do it in one hour. Can you give me that much time? I have wanted to do this for a long time, Ms. Ridge. I have already laid out all of the poses. Don't take this the wrong way, but we have never had a woman as sexy as you to work with us."

"Phil, I'm not offended in the least. As a matter of fact, I take your statement as a compliment."

"Do you care if the crew watches the photo shoot, Ms. Ridge?"

"They are welcome to enjoy the show. I was in show business for five years. I understand men, Phil."

Ruby's statement drew moans from the crewmembers as they gathered around her.

One young sailor with a bright-red beard said, "Ms. Ruby, you are the most beautiful woman I've ever seen!"

"Come here, young man!" Ruby said.

She pulled him close and kissed him on the forehead. The sailors bellowed with laughter. The young sailor's face turned as red as his hair.

"Phil, let me introduce to you my boyfriend, Lenny."

"I am glad to meet you, Lenny."

"Phil, we still want to visit the dolphins, so let's get moving," Ruby said.

"Ruby, tell me if the poses I am asking for are too sexually provocative. We are going to begin with you bending down to grab the fishnet."

"Phil, I know what you want."

Ruby bent over, exposing her breasts, with a caught-by-surprise look on her face.

"Perfect, Ruby!"

"You start shooting, Phil. I will take it from here."

Ruby moved around the boat as if the shoot had been choreographed.

"Oh, my God! You are amazing, Ruby."

"Would you like me to remove my top, Phil?"

Before Phil could respond, the crewmembers shouted "Yeah!" in unison.

"You would do that?" Phil asked.

"Here, Lenny—hold my top! Captain, are you married?"

"No, I am not."

"Then come over here and hold me in your arms in front of the captain's wheel. Give me your hand, Captain. Stand like this, and put your arms around me. Are you shooting, Phil?"

"Yes, Ruby!"

"OK, guys, will you keep it down?"

"They don't bother me, Captain. They are just being men," Ruby said.

"OK, Captain, we will do the grand finale pose. Your movement must be perfect. I would hate for the crew to see me completely exposed," Ruby said, giggling.

The remark brought on a couple of howls from the crew.

"I am going to stand behind you, Captain, and remove my bottom. You reach back with your hand and cover my private area with your palm. With your hand covering only my private area, I will move around beside you for a few very sensual pictures. The only thing I will have on will be the captain's hat.

"You should continue to cover my private area until I move back behind you and put my bottom back on. If the move is not well executed, Captain, I will be exposed. Captain, your hand is very coarse."

When Ruby moved back, she purposely stepped to the side, which caused the Captain's hand to fall and allowed the crew to glimpse her totally nude body.

The crew went crazy and applauded her for several minutes. Ruby left her top off, took a bow, and invited the crew to line up for individual photographs with her. She even allowed the men to fondle and kiss her breasts as Phil photographed them. She did decline one man's request to see or feel her private area. She smiled, kissed him on the cheek, and said, "Definitely not—not on the first date!"

I had never known a woman who could control men like Ruby could. She once remarked to me how much she loved men in general.

"Captain, Phil, I will leave you with my number. I trust that you will contact me once you have laid out the calendar. I would love to offer you some advice before you print it. I have had a great deal of experience with layout."

"We will, without a doubt, Ruby," the captain said.

"We are grateful for your help," Phil said.

"Please return when you have room to carry a few pounds of fresh shrimp free of charge," the captain said.

"Ruby, you are the most beautiful woman I have ever seen," the red-bearded sailor said.

WHERE'S LENNY NOW?

Ruby had taken total charge of the photo shoot. Phil had needed only to follow her and to push the button on the camera. She never seemed to stop directing him and performing. She loved to entertain. I never become upset with Ruby's exhibitionist behaviors. Her behavior was genuine. I could see clearly why she'd been billed as the top showgirl in Las Vegas.

She had changed my life and become the star of my story. I had been living in the past, thinking that those days had been the pinnacle of my life. In recent years, my only friends had been my daughter, Annie, and the imaginary friends and lovers I'd created in my writings. I hadn't thought I would ever bed another woman in the prime of her sexual life.

Then out of nowhere, Ruby Ridge showed up. She was less than half my age and the most beautiful, sexy woman I had ever been with. She was the kind of woman who had the ability to command the attention of any man and to give an over-the-hill man the will to start living again. Betty had convinced her that I knew how to eradicate the flaw in her that made her one percentage point less than 100 percent perfect.

I did my life's best work and cured her sexual dysfunction. The success seemed to have won me her love. I thought that the love she was giving me was a form of payment or even a temporary infatuation. After some time, I quit wondering why she'd chosen me and realized that she just might've wanted me to be her man. By the way, she had picked me out!

I would have never approached a woman with her level of stardom. The last thing I needed at that unstable time in my life was to be rejected. I decided to handle this perplexing situation by riding my euphoric high for as long as it was available to me.

I became the envy of every man who laid his eye on her. One thing I did know was that I had to live with what made Ruby the woman she was, which was, in part, her need to entertain men by exposing her body to them. One question bothered me: Just how sexually promiscuous was Ruby?

Would she go as far as to expect me to accept her if she had intercourse with another man? That thought did come to mind when the captain held her pubic area in his hand and when she allowed the crewmembers to fondle and kiss her breasts.

I had come to realize that she saw her behavior as personal and that she was not concerned with what others would think. There was no doubt that she was confident. I understood her. Furthermore, I was convinced that her long-term focus would be on us.

My conclusion was that our relationship was based on intellect. It would become what I made of it.

THE DOLPHIN HUNT

With both Jet Skis' storage compartments full of baitfish, we began our search for dolphins. Ruby led the way based on what she remembered from playing in the water surrounding Fort Myers Beach during her childhood.

"Lenny, this place had many small fish. I know that because we used to snorkel here and watch the dolphins harvest the fish. If I had a mask, I could look underwater to see if the small fish were still here. I am going to take a fish and dangle it in the water. The worse thing that could happen would be attracting a shark.

"One time a shark snatched a fish out of my hand. I was with three kids in a canoe. Wow, did we get the hell out of there. You watch for me, Lenny."

"What am I looking for, Ruby?"

"Shark fins, Lenny! The water is very clear here. Stand on your Jet Ski, and look down into the water. You should look for a large fish's dark image. I'm going to slap this baitfish on the surface of the water to make a little noise."

"That did it, Ruby. A large fish is coming our way."

"Watch this, Lenny. I'm going to hold the fish about three feet out of the water. A dolphin will jump for it. A shark won't jump out of the water. It would circle around the food source. Where is she, Lenny?"

"Looks like she is right in front of you. She's coming up, Ruby! Holy shit—she took the bait right out of your hand. More are coming, Ruby. Are we going to be safe?"

"Dolphins are smart and friendly. They know that we have food. You can start feeding them, Lenny. The dolphins will eat out of your hand.

"I am going to lay a fish on the rear deck of the Jet Ski to see if he will slide up onto the deck and let me pet his snout. See, Lenny, he will allow me to rub his snout as long as the fish keep coming."

"I counted four dolphins, Ruby."

"Try to distribute the fish equally among them. Can you take a video of me swimming with the dolphins?

"I'm going to leave my swimsuit in the Jet Ski. I will grab on to this one's fin to see if she will pull me around. She's pulling me, Lenny. Get ready. I'm going to sit on her back and ride her. Quick, Lenny. I'm on top of her, but she is diving. Did you record that? I did ride her for a few seconds."

"That will be a great video, Ruby."

I could imagine the caption on the video: "Beautiful Nude Woman or Mermaid Riding a Dolphin?"

"What do you think, Lenny?"

"This has been one exciting and fun day, Ruby. We ran wild at the beach, going from one thrill to another. Since the moment we left yesterday, there has not been one dull or boring moment. Let's turn these Jet Skis in, Ruby, and call it a day."

"I have pictures and videos of this day. I can't wait to edit these videos for our album."

"Did you say 'our album,' Ruby?"

"Yes, Lenny, I did. I have been documenting our life together since the first time we met."

"Even our sexual escapades?"

"Yes! Can we stop at Starbucks for tea and coffee and recap our fun day?"

"Sure, that would be a fine way to end this great day, Ruby."

RUBY AND LENNY TALK AT STARBUCKS

"Lenny, grab the table near the window. I will order tea with heavy cream on the side. What a day, Lenny. I might have gotten a little too much sun. You know how I work to keep my skin smooth and blemish-free. My skin had much to do with my success as a show girl, Lenny. You look OK."

"Why is that? My skin is so beat up from years of abuse that I doubt the sun could damage it any further. The upside is that your skin looks better when you're with me."

"How could that be, Lenny?"

"A portrait of you and me together could be titled *Beauty and the Beast*."

"Lenny, stop talking about yourself like that!"

"Ruby, you know the story. It is our story. The beast lived by himself because he was so ugly that people feared him. A mishap brought the beauty to the beast. She was fearful of him at first. Then she saw his wisdom and the beauty emanating from inside of him. They fell in love and lived happily ever after."

"That is a nice story, Lenny, but you are not ugly, and I insist that you never again refer to yourself that way."

"Ruby, what is the connection between Bailey, Joni, and Betty?"

"Bailey is an orphan. She never knew her mother. Bailey and Betty have developed a mother-daughter relationship mostly because they have similar backgrounds.

"Bailey calls Betty from work every day to ask how she is doing. Betty suggested that Bailey take a couple of banking-finance courses. Bailey will start school this semester. Betty has plans for Bailey to work in the bank that she and Harold are chartering. Betty intends to take care of Bailey.

"Betty raised and mentored me because my mother was never home. My mom worked sixty and seventy hours a week to try to pay my worthless stepfather's gambling debts. Bailey and Will stay busy. Will volunteers to work with veterans after his normal work hours at the VA.

"Bailey has been studying banking on her own. Betty is raising and mentoring Joni in much the same way that she did me."

"Isn't that mentally and physically draining for Betty, Ruby?"

"Joni stays occupied by playing with Jojo and Breezy for most of the day. Most of all, the clatter of little feet around the house gives Betty great joy."

"Is everything still going well with your mom?"

"She and Bob are reliving their high school days. Mom has dropped weight and is more alive now than ever before. Bob has been spending time with Betty and working with her on the banking matter. I am very happy for them."

"What about Harold?"

"I know of nothing new with the VA lawsuit. Betty and Harold spend time talking on the phone about the bank and the lawsuit. Betty expects him soon, now that his retirement home is finished."

"Should I be busier, Ruby?"

"The answer is no! Betty told me not to allow you to get involved in anything more."

"What, Ruby?"

"She insists that you and I not bother with the everyday stresses of work. She instructed me to do whatever it takes to make you happy. Lenny, you have nothing to worry about but me. I know that I cause you stress sometimes with my exhibitionist behavior."

"How could you say something so absurd, Ruby? I think you should ask me about how I feel, not decide how I feel. This is how I really feel: You are a dream come true!

"If I lived another one hundred years, I could not repay you for what you have done for me. It might not fully register with you, but it registers right at the top of my dreams' list. You performed a miracle on me."

"I don't think clinical psychology has caught up to your thinking, Lenny. All I did was come home and discover what was missing in my life.

"You performed another one of your miracles on Betty. She says that the hormone, food, and exercise regimens you designed for her enabled her to walk. She says that she desires to return the favor. To Betty, that means enabling you to do nothing but take care of the family and me. Betty knows about the tough life you have lived, Lenny.

"Lenny, all you are expected to do is lean back, buckle up, and enjoy the ride."

"I have no response to what you just told me, Ruby!"

"You don't need one, Lenny. Your actions speak for you. You have earned your pass."

RUBY'S CONFESSION AND APOLOGY

"Lenny, my only fear is that you will tire of dealing with my eccentric behavior. I become fired up when I'm performing, and after cooling down, I think I might have offended you. For example, I thought that my performance on the shrimp boat might have gone too far."

"Stop right there, Ruby! Explain what bothered you about the photo shoot on the shrimp boat."

"It now bothers me that I allowed those sailors to fondle and kiss my breasts and that I allowed the captain to hold my pubic area in his hand. What would I have done if the captain had plunged his finger inside of me? It could have started a feeding frenzy, and I would've been the prey.

"I'm no longer in Las Vegas, where security officers prevent audiences from responding aggressively. Furthermore, I apologize to you and assure you that I will not do anything that dumb ever again."

"First of all, you don't owe me an apology. Your idea about limiting your artful exhibitions to secure places might be a good idea for your safety. I assure you that I am perfectly comfortable with your need to entertain. I do not care to comment on people who are offended by the way you choose to legally fulfill your personal needs.

"Would you please get rid of that thought? Don't prevent others from enjoying the beauty of the female body. If I ever became upset with you, it would be because I couldn't find anything that I didn't love about you, Ruby Ridge. Thank you for being here with me at this time in my life. Why are you crying, Ruby? I always believed that many of my thoughts would have to remain secrets.

"I later discovered that you believe that they are perfectly sane. I know I can discuss any troubling or confusing matters with you. It would not be surprising to find out that we are both a little insane in a harmless way."

"We don't have to kneel to any person or corporation. I have all of the money we'll need for the rest of our lives. You, Lenny, have your military compensation and benefits.

"Betty will generously provide for both of us. I love you, Lenny. With the exception of our family, the rest of the world can go to hell."

"That financial news surprises me, Ruby!"

■ ■ ■

BEGINNING A LIFE WITH CALLIE AT THE TRUCK STOP (1969)

"Wake up, Lenny!"

"Good morning, Callie. What are we going to do on your day off?"

"We can drive into town and have breakfast before we shop for some clothes for you."

"How far away is town?"

"There is a small town called Willcox about fifteen miles away. There is a Western-style store that sells Levi jeans and simple clothing—nothing fancy. You will be issued security uniforms that you can wear most of the time. There is nothing here to dress up for. The clothes here at the truck stop are poorly made and expensive.

"I need a few other things that I'd rather buy in town than at the truck stop.

"We can take a shower and go."

"What about the security job?"

"Randy said that it can wait until we come back or until tomorrow, Lenny. Get yourself together first."

"You will have to drive, Cal. I don't have a driver's license—unless a military driver's license will do."

"I don't think a military license will work, Lenny. That's a problem for another time. I don't mind driving. Let's go, Lenny. I need to stop for gas. Do you need anything—maybe something to drink? Take this twenty-dollar bill, and run in and pay for the gas. I will wait outside."

"No problem. I will be back in a jiffy."

"You're not having anything to drink?"

"No. What grade of gas do you want?"

"The cheapest is good."

"How much is gas, Cal?"

"Gas is thirty-five cents per gallon, Lenny."

"Gas went up while I was gone. Take your change, Cal. Do you want me to check the oil and the other fluids?"

"That would be good. I don't recall the last time I checked them."

"You need oil and water in the radiator, Cal."

"Can you put it in? Here is ten dollars.

"Thanks, Lenny."

"You should know my secret before I freak you out. I have terrible nightmares sometimes. I might scream in my sleep or jump up in bed. My eyes don't shut totally when I sleep."

"I know where you are going with this conversation, Lenny. I did work in a hospital full of wounded Vietnam veterans. You are reliving combat experiences in your sleep, right?"

"That's right."

"Lenny, I would not have freaked out. I am familiar with what you and other young men went through. What you described is a common syndrome among combat veterans, Lenny.

"Some of the more progressive physicians say that it should be recognized as a combat disorder. However, the Pentagon refuses to recognize it, because government officials don't want to pay to treat the disorder or to compensate the veterans. Now that you have served, don't expect much out of the VA. The government got what it wanted from you, and now it wants you to go away.

"The government doesn't give a shit about you, and neither do the politicians. Their sons were exempt from service or allowed to join the National Guard. The elite make money off of wars by sacrificing mostly lower middle-class and lower-class young men.

"The dishonest media never speaks of these atrocities. The media is in bed with the politicians and relies on them to pass favorable laws that will benefit the media. The networks' advertising revenues keep them from reporting on the corporations' corruption. It's the good ol' American way, Lenny. Control the information, and you control the minds of the people."

"Makes sense, Cal. I just never thought about it. Like other Americans, I was too busy surviving to notice what was going on."

"Because you're over eighteen, I don't feel guilty for opening your mind to the truth or for fucking you."

"Damn, Cal, that's verbal assault right here on the mainland, isn't it?"

"You are right, Lenny. My passion sometimes brings out the worst in me. I am sorry, Lenny. You are like a prince who rode into my life on a white horse. I was miserable until you showed up. I will tell it to you straight, Lenny. I fell in love with you the moment I laid eyes on you."

"Did I catch you on the rebound, Cal?"

"Shut up, Lenny! I understand your confusion. You just left combat and are expected to figure out how to assimilate back into civilian life on your own. I know what I can do for you to show you my appreciation, Lenny."

"What can you do, Cal? You lost me!"

"I will nurture you until you feel comfortable in your civilian environment. Many vets don't transition well. Do you know what keeps me here at this despicable truck stop in the middle of nowhere? The truck stop's owner, Randy. He understands everything I just said, and for that very reason, you'll have a good job, Lenny."

"You don't have to treat me like a kid, Cal."

"Now you're being a little crazy. Do you believe in love at first sight, Lenny?"

"I don't know. I never thought much about that subject. For the last three years, most of my serious thoughts have been about how to stay alive.

"The army made a man of me. Before that I was just a kid. I didn't think about the things I think about now—like how easily you can lose your life. Every time a young man lost his life in combat, the thought that it could have been me crossed my mind."

"Lenny, this country takes kids and ushers them into combat before they are capable of understanding whether what they are being told to do is wrong. How can they be old enough to die for their country but not mature enough to drink alcohol? As far as I am concerned, war is equivalent to statutory rape by the government."

"I believe that in that way, war is similar to religion. A child is dragged into a church before he has the ability to make a decision about religion on his own, and then he is brainwashed with mythology.

"I want to go back to a previous question I asked before we went off on this wild tangent. It concerns the most important topic we have discussed."

"What question was that, Cal?"

"Do you believe in love at first sight? Let me give you an example that might help you answer."

"OK, Cal. I'm listening."

"When you first laid eyes on me, what came to your mind?"

"You are embarrassing me, Cal."

"How could you be embarrassed by that question after our wild sex escapade? Nothing embarrassed you. I was astounded by your lack of inhibitions. You did things to me that I had never even fantasized about, and I liked them."

"I've had a lot of practice and good teachers, Cal. But I've never had any practice with love. I remember well what came to my mind the first time I laid eyes on you. Are you sure you really want to know?"

"I do, Lenny!"

"I thought you were beautiful and I wondered what it would be like to have a round-eyed girlfriend like you to fuck. I've never had a real girlfriend, Cal. I fucked countless friendly girls in Vietnam, but no one gave me the feeling that you did."

"That's what I'm talking about, Lenny."

"Then explain it to me."

"That's love at first sight. I had a different feeling of love at first sight, Lenny. It was like yours, except it was my version of love at first sight."

"I feel like I love you now, Cal."

"I love you too, and I loved you at first sight, Lenny."

"I understand. I loved you at first sight. Give me a little leeway, Cal! I've never talked to a woman in this way before."

CAL AND LENNY GO SHOPPING, AND LENNY DREAMS OF BAGGING DEAD SOLDIERS (1969)

I turned my head away from Cal and peered out of the car's window. Not much to look at. I thought to myself that maybe the word "desert" means "nothing." The view of the terrain passing set my mind adrift. I could hear clearly the sound of helicopter blades—*plop! plop! plop! plop!*

This sound was like music to us combat soldiers. It meant that one of three important situations was about to occur. Sometimes it meant that the wounded were about to be taken to a hospital for life-saving care. Sometimes it meant that the battle-winning fire support that only an assault helicopter could provide had arrived. And sometimes it meant that there was a delivery of needed reinforcements, ammunitions, and vital supplies.

The thermometer on the inside of the helicopter fuselage read 120 degrees. The helicopter blades threw a lot of dirt around when the helicopter neared the ground. To protect my eyes, I pulled my goggles down to prepare for landing. It was the beginning of my second tour. When you extended your service for a second tour, you could request where you wanted to be stationed. If the request was within reason, it was usually granted.

I asked to be reassigned to the First Aviation Division at Bien Hoa Air Base. I was still on light duty because of a bullet I'd taken in my right leg. The wound had been a flesh wound; the bullet had gone straight through my leg, missing the bone. I could have taken the opportunity to go home, but there was nothing there for me at that time in my life.

My first light-duty assignment was to assist in the medical evacuation of wounded and dead soldiers from the battlefield. Before the huge jolly-green-giant medical center I was in landed, I heard "last chance to get your bets down, gentlemen." The seasoned members of the medical-evacuation crew were betting on how quickly I would discharge my breakfast.

I was told that rookies—and I was a rookie—would handle the dead and decayed. The more experienced would administer morphine injections to ease the wounded soldiers' pain and would provide assistance to the medical staff by loading the wounded onto the helicopter.

An American infantry company had been outnumbered ten to one and had been surrounded by North Vietnamese soldiers for more than thirty days. The company had suffered heavy casualties. The air was filled with the smell of decaying bodies and with the sound of young men screaming in pain. There were two soldiers who had been severely wounded and were delirious. One was pleading for the comfort of his mother, and one was reciting the Lord's Prayer with what he thought would be his last breaths.

I immediately noticed that several wounded soldiers were still at their defensive posts, obviously determined to fight to the end. The First Cavalry had arrived in the nick of time with artillery in tow and with armored personnel carriers loaded with fresh men. The cavalry had been supported by

M48 tanks and had driven away the regiment of North Vietnamese regulars, which had made it possible for us to bring the jolly-green-giant medical helicopter into the landing zone.

I was told to secure the uncovered dead first. There had been more dead bodies than body bags. That meant that some of the dead had been partially covered with ponchos and had been baking in the sun for weeks. I quickly removed the poncho from the first man I came to. I took a body bag from my pack and laid it out.

I had stuffed my nose with cotton that had been soaked in some substance in the hope that it would prevent me from smelling the decaying human bodies. That helped but could not entirely block the nauseating stench. I grabbed on to a soldier's arm so that I could position him on the bag. When I pulled his arm, it detached from his body. That released even more smells, and the sight of his arm ripping from his body brought me to my knees. I vomited.

"I win!" one man screamed. He had bet that I would throw up before three minutes had passed. Many men laughed.

Ernest Hemingway described dead soldiers as follows: "Until the dead are buried, they change somewhat in appearance each day. The color change in Caucasian races is from white to yellow, to yellow-green, to black. If left long enough in the heat the flesh comes to resemble coal tar, especially where it has been broken or torn, and it has quite a visible tarlike iridescence. The dead grow larger each day until sometimes they become quite too big for their uniforms, filling these until they seem blown tight enough to burst."

"Lenny, wake up! Are you OK?"

"Yeah, yeah, Cal. I guess I was dreaming."

"We are here at the general store, Lenny."

"Give me a second! Can we have coffee and some food before shopping?"

"You are soaking wet with cold sweat. You sit here while I run into the store and purchase you a dry T-shirt. Then we can get a bite to eat and talk about what just transpired."

"Thanks, Cal. Don't worry about me."

"Just relax, Lenny. I will be back in a jiffy."

Cal was quick. She opened the passenger's side door and immediately pulled the wet shirt over my head. She slid the new T-shirt over my head and pulled me close to her bosom. Holding me tight, she softly said, "It is over, Lenny. It is all over."

"I'm OK, Cal. Can we eat?"

"You are going to like this little family café, Lenny. The family who owns the café opened it in 1870, when the town became a water-and-fuel stop for the Southern Pacific Railroad. The railroad brought the first rancher and his cattle. Everything it serves is grown in the surrounding area.

"It still offers all of the original meals that it offered when it opened. The recipes and cooking procedures are the same. The cooking is still done on wood-burning stoves. The only difference is that the fifth generation is doing the cooking."

"Good morning! Welcome to the Ole Southern Pacific Railroad Café. What can I serve you?"

"Two cups of coffee and a menu, please."

"Coming right up!"

"How neat this is, Cal. I feel like I am sitting in an old train's dining car."

THE GOVERNMENT'S THIRTY-YEAR DENIAL OF THE EXISTENCE OF PTSD (1969)

"Cal, I apologize for what just happened."

"No, Lenny, you don't have to apologize. I dealt with hundreds of beautiful young men at the hospital in Vietnam. They were brave and fought for their country, just like you did.

"I helped a group of psychologists working to document the impact that combat had on soldiers. To accomplish their goal of convincing lawmakers to allocate funding to a program that would treat veterans and compensate them for their disabilities, the psychologists had to compile an inordinate amount of facts.

"The researchers named the condition 'post-traumatic stress disorder,' or PTSD. They were frustrated that the government was denying the existence of the condition, but they were determined and wouldn't give up. I read all of their findings, Lenny. I can help you learn to live with it. You will never totally repair the emotional damage.

"You can train yourself to cope and have a somewhat-normal life, Lenny. I can do that for you. Even in your lowest moments, do not think that you are not a strong man. I was falling apart from loneliness before you walked into my cafeteria. You help me, and I will help you. We are better together than we are alone. We were both alone. Now we have each other for support."

"I have been alone since the age of seventeen.

"I will never go home, Cal."

"I do not care to be alone ever again. Do you, Lenny?"

"No, Cal. I don't like being alone either."

"Now that the cat's out of the bag, you should not have any pressure on you."

"What does that mean, Cal?"

"It is a figure of speech—an idiom. I mean that you do not have to worry about me finding out your secret. Now I know it. Knowing that I do not think that you're nuts should give you some relief."

"I understand, Cal. You explain things well. Will you accept me even though I'm stupid? I will make a deal with you, Cal. I love learning. I promise you that one day, I will be the smartest man you've ever met. I have already started reading in your library.

"I have a gift for reading. The army tested me and said that my reading-comprehension test scores were very high. I was asked to extend my enlistment and to attend officers' training school. I said no, so they made me a platoon sergeant. That was mostly because of my military-school education."

"If it makes you feel better, Lenny, I will say this: If you were stupid, I would be in love with a stupid person."

"I see what you mean, Cal. You are the first woman who's told me that she loves me, and I like it, because you are saying it."

"Where did you go to high school, Lenny?"

■ ■ ■

LENNY GOES TO JAIL (1966)

"Cal, not long after I graduated from military school, my dad died. My father was one of the wealthiest men in the small town I grew up in. The townspeople respected him because of his participation in and contributions to the town's many charitable organizations. My mother continuously complained that he was wasting his time and their money on those organizations, which helped underprivileged families.

"When my father died, my mother quickly remarried. My stepfather was the son of a chicken farmer and was from a small Georgia town twenty-five miles from where we lived. He did not work on the farm with his dad. He began dating my mom while he was working construction.

"I came home from military school one summer and overheard him tell my mom that a repo man had attempted several times to repossess his car. He had not made a payment in months. She asked him how much he owed on the car. He said twenty-five hundred dollars. My mother wrote him a check on the spot and told him to go pay it off. He returned a few days later with his car packed with all of his belongings."

"Then what happened, Lenny?"

"My mother instructed me to remove his belongings from his car and to place them in her bedroom. I immediately objected. At that moment, he grabbed my shoulder from behind and spun me around. He loudly said, 'I've had about enough of you, sonny boy!'

"I told him to go to hell and left the house. From then on, he did everything possible to turn my mother against me. My mother believed everything he said. The next time I came home was after graduation. One day he told me to move my car because it was parked in his spot.

"I told him to go fuck himself. He pushed me, and I instinctively opened on him with a flurry of closed-fist blows; the first blow was to his abdomen. He was bent over; I threw a left cross to his left temple and a right cross to his right temple. I then kneed his face. Blood spewed from his mouth. He was unconscious but on his feet. A kick to his knee brought him crashing to the floor.

"I used the hand-to-hand-combat tactics I had learned in military school on him. He never had a chance. Those fighting tactics proved to be vital to my survival later, in Vietnam. I beat him badly, Cal! I did maintain enough control to keep from delivering any fatal blows. My mother thought I had killed him. I know what I did was wrong. However, I had doubts about my father's death and resented my stepfather."

"I can understand that," Cal said. "I probably would have reacted in the same way."

"My mother screamed for me to go to my room. After she'd revived him and gotten him back on his feet, he called the sheriff. He demanded that the sheriff press assault charges against me, and my mother supported his request. The sheriff examined his wounds and said that he thought his leg was broken. He informed me that I was under arrest for assault and battery. He was taken to the hospital, and I was handcuffed and escorted to the small-town jail.

"The officer on duty called the juvenile authorities in the neighboring city. The small town I lived in was not large enough to have a juvenile court. The deputy informed me that a juvenile officer from the neighboring city would pick me up the next morning and take me to a juvenile hall.

"The sheriff apologized for arresting me. He informed me that he hadn't had a choice. He and my father had grown up together and had been best friends. As he walked away, he said, 'Lenny I might have a plan.'"

"How long did you stay in jail, and how did you get out?" Cal asked.

LENNY ESCAPES FROM JAIL (1966)

"Cal, I had no idea what to do. I knew that juvenile hall was the place where they locked up juvenile delinquents until they were old enough to go to adult prison. Three different deputies came back and said hello. All of them had been friends with my dad.

"One deputy visited me a few minutes before midnight. He told me that come midnight, he would be the only deputy on house duty. He said, 'Lenny, listen to what I have to say. If you go to juvenile hall, you will be there until you turn eighteen. If you are convicted, you will probably go to the adult prison for a couple of more years. You are looking at a minimum of three to five years. I have something for you to think about for the next thirty minutes. At midnight the other two deputies on duty will be patrolling the south side of town. I will take you north to the interstate and release you. Atlanta, Georgia, is south, and Asheville, North Carolina, is north.

"'I suggest that you never come back. We were all friends with your father and decided that this was the least we could do to show him our respect. You now have twenty-five minutes to make your decision.'

"He turned to walk away. 'Stop!' I said. 'I would appreciate it if you would take me to the interstate.'"

"Lenny, were you scared?" Cal asked.

"I was both scared and confused. All I could think about was going to juvenile hall. The deputy opened my cell at midnight and led me to the jail's back door. He opened the door with his key and instructed me to sit in the front seat of his personal car. 'I don't want anyone to notice that I'm taking you to the interstate,' he said.

"He did not say much on the way to the interstate. He did ask me what I thought had caused my father's death. 'No one really offered me an answer,' I said. 'He got sick one day, came home to lie down, and died an hour later.' What I remember more than anything is what the deputy said next.

"'How long did your mother wait before she married that man from Georgia?' he asked.

"'As far as I'm concerned, not long enough,' I said.

"He said, 'I agree, Lenny. Not long enough.' I thought that he obviously suspected that foul play had been involved."

"Lenny, do you think that your mother and her boyfriend could have conspired to kill your father?" Cal asked.

"Between us, I do. There was a great deal of money involved, Cal, and I was his only obstacle. I think he played me, and I was stupid enough to take the bait.

"A couple of years later, when I was in Vietnam, I received a letter from a friend. He said that my family's homestead and property had been sold to a corporate mall developer for twenty million dollars. Furthermore, he informed me that they'd sold my dad's business for another ten million, built a ten-thousand-square-foot house on the lake, and retired.

"I will always remember the moment the deputy stopped the car at the intersection near the interstate. He shook my hand and wished me luck. To my surprise, he handed me a one-hundred-dollar bill and said, 'This is from all of the deputies.'"

PEACH TREE STREET (1966)

"What went through your mind when you stepped out of the car?" Cal asked.

"I remember how dark it was. I noticed that there were few cars on the freeway and that I was entirely alone. Cal, I had no idea which direction to go in. It was beginning to get cold. Fall was coming. I decided to go south, toward Atlanta, Georgia.

"I crossed the interstate to the south lane and stuck out my thumb. An eighteen-wheeler rolled to a slow stop about a football field's length past me. He sounded his horn, and I took off running to keep from holding him up. I mounted the running board and swung the door open. He greeted me by saying, 'Come on in, son. It's beginning to get a little chilly out there.'

"I took a seat and thanked him for stopping. He said, 'How far are you going?' I said I was going to Atlanta. 'That's the end of the road for me too,' he said. 'I've been on the road for two weeks. It sure will be good to be home with my family. I have a son in Vietnam. You look to be about his age. How old are you?' he asked.

"'I'm seventeen,' I said.

"'You know, when you turn eighteen, you will have to register for the draft. My son was drafted a couple of months after he registered. If he hadn't been drafted, he still would have joined. I tried to talk him into getting a deferment and going to college. He would have nothing to do with my idea.

"'I was in the Korean War. I try not to talk about Vietnam at home, because his mother gets upset. One of the kids in the neighborhood was killed. He was a friend of my son's. She had to go to counseling when she heard about his death. Where is your family?' he asked.

"'Atlanta,' I said, lying.

"'We will be there in about three hours,' he said. I sat quietly and listened to his country music until I fell asleep.

"His voice woke me up. 'I just passed the two-eighty-five loop, son. I will be cutting through downtown to get to Interstate Twenty. I live on the west side. Where do you want to get out?'"

"What did you say?" Cal asked.

"I knew one street in Atlanta, Cal. I said, 'Anywhere close to Peach Tree Street.'

"'I'll be going close to there, son,' he said. 'Here we are, son. Peach Tree is only a few blocks from here. My advice is to stay in school until this damn war is over.'

"'Thank you, sir, and good luck with your family,' I said. I jumped down onto the road and headed in the direction he had pointed in."

THANK GOODNESS FOR JANE (1966)

"My watch said that it was three-thirty in the morning. I was feeling tired, and I was scared. I could see a twenty-four-hour diner ahead. I decided that it would be my target. I would treat myself to coffee and contemplate my next move. I sat down and looked around. I was the only customer. A middle-aged lady walked out of the kitchen and asked me what I would like to order. I ordered coffee.

"She returned with my coffee. 'I just made it,' she said. 'I was going to have a cup myself.' It's a little boring at this time of the night. Could I join you?'

"'Sure, I would like that,' I said. She sat down on the stool beside me.

"'My name is Jane.' She stuck her hand out for a handshake. I responded by telling her my name and shaking her hand.

"'Where are you headed?' she asked.

"'I don't know,' I said.

"'Do you have a home? I would offer to take you home with me, but you look underage. I could find myself in trouble if I did that without your guardians' permission.'

"'How do you know that I'm not eighteen?'

"'I am a mother of two boys. I can tell that you're not eighteen. There is a curfew for kids under eighteen years of age here. The police will pick you up and transport you to a juvenile facility. You will have to stay out of sight until daylight. Have you had any sleep?'

"'No, I have not.'

"'I'll tell you what I can do. You can take a nap in my car. I don't get off of work until six in the morning. I will go unlock it and wake you up when I get off.'

"'Wow, thank you, Jane. How can you tell that I'm not a bad person?'

"Street kids don't wear designer clothes and shoes or go to expensive military academies. You need to take that gold military-academy class ring off before a gang member kills you for it. If you have any money, hide it.'

"'I have one hundred thirty dollars. Where can I hide it?'

"'Put it anywhere but in your pocket. If you get robbed, and chances are that you will, you will be thoroughly searched. I have worked here for ten years. I know most of these gang members when I see them. They will strip you. That's how they search people. If you resist, they will beat you. Put a few dollars in your pocket, and hand them over willingly.'

"'What about the rest of my money and the ring, Jane? That's going to be a problem.'

"'Why don't you go back home? You are obviously not cut out for living on the streets.'

"'I can't, Jane. The sheriff told me that I would go to juvenile hall and then on to prison if I went back. I beat my stepfather up.'

"'Oh, my. You will have to find a way to survive until you turn eighteen. You can come and see me when you need someone to talk to. I have customers. I must go. The coffee is on me.'"

"Lenny, were you scared?" Cal asked.

"I was scared close to death, Cal."

"What did you do next?"

"I lay down in Jane's car. Jane woke me up by tapping on the window. I sat up in the backseat. She sat down in the front seat and handed me a cup of coffee and a sausage biscuit. 'You must be hungry,' she said.

"'Thank you very much, Jane,' I said.

"'I have an idea. There is an army recruiter several blocks down, on Peach Tree Street. Check with him and see if he can obtain an age waiver so that you can join the army. My older son is in Vietnam. There is a park on Peach Tree Street too. Maybe you can meet someone who can offer you a place to stay until you figure out your next move. I will repeat what I said before. If you were eighteen, I would let you stay with me. You can come back to see me tomorrow night. Maybe by then I'll have thought of something better. My shift is from ten at night to six in the morning. I will put the seat down in my station wagon and throw a pillow and a blanket in the back.

"'You can sleep while I work again. Would you like me to drop you off at the park? It's two blocks over.'

"'Please do, Jane,' I said. 'And could you keep my money and my ring, Jane?'

"'I can do that,' she said. 'Being new in the neighborhood makes you a target.'"

"You trusted her with all of your valuables?" Cal asked.

"I didn't feel that I had any other choice, Cal. After she drove me to the park, she said, 'Put this business card for the diner in your pocket. The card has my phone number and address on the back of it. You can take the basketball that my youngest son left in my car. Lenny, be careful, and think about joining the military. Your eighteenth birthday is coming soon.'"

BASKETBALL AT THE PARK AND LORI (1966)

"The park was full of early-morning joggers. No kids were in the park to play basketball, and it was too early to visit the army recruiter. I lay down on the grass, put my head on the basketball, and took a nap.

"'Hey, buddy. You want to wake up and play ball? We've got five. You would make six. That'd make it three on three.'

"'OK, I'm in,' I said.

"'I like your ball. Can we use it?'

"'Sure. My name is Lenny.'

"'I'm Ben. Glad to meet you. Are you new around here, Lenny?'

"'Yeah, Ben.'

"'This is George, Lenny. He is our third man. Guys, we have a girl who wants to play. Her name is Lori. Lori, as soon as we pick up another player so that we can go four on four, you are welcome to play.'

"'I'll look for another girl for the next game,' Lori said.

"I thought about Lori and the other girl she brought to the game. They played as hard as the guys did. Both of them were tomboys and cute.

"During the breaks, I talked to Lori. She was a high school girls' basketball player. She told me that playing with the boys made her game stronger. She hoped to win a scholarship to the University of Georgia for women's basketball. She'd lost her boyfriend in Vietnam a few months earlier. He'd been eighteen years old.

"Her suddenly mentioning his death startled me. I planned to join soon. She looked at me and said, 'Whose heart do you plan on breaking, Lenny? That war is not worth even one young man's life.'

"I really liked her. My telling her that I planned to join the army abruptly ended our conversation. I asked Ben what he thought about the war.

"He said, 'I have a college deferment.'

"Lenny, you were hearing about reasons to not join the army. What made you join anyway?" Cal asked.

"Cal, I didn't feel that I had a choice. I had no place to go and no one. I was both confused and scared. The lights at the park began to dim. Ben said that it was time to leave. The park closed at ten."

"What did you do then, Lenny?" Cal asked.

"I asked Ben what would happen if I stayed awhile.

"He said, 'the police will tell you to leave.'

"'They sweep the park shortly after ten,' Lori said.

"To my surprise, Lori asked if I would walk her home.

"She said, 'I live with my mother a couple of blocks down the street.'

"I stuttered and said yes.

"She asked me, 'Where do you live?' I told her that I was staying with my guardian, who worked at the diner.

"'Why do you refer to her as your guardian, Lenny?' she asked.

"'Lori, I am seventeen. I don't live with my parents.'

"'I didn't know you were seventeen. That makes sense, Lenny. This is where I live.'

"Lori reached into her athletic bag, pulled out a pen and a piece of paper, and wrote her number down.

"'Call me if you want to play some one-on-one. I can take you,' she said.

"She smiled and pointed to the alley.

"You can cut straight through the block to the neighborhood diner. Good night, Lenny."

JANE TAKES A MOTHER'S INTEREST IN LENNY (1966)

"Lori had been right. The alley cut straight through two blocks and ended in front of the diner. I entered the diner and looked for Jane. When she appeared, she told me to have a seat at the bar. Jane asked how I was doing. I quickly ran through my day and told her that the next day, I was going to visit the army recruiter.

"I told her about Lori. She smiled and said, 'Hold that thought. I will be right back.' Jane returned, and I told her that Lori's boyfriend had died in Vietnam. I noticed how she was affected by that and quickly apologized. She asked me if I was hungry.

"'I'm starving,' I said.

"'Always go for the special. It is the best deal,' she said.

"'OK!' I said.

"'One special coming up,' Jane yelled. 'Lenny, when you finish eating, I should take you to my place so that you can shower and change your clothes. You are looking soiled. I don't live too far from here. We can do that during my hour-long break.'

"'That would be great, Jane!'

"'My older son, who is in the army, has clothes that will fit you. How was the food, Lenny?'

"'Jane, I did not realize how hungry I was.'

"'If your belly is full, Lenny, we can go.'

"'Jane, how long have you lived here?'

"'Since the war ended.'

"'Which war?'

"'The Great War, the Second World War. My husband died on the sixth of June in 1944 in the Normandy region and coast of France. The code name of the invasion was Omaha Beach.'

"'We studied the Second World War in military school, Jane. I know about Omaha Beach. That began the offensive that liberated France from the Nazis. Your husband was a hero, Jane.'

"'Thank you, Lenny. You are a very knowledgeable young man. I qualified for a surviving-spouse government business loan, Lenny. I took out the loan and partnered with Fred, and we started the diner.'

"'I didn't know that you were the owner, Jane. I assumed you just worked at the diner. Why do you wait tables?'

"'An owner of a small business must do a little of everything. Fred still does most of the cooking. I work the late-night shift because I don't have family at home. You know that both of my boys are gone, Lenny.

"'Fred has a wife at home, so he runs the day shift. I don't mind the late-night shift, Lenny. You clean up while I find you some clothes. Everything you might need is in the bathroom. I see that you have a little facial hair. There is a razor in the drawer under the sink. Can you think of anything else you might need? How do you feel, Lenny?'

"'Jane, I feel clean. I was worried that Lori might be able to smell how dirty I was. The clothes fit perfectly.'

"'I knew they would. You are exactly the size of my older boy. The very first thing that came to my mind when you walked into the diner was my son. You resemble him, Lenny.'

'He is lucky to have a mom like you, Jane.'

"'Thank you for the compliment, Lenny. We need to get back to the diner. Lenny, do you have a driver's license?'

"'Yes, I do, Jane.'

"'You will need the driver's license for identification at the army recruiter's office. I'm still concerned that you will run into the gang that roams this part of town. Leave your driver's license in the glove compartment of the car. If you run into them, they will take everything you have.

"'Right after you show your driver's license to the army recruiter, bring it back to the car. Do not have it on you. Do you understand how important this is?'

"'I do, Jane.'

"'You can tell the recruiter that I am your guardian.'

"'I hope you don't mind, but I already told Lori that you were my guardian.'

"'I'm glad you did, Lenny.'

"'The other kids I played ball with warned me about the gang.'

"'You have a birthday coming up, Lenny. You will be eighteen and considered an adult. Then you can join the army without your parents' permission or seek employment. Are you still OK with the sleeping accommodations?'

"'Yes, Jane.'

"'I'm going to work, Lenny. See you in the morning.'"

"Lenny, you were so lucky to find someone like Jane," Cal said. "Did you visit the army recruiter the next day?"

"I did."

"I wish I could see a picture of you from when you were seventeen. I bet you were cute!"

"Damn, Cal. You're embarrassing me."

"Tell me the rest of the story, Lenny. We have all day. I will order us another cup of coffee. Would you like a pastry?"

SHOPPING FOR TIRES AND GROCERIES WITH JANE (1966)

"Jane tapped on the window of the car. 'Good morning. I brought you a bacon-and-egg sandwich and an order of hash browns, Lenny.'

"'Wow, that sounds delicious, Jane.'

"'I have a few items to pick up at the grocery store. Would you like to come along? I can drop you off at the army recruiter's office afterward.'

"'Yeah, Jane. I would like to go.'

"'I also plan to stop by the tire store to look for a set of tires for the car. The Firestone dealer has a special on tires this week. We are here, Lenny. Are you coming into the tire store, Lenny?'

"'Sure, Jane.'

"'Yes, miss, what can we do for you today?'

"'I need an estimate for the four premium Firestone tires that you advertised, and please include the price of mounting and balancing the tires in that estimate.'

"'I need to know the size that you require. Then I will give you an estimate.'

"'This is my car,' Jane said.

"'Your total, including the cost of mounting and balancing the tires and taxes, will be one hundred twenty-five dollars. You will not find a better deal.'

"'How long will it take you to install the tires?'

"'Give me one more minute to check with the service department. OK, we can have you out of here within thirty minutes.'

"'I will take them. Can we get the payment out of the way?'

"'The car is already in the shop. Here is your receipt and your guarantee, Jane. Thank you for doing business with Firestone.'

"'Wow, that was fast, Jane.'

"'I guess we came at the right time, Lenny.'

"'I am relieved to have that off of my mind,' Jane said. 'Now we can go to the grocery store. Lenny, I would like you to know that if you need to talk, you have my attention. I am very impressed by how you are coping with your situation.'

"'I have been thinking about my situation, Jane. If the army will take me, I will join. After I serve, I can go to college on the GI Bill.'

"'Considering your present situation, that would be a good plan of action, Lenny.'

"'Jane, I am thankful for all that you are doing to help me.'

"'You are a smart young man, Lenny. I have no doubt that you will do well in life.'

"'I will find you a grocery basket, Jane. You did not purchase many groceries.'

"'I never do. I eat at the diner. I keep only snack foods and drinks at the house. Lenny, are you ready for me to drop you off at the army recruiter's office?'

"'Sure, Jane.'

"'What do you plan to do after your visit with the recruiter?'

"'I'm going to go back to the park to play ball, Jane. Have a great day.'

"'I will see you tonight. Keep an eye out for the gangs, Lenny.'

"'Bye, Jane.'"

LENNY TALKS TO THE ATLANTA ARMY RECRUITER (1966)

"'Good morning, young man. My name is Staff Sergeant Jones.'

"'My name is Lenny, Sergeant Jones.'

"'What can I do for you?'

"'I am interested in joining the army. Would you explain to me what I would be doing?'

"'Son, we are fighting a war in Vietnam. Your chances of going to Vietnam would be good. The type of training you would receive would depend on your test scores. Of course, if you joined, we would take your preferences into consideration. Men who are drafted don't have a choice. If you joined here, in Atlanta, we would send you to Fort Benning in Georgia for basic training. Do you have a training request?'

"'I have not given it much thought, Sergeant Jones. I did graduate from a military high school.'

"'Lenny, having military training gives you an advantage. You will automatically qualify to take the test for OCS, or officers candidate school, if you join for six years. If you choose not to go to OCS, you will have another advantage.

"'After basic training, depending on your score on the leadership test, you will probably be promoted to a sergeant because of your prior military training. I must remind you that we will only be able to honor your request if you possess the aptitude for the training you chose. You will be tested.

"'If you want excitement and danger, consider the infantry or combat engineering. If you like trucks, choose transportation. Request the motor pool if you like mechanics. Do you understand? I'm going to present you with a brochure that explains the different jobs, or MOSs. You can take it home and study it.'

"'What are the requirements for becoming a sergeant?'

"'You must be eighteen, have no physical impairments, and pass a literacy test. Lenny, do you meet those criteria?'

"'I won't be eighteen until next month, Sergeant.'

"'Then you will have to wait until you are eighteen or obtain permission from your parents or legal guardian. That's OK, Lenny. Waiting until next month will give you plenty of time to look over the packet I gave you. If you have any questions between now and then, just drop by. Someone will be available to talk to you, Lenny.'

"'Thank you, Sergeant Jones.'

"'Thank you for coming in, Lenny. We will see you next month.'"

SECOND DAY AT THE PARK (1966)

"It was too early for basketball. My mind was on the packet that Sergeant Jones had given me. I found a park bench to sit on and studied the packet. The minimum term of commitment was three years. If I chose a certain occupation or an MOS, as the army called it, I would need to have the aptitude for it. My aptitude would be determined by a test specific to the MOS I had chosen.

"However, the final decision about what MOS I would be trained in would be made by the army. That meant that there would be no guarantees. I understood that and thought that the right decision would be to join and to allow the army to decide where it could best use me. I knew that no matter what MOS I qualified for, I would earn educational benefits."

"Lenny, I agree that that was the best choice for you," Cal said. "You were too young and inexperienced to be on your own. I would have made the same choice if I had been in your situation. What if you hadn't joined? Then later, you could've been drafted when something important was going on in your life."

"I did think about that, Cal."

"Considering the amount of people going to Vietnam, it was just a matter of time, Lenny. At least you were in control of when you went in and when you got out. How did you survive until you turned eighteen? Tell me what you did in the meantime. I love listening to your story," Cal said.

"OK, Cal. If you're not getting bored, I will continue my story. After I made my decision to join, I tossed the packet into a trashcan and lay down under an oak tree for a nap. I dreamed of riding with my father in his car. In the dream, he told me about the trials and tribulations he'd gone through to build his business and to earn the community's respect. But mostly I remember his telling me about what had motivated him to work so hard.

"He said, 'Lenny, you will have a royal life. All of the wealth I have accumulated will go to you when I die. I want you to do good things with the money. Never forget your family and friends. I sent you to the finest private military academy, and I intend for you to attend West Point. Of course, I will support you regardless of where you decide to go to school, Lenny.

"'I have shown you, son, that respect is earned through good civic actions. I want you to carry on my legacy of doing what is right in our community.' The one thing my father did not think of was to watch out for the chicken farmer's son from Georgia. A bug entering my ear suddenly woke me from my dream. I instinctively slapped the side of my face and heard a familiar laugh. Lori was poking my ear with a blade of grass.

"'Hi, Lenny. Are you ready for the one-on-one challenge of your life? I cut out of school early today because I knew you would be here—not because I'm hung up on you or anything like that but because I want to kick your butt in basketball.'

"'You're talking trash, Lori. I'm going to send you away crying with your tail tucked in between your legs! I hope you brought your best game, because if not, you are going down, girl.'

"'Well, get off your back, and show me what you've got, big boy. Whoever wins two out of three ten-point games will be the winner. You take it out first.'

"'You fouled me Lori.'

"'I took the ball out of your hands and never touched you, Lenny. That is game one Lenny. If you can't do any better than that, maybe you should admit that I am the best and save the embarrassment of losing two in a row.'

"There's no way you can be so lucky to win two in a row. I am just getting warmed up. You are in serious trouble this next game. I'm warning you, just because you are a girl I am not going to go easy on you. Here I come. Damn, Lori, you slapped that ball into my face. That's not fair.'

"'It is fair in the game of basketball. You need to get your face out of the way when your shot is blocked. Last point, Lenny. That stripped the net, Lenny. That is it for you, two games in a row, Lenny. That's a shutout. You lost bad!'

"'You got lucky, Lori.'

"'You got fewer than eight points total. That means one thing: I kicked your butt, Lenny.'

"'OK. I admit that you won fair and square.'

"'Let's have a drink of water and walk over to the pond and talk.'

"'That sounds good to me, Lori.'"

■ ■ ■

CAL IS UPSET ABOUT LORI'S PART IN THE STORY (1969)

"Lenny, I don't know if I like where this is going. I'm becoming jealous of this Lori girl."

"She is part of the story, Cal. The story would not flow if I left her out of it. Remember that I was only seventeen years old. I guess now is the time to tell you what happened to Lori.

"She wrote me a few letters when I was in Vietnam. She was a rebel. She wrote about many matters concerning government corruption that I had never heard about before. During my second tour, I received a letter from Lori. She had become pregnant and had decided to marry the father of her child.

"She wrote me a couple of letters after she got married and told me that she was happy. In the last letter I received from her, she said she was pregnant with her second child. She and her husband were very active protesters against the war in Vietnam. They fled the United States and moved to Canada so that her husband could avoid prosecution for refusing to serve when he was drafted. After that, I never heard from her again, Cal."

I then started thinking about Mary Gibson. I never mentioned Mary Gibson in my story. I feared that Cal would not understand why Lori had shared me sexually with her mom. I did promise Mary Gibson that I would never tell anyone, and I intended to keep my promise. Mary Gibson had often written to me to express her concern for me and to tell me to make it home safely. I wrote her more than I wrote Lori. She insisted that I go see her when I was discharged.

In her last letters, she mentioned a surprise that she had for me. I was not sure whether Lori and Mary were sharing their letters with each other. Lori knew that I favored her mother, and that was all right with her. I knew that most people would've thought that my relationship with Mary Gibson was creepy.

I was only seventeen at that time. She was the assistant principal of the largest high school in Atlanta, Georgia, and almost twice my age when we first had sex. She was promoted to principal during my second tour in Vietnam.

"Lenny, wake up. Did you forget you were telling me your story? What is it with you? You fell asleep on the table before you finished the story. I let you sleep awhile. I know that the flashback took a lot out of you. However, it is time to wake up."

"I'm sorry. I did not mean to, Cal. Where was I? OK, I remember. I did observe many of the wrongs that you have mentioned, Cal. Many soldiers were aware of the government's noticeable effort to spin the truth about how the war was going. The government said it was going well for the United States, and there were no investigations into the high-ranking officials' corrupt actions. I saw the truth when I was shopping for necessary items that were available only on the Vietnamese black market, Cal."

"Lenny, most of those items were supposed to be standard-issue items. Even medical supplies were in short supply at my hospital. Corrupt private contractors sold those supplies on the black market and shared the profits with corrupt government officials," Cal said.

"The insiders and the establishment sold munitions and tangible goods to the enemy, and they made big money, Lenny. Many wars have been caused by financial incentives. Did you know that Fred C. Koch, the father of the billionaires Charles G. and David H. Koch, signed a contract to build an oil refinery for Adolf Hitler in 1933?

"The name of his company was Winkler-Koch. This oil refinery was instrumental to the Nazis' war machine. Today Koch Industries is the second-largest privately owned company in the United States, Lenny."

"How do you know these things, Cal?"

"I read, Lenny. I read!"

"Damn, Cal. That is totally amazing. I guess I should not feel guilty for swapping an M-15 for a Second World War thirty-caliber carbine with a fold-up metal stock. The carbine never misfired. When it was first issued to me, the M-15 jammed continuously. It had replaced the heavy and large-caliber M-14, which had been designed for use in the Korean War.

"Cal, the local Vietnamese, probably the Viet Cong, could modify M-15s to make them reliable. We knew we were dealing with the enemy. I couldn't have cared less. My concern was staying alive. I decided not to waste time on matters I didn't understand. I stayed focused on the day I would be discharged."

"You did the right thing, Lenny. You can't fight big money!"

"Now do you feel better, Cal?"

"I sure do, Lenny. The story was making me think that you would be leaving me to go to Atlanta."

"Lori talked about the things that you talk about. Cal, you listen to me! You mean the world to me. You are my first girlfriend, and I like the way that feels."

"Lenny, do you realize that this is the second time you've told me that you have feelings for me. It feels as good as a warm blanket on a cold day."

"I never thought about a blanket like that, Cal."

"Will you shut up, Lenny? I have one more question. Was she your first?"

"I will not lie to you, Cal. My first sexual experience was with her. She popped my cherry."

"I don't fault you for that, Lenny. I don't ever want to be alone again. Lenny, I have already told you that I loved you since the first time I saw you, and my love continues to grow every day. Lenny, promise me that you will never leave me at this truck stop in the middle of nowhere."

"I will not leave you, Cal. Now calm down."

"I'm sorry, Lenny. I do become carried away when I think about being dumped again."

"You need to give me a break. I have already told you that this love thing is all new to me, Cal. Dry your eyes, and sit up straight, and I will continue the story unless you want me to stop."

"No, Lenny. I want to know what happened."

"I hung out with Lori and a few of the guys I'd met playing ball. I stayed with them every chance I had. When I did not have an invite to sleep somewhere, I slept in Jane's car. Then I turned eighteen and joined the army."

I could tell that Cal was not going to like what happened in the last six weeks before I joined the army. I lied to Cal to keep the peace. I didn't tell her about the highlight of my young life.

For your sake, I will take a step back in time and tell you what happened during the last forty-five days before I left for the army in 1966. It was an amazing time!

■ ■ ■

BACK TO LORI AT THE PARK'S POND (1966)

This is what really went on during the last six weeks before I entered the army.

"Lenny, did you talk to the army recruiter earlier?"

"I did, Lori."

"Have you decided to join?"

"I am going to enlist, Lori. I did not sign any papers. I must wait until I turn eighteen next month."

"I decided that I won't hate you for joining. You know why I am against your going, Lenny."

"Lori, if you knew my whole story, you would agree that it is my only choice. I have nothing going on in my life."

"Since my boyfriend died, I have been adrift myself, Lenny. I intend to go to junior college next semester and to play basketball. If I don't get a scholarship to the University of Georgia, I will consider any university that offers me a scholarship," Lori said.

"I definitely want to attend a university when I finish my service obligation, Lori. I can use the GI Bill. That was a primary reason for my decision to join the army."

"I must tell you that I don't believe in the Vietnam War, Lenny. I truly can't see any acceptable reason that the United States should be involved in a civil war thirteen thousand miles away.

"A growing faction of the younger population is moving to Canada to avoid the draft. If a young man is drafted and refuses to go, he will be prosecuted and jailed. What do you think, Lenny?"

"I will admit that I've never thought about the subject. I am pretty dumb when it comes to Vietnam, especially compared to you, Lori."

"I never even heard the word 'Vietnam' until my boyfriend told me that he was going there. Once he left, I became more involved. In one of his last letters, he told me that he had begun to doubt our reasons for being there. He spoke of the shortages of supplies and said that goods were being sold to the black market by the high-ranking military officials who were living in mansions with servants and concubines in downtown Saigon.

"He thought the war was about making money by selling overpriced goods and war materials to the government by the elite who own war-material manufacturing facilities. He said that the American people were being lied to and that as long as the wealthy made money and the people didn't know about what was happening, the war would drag on."

"Wow, Lori, you know a lot more than I do. Do you hold that against me?"

"Lenny, when you go, you can write me and tell me what you have learned. If you find similar things when you're there, I might join one of those groups against the war. They're becoming very popular on university campuses around the country. There is talk of a revolution.

"I have also read about a militant group called the Black Panthers, in California. The group formed to protect minority communities from government oppression and police brutality. The Black Panthers are the antithesis of the peaceful civil rights movement started by Martin Luther King Jr."

"Lori, I have a question."

"What is your question?"

"Will you be my friend until I leave next month? We can do other things besides playing basketball."

"Do you mean that you want me to be your girlfriend, Lenny? Yeah, I guess I can. After you leave, it will be over. I refuse to allow myself to be involved in another situation like the one I was involved in before."

"I understand, Lori. Can we seal the deal with a handshake?"

"No, Lenny. I'd prefer a kiss. Now that's how you seal a deal—one kiss. Let's go see if the other guys are on the court and play some ball."

"OK, Lori. Can I walk you home tonight?"

"I would like that, my friend."

KNOWING LORI (1966)

"I am exhausted," Lori said.

"What is the problem?"

"I'm tired and hungry."

"Would you like me to go with you to eat, Lori?"

"Are you hungry?"

"A little bit."

"We can rest for a few minutes and then go to the diner. The food is on me. I have been babysitting for the neighbor the last few nights."

"Why are you tired, Lori?"

"I stayed up late to study because I was babysitting until eleven. It caught up with me, I guess. The basketball season is ending, and I still don't have any scholarships. Women's sports don't seem to be catching on like men's sports did. That is my problem, not yours, Lenny. We need to live it up, since you will be going away next month. After we eat, would you like to go swimming at the recreation center's pool? The water might be a little chilly. The pool will be closing next week for the winter. We can stop by my house for shorts for you and for my swimsuit."

"The water being a little cold will not bother me, Lori. I would love to go swimming with you."

"Let's eat first, Lenny."

"What are you going to order?"

"The diner has the best chili-cheeseburgers in Atlanta."

"Too bad Jane's not here. She would've given us a discount. She works the night shift."

"You want fries, Lenny?"

"I will have a chili hot dog with fries."

"Water is fine for me."

"Hey, Lori, is this our first date?"

"We had our first kiss and now are on our first date. You are on a roll," Lori said, laughing. "All we need to do now is go home."

"What does that mean, Lori?"

"Duh, Lenny. Think about what guys think of the most."

"Oh."

"Are you turning red, Lenny?"

"No, I know what you're talking about, Lori. I've done that!"

"I can tell that you're lying, Lenny."

"Have you gone all the way, Lori?"

"I told you that I had an eighteen-year-old boyfriend. We went steady for almost a year before he went to Vietnam. What do you think? Be quiet, and order your dog, Lenny. Don't take what I said the wrong way. I really think that you're a good-looking and very nice young man. You are the first boy I've hung out with since my boyfriend died."

"That does make me feel better."

"Lori, did they tell you how he was killed?"

"I received a long letter from his mother, thanking me."

"Thanking you for what, Lori?"

"His mother said that when he left for Vietnam, he said he was going to marry me when he came home. His mother said that I'd made him happy and that his love for the army and for me had made him a man.

"His mother thanked me for the part I had played in his transformation from a boy to a man."

"I don't get it, Lori."

"Think of it like this, Lenny, and don't blush. His mother realized that we'd been sexually active. She knew I'd been his first sexual partner. She was thankful that he'd had a sexual experience before he'd died."

"I see what she meant, Lori. Do you ever see his family?"

"I do visit them on occasion. They treat me like family. His mother told me that when she received word of his death, she prayed that I was pregnant. He was there for only sixty days before a sniper shot him in the head. It was the first and the last time I was in a church. I swore I would never get involved with a soldier again. Here I am with you."

"Lori, I am not a soldier."

"Technically, you're right, but you will be soon. I share everything with my mother. She would not be in favor of my becoming involved with another soldier."

"Lori, I promise you that I will not get killed."

"Let's not talk about this subject again, Lenny."

"We won't."

THE PSYCHOLOGY OF DEPRIVATION (1966)

"I love chili hot dogs."

"How is your chili cheeseburger, Lori?"

"I have been eating these cheeseburgers since I started high school. My mother told me that she ate them when she was in high school."

"When I was in New York, I ordered a chili hot dog, and the chili had beans in it."

"Why do you think they put beans in the chili, Lenny?"

"I guess to make more money. Beans are cheaper than ground meat."

"What did your dad do, Lenny?"

"He was a businessman."

"He told me that he went hungry during the Great Depression."

"What was that, Lenny?"

"It had to do with economics, Lori. I remember studying those years in school," I said. "It was caused by a stock market crash. I remember the dates, Lori. The Great Depression began in 1929 and ended in 1939. It was the greatest economic downturn in history. Many people lost everything they had, Lori, including my father."

"Are you showing off that expensive military-academy education?"

"I didn't mean it like that, Lori."

"I know. I was just kidding!"

"My father made a vow to himself that he would never be unable to meet his basic needs again. Not wanting to do without was the driving force behind his financial success. However, another man who did nothing but marry my mother benefited from all of his hard work. What does your mom do for a living, Lori?"

"She's the assistant principal at the high school I go to. I have to be a model student to avoid jeopardizing her reputation and position. I want to act like a juvenile, but because of the restrictions imposed on me, I can't do the things that many of the girls my age do."

"Is your situation similar to that of a preacher's daughter?"

"I don't know if I like that comparison, Lenny. But I guess that sometimes, I feel like being wild and promiscuous."

"Really, Lori?"

"My boyfriend was known in his high school as a bad boy. That was why I was attracted to him, Lenny."

"So it is true that girls like bad boys."

"In my case, Lenny, that is true. If he had gone to my high school, I couldn't have associated with him."

"Lori, my father bought my mother her first pair of shoes. She was eleven years old. Six years later he married her.

"When they built their home, she got a walk-in shoe closet with hundreds of pairs of shoes in it. Every time she went to town, she would buy several pair of shoes. I asked my father why my mother had so many shoes. He told me it was because she hadn't had shoes when she was young, because her family had been very poor. He said she was responding to a long-term deprivation of a need. Does the inability to behave the way you want to motivate you to be a rebel, Lori?"

"I believe so, Lenny. Being deprived of something causes repercussions, Lenny."

"Now you are the smart one, Lori!"

"That is called psychology. It's my favorite subject, Lenny."

SEX-EDUCATION TALK ON THE WALK TO LORI'S HOUSE (1966)

"Thanks for the dog, Lori. What's next?"

"Let's go to my house to get swimsuits."

"What about your mom? Is she going to be coming home?"

"Not for a while, Lenny. Today she has her monthly teachers' meeting. Sometimes she doesn't come home until six at night."

"Lori, you know that I went to a military academy. I haven't been around girls as much as boys who went to coed schools have been."

"I have noticed, Lenny. I kind of like being the more experienced one in this friendship. I was in your place when I first started dating my older and wilder boyfriend."

"In one of my biology classes, the professor explained the act of procreation—you know, the birds and the bees, Lori." Lori laughed.

"Why are you laughing at me, Lori?"

"Because of the way you're beginning this conversation about sex. I haven't heard the birds-and-bees story since I was an adolescent. Go ahead and finish what you were telling me, Lenny. I really am interested in your professor's thoughts on copulation."

"He said that sex is a beautiful act of trust between two consenting individuals. He then said that most religions demonize sexual intercourse and that he believed that to be wrong. He also said that the demonization of sex causes many individuals to experience problems with sexual inhibitions later in life.

"He said that young females are innately and passionately drawn to testosterone, and young males are innately and passionately drawn to estrogen. This uncontrollable passion is necessary for the survival of the species. The drive to reproduce is connected to the availability of food. The more accessible food is, the stronger the drive to reproduce will be. When food is scarce, the drive to reproduce decreases.

"That is nature's way of controlling births. In recent times, economics has also become a factor in reproduction."

"I know now why I am sexually attracted to you, Lenny. My belly is full."

"Lori, are you mocking me?"

"No, Lenny. I am impressed. You have taught me something. I see now why military schools are academically superior to public schools.

"In a public school, a teacher would never make a negative remark about religion. I also noticed that you referred to your instructors as 'professors.' In public schools, they are referred to as 'teachers.'"

"Lori, all of my instructors had Ph.D.s. We addressed each one as 'Doctor.'"

"Public-school teachers have undergraduate degrees, like bachelor of science degrees or bachelor of art degrees. There is a great difference between an undergraduate degree and a Ph.D., Lenny. My mother is an assistant principal and only has a master's degree."

THE UNEXPECTED RETURN OF LORI'S MOTHER (1966)

"This is my house, Lenny. Come on in. It could take me a few minutes to locate my swimsuit. I can't remember the last time I wore it. I will have to try it on to see if it still fits. I bought it when I had my false pregnancy."

"What did you say, Lori!"

"I was just funning you, Lenny."

"It was not funny. I was startled, Lori!"

"Here is a pair of shorts for you. This pair is too large for me. I bought it when I was literally fat, Lenny."

"I am amazed by all your trophies. Looking at these pictures, I can see that you've been an athlete since you were a kid."

"Go ahead and sit down, and make yourself comfortable while I'm digging for my swimsuit. I warned you that it might take a while. I found it, Lenny. What do you think?"

"I like the bright-yellow color, Lori."

"Tell me how it looks on."

"Do you want me to stand outside?"

"No, Lenny. I command you to sit where you are. It is OK to look, Lenny. I want you to look. It turns me on! I am undressing in front of you on purpose. I am trying to seduce you. What do you think, Lenny?"

"You are beautiful, Lori."

"Have you had a girl pose for you before, Lenny?"

"I have never been this close to a nude girl."

"I will do a few poses for you. Let me put on these sexy high heels first. I am ready. I will do a few poses that I practiced for my boyfriend. You can tell me afterward which pose you liked. Go ahead and tell me, Lenny, which one arouses you the most. It's OK."

"I like the one with you bent over, looking back at me."

"Why, Lenny?"

"It shows your uh…your uh—"

"You mean my pussy, Lenny."

"Yes, Lori. It is…uh—"

"Really exciting, Lenny? Thank you! I am going to sit in your lap. You can touch me anywhere you want. I feel something hard under me, Lenny. Is that an erection? You can remove your shirt. I will reposition myself in between your legs and slide your pants and underwear down. Don't be fearful. I know that it's your first time. I will guide you through this."

"Oh, Lori, never have I ever felt anything this good. I have never had a girl to play with my penis."

"Lie back and enjoy it, but don't come. I am going to give you head, Lenny."

"Stop, or I will come, Lori."

"OK. Think of something else. Now I am going to put a condom on you. I am going to lie on the bed and spread my legs so that you can enter me. Do not come!

"You can pull out if you think that you're going to prematurely ejaculate. You have to hold back. We have other positions to try. My favorite is doggy style."

"Oh, it feels so good, Lori."

"You feel good inside me, Lenny. Hold on while I have an orgasm. I can have many. You will be pretty spent when you ejaculate for the first time. Oh, my God, Lenny. It has been too long. That was unbelievable!

"OK, now you can mount me from the rear. That's doggy style."

"Lori, I don't know how much longer I can hold back."

"Oh, Lenny, fuck me hard. Fuck me hard, Lenny."

"I am coming, Lori."

The door suddenly swung wide open. "What are you doing to my daughter? Get off of her, gather your damn clothes, and get out of my house!"

"Mom, I seduced him! It's not Lenny's fault. He's a virgin. I'm eighteen years old and a legal adult. There's no harm being done here, Mom."

"He's seventeen and legally a minor. This will not go on in my house. I want to see both of you downstairs to discuss this matter. Get dressed now!"

She slammed the door. Lori giggled and said, "Did you finish coming, Lenny?"

"I did. What about your mom?"

"She knew I was having sex with my boyfriend. She gave me a lot of pointers on how to please him sexually. We never had sex here. We always went to his house. Mom and I masturbate together a lot.

"She has pictures of nude men with hard-ons, and we look at them while we masturbate. That's how close we are. Didn't you ever masturbate with some of your friends?"

"Yes, I did, Lori. We looked at pictures of naked women."

"This just took her by surprise, Lenny."

"I would have told her about us, but she wasn't here. I feel sorry for her. She's always horny. She doesn't have a boyfriend. After we talk, she'll get over it. I busted your cherry, Lenny. We can do all of the different positions before you leave. I even thought of some new positions to try. Do you want more pussy, Lenny?" Lori laughed and gave me a kiss.

"Damn right!" I said.

"Come here. Let me remove the condom and dispose of it. That's a nice load of come, Lenny. What a waste. I swallow." Lori dropped to her knees and licked me clean. Then she disposed of the condom. "Did you know that condoms deaden the sensation?"

"What do you mean, Lori?"

"Wearing one is the same as wearing a glove on your hand. You can't feel things as well."

"I have never felt anything better."

"It will feel much better without a condom. You'll just have to pull out. You can finish by coming in my mouth."

"Wow, Lori! Do you like it that way?"

"I prefer it that way. The best is yet to come. I don't think we'll make it to the swimming pool today, Lenny."

"That's OK with me, Lori. This was the greatest day of my life!"

THE SEX DISCUSSION WITH LORI'S MOTHER (1966)

"Lenny, my name is Mary Gibson. I would like to know more about you."

"What can I tell you, Ms. Gibson?"

"Where did you meet my daughter?"

"We met at the park, playing basketball."

"I don't have to ask whether you used protection."

"Mother, why did you even bring that up? You must have seen the condom full of come on his pretty cock when you barged in without knocking."

"How dare you talk like that, Lori!"

"Mom, get real. I like Lenny. He respects me and trusts me. I am honored that he allowed me to take his virginity. I am no doubt the beneficiary in this situation. I enjoyed every inch of Lenny."

"Lori, I can't believe you said that!"

"There was no harm done, Mom."

"Ms. Gibson, I care for your daughter. What can I say to make you more comfortable with me?"

"I'm concerned that this will get around the school," Ms. Gibson said.

"Lori told me about your position, and I understand your concern. I don't know anyone at your school, Ms. Gibson. I don't intend to make any friends, because I will be leaving next month to go into the army. You have my word, Ms. Gibson, that I will never say anything! This was my first time."

"How did you like it, Lenny?"

"Mom, you would not have believed the look on his face when I started giving him head."

"I had never been close to a nude girl, Ms. Gibson. She posed for me, like the women in some of the magazines we used to look at."

"Mom, he left something out of that sentence. When he and some of his friends jerked off, they'd look at pictures of nude women, like we do with men."

"Did you tell him about us, Lori?"

"Yes, I did. It's no big deal, is it, Lenny?"

"No. I have an open mind. I hope that I'm not being too frank, Ms. Gibson. I want to be honest with you."

"Your answers please me, Lenny."

"Mom, I intend to have more sex with Lenny. I also want to be honest with you. I will not be so stupid as to get pregnant. This will go no further than the three of us. I am asking you to allow Lenny to stay in my room and to have sex with me here, instead of out in public. It is not like we have our own private space. That way, you will know that our sex will remain secret and safe.

"We want to enjoy each other for the short time that he'll be here. This will probably be the first and last opportunity I'll have to enjoy a virgin."

"I never dreamed of receiving a request like this from my daughter. I do agree that having sex here at home would be better than having sex out in public. Times are changing. OK, we will give this a try."

"Thanks, Mom. I love you very much."

"Ms. Gibson, I think that Lori is lucky to have a mom like you. If I hadn't known better, I would have thought that you were Lori's sister. You look too young to be her mother."

"Mom became pregnant with me during her senior year of high school. She worked her way through college while she raised me. Mom is only thirty-seven years old."

"Ms. Gibson, you are very beautiful."

"Thank you, Lenny."

"Mom has not had a boyfriend in years. Her job is too demanding."

"That is true. However, once I become principal, I will have plenty of time. I think that that will happen in a year or so."

"Ms. Gibson, you can rest assured that I will always respect your daughter and your privacy."

"Lenny, will you pull your pants down for me? I know that my mom wants to inspect you."

"You mean here?"

"OK, all the way to your knees, Lenny. Turn around, and show your cock to my mom. Tell Lenny what you think, Mom?"

"Lenny, your cock looks very nice."

"Thank you, Ms. Gibson."

"Go ahead and feel how nice it is, Mom. Look, Mom—it started getting hard when you felt it. Let my mom see it fully hard before we go upstairs. Lenny, do you get excited when my mom fondles your cock? It is OK, Lenny. Tell her the truth."

"Yes, Ms. Gibson. You are so beautiful. I'm very excited."

"Mom, you have to admit that a live young cock looks better than the ones in the pictures that we look at when we masturbate.

"Lenny, let's go back upstairs and finish what we started. I have a few things that I want to teach you about how to treat a woman."

Ms. Gibson looked at me, shook her head, and laughed. "I will never forget this moment," she said. As we climbed the stairs, her mother said, "Have fun."

MOTHER-DAUGHTER THREESOME (1966)

Lori demanded that I take off my clothes when I entered the room. While I was undressing, she thanked me for telling her mother how beautiful she was. "My mother really liked you, Lenny. I would like to see my mother get laid." She went to her knees and was putting my cock in her mouth when her mother knocked on the door.

I stood there naked with a rock-hard cock. I looked at Lori, and she said, "Stand right there when I open the door, Lenny. I want my mother to see your hard cock again. I mean it, Lenny! Trust me. I know my mom. Who's there?"

"It's me, Lori. Can I come in?"

"You do as I said, Lenny."

"Come on in, Mom."

She momentarily stared at my naked body and then said, "I brought you a few things. These are some of our adult toys. Lenny might find them interesting."

"Show them to him, Mom."

"Are you sure, Lori?"

"Remember that we agreed to be open and honest."

"This is the dildo that Lori and I use when we masturbate. It can be used as an alternative when a man is not readily available, or a man can use it to keep a woman excited while he's waiting to recover from his ejaculation. This is the lubricant for it."

"Look, Mom. The dildo is about the size of Lenny's cock. I like Lenny's cock a little better," Lori said, giggling.

"Lenny, you wouldn't mind if my mom played with your cock, would you?"

"I don't know, Lori."

"Would that be all right with you, Lenny?"

"Of course, Ms. Gibson. If you want, you can play with it like Lori was."

Lori grabbed her mom's hand and placed it on my cock. Mary moaned and took a deep breath. "I agree. You are beautiful, Lenny," she said.

Lori turned her head and gave me a wink of approval. Her mother sat down on the bed and started rummaging through the box. Lori pulled me by the cock until my cock was at her mother's eye level. I was then a few inches away from her and so close to her that she could see the precome dripping from the head of my penis. Lori started stroking my cock as her mother talked about the items in the box.

"There are other things that you might enjoy in here too."

"Mom, show Lenny how to use the dildo."

"Lenny, I will instruct you on how to use it on Lori. OK, apply the lubricant to her vagina. That's good. Now insert it gently a little at a time until she naturally becomes lubricated. Lori, you need to tell him how deep you want it to go and what kind of motion you'd like."

I began pushing it in and out. "How does that feel, Lori?"

"That is perfect! Mom, this is amazing. Your being here makes it more exciting. Lenny, you have a nice erection. Mom, can I give Lenny head at the same time?"

"Anything goes in sex, Lori. This is getting to me," Ms. Gibson said. "I should leave."

"No, Mom. I want you to stay. Your being here really turns me on. Why don't you take off your clothes, Mom?"

"Really, Lori? Is that all right with you, Lenny?"

"That would be great, Ms. Gibson!"

"I need you both to swear that you will never under any circumstances say anything about this to anyone."

"I swear, Ms. Gibson."

"Mom, you know I would never."

"Ms. Gibson, you look great."

"Lenny, show her how you eat pussy."

"Sit on the bed and spread your legs, Ms. Gibson."

"Please call me Mary."

"How does that feel, Mom?"

"God, it has been a long time."

"Mom, do whatever you want. I am pleased to share him with you. I know how much stress you have at your job. You need this relief. Oh, oh, oh—good job, Lenny. You got her off by giving her head. Good job!"

"Lenny, bring your beautiful young cock over to me," Mary said. She immediately swallowed my penis.

"Mom, teach me how to swallow a cock like that."

"You said it right! You have to swallow it. It takes practice, but men love it. Watch me thrust his cock down deep into my throat, Lori."

"I am coming, Ms. Gibson."

"If I were you, Lori, I would keep Lenny busy until he left."

"Mom, we can share him. What do you think about that, Lenny?"

"I can satisfy both of you."

"Mom, you can leave for lunch and come home during the day. I can't leave school," Lori said. "You can have him all to yourself for an hour and a half. The school is only five minutes away, Mom. Lenny, what do you think?"

"Damn right. I will meet you here during lunch, Ms. Gibson. I will do anything you want me to do. You are sexy, Mary," I said.

"I will be here at about five after eleven and stay until twelve-thirty. We will start tomorrow, Lenny. You can stay over and go back and forth between our bedrooms. We can sleep in the same bed, and you can have us both. I like the idea of secret sex," Ms. Gibson said. "It is perfect for my lifestyle at this time. At his age, Lenny should be able to satisfy both of us, Lori."

"I know I can, Ms. Gibson."

"Please call me Mary, Lenny. What did you think about that blow job?"

"It was fantastic, Mary."

"This is when the toys come into play. Lenny, while you are recuperating, we can pleasure ourselves. Lenny, how many times have you jerked off in, say, a couple of hours?" Mary said.

"I jerked off ten times in two hours once. Watching you pleasure yourself is very stimulating. I will be ready to go again in a couple of minutes," I said.

"Mom, how much time do you have?"

"The meeting was adjourned so that those in attendance could go home and eat and see their families. I have only twenty minutes before I need to be back. That is not enough time to go again. Lenny, we will have to go at it later," Mary said. "You can pleasure Lori for the rest of the evening."

"What about food, Mom?"

"I am not hungry after what I just went through. I feel like a weight has been lifted off of my chest. I had four orgasms in one hour. I did not realize how badly I needed to have sex. I'm going to take a quick shower and leave.

"Lori, thank you for setting this up. I really love you. Lenny, you are a beautiful young man. I will see you at eleven tomorrow. This is between us, right?"

"You can count on me, Mary."

"Mom, I have one last request."

"What is it, Lori?"

"I want Lenny to stay here with us until he leaves."

"That would be perfectly all right with me, Lori. We will keep Lenny busy. What do you think, Lenny?"

"I promise that I can satisfy both of you."

WHITE SLAVERY? (1966)

"Lenny, I have an idea. What time will your guardian be at the diner?"

"She goes in a little before ten at night."

"Can you call her and tell her that you're going to stay at my house?"

"Is that your idea, Lori?"

"Yes, I want you to do me a favor."

"What do you want me to do?"

"I want to surprise my mom. I will wash you and manicure you from head to toe if you'll spend the entire night with my mom. Give her all of the kinky sex she desires."

"What do you mean by 'kinky'?"

"Do everything that she tells you to do no matter how bizarre it sounds. She knows more about making love than we do. Tomorrow you can show me what she did, and then we can try it."

"That's fine with me, Lori. Your mother is pretty and very sexy."

"Lenny, your doing that would make me very happy. I will draw your bath water. Is the temperature of the water good?"

"Yes, Lori. It is perfect."

"I'm going to get in facing you, Lenny. Stand up so that I can shave your pubic area. You have light hair. Your body hair is fine too. That does it for the front.

"Turn around and bend over. I want to make sure that you don't have any hidden hairs around your butt. You only had a few here and there. I shaved them. Mom is going to be so pleased when she sees you. You can sit back down now. I'm going to give you a pedicure. Let me have your left foot. OK, now give me your right foot. Now let's do your left hand. OK, now we can do your right hand. What do you think, Lenny?"

"My nails have never looked this good, Lori. Is this how men should groom themselves, Lori?"

"I don't know, Lenny. I just know what my mom likes."

"How did you find that out?"

"When we select pictures of men to look at while we masturbate, she comments on the ones who excite her sexually.

"She said that the less hair a man has, the cleaner he appears to be."

"What about you, Lori?"

"Mom and I have the same likes."

"Are all mothers and daughters as close as you and your mom?"

"I don't know the answer to that question. If they are, it is something that no one talks about. My guess is that my mom and I have a special relationship, Lenny."

"I know for sure that fathers and sons don't have this type of special relationship. My friends and I would talk about our relationships with our fathers, Lori. I know that all of my friends would give anything to be in my shoes right now."

"Lenny, I appreciate this situation and know that my mom is very appreciative too.

"I could tell that my mom really liked you, Lenny."

"I really liked her too, Lori. She is nice and beautiful."

"This situation came at the perfect time for my mom and me."

"Lori, I can't imagine a better going-away celebration."

"You finish washing while I round up the body lotions. Are you through washing, Lenny?"

"Yes, Lori."

"That only took about an hour and a half. Step out onto the mat, and I will dry you off. I forgot to shave your armpit hair. Raise one of your arms, Lenny. Mom hates hair, Lenny."

"Are you sure, Lori?"

"I promise you that I know what she likes."

"Whatever you say."

"Sit down in front of the mirror. I will dry and comb your hair. That is done. Give me your left hand. I am going to put clear polish on your nails. Look how good the clear nail polish looks."

"I have never been cleaned up like this, Lori."

"Mom will keep you clean, Lenny. She takes care of her things."

"Lori, I am not a thing!"

"You know what I mean. She is a very caring person. I want you to look perfect for her. Are you excited about sleeping with her tonight?"

"She is sexy, and she smells very good. I can't imagine sleeping with her all night. I hope I can please her, Lori. I promise you that I will do my best."

"All you have to do is what she tells you to do. She will know how to make you feel good, Lenny. Don't question her—just perform."

"Don't worry. I will not let you down!"

"We are right on schedule."

"What schedule, Lori?"

"When she comes home from work, the first thing she does is shower. I will hide you until she gets into the shower. When we hear her coming out, I will bring you into her bedroom. When she walks out of the bathroom, I will present you to her, and you can tell her that you want to sleep with her tonight.

"You will be naked with a big ribbon tied around your neck. She will be so excited, Lenny. I can't wait. What about you?"

"I'm a little nervous."

"Trust me, Lenny. This will be the best night of your life. Lie down on the bed so that I can rub this lotion on you. Getting you ready has made me so horny."

"Do you want me to screw you?"

"No, I don't want you to be sweaty."

"Do you want me to give you head?"

"No, Lenny. We don't have time. You and I will have plenty of time later."

"Mom should be here any minute. You hide in the bathroom in case she looks in on me. Let me know if you hear her open the front door to come in. I forgot to gift wrap you. Sit in the chair. I am going to tie a big blue ribbon around your neck. Wow, look in the mirror, Lenny. You are gift wrapped."

"Lori, I just heard the front door open downstairs."

"Quickly, hide in my bathroom and be very quiet. She always looks in on me!"

"Hello, Lori. How are you doing?"

"I'm fine, and you, mom?"

"I'm going to my room to shower off the dirt from being in public. Think about what we can have for a late dinner, Lori."

"Come out, Lenny! Are you ready to go? Let me comb your hair again. Now we can go to her bedroom. Be quiet, and stand here, where the bathroom light will shine on you when she opens the door. She is coming out, Lenny!"

"Oh, my God, Lori."

"Surprise, Mom! Tell Mom what you would like to do, Lenny!"

"Ms. Gibson, I would like to sleep with you tonight if that's OK."

"Lenny, you are beautiful."

"I gave him a manicure and a pedicure. He is spotless. Go to her, Lenny! Mom, Lenny will do whatever you want."

"I will take care of you, Lenny."

"I'm going to leave him with you, Mom. I will fix some coffee. Have a quickie, and then come down to the kitchen. You'll have all night with him. See you in a few minutes."

"This is the best thing ever. Lenny, tell me the truth. Do you want to be with me?"

"I really do, Ms. Gibson."

"Lie down with me on the bed. You smell very good, and look at your nails!"

"Lori said you would like them. She removed my body hair too."

"I like what she did, Lenny. I don't know what to say."

"You don't need to say anything, Ms. Gibson. I appreciate what you and your daughter are doing for me. Lori said that I should tell you exactly what I'm thinking if you ask me and that you'll tell me exactly what you're thinking and what you want.

"She told me that that's the best way to have satisfying sex. None of the guys in military school told stories like this. I was lucky to meet you and Lori. This is a real-life fantasy for me, Ms. Gibson."

"Lenny, I will gladly do away with that erection, and then we can go downstairs, have coffee, and talk this arrangement over. What would you like to do?"

"Ms. Gibson, I would like to screw you doggy-style. Sometimes it takes a woman longer to orgasm than a man. Lori already explained that to me. I will hold my ejaculation until you have had an orgasm. You'll need to tell me whether you want me to come inside you or pull out. Lori likes me to pull out and to come in her mouth. She said she enjoys it that way."

"Lori has been lecturing you on how to please a woman?"

"Yes, Ms. Gibson. She said that a man should talk openly with a woman in order to understand her sexual needs."

"Lenny, I want you to come inside me."

"That would be great. I have not experienced that without protection. Lori said to try to surprise you if you didn't have any requests."

"Surprises can be exciting on occasion. Lori has taught you well."

"Lori told me that you could teach me more than she could. She wants to learn more too, Ms. Gibson."

"The three of us will come together soon to exchange ideas, Lenny. Come here. I want to give you a hug and a kiss before we go downstairs."

"You mean that you want to make out!"

"Yes, Lenny. Let's make out for a few minutes."

"Lie on the bed beside me."

"I like making out with you, Ms. Gibson."

"Now I am ready, Lenny! I'm going to bend over this chair. Is this the right height?"

"Perfect, Ms. Gibson."

"Oh, that feels good, Lenny!" Fuck me fast and hard! The orgasm relieved my stress. You were perfect. Now you can cum inside me, Lenny."

"That felt great. Lori was the first girl I had sex with, and you were the first one I came in."

"Please call me Mary, Lenny."

"Why do you have your face on the floor and your butt in the air?"

"Your warm come feels so good inside of me. I don't want it to run out. I need to stay in this position for a few minutes. OK, Lenny, that should be long enough.

"You can put these shorts on, and we will go downstairs."

"I smell cookies, Ms. Gibson."

"Lori makes delicious cookies. Let's go."

THE FINAL DEAL (1966)

"The house smells like cookies."

"Yes, it does, Lenny. I made a large batch of chocolate-peanut butter cookies," said Lori.

"I set three coffee cups out on the table. Mom, you might want to skip the cookies. I know you are hungry. I made you a bowl of chicken soup and a salad. Lenny, will you pour the coffee? I will bring the cookies to the table for us. How did Lenny do, Mom?"

"He performed well. I feel so relieved. Lenny, I hope you are prepared to go to work. I have a lot of sex to catch up on"

"Me too," said Lori.

"Don't worry. I will do my job," said Lenny.

"Lori has suggested that you stay with us until you enter the army next month. Is that something you want to do, Lenny?"

"Ms. Gibson, I would do anything to stay with you and Lori. Lori has told me what I will be expected to do to earn my keep."

"And exactly what is that, Lenny?"

"I will be expected to help around the house and to provide sex for both of you."

"What kind of sex?"

"I am to provide whatever kind of sex is asked of me."

"Lori, I don't have any more questions. Lenny, do you have any questions?"

"I don't have any questions. This is a dream come true for me."

"There is one thing that I should let you know, Lenny. Keeping this arrangement a secret is of the utmost importance. When we come into contact with other people, I will refer to you as my visiting nephew. The less you say, the better it will work, Lenny. Do you have any questions about the importance of this rule?"

"I certainly do not, Ms. Gibson. I realize that our arrangement would not be understood or accepted by others. No one outside of this home will know about what happens between the three of us, and there won't be any exceptions to that rule.

"My job is to be of service to you and to fulfill your sexual needs until I turn eighteen, at which time I will join the army and leave your house. In exchange for my services, you will supply my basic needs."

"If Lori doesn't have any questions, we have a deal."

"I'm good with this agreement"

"Lenny, I noticed how well you make decisions."

"Making decisions was a very important part of my military-school training, Ms. Gibson. Decision-making skills are vital to good leadership."

"Very interesting, Lenny."

"Why is that interesting, Ms. Gibson?"

"Lenny, you know that I am in public education. That would be a good subject to teach. Most kids have problems making good decisions, Lenny. Thanks for giving me the idea."

"You are very welcome, Ms. Gibson."

"I would like to call Jane at the diner and tell her that I have a place to stay, Ms. Gibson. She is holding my military-academy graduation ring and one hundred twenty dollars for me."

"Lori, will you go with me to pick up my ring and my money? I would like you to meet Jane. She has been helping me out. She has a son in Vietnam."

"When would you like to go?"

"How about tonight, Lori?"

DEFENDING LORI'S HONOR (1966)

"You ready to go to the diner, Lori?"

"Lenny, it is already late. Lori has school tomorrow."

"We will come straight back, Ms. Gibson."

"Lenny, stop addressing me as Ms. Gibson. Now that we've been intimate, you can call me Mary. Call me Ms. Gibson only when we are in public."

"Sorry, I will call you Mary."

"She's right, Lenny. We need to move fast. We still have to bathe before going to bed."

"We can cut through the alley and be there in less than ten minutes. Thanks, Lori, for taking me in. Your mother is one of a kind. I don't know what to do with my ring. I can't take it with me to basic training."

"You should leave it with Mom. When you are stationed, she can send it to you. I did that with my boyfriend's gold chain."

"Stop right there! Where are you going?"

"We are on our way to the diner to see Jane," I said.

"We know who you are. You're the drifter who's been sleeping in the station wagon in the parking lot of the diner. You're the basketball player who lives one street over. I saw you play. You're pretty good for a bitch. What are you doing with this punk? I'm in charge of this territory. You should be my ho. What is your name, piece of pie?"

"None of your fucking business, mister," Lori screamed. "Now leave us alone!"

"You think you can make us, bitch? This punk here can't stop us either. I might take you home with me."

"Be cool. We don't want any trouble," I said.

"Shut your fucking mouth, punk!"

"You don't have to talk to me like that. Can't we be friends? I'll be leaving next month to go into the army. You won't ever see me around here again."

"So you're an army boy, huh? Well, why don't you get down on your knees and beg me not to take your pretty little lady home with me? While you're down there, I'll take whatever is in your pocket. She would make a nice dinner for the three of us. Come here, baby—give a real man a kiss!"

"Take your hands off of her."

"OK, guys, fuck that piece of shit up while I get some white pussy."

I lunged and struck the first one's Adam's apple. In the same movement, I cupped the second one's ear with my other hand, bursting his eardrum. From a crouching position I spun on one leg and kicked the third man's legs out from under him. Before he hit the ground, I drove a sharp open hand into his kidney.

All three lay in serious pain, begging for mercy. "You don't own anything in this neighborhood, especially not this girl!" I said. "Let's go, Lori." Not a word was said until we reached the diner.

Lori looked at me and said, "Lenny, I've never witnessed anything like that. It all happened at lightning speed. Where did you learn to fight like that?"

"I had four years of hand-to-hand-combat training in military school. We practiced all of the martial arts in gym every day, Lori. I hope you are not upset with me. I assessed that nothing we could say was going to convince them to not harm us. I had to move and use the element of surprise, since there were three of them."

"No, Lenny, I am thankful. I agree with your assessment of the situation. Those guys were definitely going to harm us. I hope they learn a lesson. You messed them up pretty bad."

"I had rather you not say anything about this to Jane or your mom, Lori."

"I agree Lenny. Here we are at the diner."

"Hey, Jane, I want to buy my new friend a piece of your fantastic apple pie."

"I was worried about you, Lenny. I have not heard from you."

"Lori's mother has offered me a room in their house until I leave for the army."

"That's wonderful, Lenny. Two pieces of pie coming up."

"You appeared out of nowhere at the perfect time. In a matter of a few days, you became my friend and saved my butt. I want to thank you again, Lenny. Recently Mom has been down in the dumps. My mom's attitude has done a one-hundred-eighty-degree turn in a few hours because of you, Lenny. She adores you! I know my mom; she will treat you like royalty."

"Lenny, the pie is on me," Jane said. "I wish you all of the luck in the world. Here is your money and your ring."

"Lenny, can I see that ring? Wow, that is impressive. Let's hurry home. Mom will probably be waiting up. She won't go to bed until we return, Lenny.

"I will accompany you to her bedroom. See you tomorrow."

"Come in, Lenny. I have drawn you a bath. Go ahead and get in. Let's wash you well and put you to bed. Stand up so that I can wash your back and behind. That did not take long. Step out onto the mat, and I will dry you off. OK, are you ready for bed?"

"I am tired, Mary."

"Is that your graduation ring?"

"It is, Mary. I want you to keep it for me."

"I will be glad to keep it for you Lenny."

"Mary, you smell good."

"Thank you, Lenny. Put your head between my breasts, and go to sleep, Lenny."

A RECAPITULATION OF WHAT WENT ON WITH LORI, MS. GIBSON, AND LENNY (1966)

How do you tell a story like this one without raising eyebrows? In the short time Lenny lived with Lori and her mother, Mary Gibson, he learned many things about the sexual desires of women. Lenny was seventeen, scared, and homeless. He enthusiastically accepted with no reservations the conditions that came with the room and board offered to him by Mary Gibson.

At seventeen, a boy's testosterone is raging. Lenny's dream job was to make two gorgeous women happy by being their secret sex slave.

The phenomenal mother-daughter relationship, sharing their sexual desires, could be a story in itself, but it would need to be told from Mary and Lori's point of view to completely understand.

Try to think of this arrangement from their point of view. They had a seventeen-year-old virgin boy willing to be their sex slave, and he would soon be leaving to go to war, where he would possibly die, as Lori's boyfriend had. Imagine how convenient and desirable that situation would've been for a thirty-seven-year-old woman too busy with her career to find a boyfriend who could satisfy her emotional and sexual needs?

Can you not feel Mary Gibson's newfound strength and elation when Lenny became her sexual surrogate? Furthermore, Mary's position as assistant principal prohibited Lori's behavior. I believe an undetectable and secret arrangement resembling Mary, Lori, and Lenny's would be acceptable to many women in similar situations.

The most interesting person in this story is Lori's mother, Mary Gibson, an on-the-rise assistant high school principal. She really took to Lenny. Her gift of shelter and love was very comforting at a turbulent time in Lenny's life.

Mary Gibson and Lenny, despite their age difference, carried on a remarkable relationship. Although, Lenny was seventeen, people guessed that he was fourteen or fifteen. Lenny knew his young-boy look was part of what turned Mary Gibson on sexually.

Mary Gibson took Lenny with her everywhere. They always held hands when they were together. She would kneel down in public, when needed, and tie his shoelace, stand up, and give him a kiss on the cheek. She would then grab his hand and off they would go again.

Mary challenged Lenny intellectually. She asked Lenny, "Do you think the secrecy of our sexual triangle is intriguing?"

"Mary, what exactly do you mean when you say 'intriguing'?"

"It means that it's our little secret, that no one will ever know, and that makes what we do more exciting."

"Like the excitement and curiosity that a spy novel presents to a reader, Mary?"

"Yes, that's close enough to what I mean, Lenny."

"Mary, I know what most boys my age would think about our arrangement."

"What would that be, Lenny?"

"Most boys fantasize about being in my situation while they're jerking off."

"I'm having a hard time visualizing that, Lenny," Mary said, laughing.

Lori liked it when Lenny spent the evenings with her mother. She said that he made her mother happy, which in turn made her happy. Lori was a senior and got out of school early in the afternoon. She would come home, and Lenny and she would have kinky sex. Then they would go to play basketball and hang out.

One day when Lori had her mother's car for the day, she drove fifty miles to the far side of Atlanta, where no one would recognize her, to have public sex with Lenny in a park. Then Lori went to a mall and rode the escalators. She wore a very short skirt with no panties.

She would step on an ascending escalator in front of a man, exposing her genitals to him. Afterward she would ask Lenny to describe the man's reaction. Lenny did not agree with this game, but he said nothing that would discourage her. Lenny did assist her. He felt it was his duty, because it was what she wanted and he had agreed to do whatever was asked of him sexually, per their agreement.

It really excited her as well as the men she chose to expose herself to. Every now and then, Lori would ask her mother if she could borrow Lenny for the night, and they would try new sex positions that she had imagined. Then they would talk and cuddle for the rest of the night. Her mother would complain the next morning at breakfast that she couldn't sleep without him.

Then she and Lori would start laughing. Lenny never said anything or laughed. He loved both of them in some enchanting way. Mary would come home every day for lunch. The minute she walked in the door, she would assist Lenny in removing his clothes. Then they would sit on the sofa and make out for a few minutes.

Mary would caress his entire body with her gentle hands. Then Lenny would reposition himself, pull her skirt up, and perform cunnilingus on her until she orgasmed. Then Mary would move to the table, where Lenny would serve her a nutritious lunch. She preferred that he remain nude until she left for work.

She said that it was their private time and that Lenny aroused her when he walked back and forth to the kitchen, serving her food. Lenny knew she was watching him, so he played the part and flaunted his genitals, putting them near her face when he served her. That would usually result in her sucking him off before she left. Because of the time constraints, they usually had outercourse.

Lenny always tried to change his performance during lunch in order to maintain her sexual interest. She really liked the way he ate her pussy. She routinely complimented him on how good he was. Lori advised Lenny on her mother's sexual fantasies. Lenny accepted the fact that his job was to encourage her to act out her sexual fantasies.

Mary had a sense of humor. She would sometimes eat quickly so that they could have intercourse. She said that after intercourse, she needed to bathe and brush her teeth before returning to work. One day Lenny asked her why. She said she couldn't return to work "smelling like cock and sperm." Then she winked and laughed.

Lenny always jumped in the shower with her to wash her back and feet. He looked forward to seeing her for lunch.

After much practice, Lori mastered the art of swallowing Lenny's cock. She referred to the act as "deep throating." However, she never came close to being as good as her mother was, and Lenny lied when she asked him if she was better at deep throating than her mother. Lori was much better at posing than Mary. Her younger, athletic body gave her more range of motion and flexibility in her poses than Mary.

Lori and her mother competed sometimes when they had threesomes. They agreed that competition would push the sexual experimentation to a higher level. Afterwards, Mary and Lori would ask Lenny to judge who performed the best. Most of the time, Lenny, would say that it was a tie, never actually declaring a winner. He remained humble, telling them that he was the winner.

Mary was good at anal sex. Lori never really got that down. Lori's pussy was tighter than Mary's. Mary's pussy tasted better. Mary's orgasms were much stronger than Lori's. Lori's breasts were nice, but Mary's breasts were picture perfect. Lenny never really acquired a taste for Lori's occasional squirting.

Lenny always looked forward to Lori's erotic poses. Lori would check out a camera from school. Lenny would spend hours photographing her. Lori found a studio in Athens that would develop them. Lenny took hundreds of pictures. She sent a shoebox full of pictures to Lenny in Vietnam. He shared them with some of his friends. When Lori married and ran off to Canada, Lenny sold the pictures for five dollars apiece.

Mary and Lori groomed Lenny on a daily basis. They enjoyed mother-daughter conversations while rubbing nice-smelling lotions on Lenny's skin.

Mary bought a table specifically for that purpose. Occasionally, they would ask Lenny's opinions on certain issues. He would try to keep his answers short, so he could listen to their conversations. Mary was very protective. Once she noticed a small cut on Lenny's cock. She asked Lori. "How did the cut happen?" Lori responded by saying she had become overexcited and bit his cock.

Mary took issue and told Lori she would have to quit sucking it if it happened again. Lenny could not help but laugh. They stared at each other for a moment and burst out laughing too. Then they both kissed his cock and jokingly said, "Does that make it better, Lenny?" Then they laughed. Lori agreed that Lenny belonged first to Mary.

Lenny lived up to his agreement. He thought a lot about how to keep Mary and Lori sexually interested in him. He was very successful with many of his ideas. How did he know when he was doing a good job? He kept track of how many times he ejaculated and how many times they had orgasms.

Lenny would ejaculate as many as twenty times, and they could have as many as fifty orgasms over a seventy-two-hour period. If those numbers began decreasing, he would make adjustments to keep them aroused. Mary and Lori would sometimes go shopping to buy him sexy apparel to wear around the house. Lenny knew he had to keep their interest until he left for the army. He felt like the sexy apparel they bought him helped do that.

Inventing new ways to have sex with Lenny became an obsession with Mary and Lori. Lenny did notice that the more he ejaculated, the quicker he could recover. He called it getting into good sex shape. Mary insisted that Lenny take zinc supplements. She said they would keep his ejaculations thick and plentiful. Only a healthy seventeen-year-old boy could have kept up with the pace.

How many men can claim that they lived the life of a concubine? Should this personal part of Lenny's life be told? Is it too much for the average reader? Does it add entertainment to the story? The most interesting question of all is, how did this event, early in Lenny's life, impact his development? After considerable thought, I decided to tell this secret part of Lenny's life exactly the way it happened and without moral judgement.

THE ARRANGEMENT SIDEBAR

The golden rule of sex is the following: When every willing player in a sexual encounter benefits, there is no "wrong." Basically, are the participants better off? Gains cannot be recorded, because of the morally unacceptable nature of how they were achieved. The gains remain the private concerns of the participants, who fear being lynched by the mob—that is, by Christian society's morality police and victimless sexual crimes.

In the United States, 75 percent of people are of the Christian faith. Today a substantial number of Americans and members of Congress persistently contend that the United States was founded as a Christian nation. They are wrong. The First Amendment to the Constitution clearly separates religion from government. John Adams, one of the founding fathers, attempted to make that separation perfectly clear when he said, "The government of the United States is not, in any sense, founded on the Christian religion."

Most evangelical Christians consider all sex but that of married couples having sex for the sole purpose of procreation to be wrong. Taking a vow to not engage in sex will not cause one's innate biological drive to disappear. That fact is evident in religious orders that require priests to be celibate.

Celibacy causes sexual frustration, which sometimes results in perverse or dangerous criminal behavior.

The best examples of this are the numerous child-molesting priests of the Catholic Church. Religious organizations have a history of persecuting consenting adults engaged in sex for pleasure. According to Sigmund Freud, "Sex is essential and part of being human. The human is first and foremost a passionate creature driven by primitive irrational forces. One passionate sexual encounter can change the course of a life, for better or worse."

The course of an individual's life is affected by the individual's psychological and physical experiences, good and bad, and by his or her environment. Lori, Mary Gibson, and Lenny accepted their unique sexual arrangement but realized that it would have been unacceptable to a majority of Americans.

So Mary, Lori, and Lenny decided to keep the arrangement private. No one suffered psychological or physical harm with their arrangement. No beneficial sexual arrangements of a positive nature are recorded and made available for study. Only sexual arrangements in which the participants are harmed and a complaint is filed are recorded.

These recorded studies of harmful arrangements are the only records available for study and form the basis of society's morality and laws. Laws are usually based on the opinions of the majority. I have never had a disagreement when I say there are more ignorant people in America than there are smart people. Then why do the ignorant majority set morality standards and legislate laws dealing with sexual behavior using records that represent sexual arrangements where people were mentally or physically harmed?

No other country in the world incarcerates a larger number of its own citizens as does the United States for sexual "crimes" that have no victims.

■ ■ ■

LEAVING CAL AT THE ARIZONA TRUCK STOP (1970)

"The food was unbelievable! Thank you for the clothes, Cal. Did you get everything you came for?"

"I did, Lenny. I think we should return home, change our clothes, and go to the gym. I suggest that after the gym, we spend the rest of the evening reading and discussing what we read."

"I agree, Cal. I want to know everything. The first book I am going to study is *Genetics of the Evolutionary Process*, by Theodosius Dobzhansky."

I couldn't believe how quickly time had passed. Cal had not stayed in the trailer for over three months. A couple of security guards had left, and I had worked a great deal of overtime. When I was not working, I was reading or working out in the gym. Randy's wife had a terminal cancer, and he spent most of his time with her. Her death was imminent.

He'd promoted Cal to general manager, and she'd taken over much of his work. Cal worked all of the time. When she was not working, she was caring for Randy's three kids and nursing his wife. She was making fantastic money and drove a new Cadillac. Cal stayed with Randy's family. We rarely saw each other. It was my day to dispatch calls and to answer the phone at the security office.

Cal's Cadillac pulled up close to the door. It was the first time I had seen her since Randy's wife had died. I opened the door for her, and she entered. She was wearing an expensive pantsuit. For the first time, I felt a sense of awkwardness. She walked straight up to me and hugged me. She said, "Lenny, this is the most difficult task of my life.

"Considering how smart you are; I know that this is not a complete surprise. I have prepared a very generous severance package for you. In this envelope is five thousand dollars. I am very sorry. Randy acknowledged that your work was excellent. I will never forget how you carried me during a low time in my life. To be honest with you, Randy and I are seriously involved and believe that it would be best for you to leave immediately. You can choose a security person to take you to the bus station or the nearest airport."

I couldn't help but notice her wet eyes. She gave me another hug and walked out of the door, crying. I had managed to earn the amount of money that had been stolen from me by the Treasury Department—and more.

I'd learned a seven-thousand-dollar lesson: that I should deny that I was a veteran. With the severance pay, I had around eleven thousand dollars with which to start my life. I'd been prepared for what had just happened. I had nothing but admiration for Cal. She'd been alone, and I had been needy when we'd met. Our temporary arrangement had filled the voids in both our hearts and minds. The truth of the matter was that we were headed in different directions.

When a permanent opportunity knocked, she seized it. Randy was definitely a very good man. He had plenty to offer. It would've been very dumb for her not to not fall in love with him. My plan had been to work for as long as possible and to accumulate as much money as I could. I'd known it would be a matter of time before I'd be forced to leave. I had read every book in Cal's library at least twice. It was time for new reading material. I had a thirst for knowledge that couldn't be satisfied.

It was time to put our arrangement behind me. I decided to ask the first man who walked through the door to take me to the bus station. I needed only one bag to hold my three pairs of jeans, underwear, socks, and five T-shirts.

I intended to call Mary Gibson. She had continued to write me while I'd been in Vietnam. In her last letter, she'd said that it was very important to keep in touch. She continually spoke of having a surprise for me. I wrote her back and promised I would call her when I completed my military service. She also had my military-school graduation ring.

It was time to call her. I couldn't have cared less about the long-distance charges. I had memorized her telephone number.

I called the operator and asked to make a long-distance call to 300-000-4345.

"Is this Mary Gibson?"

"Who is this?"

"Mary, this is Lenny. I promised I would call you when I finished my service obligation."

"Lenny, oh, Lenny, it is so wonderful to hear your voice. Where are you?"

"I am getting ready to board a bus in Arizona."

"Where are you going?"

"I am on my way to Florida to go to a university."

"You must stop in Atlanta, Lenny. I still have your military-school graduation ring."

"How are you doing, Mary?"

"I am the principal of the largest high school in Atlanta. I have been offered the position of superintendent. Will you promise me that you will stop and visit me? I have a magnificent surprise that you must see in person, Lenny."

"Are you sure I won't be an inconvenience?"

"No, Lenny. I need to see you! I live by myself. Lori left."

"Where is Lori, Mary?"

"I will fill you in when you arrive. We have so much to talk about. As soon as you arrive, call me, and I will pick you up."

"I will give you my office's number in the event that you arrive early."

"It will take a couple of days, Mary. Will that be all right with you?"

"Anytime will be fine, Lenny. The key is still under the front doormat. I am so excited."

"I will see you then, Mary. Bye."

■ ■ ■

THE RETURN TO ATLANTA (1970)

The sun was beginning to show itself when I exited the taxi in front of Mary's house. It looked familiar—not much had changed since I'd last entered her house almost four years earlier. I reached for the key under the doormat and noticed that my hand was trembling. That showed me how these steps back in time were affecting me.

I was scared. I didn't understand why. I opened the door quietly and laid the key on the entryway table like I had many times before. I made my way upstairs to Mary's bedroom and stopped. I needed to shower. I thought I should make my way to Lori's bathroom to avoid waking Mary up.

I turned and entered Lori's room. I heard Mary scream. She ran out of her room and grabbed me. "Lenny, I was waiting for you." She began to cry.

"Mary, I am filthy. Please allow me to shower." She escorted me back to her bathroom. She turned the shower on and adjusted the temperature. She then started undressing me. She was still crying. I stepped into the shower. Mary followed me in and immediately began washing me.

"You are so skinny, Lenny. Are you well?"

"I have lost weight, but I am well. Mary, you need your sleep."

"I want to be with you until I leave for work, Lenny." She dried me and pulled me into her bed and held me until I fell asleep. I did not awake until after two in the afternoon. I noticed that she had opened my bag and laid out a pair of jeans, socks, and a T-shirt.

Beside my bag was a note. It said the following:

Lenny,

    I should be home between two and three. Call me when you awake if you need to. There's plenty of food in the refrigerator. Can't wait to see you.
Love,
Mary
PS—the coffee is in the same place.

It took me a few moments to regain my composure. I asked myself how long had it been since I had slept so deeply. The bed and the smell were the same. I had a strange feeling that I was home.

I dragged myself downstairs to fix a cup of coffee and to sit at the breakfast table in front of the window overlooking the back yard. The view from the window near the breakfast table in Arizona had been of the desert. Mary had laid out the morning edition of the *Atlanta Journal*. "Finally—a newspaper with substance," I said aloud.

LENNY HAS A DAUGHTER AND LORI OVERDOSED (1970)

It was almost four when Mary walked in. Holding her hand was a beautiful child. She turned to her and said, "Would you go upstairs and find your hairbrush, Annie?" Annie skipped away.

"Whose child is that, Mary?"

Mary grabbed my hand, looked me straight in the eye, and said, "She is your daughter, Lenny.

"She is three years and three months old, Lenny. I was beginning to think that I was not going to hear from you. Why did it take so long for you to contact me?"

I was paralyzed. Mary shook me and said, "Say something, Lenny. She is the surprise that I needed to show you in person. OK, I will do the talking, Lenny. I will tell you the short version for now.

"The details can come later. In the beginning, I was not going to tell you that you had a daughter. I changed my mind after a great deal of soul-searching. Telling you is the right thing to do. I don't expect support. I was prepared to raise Annie on my own. I want to be honest with you. I want to tell you to your face that I love you, Lenny!

"If you can find love in your heart for me, I want you to stay with Annie and me for the rest of your life. Remember that I insisted that you ejaculate in me? Do you remember telling me that I was the first woman you had ejaculated in? I believe that you impregnated me the first time you ejaculated in a woman. Knowing that that had been your first time made the pregnancy sacred to me. I wanted you to impregnate me. I didn't know why. I just knew I did. When Lori died, I understood why.

"I don't know how I could have survived losing Lori without Annie. Lori died almost two years ago from an overdose. Annie gave me the courage to move on. Now can you talk, Lenny?"

"Yes, Mary, but I don't know what to say. Mary, I can't believe that Lori is dead."

"She was buried not far from here. You can visit her grave."

I broke down. "Oh, my God, Mary. I am sick of death!"

LENNY DECIDES TO STAY WITH MARY GIBSON IN ATLANTA (1970)

"Would you like to take Annie to the neighborhood park with me? Maybe we can talk more while she plays."

"Good idea, Mary. This park has been renovated since I was here, Mary."

"Yes, Lenny. The neighborhood has become a desirable place to live.

"When I was bathing you, I noticed a large scar on your thigh and a scare on your chest, Lenny."

"I was shot in the leg in the Battle of Bien Hoa. The scar was acquired in a struggle with a North Vietnam soldier, Mary."

"Are you going to be all right?"

"The bullet missed my bone and the knife fight I won. I should be fine, Mary. I have no knowledge about or experience with this kind of domestic situation. Please tell me how you see this scenario working out for all involved, including the child. Tell me what you would like me to do. After you share your thoughts with me, I will hopefully make a logical decision, Mary."

"I see that you have returned with wisdom, Lenny. I will tell you about my wishes as well as about what I believe is possible. I have done my homework on this topic. I knew it could be the most critical decision of my life. I am sorry that you have not had the many hours I have had to arrive at a conclusion. I do have faith that we will make the right choice."

HORMONE SUPPLEMENTATION FOR MARY GIBSON

"Lenny, I have addressed the age difference between us. I made an appointment with an endocrinologist. I asked her how menopause would affect a relationship with a man twenty years my junior. She told me that I would lose my sexual drive beginning with perimenopause. She explained that a young male partner would be at his sexual peak. During menopause, women tend to put on weight and to lose muscle definition. She referred me to a physician who specializes in hormone-replacement therapy, which originated in Germany. The physician's advice was to exercise and to restore my estrogen, progesterone, and testosterone levels to the levels they were at in my youth. If I do that, we could be compatible for years. She told me that new research on hormones has opened the door to extending sexuality, decreasing the likelihood of contracting diseases, and promoting longevity in both genders."

MARY DISCUSSES HER PRIOR RELATIONSHIPS AND SUGGESTS THAT LENNY ATTEND A UNIVERSITY (1970)

"Lenny, you asked me what I wanted, and I will tell you. I have dated men closer to my age. For some strange reason, I keep coming back to you. I love you, and I want you to stay with Annie and me. Do you want me to continue?"

"By all means, Mary."

"Lenny, I know how much you want to continue your education. Some of the finest schools in the nation are within walking distance of this house. Georgia Tech is one example. In my perfect world, you would enroll in one of those universities.

"The GI bill will pay for your education. I make a six-figure income, and the house is paid for in full. We will experience no financial problems. Lenny, I pay a ridiculous amount of money for Annie's day care. I suggest that you attend afternoon and early-evening classes so that you can spend quality time with our daughter, which will eliminate the need for day care altogether. That would be your contribution to the household.

"We would be a family during the evenings, weekends, and holidays. I ask you try my plan on a trial basis. I do realize that you became a man over the last three years. Do you still think I'm attractive, Lenny? I would like to hear your comments without further ado, Lenny."

MARY, ANNIE, AND LENNY, PLEDGE TO MAKE A LIFE TOGETHER (1970)

"I must confess, Mary, that I had a brief relationship before returning to Atlanta. It didn't work out. Even during the height of that relationship, I thought of you and Lori. I never imagined that my forty-five-day-long fantasy would become permanent.

"I was satisfied that time would live on only in my memory. Annie will enter into my decision. Ironically, I did read a book on menopause. I understand the value of hormones. I did think of our age difference from time to time. What I could not figure out was why it did not seem to matter.

"We enjoyed each other at all times, not just during sex. I can appreciate your concern about menopause and your willingness to eliminate a possible problem down the road. If you are willing to accept my youthful shortcomings, I will be your partner and the practicing father of our child.

"With the universe as my witness, I swear that I still believe that you are the most beautiful woman in the world. I pledge to honor you and our child with maximum dedication. I don't believe that we should ever question our age difference again. This relationship is right for us, and that is all that matters. Mary, how will you introduce me to others now?"

"If it is OK with you, I will introduce you as my husband, who just came home from Vietnam. I couldn't care less about whether they will talk about how much younger you are. You are a wounded veteran. You can't get more grown up than that."

"Should I refer to you as my wife?"

"I would be proud to be known as your wife, Lenny. For Annie's sake, I would like to get married as soon as possible. We can get married at the courthouse this week."

"Mary, I agree—the sooner, the better."

"Do you think Annie will like sports?"

"I don't know, Lenny. I think that for now, you need to learn how to play with dolls."

"When can we announce to Annie that I am her father, Mary?"

"I am not sure that she will understand that at this time. In time she will, Lenny."

"I am so excited, Mary. When can I have my first kiss?"

"There is the Lenny I remember. Lenny, you will get the full brunt of my love tonight! I am so happy to have you back in my life. I have dreamed of this day for over three years."

"Mary, I was alone for the last three years. Now I have a home, a beautiful wife, and a healthy child!"

"Yes, and I know Lori too would have been happy. She did see your child before she died. She could not get over how much she looked like you. Lori loved you too, Lenny. She made me promise that I would bring you home. It hurts me that she is not present at this reunion."

"I too am sad, Mary. She too was always on my mind. I loved Lori, Mary."

"We need to catch up after three years apart, Lenny."

"Mary, I am looking rough. I need to manicure myself so that I can meet your standards."

"We will take care of that first thing."

"I also need books about children."

"I have several that you can start reading. Lenny, slow down. You can't do everything all at once."

"I don't want to disappoint you, Mary."

"Lenny, tonight is for reigniting our love and nothing else."

BRINGING A FAMILY TOGETHER (1970)

"What a night, Mary! At what time do you wake up Annie?"

"She gets up about forty-five minutes after I do. That gives me time to dress."

"Can I help you dress her? I would like her to know me, Mary."

"I will show you her clothes and personal belongings when she wakes up."

"While you are dressing I will go downstairs and make coffee, Mary. I will be back in a jiffy."

"Don't bring the coffee back to the bedroom. We have time to sit at the table downstairs, Lenny. I will be right there."

"That was quick, Mary."

"Sit down, and I will pour you coffee."

"Mary, now that we have a family, don't you think that I need a pair of pajamas? I see that you are wearing an elegant house gown."

"That would be a good idea, Lenny. We will add pajamas to the list of things to buy as soon as possible."

"Mary, I must warn you that I have terrible dreams about my combat experiences. Don't allow my dreams to scare you. Wake me up as quickly as possible. I intend to make an appointment at the VA and to discuss them with a psychiatrist."

I later discovered that the VA did not welcome my request for help. It was for that reason that I initially chose to study psychotherapy. I had a need to understand why I continued to have horrid dreams about death and combat.

"I want you to know that I had several boyfriends while you were gone, Lenny. I had to imagine that they were you to avoid becoming sick to my stomach. Now that you are home, I wanted to tell you that. If one of them called or if we bumped into one of them, I would not want you to be surprised, Lenny.

"None of the men I dated pleased me, Lenny. I always had the feeling that something was missing from those relationships. I was in love with you, Lenny. At first I couldn't accept that, because of your age. Over time I came to the realization that I had not simply had a fascination with you.

"I was truly in love with you. All of the signs were there. We went everywhere together. We had unexplainable chemistry, Lenny. After three and a half years, our connection still exists."

"I had similar feelings after I left, Mary. I have no desire to hold any of the relationships that you had against you. I can handle the situations you described without becoming jealous or having negative thoughts."

"Thank you for understanding, Lenny."

"I don't require much to go back to school. I have money and can secure schoolbooks, supplies, and other essentials."

"I hear Annie. It's time to go. Good morning, Annie! Are you ready to go play with your friends? First we need to get dressed. Do you like this dress, Annie? Lenny, hand me her shoes. Look in the second drawer in that chest, and hand me her panties and socks. Pick out ones that will match this yellow-and-white dress.

"Annie, do you know who this is? This is your daddy."

"Daddy," Annie said.

"Yes, Annie. This is your daddy."

"Are you hungry, Annie?" I asked.

"Breakfast," Annie said.

"What does she eat for breakfast, Mary?"

"I like to fix her a nutritious meal before she goes to day care. She plays all day with the other kids. A good breakfast is mandatory. I would prefer to pack her lunch, Lenny—something more nutritious than peanut butter and jelly and cookies."

"Tell me what she will eat, and I will start preparing her lunch."

"That would be great, Lenny."

"For breakfast, I usually cook her an egg with cheese and pour her a glass of milk. She likes butter on her toast."

"I will make it a priority to orient myself to the kitchen, Mary."

"Actually, Lenny, everything in the kitchen is the same as it was when you were here. We have a lifetime to put it all together, Lenny. Having you here has already energized me. Even though I'm an atheist, I prayed for this scenario for three years, Lenny."

"That has never come up, Mary. I was concerned that you might not approve of my atheist beliefs."

"Lenny, will you hold her hand and see if she will walk down the steps?"

"Here we go, Annie. You did well. Can you sit here? Your mom is fixing your breakfast."

"Put this bib on her, Lenny, or she will be wearing her breakfast to day care. You can pour her milk. I set it out on the counter."

"Lenny, would you like to feed her? If you don't, she will elect to play with her food."

"Mary, she ate almost all of her breakfast. She is a pretty good eater."

"Can you run back upstairs and get her light-blue jacket? It is hanging in her closet. She will need it if they go outside."

"Annie, who is your best friend?"

"Joe," Annie said.

"I am going to slip into a dress. I will be back in a minute, and then you can put your jeans and a T-shirt on."

"That was fast, Mary."

"Lenny, go get dressed. We are running a little late. Secure her in her car seat, please. Lenny, did I tell you Annie's last name?"

"Is it Gibson, Mary?"

"No, Lenny. I gave her your last name—Lewis."

"Are you kidding me, Mary?"

"I thought that if you failed to make it back from Vietnam, you would not be forgotten."

"Wow. I am honored, Mary!"

"The day care is only about a mile from the house. I will park here. You can unbuckle Annie and remove her from the car. Come with me into her day-care center, Lenny. I will introduce you to the staff."

"Hi, Annie. Hello, Ms. Gibson."

"Ms. Walker, this is my husband, Lenny. He just came home from Vietnam."

"Welcome home, Lenny."

"Thank you, Ms. Walker."

"Lenny will be picking up Annie when I am busy."

"That will be fine, Ms. Gibson. Could I ask you to take a minute to sign the pick-up authorization document?"

"Yes, of course. Annie, give Mom a kiss."

"Can I have a kiss too, Annie? She gave me a kiss, Mary."

"Bye, Annie. You have fun. Lenny, do you have a driver's license?"

"Yes, Mary, but it is an Arizona license."

"Drop me off at work and go get a Georgia driver's license. You can also go by the admissions office at the university. The park you played basketball in is part of the university now. Someone there can direct you a couple of blocks over to the DMV."

"What bank can I open an account at? All my money is in my bag at your house."

"You can circle back around and pick up your money and open an account at the university's bank. That's where my account is, Lenny. Later I will add you to my account. They have an annex on the campus. I have a meeting at three. You can pick up Annie from day care and swing back around for me. I should be out of the meeting at around four-fifteen. You can wait in my parking space at the school. I have a reserved parking space with my name on it. You should have no problem finding it. I'll be able to see you from my office."

Things have a way of working out when they are meant to be. I completed everything Mary had ask me to do in time to pick Annie up at day care. Actually, I arrived at the day care ten minutes early. This gave me time to see what everyone was doing for the last ten minutes of their day.

"Hello, Ms. Walker. Is Annie ready to go?"

"She is at the drawing table. You can sit for a minute before you leave."

"Hi, Annie. Show me your drawing. This is lovely. I have no idea what it is. I like the color you selected, Annie."

"Dog, Daddy. Dog."

"OK, it's a big red-and-blue dog. Annie, would you like to go get ice cream with Daddy?"

"Ice cream, Daddy," Annie said.

"Time to go, Annie. Hold my hand. Bye, Ms. Walker."

"Hold on, Lenny," Ms. Walker said. "You forgot Annie's jacket."

"I will order you vanilla ice cream, Annie. It will be less likely to stain your clothes. We can sit here and eat our ice cream. Now let's go to the park for a ride on the merry-go-round."

How quickly life can change! I'd been headed to Florida to go to school. I'd stopped in Atlanta to visit Mary and had reignited a romance and discovered that I had a three-year-old daughter. Then I made a life-changing decision to stay and become a family man.

Everything happens for a reason. I watched Annie go down the slide, hit the bottom of it, and roll over. She jumped up, looked over at me, and laughed, and then she went up the steps for another slide. "That's my daughter," I thought to myself. In just two days, she had started calling me "Daddy." I had just turned twenty-one years old, and my forty-one-year-old wife was the principal of the largest high school in Atlanta, Georgia.

"Time to go pick up Mommy, Annie. Let's go now! Put your jacket back on. Wow, Annie. I hope your mommy won't be disappointed that I allowed you to get dirty."

"Go find Mommy, Daddy," Annie said. I found her parking space near the main entrance. Like Mary had said, I could see her window. I flashed my lights to see if she would notice me.

"Mommy is waving from her office window, Annie. Can you see Mommy? Right—there she is! Do you see her?"

"Hi, Annie and Lenny. You drive, Lenny. It has been a very long day. What did you get done?"

"I got everything that we talked about done."

"How long did it take to get a driver's license?"

"I was in and out within an hour."

"That has to be a record," Mary said.

"I enrolled in school and will start next semester."

"When does the semester start, Lenny?"

"Here is my schedule, Mary."

"Do you need to stop for anything?"

"I want to go home and take a bath. I'd prefer to have a comfortable evening with you and Annie. Lenny, I am so happy that you are here with Annie and me."

"I have everything, Mary. I have you and Annie and will attend the perfect university. Mary, I should start looking for a car. I have the money to buy a nice used car. What do you think?"

"I think situations will arise that will require us to have a second car."

"OK, I will start looking, Mary."

LENNY COULD NOT HELP BEING PISSED OFF (1970)

On May 4, 1970, an event at Kent State University received my serious attention. The Ohio State National Guard fired on student protesters. Four students were killed, and nine were wounded. President Nixon had previously announced the de-escalation of the war in Vietnam.

However, on April 30, 1970, President Nixon had announced the Cambodian Campaign, a plan to bomb and invade Cambodia. The protestors saw that move as an escalation of the very unpopular war. An American theologian named William Ellery Channing said the following about powerful leaders: "The cry has been that when war is declared, all opposition should be hushed. A sentiment more unworthy of a free country could hardly be propagated. If the doctrine be admitted, rulers have only to declare war, and they are screened at once from scrutiny."

The administration's strategy was to destroy the North Vietnam Army in Cambodia in order to prop up South Vietnam before the United States left South Vietnam. I knew that his announcement was a lie. We had been bombing Cambodia since 1965, and I personally had been in Cambodia on secret missions during 1967 and 1968.

During the three-month campaign, we dropped more bombs on the North Vietnamese supply trails in Cambodia than we did on Japan during

World War II. This indiscriminate carpet-bombing killed hundreds of thousands of Cambodian citizens. The dishonest mainstream media never reported on this atrocity. I had vowed that I would not become involved in any protests against the war.

My objective was to maintain a GPA of three and a half or higher so that I could obtain an academic scholarship to graduate school. The atrocious killing of innocent students, the killing of hundreds of thousands of innocent Cambodians, the government's blatant lies, and the ungracious treatment that I received from the VA hospital convinced me to participate in an on-campus Vietnam protest organization and to criticize Veterans Affairs.

ACCOMPLISHMENTS (1975)

Annie and Lenny routinely visited Lori's grave. He told Annie about Lori and especially about how well she'd played basketball with him on the very same court that they played on. Annie considered her to be her older sister. She remained a part of the family in spirit.

Mary had continued to progress in the world of education. The DeKalb County school board hired her to be the superintendent. Mary Gibson was then making a high six-figure salary. A local TV reporter interviewed her and asked her what the secret of her success was. Her response was "the amazing love given to me by my husband and daughter."

After a considerable delay, Lenny received his master's degree in human biology, the discipline closest to evolutionary biology. He ordered most of the textbooks used to teach that controversial discipline from UC Berkeley and studied it on his own. A strong evangelical lobby in the United States opposed the teaching of evolution in state-supported schools. It was clear to the evangelicals that the Bible said that the earth was only six thousand years old. Scientific evidence disagreed with that absurd biblical myth. The only explanation I can come up with for such a stupendous belief by so many is a quote from George Orwell's book, *Nineteen Eighty-Four*: "Ignorance is strength."

MARY AND ANNIE APPROVE OF LENNY'S NEXT GOAL (1978)

Lenny requested that Mary and he have a sit-down discussion about his next goal. Without hesitation, she suggested that Lenny continue his education in a Ph.D. program. He responded that he had spent his GI bill and savings.

"Lenny, the last seven years have worked perfectly for Annie and me. You said you were content with our family arrangement. Has something changed?" she said.

"No, Mary, but what about becoming a financially productive member of the family?"

"Lenny, do I need to remind you that I make ample money? We need a Ph.D. in this family. I suggest that you begin looking for a good program here in the Atlanta area or at the University of Georgia in Athens, which is only fifty or so miles away. The money is of no consequence. What do you think your father should do, Annie?"

"I agree with you, Mom. I know Dad's dream is to get his Ph.D. He told me that several times, Mom. I have grown fond of the additional home-schooling that Dad offers me. I would like to continue our study sessions. They are responsible for my straight-A average."

"Lenny, the family has spoken. This matter is settled."

"Thank you, Mary. I will begin my search this week."

Regardless of where life takes Lenny, he always ends up in the presence of a loving, intelligent woman, and in Annie, he found a younger woman with say-so in his decisions. The ones we love profoundly influence who we are. It is critical to choose a partner who has traits and desires similar to yours.

LENNY RECEIVES TWO LIFETIME AWARDS (1983)

During this period, life was similar to the typical American life, or at least to what the typical American life was thought to be. It was a time of opportunity. People could achieve almost any goal with hard work. It was time to enjoy the benefits of family life. Lenny was fortunate to have a wonderful wife and a beautiful, healthy daughter who supported his thirst for knowledge.

Lenny found a Ph.D. program that offered the challenge he was looking for. The committee approved his dissertation. The program was slow moving but thorough. It offered him time to keep the house, plan meals, run errands for Mary, and spend quality time with his new buddy, Annie. Lenny was the original stay-at-home dad. It was a wonderful life.

By the time Lenny received his Ph.D., Annie was a teenager. She had become a good basketball player and a straight-A student. Annie and he played basketball a couple of times a week on the same court that Lori and he had played on more than a decade before. Annie actually referred to the court as "Lori's court." During that time, Lenny tried every medication prescribed to him by the VA to deal with his nightmares about his combat experiences.

Lenny noticed that all of the drugs had one thing in common: Each drug's side effects were as bad as—if not worse than—the nightmares. What disturbed him the most was that the medications treated only the symptoms. He investigated the process of drug development. It was clear to him that the pharmaceutical corporations had little interest in developing drugs that cured people. Their true focus was on developing drugs that treated symptoms.

Lenny made his decision to stop taking medications and to concentrate on coping with the disorder. He did go through a period of withdrawal that actually strengthened his resolve to not put those toxins into his system ever again.

The VA later welcomed Vietnam veterans and awarded Lenny a service-related disability. He received a compensation check each month. The benefits covered college tuition for Annie and provided him with free medical and dental care. He took the hush money. Lenny's rationale for doing so was that they were finally acknowledging his contribution to the war. Lenny learned a lesson: Don't trust the government!

SLICK-TALKING GOVERNMENT PUNDITS TRICK THE PUBLIC

I don't think that the government ever wants to give up anything, but sometimes too many people find out the truth and embarrass the government into doing the right thing for its constituents. History has proved that the government's representatives use their media access to oppress the people by distributing disinformation. That's what Veterans Affairs did.

The VA decided to admit that it had neglected veterans and later collaborated with the mainstream media to convince the public that the problem had been solved. Telling the public that something is being done saves the government money.

One must note that the public did not have inspectors who could ensure that the VA's promise to improve veterans' care would be fulfilled. We had no other choice but to take the government's spokespersons' word at face value even though the government continued to be caught in lies about matters of public concern on a regular basis.

I would like to quote a Roman playwright named Terence: "There is a demand today for men who can make wrong appear right."

MARY AND ANNIE AGREE THAT LENNY SHOULD STAY HOME AND CONTINUE TO SCHOOL ANNIE

When I informed Mary of my award, she smiled.

"Mary, what does your smile mean?" I said.

"I think the VA made the right decision. Lenny, you sacrificed for our country, and you've earned a pass. This is an acknowledgement of the country's appreciation of you and compensation for the injuries that you sustained.

"Now you can continue to pursue your passions: reading, writing, and learning. Maybe you should write a novel."

"Mary, I would like to take a few graduate courses on psychotherapy."

"You can practice on me, Lenny," Mary said, laughing. "Annie and I think that you are the perfect person to run the house. You are the nucleus of this family, Lenny. Annie and I don't think that we should fix what is not broken. We love your being home to take care of us."

MARY IS HESITANT TO APPROVE LENNY'S THESIS ON SEXUAL DYSFUNCTION (1989)

In the years that followed, Annie graduated from high school. In 1989, she was a senior in college. I continued my pursuit of psychotherapy and earned a master's degree. My thesis was on sexual dysfunction. Mary Gibson had contributed to my thesis with her hands-on sexual tutoring before I had entered the army.

I want to express my admiration for her by using a pragmatic phrase that anyone could understand: Mary Gibson broke me in right! Because of her, I didn't develop any inhibitions, and I learned to enjoy nature's wonderful gift of intimate sexual expression. I cannot deny Mary's contribution to that.

As a matter of fact, I acknowledged Mary Gibson and her late daughter, Lori Gibson, in the foreword of my thesis, which Mary was, at first, hesitant to approve. I think her hesitation was more about the possible effect on her reputation than about the content itself. After all, she was the superintendent of the local schools.

CHRISTIANITY, HYPOCRISY, AND PERSECUTION

I believe that Christianity's animosity toward the act of sex is caused by a "confusion factor." Our innate human obligation to reproduce overwhelms Christianity's unnatural teachings on abstinence. A person's internal struggle with guilt emanates from a lifetime of believing that sex can lead to psychotic behavior or cause ill effects to an individual's self-esteem.

Now I'll quote an English author named Aldous Leonard Huxley, who had a little something to say about Christian hypocrisy: "The church allows people to believe that they can be good Christians and yet draw dividends from armament factories, can be good Christians and yet imperil the well-being of their fellows by speculating in stocks and shares, can be good Christians and yet be imperialists, yet participate in war."

In my readings, I came across a perfect example of a Christian atrocity. In 1209 a Catholic army massacred twenty-thousand people in the city of Beziers, France, in order to eradicate heresy. The Catholic priest in charge was not sure of which people were faithful and which were heretics, so he gave the order to kill every man, woman, and child. He told his Christian slaughterers to let God sort them out.

That was one of the thousands of slaughters of millions of people ordered by Christians and those of other faiths throughout history. Nations under the influence of religion pass surreal laws. These laws are used to justify waging wars, plundering, and killing dissenters.

I say that if you show me religion, I will show you ignorance. If you show me ignorance, I will show you intolerance, discrimination, persecution, and genocides ordered by God or in the name of God. Beware of the devil in sheep's clothing!

THE FINAL PLAN (1990)

I completed my self-directed study on human evolutionary biology from the University of California, Berkeley. My interest then became health care, and my activity, doing resistance exercises. Mary planned to retire a few months before Annie's graduation.

Annie had been accepted into the graduate program at Yonsei University in Seoul, South Korea, and would start the following fall semester. To commemorate the family's accomplishments, Mary reserved a cottage in Fort Myers Beach, Florida, for the summer. Mary and I made our way to Connecticut for Annie's graduation. Annie had spent the last four years at Wesleyan University in Middletown. I don't know who was nervier, Annie or us. We were excited as she was. She had planned every moment for us. We gave no resistance to her demands. After all, it was her main event.

Mary lost her appetite the day before graduation, and I failed to sleep the night before. After the ceremony, we shared a bottle of wine. Mary found her appetite, and I found sleep later that evening. Nothing about the graduation bothered Annie. She was excited about spending the summer in an oceanfront cottage in Southwest Florida.

THE DRIVE BACK TO ATLANTA AND MEMORIES (1990)

We spent a day packing Annie's possessions and carrying boxes to UPS to give us room in the car for the ride home. We needed as much room as possible for the three-day drive from Connecticut to Atlanta.

Mary and I waited in the car. Annie took a few minutes to hug the friends she had spent time with over the last four years. We were solemn when we drove Annie away. She told us stories that she and her friends had shared over the last four years.

I have similar memories of the day Mary and Lori took me to the army recruiter's office. We had said our good-byes, and I had watched them drive away.

In Vietnam I recalled, from time to time, the comforting hugs and kisses that I received from Mary and Lori the day they dropped me off at the army recruiter's office.

Those few last minutes at the army recruiter's office were the only mental caption I kept of the first eighteen years of my life. I can't help but think back to how it all started. When Mary and I fell in love, she was forty, and I was twenty-one. That was after I returned from Vietnam. I believe we actually fell in love before I left.

MARY CRUISES THROUGH MENOPAUSE WITH HORMONE SUPPLEMENTATION

I was now in my forties, and Mary was over sixty. Cal had had a book that explained menopause, the change that females go through somewhere between forty and fifty years of age. After reading everything in her library twice, I read the book about menopause, and, man, was I glad that I had.

When Mary brought the subject up, it surprised her that I had an understanding of it. Because of my reading about the subject, we blew straight through our discussion about the difference in our ages.

Mary, who was broad minded and highly educated, had decided to replace some vital hormones to prevent or minimize the negative symptoms of menopause. Bioidentical hormones had recently become available. Mary said that they were much better than the synthetic ones that the pharmaceutical companies had been pushing in the beginning. Some experts proclaim that "the change" is a primary reason for middle-aged divorce. In most cases, a woman's creativity and sexual drive is severely dampened.

During menopause, women's interests are subject to change, and they can struggle to become more independent, maybe by seeking new careers. Their bewildered husbands can be resistant to those changes. But resistance is futile, and arguments ensue, and in many cases, this can lead to divorce.

I do believe that the hormones played an important part in Mary's sexual drive. Most of all, I gave Mary credit for her strong understanding of the new state of mind that had been forced upon her by nature's law. I am proud to admit that we were still madly in love with each other and that our sexual functionality was as good as ever.

■ ■ ■

SPENDING THE SUMMER IN FLORIDA (1990)

"How long are we going to stay at home before we leave for Florida, Mom?"

"No longer than it takes us to pack up and shut the house down. Don't pack too many clothes, Annie. You will be in your swimsuit most of the time. I don't see us leaving the cottage or the beach except to eat.

"My concern is avoiding sunburns, Annie. Sunburns can be dangerous. During the first few days, it's crucial to gradually build a base tan to protect the skin from burning. The cause of melanoma—or skin cancer—is not the sun. The sun provides vitamin D. The culprit is overexposure to the sun's ultraviolet rays. I do not recommend sun blocks, which have toxic ingredients."

"Mary, how does it feel to be retired?"

"Yeah, Mom. How does it feel to not go to work?"

"I don't know. I guess it hasn't set in yet."

"What will you and Dad do when I'm in Korea?"

"We have talked about traveling. Dad and I talked about buying a small motor home and touring the United States.

"Annie, your dad and I have not left Atlanta very much since he came home."

"I think you and Dad should travel," Annie said. "I plan to travel all of Asia during the summers and the holidays. I'm hoping to find a scuba-certification center while we're in Fort Myers, Dad, and to acquire a diving certification before I go to Asia. I have a friend who did scuba diving in several of the seas of Asia.

"She said the water was perfectly clear. She had an underwater camera. The pictures she took were amazing, Dad. I think scuba diving would be exciting."

"Make sure to take pictures when you visit Vietnam. I would be interested in seeing how the country has changed, Annie.

"I would love to visit with your mother someday."

"Maybe you and Mom could meet me in Vietnam one summer."

"I would like that, Annie. Seeing peacetime Vietnam would serve me well."

"Would you like to do that, Mom?"

"I would love to meet you in Vietnam, Annie."

PURCHASING A MOTOR HOME FOR THE FLORIDA TRIP (1990)

"Maybe we should change our minds about touring the United States, Mary. The ride from Connecticut to Atlanta wore me out."

"That's one more reason to travel in a motor home, Lenny."

"Mom, are we leaving tomorrow?"

"We have to stay until UPS delivers your belongings from Connecticut. Your boxes will be here tomorrow or the next day. You can unpack what we have in the car and start a list of your must-take items in the meantime. I will pull some food out of the freezer to thaw for dinner."

"Mary, I am going to have the car serviced and checked over tomorrow morning. Annie, you can go with me."

"No, Dad. I want to sleep in."

"Lenny, don't forget to go by the post office to arrange for our mail to be forwarded. The address of the cottage is lying on the breakfast table."

"Good morning, Mary! I have a cup of coffee for you."

"Thank you, Lenny. I have been thinking about our drive to Florida. I do not look forward to another long trip."

"What do you think about purchasing a motor home for the trip? After the summer, when Annie leaves for Korea, we can do some traveling…to wherever."

"It sounds reasonable, Lenny."

"Then why don't we go take a look?"

"That's fine with me, Lenny. While I dress, you can write a note to Annie explaining our plans for today."

"I left Annie a note and wrote down the addresses of motor-home dealers."

"I don't believe we'll need one of those huge motor homes, Lenny. It will just be the two of us, and I want to be able to drive it. I would not be comfortable driving one of those bus-sized motor homes, Lenny."

"We can pull Annie's small car behind it. When we set it up, we can use her car to run around locally.

"I think we can educate ourselves on the fly about the motor-home conveniences we will need, Mary."

"What do you mean by that, Lenny?"

"After we look at a few different motorhomes, I am sure we will become more knowledgeable of our needs."

"That makes sense, Lenny. Turn in here. This is the third dealership on our list. Lenny, I did not realize how many different kinds of motor homes there were. After looking at every style, I prefer this one, Lenny."

"We never disagree, do we? I too favor this one, Mary."

"If you agree, I will make an offer on it, Lenny. I am going to offer twenty-five percent less than the sticker price based on the guide for purchasing motor homes."

"Mary, inform the salesperson that we will need a towing package."

"I will tell the salesperson that this is a one-time offer, and we will pay cash now. Our salesperson said that he is going to take the offer to the manager. If he refuses, we can look again at the other one we liked, Lenny."

"Fine with me, Mary. We can always come back. How long should we give the salesperson to give us an answer?"

"I think fifteen minutes is ample, Lenny. Here he comes now."

"Ms. Gibson, the manager said that if you could come up two thousand dollars, he would accept the deal."

"We refuse to pay any more than our offer. Thank you for showing us the motor home. We can now go and take another look at the other one we considered. Do you want me to drive, Lenny? Lenny, stop the car. The salesman is running after us."

"Hold on, Ms. Gibson. The manager says that we can do the deal if you can close it now."

"Let's do it, then," Mary said.

"Ms. Gibson, thank you for your purchase. We can have the home ready in an hour or less. You can sit comfortably in the customers' lounge."

"This might be the best time to load the car onto the auto-tow. If I have any questions I can ask someone in the service department."

"Good idea. That way we can do our maiden voyage together. Lenny, that didn't take long."

"How does it drive Lenny?"

"Like a dream, Mary. I will park in the driveway close to the house so we can load."

"Annie, come out and look over the motor home."

"UPS delivered my belongings, Dad."

"Now we can load what we are taking into the motorhome tonight and leave early tomorrow morning."

"I will unload your car, Mary, and mount Annie's smaller car on the auto- tow. This is it for tonight, people. Tomorrow is the big day."

WHAT DOES "NORMAL" MEAN? (1990)

I always volunteer to drive. Driving satisfies my addiction to daydreaming. The drive to Florida was no different. I slipped comfortably into my thoughts while the other occupants of the car passed the time by making conversation. In most cases, I was left out of it.

Not long after I began living with Mary, I became concerned about what my peers at the university thought of me. I was perturbing them. It appeared that I was disagreeing with them increasingly more often as we brainstormed how to save the world.

I was discontent, so I decided to visit my adopted mentor, Dr. Roberts, for advice. I knocked and was invited into his office. I noticed that he could sense that something was troubling me. He instructed me to close the door and to sit down. He poured me a glass of cold tea from his office refrigerator and said, "Lenny, what is your trouble?"

I immediately thanked him for seeing me without an appointment. He said, "Lenny, when you don't ask in advance for a time to discuss something with me, I know it can't wait. So let me hear what is going on with you."

"Dr. Roberts, I have a problem with agreeing with my friends. I disagree with my friends on almost every subject that we discuss."

"How so, Lenny?"

"Well, Dr. Roberts, I am increasingly in disagreement with them on political and social matters. I find that I'm sometimes the only person who dissents. That is causing me to be viewed as a rebel among my friends. If I continue to disagree with them, I will end up with no friends."

"I see, Lenny," Dr. Roberts said. "I think you need to take into account the fact that you are married to a very well-known academic scholar who works as a superintendent of the Atlanta public school system.

"Your exposure to this brilliant woman separates you from your young and inexperienced friends. You have a more mature perspective on matters. Your position will require you to adjust your personality so that you can fit in with your friends at school and then, later, to readjust it when you get home to your family."

"You mean that I should have two different personalities, Dr. Roberts."

"Sure, Lenny. For example, an employee interacts differently with his employer than with his friends."

The thought slammed my mind. I quickly stood and thanked Dr. Roberts several times before he dismissed me with a big smile on his face. Dr. Roberts reminded me of how fortunate I was to be in my situation, to be married to Mary Gibson, and to have a child. I didn't have to disagree with others all of the time or during my irrelevant conversations with my young, inexperienced school friends.

I have been blessed when it comes to relationships and mentors. No matter where I end up, I always find a mentor to turn to for wise advice. If this is true and if God exists, he loves atheists too.

"For how long do you intend to drive before camping, Lenny?"

"Annie, look at the camping guide, and tell me when the next RV park is coming up. I would like to park and set up before dark."

"There is a Yogi Bear campground at the next exit, Dad. It has plenty of amenities."

"Sounds OK—does anybody object? I did not think so. It was a good idea to bring our mattress onboard, Mary. I sleep as well as I would if we were home."

I arose early and disconnected the RV. "We are ready to roll, everybody. We can make coffee on the road."

"Dad, will we be there today?"

"No, Annie. We will stop one more time. We want to arrive at Fort Myers Beach during the day. That way, we will have daylight when we unload the RV and settle in."

I loved driving. It was my time to gather my thoughts and to go places. I was concerned for Mary. She was showing obvious signs of not knowing exactly what she should've been doing.

Mary, who had had a busy everyday agenda, found herself with no tasks or ongoing obligations. I believed the beach would expedite her adjustment to her retirement. I planned to keep her as busy as possible, not with work but with relaxation. I was convinced that the sunshine, the saltwater, the pure air, and the vacation atmosphere would bring her around before the summer's end.

I was not at all worried about Annie finding ways to enjoy her vacation. She had already said that it would be her last tango in the States before she left for Korea. She was not going to leave with us. At the summer's end, Mary and I were going to escort her to the Southwest Florida International Airport for her departure to Korea. If Annie's leaving for Korea was bothering me, I am sure it was worrisome to Mary. Mary did tell me that Annie's presence gave her the strength to carry on after Lori's drug overdose and death. I chose at this time to not speak to her on this matter. I hoped that by summer's end it would work its way out.

THE COTTAGE ON THE BEACH (1990)

I was impressed with Fort Myers Beach. The yearly average temperature was seventy-four degrees. The average low temperature was sixty-five degrees. A long-sleeve shirt could sustain you on a few cool days during the winter months. One could live there without an automobile. At its widest point, the seven-mile island was only a quarter of a mile wide.

Every basic need was within walking distance. If one had a time constraint, he could ride a bicycle to wherever he needed to go. However, the winter months did become a little crowded with snowbirds escaping the extreme cold temperatures up north. Mary reminded me on a regular basis that we should consider retiring in Fort Myers Beach.

Mary had not worn shoes over the last three weeks. She had bought new swimsuits to keep from having to unpack her suitcases. She had carefully cultivated a perfect tan, and she counted every calorie and exercised on the beach every day. The minute we arrived, she increased the amounts of testosterone, estrogen, progestin, and pregnenolone that she took.

She was as sexy as ever. More interesting than her looks was her ever-evolving character. I suspected that her youthful and trendy behavior was the result of her being in the presence of high school students—teenagers—throughout her entire career. Her thinking and tastes were like those of a trendy woman in her late twenties. She preferred to socialize with young adults.

I noticed that Annie and Mary played well together. Mary sometimes made the beach club rounds with Annie. They reported to me that they had drinks and danced. It pleased me to hear they were having a great time together.

Mary said to me more than once that we had already benefited from our past experiences. "Let's us do something that we have never done," she said.

She insisted that young people offered the excitement of something new, and that nothing was more thrilling than a first-time new experience. Mary's advice for staying young was to have more young friends than old friends and to resist routines. As for me, I liked relaxing on the beach with a good book that advocated fresh new thoughts, working out with Mary, and hanging out with Mary and Annie.

Annie managed to obtain a certification for scuba diving, which she would need if she went scuba diving in Asia. Our family ritual was sitting on the patio and watching the sunset. We would sometimes go to the docks and barter with the fishermen to get fish. Annie enjoyed haggling over prices with them. She was fascinated by the speed and precision with which they cleaned them. It was clear that fresh-caught fish tasted better and were more nutritious than the frozen fish sold at grocery stores.

The sun, salt air, physical activity, fresh food, and lack of everyday stressors physically and mentally rejuvenated us.

I had not heard a complaint from any family member since our arrival. Time sure rolls by when you are having fun in the sun on an island in paradise.

ANNIE LEAVES FOR KOREA

Annie had her bags ready to go. We planned to ship her larger bags after she left. There was a limit on what could go with her. We had given her money so that she could purchase most of her clothes upon arrival. Annie liked the idea of purchasing clothes that would be fashionable in Korea. The closer we came to leaving the cottage, the more solemn Mary became.

She extended her arm between the two front seats to hold Annie's hand. Her motherly concern was quickly surfacing. I intervened and reminded Mary that Annie had been looking forward to this for years. Annie leaned forward and hugged Mary's neck and told her that she loved her and that everything would be fine. It was the last leg of her education, and soon she would find her own way.

That is how life works. Mary would not release her hold on Annie at the boarding area. I raised my voice and forced Mary to let go of her. Annie gave me a sign that she approved of my action. Annie kissed me, kissed Mary one more time, entered the boarding tunnel, and soon disappeared into the aircraft.

Mary fell to her knees. I pulled her to her feet and led her to the nearest seat. She was having difficulties catching her breath. She looked into my eyes and said, "I lost Lori, and now I am losing Annie." I said nothing and allowed her to let it out. I held her tight until she regained her composure.

"Mary, let's go!" I said.

We exited the terminal and walked to the car. Mary apologized. When she regained her composure, she said, "Lenny, I knew this day would come. I thought I was better prepared for it. I don't guess that I was."

"Mary, we will be all right. We have each other, and we will write her together every week. Now that you are retired, we will have many new horizons to explore. To start, you can take up basketball and replace my partner, Annie."

"I don't think so, Lenny. I want to take better care of my knees. Maybe we should find another activity that will be less brutal on my joints," Mary said, laughing.

"Now that's the girl I love! Let's go take care of life, Mary."

"Lenny, you load the car onto the hauler. I will round up everything in the cottage. We will eat out tonight and leave tomorrow morning."

Loading the car allowed me to slip into another thought about family. Friends come and go throughout one's life. Family is in a class of its own. A thought came to my mind: Family is with you through thick and thin and good and bad.

■ ■ ■

DEPARTING FORT MYERS BEACH (1991)

"Lenny, I will make coffee in the motor home. Take your morning shower, and lock the door on your way out. Don't forget to leave the key in the mailbox. We need to stop by the post office to have our mail forwarded back to the house in Atlanta before we leave town. Our neighbor will collect our mail and send it to us.

"When we are home in Atlanta, we can get a private mailbox, Lenny. Then we can call and request that our mail be sent to our campsite."

"I like that idea, Mary. I asked Annie to call our neighbor and to leave a number we can reach her at."

"Lenny, we should look into purchasing one of those new cell telephones."

"We can look into that too. The RV parks are wired for telephones. If we stay for a month or so, we can have a telephone installed."

"We will eventually figure out a system, Lenny."

"Where do you want to go first, Mary?"

"Let's go to the Keys for a while, and then we can do Disney World. Once we have a number for Annie, we will be free to go wherever. You know, we can call our neighbor and ask if Annie has called."

IN RETROSPECT (1991)

Good things seemed to have come to us suddenly. Mary retired from public service. Her retirement benefits were adequate. Her house had been paid off for years. Lenny's disability benefits eliminated the tax burden on the house. He would receive disability compensation for life. The only monthly payments were for insurance on the house and cars. Because of her scholarship, Annie owed nothing on education.

"Mary, what should we do with our money?"

"What do you mean, Lenny?"

"Well, should we allow the money we don't spend to add up in our account, or should we look for investments?"

"Good question, Lenny. Personally, I never looked this far ahead. I am amazed by how quickly time has passed.

"Lenny, it seems like yesterday that you walked into my home in the middle of the night. You had been gone for over three years. That moment will always be front and center in my memory. When you were in Vietnam, I thought of you every day."

"Mary, it did not take me long to realize how important you were to me. I grew up fast in Vietnam.

"Stopping at the truck stop in Arizona was necessary to my survival. I was hungry and broke. I see it now as a step in the right direction."

"If it means anything to you, Lenny, I agree with you."

"Thank you, Mary. I will never forget the morning you appeared in the kitchen holding Annie's hand and announced that she was my child. I immediately knew that we would make a life together."

"Lenny, I think we should postpone the finances question for now. Let's enjoy our nomadic life."

"Mary, you choose a place to camp."

"I have already found one that has five stars in the RV guide. The campsite has all of the amenities we like and access to the ocean. Turn at the second exit."

SETTING UP CAMP IN KEY WEST (1991)

"Lenny, I'm going to the office to obtain information on things we can do here."

"I will stay here and set up camp."

"Do you need anything from the store?"

"No thanks, Mary. Oh, you might ask about installing a telephone, Mary."

Mary left.

"That was quick! What did you find out?"

"The sites are wired for telephones. I gave them a one-hundred-dollar deposit. All we need to do is connect the cable to the RV. The telephone should be on tomorrow. I have other good news to report. The store looks like a dive shop. We can harvest spiny lobsters on the beach. You can purchase snorkeling gear at the store and get a license."

"If you have never snorkeled, you can take a couple of lessons in the pool before you go out. The camp has boats that can take you to where the lobsters migrate. Each person is allowed to harvest six per day."

"Wow, Mary, that sounds like fun—and good eating. I need to locate the telephone. I can't remember which bin I packed it in."

"I remember, Lenny. You packed the phone in the first bin, on the left side."

"How did you know that, Mary?"

"You placed the iron in the same bin. We will need it if we go out to eat. Our clothes will be very wrinkled. They have been packed in those suitcases going on two months."

"I picked up a boat-departure schedule. I want to do this. Do you, Lenny?"

"I think it would be a great experience. A boat goes out every hour. The normal harvest time is in an hour. The lady could not stop talking. I suppose her way of repaying me was telling me to go out on the first boat. The people on the first boat usually gather the most."

"Why do you think she gave you a tip?"

"Lenny, do you remember our talk about friends? We agreed that people need others to listen to them. People will consider you a friend if you spend time listening to their stories. Not too many people have relationships in which each party gets equal talking time. Most relationships are made up of a talker and a listener. Too many people have no one to talk to. She definitely needs a listener."

"I don't know what I would do without you, Mary."

"Lenny, we are so lucky to have our relationship."

"Mary, have we ever had a problem in our decades together? Have we ever had an argument? Maybe we should have an argument to see how it would feel, Mary."

"I totally disagree with that idea," Mary said, laughing. "Don't try to fix what is not broken, Lenny. Let's go purchase lobster-fishing licenses and the gear we'll need to catch a few of those tasty critters. I also purchased a brochure about all of the different ways to cook spiny lobsters."

CATCHING SPINY LOBSTERS IN KEY WEST (1991)

"Are we supposed to wake up this early on vacation, Mary?"

"I don't think we are on vacation, Lenny. Let me remind you that we are retired."

"I was hoping that I would not see early mornings ever again."

"I know what you mean, Lenny."

"I have our gear."

"We'd better hurry before the boat leaves us."

"When you bring a lobster to the boat, our guide will measure it. If the lobster is too small, it will be released."

"Mary, I'm going to catch only large ones. How much freezer space do we have?"

"Twelve lobsters—our combined limit—would take up all of our freezer space. That amount would feed us for a few days."

"We barely made it on time. Another minute and we would have missed the boat, Mary."

"This is where we get into the water, Lenny. Good luck."

"How many have you caught, Mary?"

"I have four."

"Damn. I only have two. Take me to your area, Mary."

"No, Lenny. You find your own area. I'm at my limit now. I will wait in the boat for you. You had better hurry. The boat leaves in less than ten minutes."

"I got my limit, Mary."

"What took you so long?" Mary said, laughing.

"Shut up, Mary. You were lucky. We are ready to go now."

"Thank you for the wonderful experience."

"You are very welcome. How long do you folks plan on staying with us?"

"We will stay for as long as we're having fun."

"Then maybe you would enjoy going on a fishing charter. The departure times are posted on the store's bulletin board."

"Thank you again. We will give it some thought."

"You take the lobsters, Lenny, and I will carry our diving gear. I can't wait to cook these lobsters. You boil the water, and I will go to the store for butter."

"Mary, come straight back. The water doesn't take long to boil."

"I'm back, Lenny. You can dip the lobsters now. Four is plenty for us. Don't cook any more of them. I am full."

"So am I, Mary."

"The telephone is working. I'm going to call our neighbor to see if Annie left a number that she can be reached at. It would comfort me to know that we have a way to reach her in emergencies."

"I need a nap."

"Lenny, are you still awake?"

"Yes, what can I do for you?"

"The neighbor had a number for Annie. I wrote it down in the telephone book. Lenny, it looks like a thunderstorm is coming in.

"The lady working in the store told me that when a storm comes in, the high, choppy surf pushes shells onto the beach. While you are napping, I'll go to the beach to see if I can find a few shells. I will see you later."

"If I'm still asleep when you return, wake me up."

"OK, Lenny."

LIGHTNING STRIKES (1991)

"Damn, who is beating on the door?" I thought. "They don't want to give up. I guess I should see who is there."

"Here I come! Who is it?" I said.

"It's the sheriff. Will you open the door, sir?"

"I'm sorry. I was asleep. What can I do for you, Sheriff?"

"Sir, are you with a woman in her late fifties or early sixties who has light-brown hair and is wearing a white swimsuit?"

"Yes, sheriff. That sounds like my wife, Mary."

"Sir, would you mind stepping outside?"

"Sure, sheriff."

"Sir, my deputy will fill you in on what we know."

"Tell me, sheriff. Has something happened to my wife?"

"Sir, we suspect that your wife was struck by lightning on the beach. She has been transported to the local hospital. This is the address of the hospital.

"If you go now, I will give you an escort, and you can do the paperwork there."

"Let's go, sheriff! This can't be real. What are the chances of being struck by lightning? I'm sure that she is all right."

I found a place to park and headed for the emergency room.

"I am here to see Mary Gibson. I was told she might have been struck by lightning."

"Are you her husband?"

"Yes, I am."

"We need you to fill out this paperwork."

"Can you tell me how she's doing?"

"Mr. Gibson, she is in intensive care. You must wait out here. The doctors are doing everything they can. Lenny, there seems to be a problem with your name."

"What do you mean?"

"Well, your IDs say that your name is Lenny Lewis."

"I know that. Mary did not want to take my name. She is a very independent woman. We are married. Our child goes to a university in Korea."

"Mr. Lewis. I have the paperwork I need. I will leave you for now. Good luck!"

"Thank you, sheriff.

"Are you the person in charge of the admissions desk?"

"Yes, sir, my name is Ms. Ruth. What can I help you with, Mr. Lewis?"

"I need to know how my wife is doing."

"Mr. Lewis, bear with us. Your wife is still in the operating room. When the doctors finish their procedures, they will send someone out to explain what they are doing to save your wife's life."

"Do you mean that her life was threatened?"

"She was diagnosed as critical and taken to surgery immediately after she was admitted, Mr. Lewis. That's what we know at this minute. Please take a seat. I will notify you if we hear anything further. Our social worker will be glad to assist you."

"Hello, Mr. Lewis, my name is Ms. Ross. I work for the hospital. I can assist you with everything from getting information about the hospital's policies to finding food and lodging. And I do have a good ear for listening. I was told your wife is in surgery. She was struck by lightning. Is there anything I can help you with? I understand that you're experiencing a high level of stress and that you're waiting for a report on your wife's condition."

"When will we hear something from one of the physicians working with her?"

"Mr. Lewis, as soon as the surgery is over, the surgeon in charge will come into the lobby to inform you of the state of the patient—that's the policy. I will sit with you awhile to answer any other questions that you have. Well, I might have been premature in telling you I would sit with you awhile. The admissions desk is summoning me. I will answer their call and come back, Mr. Lewis. Hello, Becky, what did you need me for?

"Ms. Ross, I just received a brief call from the head-surgery nurse. She told me to let you know that the surgeon is cleaning up and will be out to see Mr. Lewis. He has bad news. Prepare for the worst."

"Thank you, Becky."

"Mr. Lewis, my name is Dr. Bennett. I am the chief surgeon. We did everything we could. Your wife did not make it. I am sorry, Mr. Lewis."

"Goddamn it. Goddamn it! Why her? Why not me? Mary has done nothing but good her entire life. Oh, no, I will not accept this."

"Mr. Lewis, please get a grip!" advised the social worker. "Do you have any family I can call for you?"

"Only our daughter. She is in Korea. Can we get in touch with her?

"I have her school phone number at the campsite."

"There is a private lounge for this purpose. We can go there until we make a plan. I will go with you, Mr. Lewis."

"I can't drive at this time, Ms. Ross."

"Then let's go, Mr. Lewis. Can I call you Lenny, Mr. Lewis?"

"Please do, Ms. Ross. I have to pull myself together."

I thought back to the debilitating confusion I'd felt when I'd returned from Vietnam. I'd suddenly found out that the very people I'd thought I was fighting for hated me. The first time I was spit on, I was in a crowd of American protesters. I was incarcerated by a federal agency because I was a Vietnam veteran. The first time I was discriminated against, it was because I was a Vietnam veteran. When I first asked for help from the VA, I was ignored.

I was distraught, and suicide crossed my mind. I had to lie on my application to college and say that I was not a Vietnam veteran. Even to the day of Mary's death, I harbored guilt and suffered from horrid dreams about the combat I had experienced in Vietnam. If I had survived all of those experiences, I could surely survive Mary's death. I had Annie to think about. I had to remain strong for her.

THE FINAL ARRANGEMENTS (1992)
"Ms. Ross, I truly appreciate what you have done. I am prepared to confront the situation as it exists. Whom should I talk to about arranging the disposal of my wife's body?"

"I have the forms, Mr. Lewis. Are you sure you can deal with this matter at this time?"

"I am, Ms. Ross. Actually, I dealt with similar situations in Vietnam. But this situation is more difficult."

"Mr. Lewis, this is the release form for her personal belongings. She was wearing a wedding ring and a diamond pendant necklace. Where do you want the body to go?"

"Ms. Ross, I would like her body to be picked up by the nearest cremation company and would like her ashes to be returned to me as soon as possible."

"I have a list with me. Would you pick one, Mr. Lewis?"

"Show me a cremation company that works fast and is close by."

"This company is only a block away and has been in business for several decades. You can call the company from this phone. Here is the information that you will need to supply them with.

"You will have to meet them and sign their paperwork. A representative will come to this room within a few minutes. Are you sure that you are up to this?"

"Yes, I am, Ms. Ross."

"I will dial it for you, Mr. Lewis."

"Thank you."

"I will be in the designated room. Mr. Lewis, how long did they say it would take for the representative to show?"

"He said no longer than fifteen minutes."

"I will stay with you until he shows."

"Thank you, Ms. Ross."

"Hello, I am John Hammond. Are you Mr. Lewis?"

"I am."

"Mr. Lewis, I represent Hammond Funeral Services. I have the paperwork in order for you. Mr. Lewis, I am sorry for your loss. You will need to sign this document before the hospital will release the body to Hammond Funeral services. The second page denotes money owed to Hammond Funeral Services.

"There is an added rush charge to have her remains by noon tomorrow. We request that you come by and take care of the payment within the next hour or so. That will enable us to return her remains to you by noon tomorrow."

"Mr. Hammond, do you prefer a check or a credit card?"

"We would prefer a check."

"I will go to the RV park, get my checkbook, and come straight to the address on the paperwork."

"That sounds fine, Mr. Lewis. I will see you shortly. Good-bye."

"I'd better go. Thank you again, Ms. Ross."

"It was my pleasure, Mr. Lewis. Here is my card. Call me if you have a question."

I needed time to think about how to present this mishap to Annie. The first thing was to take care of the cremation company. Then I could return to the RV for some quiet time and separate my thoughts from my emotions.

■ ■ ■

PREPARING TO BREAK THE NEWS TO ANNIE (1992)

I was impressed by how I had taken care of the cremation. I had not shown discomfort while taking care of the bill. I had wept on the drive back to the RV park. My concern was strictly for Annie. How would I break the news to her?

The telephone was working, and Mary had written Annie's number down in the phone book. I looked at the number that Mary had written and hesitated. I had never felt so blue. First, I decided to call the local VA clinic to see if I could get an emergency appointment with a psychiatrist.

In recent years, the VA had come to recognize Vietnam veterans. I hated taking medication. However, I knew that it might be a good time for a sleeping medication or for something that could calm my nerves temporarily. After I explained the situation, I was given an emergency appointment for the next afternoon.

I decided that it would be best for me to deal with picking up Mary's remains and seeing the VA psychiatrist before I contacted Annie. I also wanted to ask the psychiatrist for advice on how to break the news to Annie. Annie would fly into Miami International Airport. The airport was only fifty or so miles from the camp.

I decided to pick Annie up and to bring her back to the campsite so that we could plan our next move. It was the one time when I could justify drinking. A couple of glasses of brandy took the edge off the worst day of my life.

I wondered whether I could find 150-milligram tablets of trazodone HCl in the bottom of my shaving bag. I remembered seeing a couple of them lying loose in my case at some time or another. I dumped the contents of the bag onto the table. There they were! There were my sleeping aids for the night.

I recognize that drugs are only temporary fixes for problems. The idea was to use a drug as a crutch for a short period of time while developing a permanent and acceptable psychological coping mechanism to deal with the despair I felt. Sleep was important. I needed to maintain a margin of lucidity and physical strength and to remain strong for Annie.

THE DAY AFTER MARY'S DEATH (1992)

Thanks to the trazodone, I slept for eight hours. First thing in the morning, I went for breakfast at IHOP. To keep my mind occupied, I read a local paper while I was waiting for my food. I read only the sports and entertainment sections. I didn't need any other problems weighing on me. I intended to tiptoe through the day to conserve energy. The last time I had been that lonely had been over two decades ago, when the sheriff had dropped me off on the interstate, given me a hundred-dollar bill, and said, "Lenny, don't ever come back."

I had been seventeen years old. I remember that it was the end of the summer, and the air was cool. I had only a light jacket. Knowing that it would be cold soon, I made my decision to go south, toward Atlanta. That was where I met Lori. She took me to her home, where I had sexual relationships with her and her mother for more than a month.

The next time I felt totally alone was on the bus headed for Fort Benning, Georgia, for basic training. Over the next three years, two of which I spent in Vietnam, I focused on my missions and on staying alive.

Occasionally, I would think about Mary Gibson. I did not realize at that time—maybe because I had never been in love before—how much I missed her. I received letters from Mary and Lori. I assumed they were letters of support. None of their letters ever gave me the idea that either considered me to be more than a friend. Looking back and reading in between the lines, though, I can see that Mary's letters did imply that she thought of me as more than a friend.

I now know that she thought that I was young and that I might think she was weird if she said she loved me. Mary Gibson was a respected professional in the Atlanta school system. She even told me in her letters that she had boyfriends but that she was never as intimate with them as she had been with me. She did make me promise to memorize her telephone number and to call her when I returned.

The next time I experienced a surge of loneliness was when I exited the plane from Vietnam. Family members and loved ones were present to welcome the soldiers I arrived with. No one was at the gate waiting for me.

"Sir, would you care for another refill?"

"How many is that?" I asked.

The waitress smiled and said, "I think that is six."

"No, thank you. I must be going. I lost track of time. Do you have my bill?"

"Yes, sir. Here it is, and thank you for coming in." I glanced at my watch and noticed that it was noon. Sorrow immediately overwhelmed me. It was time to go to the mortuary and to obtain Mary's ashes. I lost control and bellowed in pain. The waitress ran to me and asked if I wanted her to call an ambulance. I apologized and told her that my wife had been struck by lightning and had died.

She gasped. "Everyone has been talking about that unfortunate woman. I am so sorry." I walked to the cashier to pay my bill.

When I presented the check, the manager picked it up off the counter and said, "This one is on us. We all feel your pain." I walked out before I broke down crying. The waitress followed me out. She asked me if I was going to be all right. She handed me a small package of Kleenex and gave me a hug.

I become so weak that I was not sure that I could reach the car. The young waitress opened the door and offered to sit with me awhile. I declined her offer and thanked her again. I started the car and headed out to the highway in the direction of the mortuary. I asked myself why my thoughts always revert to Vietnam during crises.

The only answer I could come up with was that I'd been introduced to calamity at a young age in Vietnam before my character had fully formed. My experience in Vietnam was an integral part of me. Combat had caused my behavior to swing to the opposite side of the pendulum. I began to avoid controversy so much that on occasion, Mary would say, "Lenny, you need to take a stand!"

I never verbalized to Mary what I just expressed. I was very protective when it came to Mary's feelings. She was without a doubt the most eloquent person I'd ever met in my life. I preferred to serve her. When Mary smiled, I smiled. This mortuary was one place I'd never thought about visiting. I had often thought what Mary would do with me if I died until one day I told her that I preferred to be cremated. That's when she informed me that cremation was her wish too.

I parked the car. Walking from the car to the entrance of the mortuary, I developed a severe headache.

Mr. Hammond met me at the front door and without hesitation handed me Mary's remains.

"Thank you, Mr. Lewis. If we can do anything to make you more comfortable, don't hesitate to ask."

I responded by saying, "Do you have an aspirin?"

"Of course I do, Mr. Lewis."

"Here is a bottle. Take as many as you like. Right there is a water fountain."

"Thank you, Mr. Hammond, and good day"

I had never wanted to remove myself from a place more than I did at that moment. I felt like running to the door. The mortuary was dark. The warm, bright Florida sun had never felt so good on my face.

I placed Mary's urn between my legs and sped out of the parking lot. My next stop would be the VA clinic. But where would I place the urn while I was in the VA? I didn't think there was any certain place that you were supposed to put an urn. The seat looked to be OK.

I made my way to the appointment station.

"I have an appointment with Dr. Atoms," I said.

"Dr. Atoms is expecting you. Follow me, Lenny."

"Dr. Atoms, I'm Lenny Lewis. Thank you for seeing me."

"Tell me what's going on with you, Lenny."

"My wife got struck by lightning on the beach yesterday. I just picked up her ashes at the mortuary. Now I have to call our daughter in Korea to tell her. It is taking all of my strength to cope with this."

"I saw that on the news, Lenny. Florida leads the nation in people getting struck by lightning. Lenny, are you thinking about harming yourself?"

"Doc, are you speaking on the part of the VA or on my part?"

"Lenny, my concern is for the veteran. I need to ask you if you would like to come to group therapy until you can deal appropriately with this tragedy."

"Not at this time, Dr. Atoms."

"You mentioned your daughter. Have you spoken with her?"

"No, I thought I would run my thoughts by you first and ask you for suggestions. I intend to call her when I leave."

"Lenny, I reviewed your records. You are not a stranger to sudden deaths. Where do you feel vulnerable?"

"In my heart, Doc! I felt sorrow for my men who died in combat, but Mary's death has affected me in a way that I can't explain. Her death affects me personally. I'm not going to do anything stupid, Dr. Atoms, but I doubt that I can recover from this blow. My fear is that I'll never care about anything ever again."

"Lenny—or should I call you 'Doctor'?—I suggest that you try to ignore your emotions for now. You have a daughter still in school. She will need your immediate support and guidance."

"Thanks for reminding me."

"I had your records faxed over from the Atlanta VA clinic. I'm impressed by your academic accomplishments. I wish we had time to discuss evolutionary biology. Lenny, can I prescribe you an anti-anxiety medication?"

"I appreciate the offer, but I respectfully decline. But you could prescribe trazodone HCl. Lying down in my bed without the love of my life for the first time in twenty-one years will be a challenge. This is a difficult time for me."

"I agree, Lenny. Are you on your way back to Atlanta?"

"After I pick my daughter up at Miami International, we will share a long ride back to Atlanta."

"What about your family's assets?"

"I will suggest to Annie that we sell the house and put the money in a trust so that she can pay for her schooling and then start her life. She can do whatever she chooses to do with the money in the bank. Annie can have our savings too.

"I can get by on my compensation money. Annie is in school in Korea. I suspect that she will be there for five or six years. She intends to get her doctorate degree. I will go back to Fort Myers Beach, and I will write. Mary and I fell in love with the island."

"Lenny, if that is your plan, I suggest that you check in with my college roommate. He practices psychology at the Fort Myers VA clinic. I first started there and later transferred to Miami. My wife has family here, and she insisted that we move. I'd also like to give you another veteran's name. I know that you would have a lot in common with him. Take his name and number. Give him a call, Dr. Lewis. He was more like a friend of mine than a patient…very smart man. Everybody called him 'the Veteran.'

"Here is your prescription and my card. I wrote my personal telephone number on the back of the card. Call me night or day. You are going to be all right."

"Thanks, Dr. Atoms."

"Thank you for your service, Lenny."

Dr. Atoms reminded me of my obligation. He was the first professional to call me Dr. Lewis. Few Ph.D.s refer to themselves as doctors, because when they do, other people often assume that they are medical doctors. To me, that would be an insult.

INFORMING ANNIE OF THE DEATH OF HER MOTHER (1992)

The most stressful part of the day was still to come. I did not look forward to calling Annie. The obligation was beginning to wear on me. I will never forget my drive to the campsite that day.

The moments before I called Annie will always remain vivid in my mind.

"My name is Lenny Lewis. I am the father of the student Annie Lewis. How quickly can you summon my daughter? I request that someone keep company with her after I inform her of the tragedy at hand."

"Mr. Lewis, I need one moment to verify your identity. Can I have your date of birth? Thank you, Mr. Lewis. Please hold. I will return as soon as possible…. Thank you, Mr. Lewis. How can I help you?"

"Annie's mother, Ms. Gibson, has died. I would like to make arrangements for Annie to come home immediately. I request that she be excused from class and allowed to return home."

"That is an acceptable reason for a student to leave school and to return without facing an academic penalty. What would you like me to tell your daughter?"

"How long would it take you to bring her to the phone?"

"If she is in her room, it will take a runner five minutes to reach her, and then it will take her five minutes to get here."

"If that is the case, send a runner, please. Tell him that this is a very serious matter and that she must come to the phone without delay. Do not tell her about her mother's death."

"I will do as you wish, Mr. Lewis. The runner has left the building."

"Is there anyone who can comfort my daughter after I tell her about her mother's death?"

"I will summon a professor who works with students experiencing crisis situations. Hold for a minute or so Mr. Lewis.... Thank you for holding, Mr. Lewis. Professor Ji-hoon is on his way. Thank you for your cooperation. I will stay on the line with you until the runner returns."

"Is there someone there who can make her flight reservation? She has a credit card to use for payment."

"Yes, Mr. Lewis, I am authorized to make flight reservations for students. I'll just need her permission."

"Can you have the permission form readily available?"

"Yes, Mr. Lewis. I have it in my files."

"Please have it ready for her to sign. Will you please call me at this number, 239-xxx-2302, when her flight has been confirmed? I request that you book her a seat on the first available flight to Miami International."

"Yes, sir, Mr. Lewis. Here is your daughter, Mr. Lewis."

"Dad, what is so important—"

"Annie, listen to me. Go back to your room, get your credit card, and give it to the lady I've been talking to.

"She will reserve you a seat on the next flight out. Do you understand what I just said?"

"Yeah, Dad, but what's the hurry?"

"Annie...Your mom is dead. Annie...Annie, are you there?"

"No, Dad. No!"

"Yes, Annie. I will meet you at the Miami airport."

"Mr. Lewis."

"Yes, I am here."

"We will take care of her. Dr. Ji-hoon is with her. I will call you back when I have made her flight reservation."

"Thank you. Please hurry."

I decided to have a glass of brandy and to concentrate on remaining calm while waiting for her call. I thought back to my reaction when Mary informed me of Lori's death. I wondered how Mary had managed to move on.

I remembered that she'd admitted that Annie had given her strength. She had been alone in much the same way that I was. Mary would have expected me to hang tough and to help Annie—and that was exactly what I was going to do. When Lori had died, Mary and Annie had each other. Then Mary died, and Annie and I had each other.

The phone rang. "Mr. Lewis, we were successful in finding Annie a flight that leaves immediately. She is on her way. She will be landing in Miami International on Korean Air flight five-five-six-five at five in the evening (Eastern Standard Time). We will be looking forward to Annie's return. If there are any questions, please don't hesitate to call."

"Thank you, and good-bye."

FACING THE INESCAPABLE (1992)

I wondered how I would make it through another night. I decided to go for a jog on the beach. I needed to burn off some nervous energy and to contemplate my next move. When tragedy takes me by surprise—and it has countless times—I always try to connect the current happening to one in the past.

My past experiences allow me to scrutinize tragedies with more savvy. Mary's demise had totally blindsided me. Her death had taken me by surprise and temporarily paralyzed me, which had never happened to me in combat.

When on patrol in Vietnam, I always considered the possibility that we would be ambushed. The Viet Cong's training and equipment were inferior to those of the Americans. Their tactic was to ambush us and to kill as many as possible. Then they would hide. To survive, a unit would have to quickly recover and retaliate.

The men I led trusted that I could make life-saving decisions quickly enough to counteract ambushes. That had been part of my training in military school. I was known to be cool under fire. I thought that my combat experiences might benefit me when I picked up Annie. I vowed to be strong and cool under fire and to lead Annie through this crisis.

I knew that would've been what Mary would have asked of me. I decided that when I returned to the campsite, I would flush the one trazodone I had and trash the prescription Dr. Atoms had just written me. I no longer needed a crutch to face the way things were!

I had difficulties going to sleep. I reviewed my decision and stuck to it. I slept for almost seven hours. I realized that the next days could be the most important days of my life. I had to get them right! Annie's life was just beginning. My counsel on this matter would affect Annie emotionally for the rest of her life.

THE FINAL CHAPTER IN ATLANTA (1992)

It was time to meet Annie at the airport. I knew that it would be a difficult reunion. Her flight was on time. I waited at the gate for her.

"Annie, Annie, here I am!"

"Oh, Dad, what are we going to do?"

"Annie, do you have other bags?"

"No, Dad. I brought only what I could carry on. Can we get out of here?"

"Yes, I parked close by."

"I want to be strong for you, Dad. I have been coaching myself on how to remain calm.

"I cannot imagine what you have gone through. Was she able to speak after the lightning struck her?"

"I was told that she never regained consciousness and never suffered."

"What did you do with her?"

"I carried out her wishes, Annie. I had her cremated immediately. We have each other, Annie. We will get through this together. Annie, I am so proud of you. I expected you to be hysterical. Your courage will help me cope with this unexpected tragedy. I need food, Annie. Have you eaten?"

"No, Dad. I lost my appetite."

"Let's stop and try to eat something to keep our strength up."

"OK, Dad. I'll try."

"This restaurant looks good, Annie. Where would you like to sit?"

"Near a window would be fine."

"How do you like Korea?"

"I love it, Dad. The people are so nice. I like all of my professors, especially the one I was assigned to."

"Annie, we have plenty to take care of. First of all, what do you want to do with your mom's ashes?"

"You want me to make that decision, Dad?"

"Yes, I do."

"I think they should be spread out over the ocean surf."

"Will you attend to that when we get back to the camp in Key West, Annie?"

"I think I can do that."

"Next, what do you want to do with the house in Atlanta?"

"What do you think we should do with it?"

"The house should be sold, and the money placed in a trust for you, Annie. I don't intend to live there—too many memories. I'm going to move to Fort Myers Beach."

"Dad, I understand. I couldn't live there myself."

"Your mother's portfolio should be transferred to you. You can use that money for your retirement. You can use the money in the savings account to pay for any and all expenses while you are attending school."

"What about you, Dad?"

"I would like to keep the RV and live in it for now if that suits you, Annie."

"I want you to have it, Dad."

"Thank you. And I'll have my military compensation. I came to your mom with nothing, and she shared her life with me. Those memories will carry me for the rest of my life. As long as you are taken care of, I will be content. When do you need to be back at school?"

"If I go back within two weeks and make up the time I missed, I won't have any setbacks, Dad."

"I knew that, Annie. I don't know why I asked. Then that's what you should do."

"Let's eat, and after, we'll get busy, Annie."

"Dad, I love you!"

"I love you, Annie."

Annie and I returned to Atlanta. There was no formal will to slow us down. Mary and I did file a notarized agreement in the courthouse stating that if one or the other died that that the surviving spouse would take ownership to all monies and assets. It further stated that if Mary and I both died that everything would go to Annie.

The house was in a highly desirable neighborhood. It sold in the first week it was listed. The house furnishings were donated to the Salvation Army. We sold Mary's car to a neighbor. Annie insisted that I keep the money from the sale of Mary's car and that I tow her car behind the motor home. We hired an attorney who was a neighbor to oversee the transfer of all monies to Annie's trust. We managed to schedule a flight for Annie within the two-week period given to us by the school.

I turned and took a last look at the house we had lived in for over two decades. To avoid dwelling on years gone by, I forcefully focused on the present. I drove Annie to the airport. We hugged and said our good-byes. We cried one last time together. We both knew we would always stay in contact. However, we realized for the first time that we would no longer live together. Annie was a grown woman and would move in her own chosen direction. I would search in Southwest Florida for a new purpose in life.

I thought about all of the movies that end with the main character riding off into the sunset alone. Life has a way of beginning, climaxing, and starting all over again for me. This time, I decided to take myself with an open mind and no plan to a subtropical environment. I would set up my living camp and allow the environment to choose my next adventure. I had returned to Atlanta on a Greyhound bus. I would ride into Fort Myers Beach with a motor home and memories.

■ ■ ■

FORT MYERS BEACH (1992 TO PRESENT)

I set up camp in an RV campground in Fort Myers Beach. The RV brought on too many memories of Mary. I sold it and moved into a small apartment. I thought about Dr. Atoms' suggestion that I call the Veteran in Fort Myers Beach. The first call I made was to the Veteran.

I intuitively felt that it was the right thing to do. The Veteran answered my call. I relayed to him that Dr. Atoms had advised me to contact him. He was elated and insisted that we meet immediately. The Veteran and I agreed to meet at a coffeehouse the very next day. We instantly became friends.

Our military experiences had been almost identical. We had even been in Vietnam at the same time. We agreed that there was a possibility that we'd been in the same places from time to time. We even could have patronized the same bar and whorehouse. We agreed that our similar views had been influenced by our similar experiences.

He welcomed me into his home and introduced me to his mother, Betty. Betty's husband had lost his life in World War II. Betty was a very intelligent woman. Betty contributed facts to every discussion we had. The Veteran and I investigated many landmarks in Southwest Florida. In time, I found that I was comfortable with my new Southwest Florida life.

I continued to hear from Annie over the years. She remained in Korea after she finished school and went to work for a major technology company. I continued to read and to write articles on health even though no one was interested in them. But the Veteran had an interest in health. Without his interest, I would have probably lost interest in health and started writing romance and spy novels.

Americans want to be entertained, not educated. A woman once said to me that the less you know, the less you have to worry about. I had no reply for her. She took pride in her stupidity. How did I respond to that kind of advice? I didn't. I walked away. Betty's health improved, and she became deeply invested in our conversations.

THE LATEST FAMILY NEWS
"Hi, Betty. How are you doing today?" Lenny asked.

"I have been consolidating Lewis's medical records for Harold. Test results clearly show that the VA ignored five of Lewis's critical conditions."

"Betty, have you done your research on the number of wrongful-death lawsuits the VA has taken to trial?"

"There have been only a couple, and they were years ago. The VA prefers to settle out of court. The VA's lawyers know that they are at a disadvantage when they go up against a wrongful-death lawsuit, especially if it concerns a disabled veteran. The VA's inept veterans' care reputation is well known. A jury will normally support a veteran's family even if the jury has doubts about what happened."

"Do you still expect the VA to offer to settle?"

"As you know, the VA's attorneys have already offered five million dollars. They will raise their offer when they realize that we are ready and willing to go to court.

"They know that a sympathetic jury could award me the full twenty-five million. Plus, the VA's worst nightmare is negative publicity. Harold has been in contact with the VA's lawyers for the last month. He expects them to make an acceptable offer any day now."

"Betty, what would be an acceptable offer?"

"Harold and I decided that an acceptable offer would be no less than twelve million."

"What's going on with the bank charter?"

"The state has investigated the stockholders' backgrounds per Bob's suggestion. I don't foresee any problems with them.

"Talk about scrutiny. The background checks go far beyond criminal records' checks. The state's banking commission is still reviewing the charter. Harold and his friend who specializes in bank charters spent a great amount of time drawing up our charter. Harold said the charter is a work of art.

"The process itself is traditionally slow. Like Lewis used to say, you have to hurry up and wait."

"Ruby wanted me to ask you if you needed anything. We are going shopping for a few things."

"I wonder if a heating pad would soothe the arthritis in my shoulders."

"Heating pads cost very little. You can't go wrong with trying one. We will bring you one."

"Thank you, Lenny. I will look forward to giving it a try."

"Any word on when Harold will be here?"

"I'm glad you brought that up. I'm supposed to call him today to discuss that very subject. I will let you know when he's coming. Lenny, Ruby is the most beautiful woman in Fort Myers."

"You won't get any argument from me, Betty.

"Are you ready to go and turn some heads, Ruby?"

"You know me, Lenny."

"Do you know where we can find a good heating pad for Betty, Ruby?"

"Are you in pain, Betty?"

"No more than normally. There's no reason to be alarmed. It is the same nagging pain I've lived with for years."

"Betty, will you stop working for now? You have been at that computer all day."

"I think you're right, Ruby. I have a good book to read. You kids have fun. I will be in bed before you return.

"I will see you two in the morning for a cup of tea. Oh, Ruby. I almost forgot. You had three phone calls today. One was from a Mr. Porter, with Windy Beach Stores, and another one was from a salty-sounding shrimp-boat captain. I wrote both numbers down for you. The numbers are on my desk in the call-back box."

"Thank you, Betty. I can deal with them tomorrow."

"I thought about not telling you about the third person who called. I know that that would not be right. Adolf called from Germany.

"Lenny, you had a phone call from Art Ray. He called to inform us that he has decided to run for sheriff. He and I had an extensive conversation about his campaign. I told him we would set up a financial committee to collect money, keep records, and disburse the funds. I also assured him that the family would be a major financial contributor. Lenny, we need a sheriff who's friendly with the family."

"Wow, Betty! The family is becoming political?"

"Indeed, Lenny."

THE WINDY BEACH STORE'S FASHION SHOW, THE SHRIMP-BOAT SHOOT, AND WALMART

"Lenny, what do you think about me doing the swimsuit fashion show for Windy Beach Stores?"

"I don't, Ruby!"

"What do you mean?"

"I mean that it is not up to me, Ruby. The decision is yours. You know that I only want you to do what you will enjoy doing. If you're happy, I'm happy. If you're not happy, I'm not happy."

"I will contact Mr. Porter and listen to his ideas, Lenny."

"Ruby, I would like to see the shrimp-boat calendar's layout. Would you?"

"I would love to see the photographs, Lenny. It was a wild and sexy photo shoot. I was living totally in the moment."

"Where can we find a heating pad for Betty?"

"At any department store."

"Would Walmart have one? We need dog food too. We can go there for those items. I hate that store."

"I have to admit that one-stop shopping is convenient, especially if you're like me and don't like to shop. During the rise of Walmart's popularity, the store boasted that it sold only products made in America. The claim was short lived. 'We only sell Chinese products' could be the store's slogan now. How quickly the American consumer forgets."

"No one really cares about where products come from. The only things that matters are their prices."

"I certainly agree, Ruby."

"Lenny, you need to support me when I tell Betty that she needs to slow down. She is trying to do too much. I realize she is concerned about having everything in order for Harold."

"She is stressing herself out. I agree. We will both talk to her when we deliver this heating pad. Is there anything we can do to lighten her load, Ruby?"

"No, Lenny. I have already offered to help her. She quickly refused. Betty is a human dynamo."

ODE TO HAROLD

"Betty, give this heating pad a try. It should lie comfortably on your shoulder. Is this the shoulder that bothers you the most?"

"Yes, Ruby. I have news."

"What news, Betty?"

"I got a call from Harold. He is on his way to the VA's regional office in Tampa to meet with the VA's lawyers."

"What does that mean, Betty?"

"I am sure that the VA is going to make another offer. Harold said he would call me after the meeting. I need to forward this paperwork to him. Do you guys want to help? You can scan this stack of documents for me."

"We will do that while you take a break, Betty."

"Ruby and I think that you should slow down, Betty,"

"OK, I do need to break and feed Jojo and Breezy."

"We were thinking that you should permanently slow down, Betty."

"OK, after the VA settlement, I will consider it. Did you pick up dog food?"

"Yes, we did."

"Betty, I have heard you talk about Harold many times. What makes him such a great trial lawyer?"

"Harold could have been a successful politician. Good politicians are excellent orators.

"Politicians spend hundreds of thousands of dollars to manipulate their constituencies with their words. The politicians who hold higher offices are the better wordsmiths. They have mastered the art of giving speeches. In the world of politics, getting elected is everything. Once you get into office, you can do whatever you want.

"Harold has that gift. He is a master of persuading juries to vote his way. In the world of law, winning court cases is everything. Harold represented many high-profile cases and rarely lost. Lawyers who consistently win large awards can demand high fees. Harold was one of the top-ten highest-paid lawyers in Michigan.

"When Harold retired, his son took over the firm. He is helping Harold with my case."

RUBY RETURNS HER PHONE CALLS

"Ruby, you have not picked up your messages. I see that all three of the reminders I wrote are still in your tray," Betty said. "Have you decided not to call them back?"

"You are right, Betty. I will do that now. I will call Adolf last. Germany is about seven hours ahead of Florida. I'd rather talk to him after his work hours, when he will not be disturbed by ongoing business.

"I would like to talk to Mr. Porter, please. My name is Ruby Ridge. He is expecting my phone call. Yes, miss, I will hold."

"Hello, Ms. Ridge. Thank you for returning my phone call. I presented the idea of having a swimsuit fashion show to the board. The board was in favor of promoting the event.

"However, two of the board members were concerned about your past profession. The board suggested that you participate as an advisor only."

"Mr. Porter, will you tell me exactly what they said?"

"In all honesty, Ms. Ridge, they are concerned about your burlesque career."

"Mr. Porter, what does my legal career have to do with it?"

"A couple of the board members were concerned about Windy Beach Stores' reputation."

"Mr. Porter, can you please refrain from beating around the bush and tell me exactly what those two board members' objections were?"

"They voiced moral objections to your participating, Ms. Ridge. They are devout evangelical Christians."

"Mr. Porter, the swimsuit I received from your inventory was the most expensive suit you had. The bottom is made up of no more than a patch and a few strings. The top covers only my nipples. How do those two Christian board members justify carrying a suit so revealing?"

"I cannot speak for them, Ms. Porter."

"Then can you pass on my decision to those two board members?"

"I can, Ms. Ridge."

"I refuse to be in the presence of their hypocrisy and ignorance. Thank you, Mr. Porter, and good-bye! I need to calm myself down with a cup of warm tea."

"Ruby, you look flustered," I said.

"Windy Beach Stores just pissed me off. They wanted me to advise on the fashion show but not to participate in it. The two Christian board members objected to my participating for moral reasons. They were concerned about my background in burlesque. In a nice way, I told them to go fly a kite. Of the two hundred seventy or so large religious groups, Christians seem to be the most hypocritical.

"If you ever live in or visit a 'dry county,' you will notice how many liquor stores and adult cabarets border the county line on the side of the 'wet' county. Christians can cross the street into the next county to see adult entertainment and to purchase alcohol to sneak back into the privacy of their own homes. They think that if no one sees them sinning, they are good Christians."

"I know, Ruby. Everyone you affiliate with knows about your past, and frankly, none of us give a damn about Christian hypocrisies. You know you can't change their two thousand years of ignorance. Now can you set aside all of these unnecessary concerns, Ruby? Have you spoken to the shrimp-boat captain?"

"As soon as I compose myself, I will give him a call. I made two cups of tea. Would you take a cup to Betty?"

"I will, and then I will come straight back, Ruby.... OK, Ruby, I have returned. I have a concern."

"What is your concern, Lenny?"

"Ruby, my concern is you. I have never seen you so emotional. May I remind you that we don't need those people's approval of anything in our lives? I say, 'Fuck them!'"

"Wow, you are so right, Lenny. How did I allow something this petty to stress me out? I will not give one more minute of thought to the convictions of religious hypocrites.

"Wherever religion dominates, so too do ignorance, intolerance, and persecution. Not one more minute will I waste thinking about this situation.

"I will call the shrimp-boat captain now, Lenny."

"Ruby, did that phone call go better than the one with Windy Beach Stores?"

"Lenny, I can tell you without a doubt that it was great. The captain asked if we could meet him in downtown Fort Myers. The captain was excited to hear from me. He said his publisher was transfixed to the prints.

"The publisher said that he had never seen a sexier model. The captain warned me that the publisher intends to hire me to do photo sessions for other advertising clients. He informed me that the agency represents Valerie's of Hollywood and Rita's Secrets.

"Lenny, both of those corporations are well known internationally. They represent the standard in women's evening wear and lingerie."

"When will we meet the captain, Ruby?"

"I agreed to meet the captain and the agent tomorrow for lunch."

FAMILY GATHERING

"How is everything going with you and Ruby?"

"I am living a dream, Will. Wait until you see the pictures of her in the shrimp-boat calendar."

"I can imagine them, Lenny. I felt like a stud when Ruby took me to Starbucks for coffee. She captured the eyes of everyone there.

"It was the first time I had ever felt the envy of other men and women, Lenny. I don't know if Bailey will allow me to hang up one of Ruby's calendars in my man cave, which is the garage," Will said, laughing. "I started to think about why men marry, buy homes, and live in their garages."

"Do you know when Bob and Gloria plan to marry?"

"Uh-oh. Has no one told you that they got married last week?"

"No, Will. Why weren't we invited?"

"No one was invited, Lenny. They decided to be married by a magistrate to avoid having to deal with a wedding. Bob and Gloria got married on the spur of the moment. They will be stopping by later. When we left, Gloria mentioned that they're planning to visit."

"Hey, Ruby, did you know that your mom and Bob are married?"

"What?"

"Yeah, Ruby, they're married."

"Bailey, is that true?"

"Yes, it is, Ruby. I just told Betty. She did not know."

Will said, "They are planning to come by, Ruby."

"I sure hope they had a good reason for not allowing us to go to the wedding, Bailey. Bailey, would you like to show me how well you can do the fox-trot?"

"Sure, Ruby. Betty, can you put some music on?"

"Damn, Will, they are good."

"She does much better with Ruby than with me. Bailey says that I have clubfeet."

"You are not alone. I gave up," I said.

"Bailey does all of the ballroom dances well. She has spent time with Ruby. I learn them from Bailey. I like the break-dancing moves that Ruby showed me.

"I need to get in better shape before I can improve. You need to be super-limber and athletically fit."

"Break dancing would be impossible for me at my age," I said. "However, I enjoy watching it. Will you give me a hand with these grass-fed and grass-finished rib-eye steaks, Will? Ruby and Bailey can marinate them, and we will start the grill.

"Will, take a couple more steaks out for Bob and Gloria."

"Lenny, I am going to call them and inform them that we have started cooking," Ruby said. "Betty, I just spoke with Gloria. She informed me that she and Bob are on their way."

"Good. I really have a lot to talk about with Bob."

"Betty, try to keep the business talk short," Ruby said. "We have not had a family gathering since before we went to historic downtown Fort Myers."

"I agree, Ruby. It is time for our regular social schedule to return. Oh, I almost forgot, Lenny. Art called and said that he and Barbara will not be coming. They are too busy organizing his campaign for sheriff."

THE BANK CHARTER'S DETAILS AND BOB AND GLORIA'S MARRIAGE ANNOUNCEMENT

"Bob and Gloria are here, everybody. I will get the door," Bailey said.

"Hello, Betty. How are you doing?"

"I have been working overtime on the bank charter. We are really making progress. All of the paperwork is in. Bob, I need your input on the employee manual."

"Betty, I would enjoy creating a good manual. For years, I used manuals written by someone outside of the banking industry. It would be my pleasure to create a complete bank-policy manual. A good one will eliminate many employee-management disagreements. Betty, what else can I do?"

"You should start your search for appropriate furniture and electronics for the bank and for your office. We hired a company to compile statistics on the areas in need of a local bank. We will use those statistics to look for possible sites with our realtor. Finding a vacant building that we could renovate would save time and money. However, if that is not possible, we will build one.

"The bank charter should be approved in the next thirty days or so, Bob."

"That is the best news I have ever heard, Betty. What do you think, Gloria? You'll have your dream job too—you'll be a bank administrator."

"Oh, Betty, we are so grateful."

"I promised Ruby that this would be a social event and that I would not burden you with too much business."

"Come back to me at your convenience, and we will tie up the loose ends, Bob. We need an explanation for your secret wedding, Gloria."

"A magistrate whom Bob does business with mentioned that if we went down to the courthouse, he could marry us in a matter of minutes. Bob called me, and I took an hour off, and we met and tied the knot. It was a reflex, not a plan, people."

"We dispatched Will to retrieve a cake. This gathering will act as your wedding party."

"This is so nice of all of you."

"What will it be, Bob and Gloria? Beer, wine, or champagne?"

"Lenny, will you open the door for Will?"

"How did you get your hands on a cake that nice?"

"I got lucky. Some couple canceled their wedding, and I took their cake. Even better, I bought it for half price."

"Gloria, look at this cake!"

"Wow, Will, it is beautiful," Gloria said.

"Listen up, everybody. I propose a toast to Bob and Gloria. May they live happy ever after."

BETTY AND LENNY DISCUSS ADOLF AND HAROLD

"Lenny, is Ruby still sleeping?"

"She was up most of the night talking to Adolf, Betty."

"Well, have a cup of coffee with me."

"I would enjoy that, Betty."

"Do you ever wonder why Ruby continues to talk to Adolf? I find it hard to believe that it doesn't bother you. It bothers me, Lenny.

"I am going to confront her with my concerns. She is cohabitating with you. She has to know that communicating with him is disrespectful to you."

"Betty, I said at the beginning of this relationship that I couldn't believe she'd chosen me. She could have any man. I live this dream every day. Before she entered my life, I had accepted that my time for love had passed. I am in far over my head with her."

"Lenny, I am under the gun too. Harold will be here soon. I worry that I have become too old and feeble to please him."

"Betty, he is old and feeble too. I am sure he is in need of companionship. He knows that you are intellectually on par with him. It would be impossible for either one of you to find a more compatible companion. You two have spent years together. There are no secrets. You know each other. Just be, Betty!"

"Thanks, Lenny, for reminding me of that."

LE MOIRÉ CAFÉ

"Good morning, people!"

"Good morning to you, Ruby!"

"Lenny, we need to get dressed to meet the captain and the publisher. You should look your best. I have an outfit that I wore for special occasions in Vegas. It attracts attention."

"What do you think I should wear, Ruby?"

"I already gave that some thought too, Lenny. I pulled your blue suit out and hung it up. It goes with my outfit. I want to steam the wrinkles out of it, and then it will be fine."

"I will steam it, Ruby, while you are getting ready. Betty, do you know where the steamer is?"

"The steamer is in the kitchen pantry. Be sure that you use distilled water. There is a gallon of distilled water in the pantry too. I would hate to see you stain your suit with the minerals that are present in tap water. You two will be the talk of the town," Betty said. "The café you are meeting them at is the Who's Who of fashionable people in Fort Myers. Who do you think chose Le Moiré Café?"

"I'm sure the agent chose the meeting place. I can't imagine a shrimp-boat captain setting up a meeting there. Betty, would you like to come?" Ruby asked. "It would be an opportunity to wear one of those beautiful Neiman Marcus gowns in your closet. Any one of the three would be perfect for this occasion.

"It would probably give you a chance to see some of your old friends. You really have not been out much since you restored your health. How long has it been since you last had tea at Le Moiré? A soon-to-be chairman of the board of a local bank should have some exposure."

"Too bad Harold is not here to go with us."

"I will not give you an opportunity to say no, Betty. I insist that you come," I said.

"I don't know, guys. It has been a couple of decades since the last time I was at Le Moiré. It used to be my hangout, Ruby."

"This will not turn into a debate. The matter is settled. Go ready yourself, Betty," Ruby said.

"OK, I am excited. Thank you, guys!"

"Wow, you ladies look fantastic."

"It has been a while since I have seen you in a suit, Lenny."

"What do you think, Betty?"

"He does not look like the same man, Ruby."

"Is that good or bad, Betty?"

"Lenny, quit playing; you know what I'm saying. A suit makes a man look more serious. Lenny, we can take my Escalade, and you can drive.

"Lock the dog door so that the dogs will stay inside while we're gone. I don't like leaving the dogs out when we're gone. The fence has a couple of holes in it. The fence people will be out soon to replace parts of it and to install a new automatic gate opener. They are also going to fence in a half acre and install a prefabricated shed at the rear of the property."

"What is the enclosure for?" Ruby asked.

"I am going to purchase a pony for Joni, Ruby."

"Betty, that is such a nice thing to do. Does Bailey know?"

"No, she does not, Ruby. It will be a birthday present, and I want it to be a surprise."

"I understand, Betty."

"Betty, how large is your lot?" I asked. "I noticed that your lot is larger than any of the others in this neighborhood."

"I purchased three acres. After I bought my acreage, the developer cut the rest of them down to one acre. I built the first house in this neighborhood, Lenny."

"Your property might be the only one without a dock. You are located on a deep-water canal. A boat can take you out to the ocean."

"I never had any interest in boats. Lewis thought about building a dock and buying a boat. I don't know what stopped him. Maybe that's something that would interest you and Ruby."

"Don't look at me, Lenny. The only time I was ever on a boat was when we did the shrimp-boat photo shoot. I am totally incompetent when it comes to boats. OK, here we are."

"Go ahead and do valet parking, Lenny. There's no reason to park a mile away."

"Good day, sir, will you be having lunch?"

"We are supposed to be meeting a boat captain and a Mr. Steinberg."

"Yes, sir, they are expecting you. I will lead you to their table."

"My God, how lovely you ladies look," the captain said. "Mr. Steinberg, this is Lenny and Ruby and, I am guessing, the lady of the family."

"My name is Betty, Mr. Steinberg. I just came along for the Le Moiré experience."

"Please sit down. Ruby, I have to say that I have never seen a woman as photogenic as you. May I ask how tall you are?"

"I am six feet tall, Mr. Steinberg. Can we order? I apologize for my hurry."

"Waiter, we would like to order."

"Thank you, Mr. Steinberg. I will be right back."

"My staff did a little research on you. You were billed as the top showgirl in Las Vegas for five years running. You have a master's degree in dance from one of the more prestigious universities. Allow me to cut to the chase, Ms. Ridge.

"My company wants to contract with you for a series of video and photo shoots. We are the number-one modeling company in the southwestern part of the United States. Here is a list of a few notable clients we represent. This is not an appropriate time to discuss a contract. I simply wanted to meet you, to have an informal conversation with you, and to present you with this packet of information.

"You can come to our office and discuss this information before you sign a contract. I have been in the modeling business for a long time and have never seen a woman more striking than you, Ruby Ridge. You are one photo session away from being an international star.

"I am not concerned about how you would perform in a studio. You are a proven professional. That's all I want to say at this time. Let us enjoy our meeting, people. Everything is on me."

"Thank you, Mr. Steinberg."

"Betty, my God—is that you? Where have you been?"

"Lucile, I have been in my own little world."

"Betty, take my personal card, and give me a ring. We have a lot of scuttlebutt to catch up on."

"Mr. Steinberg, it has been a pleasure. Thank you for the food and drink. I will read your information and give you an answer soon."

"I will look forward to your call, Ruby."

"Mr. Steinberg, thank you for the tea and the hospitality," Betty said.

"Betty, I will definitely do business with your bank. It was a pleasure to meet you. Lenny, you are one lucky man. Don't take my compliment the wrong way. I hope that we can become business partners in the near future."

"Betty, I saw that you ran into an old friend."

"Lucile and I hung out at this café years ago. She keeps up with the social scene around town. She can tell you who is doing whom. I have to admit that she is a lot of fun. If I ever find a minute, I will call her and spend an afternoon with her."

"Ruby, what do you have to say about your meeting with Mr. Steinberg?"

"Betty, my gut reaction is that he wants a long-term commitment. He is not going to get one from me. I worked for businesses that were similar to his but much larger. I don't have a damn thing to prove. If I do a photo shoot, I will direct it from the beginning to the end. Betty, you and I can review the information and the contract. I have reason to believe that the contract will require more of me than I am willing to give.

"What do you think, Lenny?"

"Ruby, you have already been to the top of the mountain. I don't see you committing to a contract. You don't need the money. If it doesn't offer you fun and excitement, don't waste your time with it."

"I thought the captain was a real gentleman," Betty said.

"OK, guys. I think we have made a decision. I will allow the shrimp-boat calendar to be published but will not allow any of the photos to be used for anything else."

"I second that motion," Betty said. "Looks like the nays have it. You will reject the deal!"

"I am going to go to bed a little early tonight. Tomorrow morning, I will go to the gym and work off some of this stress."

"Lenny, are you ready for bed?"

"No, Ruby. I need a little private time in the library. I will try not to wake you when I do come to bed. Love you…good night."

■ ■ ■

LENNY'S FINAL RECIPE FOR GOOD HEALTH

Many years of my life have been devoted to trying to come up with a simple health program. My idea was to establish a common-sense approach that individuals could use to make good health decisions without needing to study health for years first. Given common-sense thinking and basic information, an individual should be capable of making healthy choices.

I believe that my program will help people accomplish that goal. Of course, I can't list everything that is bad for you. But I can offer advice that will help individuals achieve good health if they apply some common sense.

Any researcher would agree that every individual is as unique as his or her fingerprints and DNA. For that reason, an individual must find what works best for him. Understanding how we live today and how we lived hundreds of thousands of years ago can help a person make better decisions about eating and living.

In the future people will choose their foods based on their genetic make-up. This information will reveal a family's geographical origin. Different population groups are hardwired to a specific diet.

Knowing what causes diseases could help prevent diseases.

An individual who uses common sense can personalize his or her health plan and make it fit his or her specific needs. Knowing one's medical family history can make it easier to assess one's health. If an individual knew a thousand years' worth of his medical family history, he could ideally avoid contracting certain diseases.

However, that is an impossible dream. So we must move on to the next-best possible goal: investigating ancient history. The particular area of the world that one comes from is very important, as that is the environment that his family adapted to. We only recently developed the means to travel thousands of miles in search of better lives.

The study of the environmental factors that influence genes to express themselves is called epigenetics. Cultural evolution's influence produced genetic confusion. Gene expressions became erratic, and new mental and physical diseases developed. One concerned with his health should eat and live his life as similarly as possible to those in the environment that his family originally evolved in.

Note that if a fruit, vegetable, or animal cannot live on its on in the wild, it is not truly a food that humans naturally consumed for thousands of years.

Another theory is that contemporary vegetables and fruits can be toxic to one's health. You might ask how that could be. Today's vegetables and fruits are superhybrids. They are not even close to the ones eaten by our ancestors. A comparative analysis of wild vegetables and fruits (which have very low glycemic values) and the conventional vegetables and fruits (which have very high glycemic values) would prove that modern fruits and vegetables are nutritionally entirely different from those of the Paleolithic age.

The glycemic-index chart rates foods, including vegetables and fruits, according to the rates at which they break down into sugar and enter the bloodstream. On the chart, zero represents the slowest breakdown rate, and one hundred represents the fastest breakdown rate. The point here is that modern hybrid vegetables and fruits quickly break down into glucose (sugar) and flood the bloodstream at rates that many bodies can't handle. Too much sugar in the bloodstream is a serious problem.

This is where things become interesting. Man survived a ten-thousand-year-long ice age with literally no vegetation. Some researchers question whether we even need to consume plants, stating that the body runs more efficiently off fat. After the ice age ended, our ancestors ate wild fruits and vegetables only when they were in season and in small quantities.

Today's high-sugar, low-fiber hybrid vegetables and fruits are available all year. Also, the daily overconsumption of hybrid fruits and vegetables promotes obesity, diabetes, and inflammation, which are gateways to ill health and chronic disease.

Eat these modern hybrid vegetables and fruits in moderation.

Even worse things can be said about energy drinks and processed foods. Energy drinks were developed to quickly deliver sugar to the cells of athletes pushing their bodies to their limits. The average sedentary adult cannot tolerate the continuous onslaught of excess sugar and energy. Energy drinks cause metabolic diseases in sedentary adults. Processed foods are cheap man-made foods that are high in sugar and low in nutritional value.

Enzymes are responsible for all of the chemical reactions in the body. It's good to know that raw vegetables can furnish their own digestive enzymes and break down into sugar at slower rates. Raw vegetables do not deplete the body's finite supply of systemic enzymes. Hydrochloric acid, digestive enzymes, amylase, protease, lipase, and cellulase supplements are recommended for individuals over forty years old.

Inside every human's digestive system live trillions of friendly bacteria necessary for life. These bacteria manufacture vital nutrients that we cannot extract from food or manufacture on our own. They support our immune systems and aid in digestion. Recent research indicates that these bacteria affect the central nervous system through the longest cranial nerve, the vagus nerve, which runs from the brain stem to the abdomen.

The antibiotics in conventional domestic meat kill these bacteria. Chemicals in processed foods also devastate them. This microflora imbalance is known as "dysbiosis." Routinely taking a probiotic supplement and regularly consuming fermented foods can reinstate the population of bacteria.

Now what do we know? Cultural evolution changed the foods people ate. This drastic environmental change affected our health. Let's identify some of the modern foods that our bodies are not adapted to and remember that these foods may cause ill health. If possible, shun all products with added sugar. Eliminate fruit juice. Pulp-free juices can have high glycemic rates. Our ancestors did not juice their fruits or vegetables.

In the past, the technology to process vegetable oils did not exist. Highly processed oils are toxic and give fat a bad name. Remember that Mother Nature makes no bad fats—only men make bad fats. Animals that are fed corn and grains and given manmade chemicals that expedite their growth are toxic. Our ancestors did not eat animals like those. Eat grass-fed and grass-finished meat that is pesticide-and fertilizer-free. Fish raised in unnatural, artificial environments are less nutritious and are toxic. Eat wild fish only.

The way meat is cooked is important. The chemical reaction that turns meat brown on the outside is carcinogenic (that is, cancer causing). Do not allow meat to brown or char. Do not fry it. Processed grains (like bread and pasta) became available during the later part of the agricultural revolution. They cause hunger, are calorically rich, are difficult to assimilate into cells, and have high glycemic rates, so they cause insulin levels to spike. Eat in moderation! Avoid using antibacterial soap.

When possible, avoid chemicals in food, clothing, plastic containers made wth bisphenol-A (BPA), and the environment. Exercise your mind and body, sit up straight, practice proper posture when standing and walking, sleep for between six and eight hours each night, and manage your stress.

Scientists have concluded that the common diseases today are mismatched diseases, meaning that our bodies are mismatched to today's environment. This clash between the environment and our genes results in preventable mismatched diseases. Some of the more common mismatched diseases include type 2 diabetes, obesity, high blood pressure, osteoporosis, arthritis, back pain, flat feet, anxiety, asthma, acne, irritable bowel syndrome, and some heart disease and cancers.

If one wants to hear the full history of food, I suggest Nora T. Gedgaudas's book *Primal Body, Primal Mind*.

It was time for me to go to bed. I hadn't intended to stay up late.

"Lenny, I am concerned. Is something bothering you? You have never worked all night before."

"I apologize, Ruby. I was focused on developing a health program that would not require years of study to understand. I designed a simple program that anyone could understand. It offers common-sense methods that will help people choose good foods and the right activities and minimize their stress."

"You have often talked about doing that. I know what this means to you, Lenny. Come to me so that I can congratulate you in an intimate way and relieve your stress."

"Oh, my God!"

■ ■ ■

THE DRIVE TO THE VA REGIONAL HOSPITAL

"Hello, Ruby…Ruby, will you wake up please?"

"OK, Betty. I'm coming."

"Morning, Ruby. I'm so sorry that I woke you up. I waited as long as I could. It is already nine. Harold called me this morning from Tampa. He is in need of some original documents. I must take them to him. He needs them to close the deal. Can you quickly dress and deliver them to him?"

"I will wake Lenny, and we will hurry, Betty. Get up, Lenny; we have a mission that can't wait. We need to take documents to Harold in Tampa."

"Can't you fax them or email them?"

"Betty says that he must have the originals. While you are getting ready, I will make some coffee to take with us."

"I will come as soon as possible, Ruby."

"Betty, Lenny was up last night late working on his book."

"You don't look ready, Betty."

"I'm not going, Ruby. It would be too much of a distraction. Harold is going to ride back with you. I will welcome him here. He is excited about seeing his new home. He is leaving his house and everything else to his family. He wants to purchase everything here."

"What about the lawsuit, Betty?"

"You will know about the result before I do. I think that once you deliver these documents, a final decision will be forthcoming."

"The VA's attorneys already vowed to settle this matter today. I think that they are waiting for these documents. Don't call me before Harold does. I know that Harold wants to be the one to tell me the final amount of the settlement."

"I understand, Betty."

"Where is Lenny?"

"I'll check on him, Betty."

"Never mind, Ruby. I am ready to roll."

"I'll drive, Lenny. You only had a couple of hours of sleep. You can stretch out in the back of the Escalade and sleep for another three hours on the way to Tampa."

"Thanks, Ruby. I won't argue with that."

REFLECTIONS OF LENNY'S LIFE

As I lay in the backseat of the Escalade, my mind meandered down the pathway of my life. The events I was reliving were indications of what was permanently parked in my mind. My mother had betrayed me for her new lover soon after my father had mysteriously died. I had become homeless at seventeen years old.

The most damaging event was Vietnam. While I was in Vietnam, Lori Gibson, the daughter of Mary Gibson, died of an overdose. She had taken my virginity when I was seventeen. Then there was Callie, who rescued me, loved me, and disposed of me.

The event that caused me the most pain was the death of my wife, Mary Gibson, who had been struck by lightning. I managed to carry on but was often reminded of what she had meant to me. Then the Veteran died. Miraculously, each ordeal ended with my being taken in by another generous person or group of caring people.

I couldn't help but wonder whether some unknown force had kept me safe for some higher purpose.

The things I saw and the things I did shaped the person I became.

Ruby's regular telephone conversations with Adolf disturbed me. For a long time, I thought nothing of them. The month before, he'd flown into Fort Myers, and Ruby had spent the entire day and night with him. I became concerned. She never said one word about it to me. Betty's mentioning it had brought it to the forefront of my mind.

I knew that if something troubled Betty, it should be a concern of mine. Betty had a great sense of balance with those things. Several times I came close to saying something to Ruby. I felt that saying something would've been like showing jealousy. I knew Ruby would not accept that behavior. I found it strange myself. I had never felt jealousy before in my life.

I asked myself why I was feeling insecure at my age. I knew that I had post-traumatic stress disorder. I had accepted that the pain of combat would be a part of me for the rest of my life. PTSD had nothing to do with my becoming jealous.

I did know that whatever was going on with me needed to be sorted out. Going to Vietnam and losing Mary Gibson were all that I could deal with. Losing Betty and Ruby would be my third strike, and after three strikes, you are out. That's the rule in many games in life.

THE VA REGIONAL HOSPITAL WITH HAROLD

I wondered how long I had slept for and where Ruby was. It looked like I was in the parking lot at the VA. Four hours had passed since we'd left Fort Myers. I decided to see if Ruby would answer her cell phone.

"Hi, Ruby."

"Hello, sleepyhead."

"What is going on?"

"I am waiting outside of the mental-health ward's conference room."

"Did you deliver the documents to Harold?"

"I did, Lenny. The lawyers are talking now."

"What floor are you on, Ruby?"

"I am on the fourth floor, section two B."

"I will be right there!"

"Can you fetch me a cup of coffee, Lenny? I don't want to leave my station for fear of missing Harold."

"OK, one large black coffee is coming up. Here is your coffee, beauty. How did you identify Harold? I have no idea what he looks like."

"Betty showed me a picture before we left."

"Did you talk to Harold?"

"Just for a minute."

"He said that the VA's lawyers were working out the details."

"What else did he say?"

"He said, no movie rights or publications would be a part of the deal. The VA is concerned about publicity."

"What does Betty think?"

"I know that Betty and Harold have spoken about this for hours. They have been dogmatic. Harold is the messenger. You can bet that Betty is on top of everything. Her body is worn down, but her brain is as sharp as a razor."

"How long has it been since Harold has seen Betty?"

"Quite a while, Lenny."

"Does he realize that Betty has changed physically over the last ten years?"

"I think that they are pretty much the same."

"What are you saying, Ruby?"

"Harold looks almost like Betty. He uses a cane to get around. He is in no better physical shape than Betty. Like Betty, his mind is sharp, but his body is worn out.

"Lenny, trust me—they are a perfect match. I will tell you a secret. Don't ever say anything about it, OK?"

"I promise, Ruby."

"They swapped nude pictures before they committed to each other."

"No shit, Ruby."

"No shit, Lenny!"

"How do you know?"

"I took the pictures, Lenny."

RUBY CONFESSES HER DISGUST

"Ruby, did Harold give you any idea of how long this conference might take?"

"All he said was that it would be a while. By the way, Ruby, can you tell me why you're no longer interested in working with the Boys and Girls Club of America? You said nothing after meeting with the board of advisors."

"You are right, Lenny. I lost all interest in it after I met them."

"Would you explain why, Ruby? I thought you and I would be working together on this matter."

"I did not want you to have to listen to such BS. Those people really pissed me off, Lenny! This nice Christian chairwoman and her cohorts objected to the idea of me working with kids."

"What do you mean, Ruby?"

"She said that because of my past profession—which the chairwoman said was burlesque—I would be a bad example for the kids. I was so caught off guard and offended! This organization's mission is to beguile these young boys and girls into joining the Christian religion before they can make their own choices.

"That is the reason that I no longer desire to do anything for that organization. However, I do worry for the kids."

"You did the right thing by saying nothing further, Ruby."

"You know how I feel about Christians, Lenny."

"The same way I feel, Ruby. Show me religion, and I will show you bigotry and ignorance. You can't negotiate with someone who believes in talking snakes, Ruby. It amazes me that our society applauds the mental rape of children."

WAITING-ROOM SCUTTLEBUTT

"This place creeps me out, Ruby. The last time I was at this hospital was when I brought the Veteran in for an evaluation. He unexpectedly died. On the way home, I tried to do a good deed and ended up getting knifed in an attempted robbery. Then I had to return to the emergency room to be sewed up. Nothing good happens here."

"Lenny, don't think that it will always be this way. I have a feeling that today is going to be different. I get excited just thinking about this settlement. The settlement is a done deal. The debate now concerns the amount.

"Betty said that they would not accept a penny less than twelve million dollars. She said that they would've gotten twenty-five million dollars if they'd gone to court. The problem with going to court is the time involved. It could take between three and five years. Harold and Betty will take half of that amount to settle now."

HAROLD'S DEBUT

"The conference room's door just opened, Ruby. They are coming out."

"Harold, this is Lenny."

"I've heard about you from Betty."

"Harold, do you have any bags?"

"I have only one bag, Lenny. Betty insisted that I not pack many clothes. She said she wanted to take me shopping for clothes for Florida."

"I will help you with the bag, Harold."

"Thank you, Lenny. The bag is in the corner of the conference room."

"Ruby, God—you are a beauty! Betty tells me that you have been like a daughter to her. As a matter of fact, she talks about her family every time we talk. She says it is a potpourri of talents and intellects.

"Betty talks mostly of the loyalty of her family members. She told me that the family adopted a slogan, 'one for all, and all for one,' from Alexandre Dumas's book *The Three Musketeers*. When Betty told me that, I said, 'Betty, that sounds more like a cartel than a family.' She ignored my reply. I now understand why."

"Is this all you brought, Harold?"

"That's it, Lenny. Can we go now? I hate hospitals."

"Lenny just said that they creep him out," Ruby said.

"Well, Lenny, we agree on that."

"How did the meeting go, Harold?"

"It turned out to be close to perfect, which reminds me that I promised Betty that I would call her the minute the meeting ended. Can we sit here? Hello, Betty, it is a done deal. The money will be electronically wired to the corporation's bank account. God, I love this business when I win. The transfer will take ninety days at the most. I have the details in my briefcase. We settled for fourteen million."

"Harold, you are still the best!" Betty said.

"We will dance tonight, Betty. We will be investing the money from the settlement in a community bank, so I submitted a tax waiver. That's right, all fourteen million, Betty. Let me go so that we can head your way. I can't wait to see you. I love you too. Bye."

"Wow, Harold, that is what I would call a home run."

"I would call it a home run with the bases loaded. They got off easy, Lenny. The VA knows it. Those physicians made numerous mistakes, and they were documented. We could've filed criminal charges against two of those damn doctors. Our not insisting on criminal investigations was instrumental in bringing the VA to the negotiating table.

"Lewis's death was a Goddamn shame, Lenny. I loved that boy like he was my own. Betty was a workaholic. He stayed with me for most of his young life. I virtually raised Lewis. Betty said that she would not have survived his death if it had not been for the family. She specifically named you and Ruby.

"I owe you guys a thank-you for saving my gal. Once we open the bank, I am going to officially retire. What a nice day. When I left Detroit, it was snowing."

"Harold, welcome to paradise."

EVERY FAMILY MEMBER BECOMES A MILLIONAIRE

"This is the Escalade that Betty bought? Betty told me about it. She said she could teach me how to work all of the newfangled technology. My generation is ignorant of today's technology. My son took over my law firm and brought it into the twenty-first century. I reciprocated by showing him what can't be taught in law school. I mean that I showed him the ropes and introduced him to the right people. That's still how you get things done. Betty and I made a fortune over the years.

"I have not eaten. I become giddy when I am hungry. Could we make a quick stop and grab a bite to eat? Lenny, would you recommend something healthy? I realize that it will be difficult to find healthy food on the interstate. However, we can select the least bad food."

"Take exit two fifteen, Ruby; there is a country restaurant that serves locally grown food."

"It looks quaint, Lenny. Reminds me of my grandma's kitchen," Harold said.

"The food will taste like your grandma's too."

"Lenny, how did you find a place like this?"

"The Veteran and I would search for better places to eat when we drove to and from the VA hospital. We refused to stop and eat at the fast-food places along the interstate."

"Lenny, who is the Veteran?"

"I am sorry, Harold. That was what I called Lewis. He was the best friend I ever had. He helped me accept the death of my wife when I first came to Fort Myers."

"I heard about that most unfortunate accident. She was struck by lightning. I know that you and Ruby returned the favor by helping Betty cope with Lewis's death.

"I heard the story from Betty. Betty has told me about the people she calls her family members."

"Harold, Betty is the head of the family. Everyone goes to her for advice, and rightfully so."

"Who is Bailey?"

"Betty looks over Bailey as though she were her own child."

"Betty has plans for her in the bank. She has a master's degree in finance, and she is taking additional courses in banking."

"That's right, Harold. Betty has everything lined up."

"I hear that," Harold said. "I have the final legal paperwork for the charter in my briefcase. I guess we are in the banking business now."

"Did I hear you say 'we'?" Ruby asked.

"Betty hasn't told you?"

"Told us what, Harold?"

"She is assigning each one of you a million dollars' worth of stock in the bank. That should be good news for both of you."

"I have to admit that that comes as a surprise."

"A million dollars is a nice surprise," Harold said, laughing. "It is not every day that one receives a million-dollar gift."

"Harold, I already have a million dollars," Ruby said.

"Now you have two million, Ruby. Lenny, is this your first million?"

"I guess so."

"Betty did not want any members of the family to have less than a million dollars."

"You mean that everyone in the family will be receiving a million dollars' worth of stock?"

"Yes, Lenny, that is the way that Betty wants it to be, although Betty does not want them to know that until the bank is up and running. So this is to be our secret until then."

"Holy crap, Harold. Betty isn't going to give away all of her money, is she?"

"I don't think you have to concern yourself with that. Betty has many millions more."

HAROLD ENJOYS COUNTRY COOKING AT BETSY'S

"How did you find this place, Lenny?"

"The Veteran and I would exit the highway and ask the locals about down-home restaurants."

"What are pot roast and boiled cabbage, and what is the ham steak and sweet potatoes special?"

"What is your question, Harold?"

"I have never heard of any of this. What should I order, Lenny?"

"I recommend the pot roast."

"All right, ma'am, that's what I will have."

"Times three, miss. Thank you. Harold, I guarantee that you will enjoy every bite. Every bit of food on this menu is grown and cooked here. Betsy says that she doesn't own a can opener."

"What does she mean by that?"

"Everything is fresh. Nothing comes from a can."

"I did not think that that was possible today, Lenny."

"If her goal were to maximize her profits, it would not be possible. Betsy enjoys some profits but lives with a lower income because she will not compromise on delivering quality food. The rolls and butter are made here too."

"Do you mean that she churns the butter here?"

"That's right, Ruby. Here come the rolls and butter now. I forgot to tell you about the fresh honey."

"I can smell the freshness."

"Ruby, that smell is the wood-burning stove that your food is being cooked in."

"My God, this is good, Lenny."

"Ruby, what do you think?"

"That's the sweetest honey I have ever put on a roll."

"Thanks, Lenny. You have introduced me to a unique dining experience, and the food is absolutely delicious."

"You guys, don't fill up on rolls. You need to save room for the pot roast and cabbage. They will melt in your mouth."

"Hello, Lenny!"

"Hello, Betsy!"

"I have not seen you in a while. Where is the Veteran?"

"The veteran died."

"Oh, my God, Lenny. I suppose that that's the reason that I haven't fed you in a while. I am so sorry. When you two first started stopping in, I thought you were brothers. You were so close to each other. You tell his momma that I will pray for him."

"I will, Betsy."

"Enjoy the food, and come back to see us. I have homemade pies. You can take one with you. The pecans in the pie came from the tree behind the restaurant."

"Is Betsy the owner?"

"Yes, she is, Ruby."

"I have not seen this type of hospitality since I was a kid, and believe me, that was a long, long time ago."

"Harold, do you drink coffee?"

"I drink coffee religiously."

"Make sure that you get a cup of coffee to go."

"Why is that?"

"You will see when you drink a cup of coffee made by a one-hundred-year-old percolator."

'This was a wonderful experience, you two," Harold said. "I have to pay the bill. I would not be comfortable if I didn't. Betsy's cooking hit the spot and satisfied my ready-for-something-new appetite. And you are right about the coffee.

"What do you think, Ruby?"

"I have never tasted coffee like this before. It's almost like a new kind of food."

"You nailed it, Ruby. The coffee is almost a food in itself. She should go national with this coffee."

"I don't think she could find enough one-hundred-year-old coffee percolators to do that," Ruby said, laughing. Harold chuckled too.

"It has been a long day for a man of my age. I am going to lean this seat back and take a nap. I want to restore my energy so that I will be fresh when I meet Betty."

"Be our guest. Lenny, will you let me drive awhile?"

"I think so, Ruby. I'll pull over at the next rest stop. I would like to listen to this audiobook by David Perlmutter. I will use earphones. Hand me the set of earphones in the console."

"I liked his first book, *Grain Brain*. I too would like to listen to his new book, *Brain Maker*."

"We're home, Harold. Take a look at the addition. That is your part of the house. You're going to love it. You have an amazing dwelling."

"I can't wait to see it," Harold said.

"Betty is waiting at the front entrance for you, Harold. Let's get going!"

"Are these your dogs? Do they have names?"

"The shepherd's name is Jojo, and the poodle's name is Breezy. They are part of the family too."

"I think Betty failed to give them a million dollars," Harold said.

"Hello, Betty. He is all yours," Ruby said. "Lenny, let's change our clothes and go to the gym."

"I will race you, Ruby. The last one dressed will have to wash clothes tonight…. You lose, Ruby."

"I had a phone call, Lenny."

"What are you saying?"

"We will have to do it again."

"No way. You lost, Ruby. I expect you to wash the clothes tonight."

"That is not fair, Lenny. You drive."

HAROLD AND BETTY TAKE VOWS

"Betty, I can't believe how well everything came together. My living quarters exceed all of my expectations. The swimming pool is something that I never thought was possible. It will be nice to not have to go to a gym to swim early in the morning. I can even adjust the water temperature to my liking. I would have never been capable of designing such a convenient space. You will need to show me how to use all of this smart technology.

"I never imagined living in a smart home. Lenny and Ruby are exceptional people. I am sure that the rest of the family will be similar. In your family, you have a president of a bank, an administrative assistant, and a bank accountant."

"My realtor found a location for the bank. We have already closed on the building, Harold. You can take a look at it tomorrow."

"OK, that sounds good. You have done all of the work, Betty."

"You know better than that, Harold. You secured fourteen million dollars and prepared the paperwork for the bank."

"I can't take all of the credit, Betty. My son and his staff contributed to the work."

"Do we owe him, Harold?"

"He was glad to do it. He knew it would cause me to retire and to leave his law firm."

"I am so happy to be here with you, Betty. I would like to change my plans."

"What do you intend to change, Harold?"

"As you know, I was planning to go back to Michigan to clear out my home. I will ask my son to take care of all of that. Goodwill can clear the house of my belongings.

"He can hire a company to get it ready to be sold and then sign it over to a realtor. I don't care to go back. My home here is beautifully decorated, and we have already agreed to purchase some attire for me. Why should I return to my lonely way of life and to that freezing weather?"

"Oh, Harold, I couldn't agree more. Welcome to paradise!"

"Betty, let's quickly put this bank together. Then we can spend the rest of our days enjoying each other and the wonderfully talented people you have come to call your family.

"Betty, I have loved you for the better part of my life. I never stopped believing that one day, you would want me."

"Harold, I am so lucky that you never gave up on me. I will make you a happy man."

"And I will make you a happy woman."

HAROLD'S FIRST DAY

"Good morning, Harold. Bob is going to meet us at the bank."

"Bob?"

"Bob is part of the family. He is the president of BA&C Bank."

"Oh, I am so sorry. I knew that, Betty."

"The realtor has all of the records concerning the property. I have the reports on the businesses and the average income of the residents in the area.

"The architectural firm that I hired has already drawn up the building's blueprints. A representative of the architectural firm will be there to meet Bob, who will advise him on the bank's floor plan. The agency I hired strongly suggested this location. The purchase is complete, Harold.

"This will be the first gathering of our team on the premises. I have keys for everyone. I will introduce you to everyone involved, and then we'll begin our work."

"I'm ready to go if you are, Betty."

"Do you still drive, Harold?"

"Of course I do, Betty."

"Then you can drive our new Escalade. Don't worry about the new-fangled gadgets. I will introduce them to you as we go. There is one more serious piece of information that I need to tell you. I promised a friend of Lenny's that we would finance his run for sheriff."

"A high profile will come with the bank. It will be necessary to have a friend in politics, Betty.

"You will need to be patient with me when it comes to technology. I have changed my opinion on technology, Betty. What a great invention that swimming pool is. I swam a quarter of a mile this morning and never left my home. Afterward, I lay on the automatic-massage table for fifteen minutes. I never knew those fantastic amenities existed."

"I am introducing you to the twenty-first century, Harold."

"I know for sure that we don't owe my son anything for his legal help. But I think he would gladly pay you, Betty, for looking out for me. You have relieved him of that duty."

"Lenny and Ruby said that they would be ready. We still have a little time before the others are to meet us at the bank. Give me a minute to check on Lenny and Ruby. Go ahead and fix yourself a cup of coffee. The condiments are all on the table. Ruby, are you two up?"

"Yes, Betty. We will be ready in five minutes. See you in the kitchen."

"They are on their way, Harold."

"That's good. I really like them. Good coffee, Betty. Did they ever bring you coffee from Betsy's?"

"Lenny and Lewis would bring me a pint every time they stopped. It is the best coffee I ever tasted."

"That's exactly what I thought, Betty. It has a great flavor to it."

"Good morning, Harold. How was your first night in your new abode?"

"It was pleasant. You guys will have to show me how to work all of the bells and whistles."

"I did figure out how to raise the window shades with the remote."

"Betty is responsible for designing most of your place. She knows more about it than anyone."

"If everyone has his or her coffee or tea, let's roll."

"Harold, this is one important day."

"You are dead on, Ruby."

"I never thought I would be one of the owners of a bank."

"Life is full of surprises."

"Harold, what do you think has changed the most in the last fifty years or so?"

"Culturally speaking, I would say that everyone is more specialized and dependent on others. People used to be more versatile. A man would be expected to do almost everything on his own. He'd only occasionally go to others for advice or help."

"What are some examples of what you're talking about?" Ruby asked.

"Nowadays, many people don't even change their flat tires. They call road service. People don't even negotiate when they're buying their own houses. They hire agents. People used to settle their own personal disputes.

Now they hire counselors, arbitrators, or lawyers. Everyone is dependent on someone else in almost every area of his or her life.

"Just look at what we are doing here. We'll be establishing and operating a bank thanks to many different talented people. Putting a team of qualified people together is an amazing accomplishment in itself. The credit belongs to Betty."

"I see what you're talking about, Harold. I understand your reasoning."

"Ruby, nothing is simple anymore. Betty, I am looking forward to meeting Bob and Gloria."

"I'm not sure whether Gloria will be there. She will probably stop by tonight. Bob and Gloria live next door. Will and Bailey live in their apartment. I suspect that they will come over to meet you tonight, Harold."

THE CITADEL BANK BUILDING

"Betty, this building is three stories tall."

"In this part of town, you have to build vertically because of the high property values. It has enough room for two drive-up windows—maybe three. Looks like everyone is here. You two can exit through the front door of the building."

"Lenny and I will park the car. We will be right behind you."

"Harold, this is Alice Smith, our realtor, and this is Joyce Freeman, our architect, and Frank James, our contractor. This is Harold, our attorney. I am Betty Anderson. I'll be the coordinator of this project. All money requests will go to me or to my assistants. My assistants are Lenny Lewis, Bailey Darby, and Ruby Ridge.

"If I'm not available—or, God forbid, if I'm no longer here—my heir will continue this project as planned. This site is owned by Citadel Corporation and has been approved for a bank charter by the state of Florida. The bank's name will be Citadel State Bank, or CSB. Harold, meet Bob Richburg. Bob will be our president.

"Joyce, you will be working closely with Bob on designing the interior of the bank. You two should meet and then turn the plans over to Frank as soon as possible so that he can go to work. Joyce and Frank, ASAP, I hope to see a nicely designed sign in the front stating that this building will be the home of Citadel State Bank. I have keys to this building for all of you. If there are no other questions, let's get busy, ladies and gentlemen."

"Betty, what does the third floor look like?" Harold asked.

"It was mostly office space. It has nice picture windows. Bob selected a corner room for his office. There is plenty of space for you to have an office in the bank, Harold. Would you like to take a look? We will have to take the stairs. The elevator's inspection sticker has expired."

"I would like to take a look."

"The staircase is in the rear left corner, Harold."

"Let's go, Betty. Those three flights of steps were more difficult than I thought they'd be. I see that a couple of chairs were left behind. Let's sit down and catch our breath, Betty. You know, Betty, having a small office space for legal work might be the way to go for me. I really like the view up here."

"In the next day or so, you need to go by Joyce Freeman's office and tell her to draw in an office for you."

"I will do that, Betty. Oh, what a life we have had. You and I have been together for a lifetime."

"I believe that our life's just beginning. After the bank is running on its own, we will have no distractions.

"The family will be capable of doing business without us. You and I will have every day to explore Florida."

"Betty, you put together a remarkable group of people. My only regret is that we didn't do this ten year earlier. I have loved you for more than fifty years, Betty."

"And I have loved you since the first day you walked into my library and asked me to show you around. Do you remember that day, Harold?"

"I remember that day as well as I remember yesterday."

"Are you ready to go back down? Let's hold on to each other and slowly make our way down. I suspect that Lenny and Ruby are looking for us by now."

TRAGEDY STRIKES

"Lenny, I can't find Betty and Harold."

"I thought they went outside."

"I walked around the building and didn't see them. Where do you think they could be?"

"I've been talking to Joyce for the last twenty minutes or so. Have you looked upstairs?"

"No, Lenny."

"The elevator isn't working. You'll have to use the staircase. It is located in the rear left corner of the building."

"OK, I will go see."

"Joyce, how long will it take you to draw up the plans?"

"Once I meet with Bob, I'll be able to complete them in a couple of days. Frank can bring his crew in next week. Lenny, someone is screaming!"

"That sounds like Ruby. It's coming from the staircase. Let's go!"

"Oh, my God! Oh, my God! Someone call nine-one-one. We need an ambulance."

"I'm calling," Frank said.

"Ruby, get a hold of yourself, and hold Betty's head up."

"She's still breathing, Lenny."

"I have Harold. He's not breathing. I will start CPR. Joyce, see if you can find something to use to wipe the blood off of Betty's face."

"What happened?"

"It appears that they fell down two flights of concrete steps."

"Everyone move back. The EMT crew is here. Give them Betty, Ruby, and stand back. Hurry, Ruby! We will follow them to Memorial Hospital."

MEMORIAL HOSPITAL

"Why can't I find a parking space, Ruby?"

"Try looking farther back. It would be quicker to park far away and to walk to the emergency room than to find a close parking space."

"OK, Ruby, go. I will be on your heels."

"The EMT has already brought them in, Lenny. I'll check in with the front desk and inform them that the family is here."

"Ruby, I'm beginning to believe that the hospital is my second home."

"How long were they lying in the stairway before we found them, Lenny?"

"It couldn't have been more than five or six minutes, Ruby. I had no idea that they'd gone upstairs. I was having a conversation with Joyce. I didn't notice that they were gone."

"This is not our fault, Lenny. I have your debit card. There is a coffee machine. Lenny, I am going to throw up."

"I will ask the nurse at the front counter for something that can settle a nervous stomach."

"I have to go."

"Ms. Ridge is in the restroom, nurse. She has a nervous stomach. Is there anything you can do?"

"Mr. Lewis, I will attend to her. I can give her bicarbonate to absorb the excess acid in her stomach."

"Thank you. I'm going to sit down."

"Breathe deeply, and concentrate on calming down, Ruby."

"Mr. Lewis, Ms. Ridge, my name is Dr. Crane. We could not revive Harold Williams. I am sorry for your loss. Betty Anderson is stable for the moment. She has a broken back, a broken arm, and a mild concussion. She is a very tough lady. We will alert you to any changes in her condition."

"Oh, Lenny. I'm scared."

"Ruby, lay your head on my shoulder, and relax. It will help release some of your anxiety."

"Why do things like this happen? Harold just arrived. It's unimaginable that he's dead. Betty was so happy to have him here. Now Betty fears for her life. What's going to come of all this? They had so much going on."

"Sorry it took so long," Bob said. "I called Gloria. She insisted that I pick her up."

"Ruby, how is Betty?" Gloria asked.

"We just spoke with Dr. Crane. He said that she was stable for the moment. Gloria, Harold is dead."

"Oh, no, Ruby! Lenny, we spoke with Will and Bailey. They are on their way. There they are now."

"Ruby, can you help me with Bailey? She's hysterical."

"Bailey, please sit here with me! Will, do you have any wipes for her face?"

"No, Ruby."

"Go to the nurses' station, and ask for some Kleenexes."

"Ruby, what are we going to do if Betty doesn't make it?"

"Bailey, the doctor said she was a tough lady. She is stable. We will get through this together."

"Bob, this might not be the right time to announce this, but I think that it might help. Lenny is Betty's heir and is in charge."

"What are you saying, Ruby?" I asked.

"Betty told me that some time ago. She didn't think it was the right time to let you know. I told her that I wouldn't say anything unless there was an emergency, and in my opinion, this is an emergency.

"All of the legal documents are in Betty's safe, and I have the combination. Bob, everything will go on as planned. Betty prepared for this kind of happening. She was concerned that her or Harold's age would become a problem. Here is the way things are set up: Something happened to Harold, so all of Harold's assets will go to Betty. In the event that something happens to Betty, all of Betty's assets will go to Lenny.

"At this moment, Betty has inherited Harold's assets. Since Betty is incapacitated, Lenny is in charge of everything, and that includes the money, in case anyone was wondering. Everyone else's situation will remain the same. We will talk no more about this."

"I'm nauseous now, Ruby. I need to go to the restroom."

"Bob, will you go with him?" Gloria asked.

"No problem. Lenny, what's wrong?"

"I'm shocked by what Ruby said. It makes me want to throw up. This hasn't happened to me since I was in Vietnam. I would develop knots in my stomach when I lost one of my men, and sometimes I'd throw up. It's a nervous reaction, Bob. I'll be fine in a moment or two. Betty's responsibilities are immense. If something happens to her, I'll need you to back me up, especially with the bank."

"Lenny, you can count on Gloria and me."

"Thank you, Bob."

"We'd better get back in case Dr. Crane returns."

"Mr. Lewis and Ms. Ridge?"

"Yes, Dr. Crane."

"Ms. Anderson is awake and is asking for you. Normally, we don't allow patients in her condition to have visitors. But she insists that she be able to see you. I would ask that you make your visit brief. She is very weak and goes in and out of consciousness. Please follow me. I will take you to her."

"Lenny and Ruby, I love you both. I know that Harold is no longer alive. I want you to know that I will be all right. I will be in heaven with Lewis and Harold. I want you to make our dream of opening a bank come true. Lenny, you are my sole heir. I trust that you will take care of the family in the same way that you took care of your young troops in combat.

"Lenny, I love you like a son. I must go now. The Lord is calling me. Will you and Ruby hold my hands?"

"Hold on, Betty. You are not going anywhere."

"I'm tired."

"Ruby, quickly push the call button. The monitor is showing a flat line."

"Step back, sir. Let me in here. She is gone. I am very sorry. We have to ask you to leave. There's nothing you can do. Someone will join you in the waiting room to explain what will happen next."

"Ruby, stand up!"

"I can't walk, Lenny."

"Nurse, will you assist Mr. Lewis with Ms. Ridge?"

"What's going on, Lenny?" Gloria asked.

"Betty died."

"Oh, my God."

"Gloria, will you help me with Ruby? I will need to fill out the final paperwork. I have become an expert at closing out a life. Bailey, you stay with Ruby and Gloria."

"Bob, can you and Will help the women and get them home? I will stay and finish up the hospital paperwork and be there soon."

THE SHOW MUST CONTINUE

"Lenny, everyone is here. They know that you are Betty's heir."

"Hello, Alice, Roy, and Frank. I'm glad you stopped by."

"Lenny, we are in shock. We all spent time with Betty, and we all saw her as a friend."

"Thank you, Roy. It is important that you all know that nothing is going to change.

"I hope all of the contractors involved will start this project in accord with Betty's agenda. Bailey and Will, can I have a few minutes with you in private? Gloria, will you please serve our guests drinks? Ruby, if you are up to it, give Gloria a hand. Bob, give me a few moments with Will and Bailey. Then I would like to have a private moment with you.

"I will make this quick. Bailey, I intend to carry out Betty's wishes. I know Betty spoke with you about managing the accounting department at the bank. I want to ask you to give your notice at the VA immediately. You will receive comparable benefits, a twenty percent raise, and one million dollars' worth of stock in Citadel State Bank.

"I need you to manage the payouts and to organize the documents from the companies involved in the ongoing plans. When can I have your decision?"

"Lenny, Will and I talked about this with Betty. We both agreed that it is an opportunity of a lifetime. I'll need just one day to give my resignation to the VA. I will be at your service the day after tomorrow."

"Betty never mentioned giving us a million dollars. Does that mean we're millionaires?" Will asked.

"Yes, Will. You and Bailey each have a million dollars' worth of stock in Citadel State Bank.

"Your contracts will require you to work for thirty-six months before you can leave the company and sell your stock. Will, your conditions are the same as Bailey's. You must wait thirty-six months before selling your stock.

"It was Betty's wish to give you each a million dollars. Writing the contracts is my job, and I will need to prepare them. If you have no more questions, I would like you two to stop by after work and sign the contracts. Will, you are not being left out! We will find a position for you. Do you two want to have a drink and hang around to comfort Ruby? Bob, can I have a quick word with you?"

"What can I do for you, Lenny?"

"I intend to carry out Betty's wishes."

"What does that mean, Lenny?"

"You know that you are the president of the Citadel State Bank and that you are a voting member on the board. What you don't know is that Betty gave you one million dollars' worth of stock in the bank. Bob, congratulations. You are a stockholder."

"This is unbelievable. Can I tell Gloria?"

"Of course, Bob. You can inform her that she too was given a million dollars' worth of stock."

"I am flabbergasted, Lenny."

"Let's have a drink and comfort the women, Bob."

"Ruby, are you doing better?"

"Yes, Lenny. I am sorry. I was overwhelmed by my emotions."

"How can I help you?"

CRACKING THE SAFE AND RUBY'S CONFESSION

"Ruby, when our guests leave, we can open the safe and begin studying the documents."

"Everyone has gone, Lenny. I will open the safe."

"Write the combination down on this piece of paper."

"Look, Lenny—cash!"

"Count it while I read Betty's last will and testament."

"Lenny, there is one hundred thousand dollars here, and there are two trays of heirlooms and jewelry. There is a check in her checkbook signed and made out to Art Ray's campaign. It's for two hundred fifty thousand dollars. Betty was really serious about getting Art Ray elected as sheriff. Today's date is on it.

"She must have signed it before going to the Citadel building. Do you think Art was planning to pick the check up today?"

"I know they spoke on the phone at some point during the last few days. When I catch up with my work, I will give him a call, Ruby."

"There's a gun in here too."

"Careful, Ruby."

"I know everything about this handgun, Lenny. This is a thirty-eight-caliber snub-nose Smith and Wesson, and it's loaded. It's the same kind that I learned to shoot when I was a kid. I can't imagine what Betty would be doing with this weapon. Do you remember the story I told you, Lenny?"

"Oh, yeah! I'm glad he died before you had the chance to kill him. I will attend to the weapon, Ruby. See if there is a permit for the weapon in the safe. Betty's will states that if something happens to me, Bob and Bailey will be the custodians of the estate, and its assets will be divided among the family and managed according to her instructions. It is quite extensive, Ruby. I will take time later to study this part of the will. Looks like Betty took care of every possible situation.

"Ruby, the mystery here is that this will was written a few days ago and clearly states that it supersedes any previous wills. Furthermore, she filed it with the county's recorder. Here is the receipt for fifty dollars and the filing number. I am the sole heir. I don't understand why she didn't leave you an inheritance."

"Lenny, I accompanied Betty to the county recorder's office. I know why she made you her sole heir. I had a personal talk with Betty last week. She expressed great dissatisfaction with my actions, Lenny. She told me that she loved me but that she was going to remove me from her will. I felt her decision was justified."

"Well, Ruby, do you intend to let me in on the little secret that was so important that she removed you from her will?"

"Betty planned to accompany me when I told you this. I am so sorry, Lenny!"

"What the hell are you talking about, Ruby? This is not the time for guessing games!"

"Lenny, I'm pregnant with Adolf's child."

"No way, Ruby! I will not accept what you just said."

"It's true, Lenny. I will not abort the child. I told Adolf, and he's flying into Fort Myers. He'll take me to Germany, and we'll get married. His family has already planned the wedding and the celebration. I made the decision. It will be the best thing for the child.

"I do love you, Lenny, but a child should be with his or her biological father. That's the reason Betty removed me from her will. You will find another document giving you my million dollars' worth of stock along with a check for one million dollars. I signed the Honda Fit and the Honda Odyssey over to you, Lenny.

"Betty's Escalade is also yours. Betty inherited Harold's wealth when he died. Betty told me that if something happened to her, your assets, which include Citadel Corporation's assets, would exceed two hundred million dollars. That's not counting Betty and Harold's accidental death policy you will need to look into. Her wish was for you to continue the family's plans if something happened to her and Harold. You should contact Harold's son for legal advice. Everything I just said is explained in this document, Lenny. I require nothing. Adolf is a multibillionaire."

I had no words for Ruby. She stayed clear of me until the limousine pulled up to the front door early the next morning. Adolf's bodyguard exited the car and proceeded to the entrance of the house. His knocking on the door seemed to go on forever. Time froze. Ruby carried only a handbag as she slowly walked down the hallway to the front door. She stopped short of the door. She turned to me and, crying, she ran into my arms. She kissed me and said, "I will always love you. Please forgive me, Lenny." She released her hold on me, and without looking back, she entered the limousine and disappeared.

■■■

About the Author

Jerry Lewis is a Vietnam veteran, Florida State University alumnus, Florida resident, and lone wolf.

Made in the USA
San Bernardino, CA
29 April 2017